THE SHADOW GIRLS

THE SHADOW GIRLS

LUCIENNE DIVER

FALSTAFF
BOOKS
WWW.FALSTAFFBOOKS.COM

To anyone who's ever been down and risen again. To all the phoenixes out there.

A NOTE FROM THE AUTHOR

In The Shadow Girls, I set out to tell a tale of characters rising from their ashes, determined not only to survive their burning but to use their still-blazing embers to change their world, though one may actually set it on fire. This means that my main characters have been through some things. I've done my best to represent their circumstances honestly and for certain events to be implied and to occur off-page, as it's not my intent to traumatize my readers. However, I must provide a trigger warning for spousal abuse, sexual assault, bigotry, and personal loss. I will have resources listed at the end of the book for anyone who might need or want them for themselves or someone they know.

I hope you will enjoy The Shadow Girls, which is meant to show how strong and resilient we are, to bring us up rather than hold us down.

Sincere love to all who turn the page and understanding to those who choose otherwise.

Lucienne Diver

PROLOGUE

SIX YEARS PRIOR

Ulan

Ulan had twice disentangled Sophie's fingers from their death grip on her cloak, wound so tightly in the fabric they'd waste valuable time getting free of each other once they were called to aid the wounded on the battlefield. She finally seized Sophie's hand in hers but regretted it as she immediately lost all feeling in her fingers. Ulan's other hand clutched the bag resting against her hip that contained her bandages, needles, stitches, and poultices that might save the saveable.

The way things were going, she was terrified there wouldn't be anyone left alive for them to minister to. The last battle had been…not a battle so much as an ambush. The Frizenzian people were fierce in the defense of their land, and they knew it more intimately than the Jucari.

She wasn't sure whether the Frizenzian princess had truly done what they'd said—poisoned her royal husband as soon as he got her with child so that she'd have sole control of the heir-to-be. How could she know it would be a boy? Or that she wouldn't need a spare? And the rumors that came out of Alban Castle were dark. Nearly anyone could have wanted King Cyril dead. His younger brother had certainly been quick enough to seize power, almost as if poised. Not that anyone would so much as whisper such a thing. Not if they valued their lives.

In the end, it didn't matter what had started the war. They fought because the new king demanded it. Because they had no choice.

People like Ulan and Sofie and Reynal never did.

She and Sophie and the other stitcher-women had spread across the foothill above the valley to keep fretful watch on the massive battle below, but it was really only Reynal she was desperate to find. Even knowing the likely futility, Ulan sought some sign of him – his tall, lean form, his gentle gray eyes, the gouge in his right cheek that disappeared into a dimple when he smiled at her.

Her stomach lurched at the thought of never seeing that smile again, and she cupped a hand there, as if that would steady the upset.

But her gorge wasn't the only thing rising. She felt it like a tremor through the land, the sense of their very foundations coming unmoored. Beside her, Sofie cried out and dropped fully to the ground, trying to drag Ulan with her, but she wouldn't go. Sophie released her hand then, and Ulan was left alone in silent vigil.

Below them, a mist rose from the floor of the valley, brown and thick, fecund and alive. Anima, the very substance and soul of the land gathering and forming into a solid force. The grass, weeds, flowers and trees, and everything tied to them, all that crawled, slithered, skittered or scurried withered and died. Their very spirit was stripped away and reformed by their great and terrible magic men, the mageri, into a monstrous battle beast.

A mighty Torvus was coalescing before the Jucarian army, created from the pillaged lifeforces, becoming as physical as all that had died to create it. It rose nearly three horses high, its chest four oxen abreast. It trembled the earth when it scraped its massive clawed hooves along the ground, head lowered in preparation to charge their Frizenzian foes. It snorted a massive gust from its nose, expelling some of the substance from which it was made, which flew up to complete razor-sharp horns that matched its lower set of tusks.

The Torvus bellowed a war cry before charging, expelling more of the mist that puffed like steam out of flaring nostrils. It rushed the coming army, head thrashing left and right, catching horsemen and mounts on its massive horns or knocking them to the ground with its tusks, cutting their legs out from under them. Ulan clenched her own hands, hating the bloodshed while glorying that the Torvus was on the Jucari side, and she wouldn't have to watch anyone she'd ministered to fall to it.

The Frizenzian army began to falter. Trained warhorses balked and bucked. The formation divided, desperate to avoid the monstrous beast. In the divide stood one of the Frizenzian mageri, obvious from his wild, untouched hair and dangerously pointed staff. He faced down the charging Torvus.

The beast bellowed loudly enough to shake the sparse trees on the mountainside, and Sofie clawed again at the hem of Ulan's dress, urging her to the ground. She dropped, but only to her knees. Ulan grabbed at Sofie's clutching hand to still it, and to comfort her, but she couldn't look away from the battlefield.

The Frizenzian mageri stabbed his staff into the ground, trying to cut off the flow of energy the Jucari were drawing. Given the size of the Torvus, Ulan was sure it must be too late, but the Frizenzian's staff took on a glow, becoming a lodestone for the ani-mist bleeding off the Torvus where the soldiers had pierced it as they were flung from their horses.

The escaped anima collected around the mageri's staff in thin wisps and whirls. His lips moved as one hand burrowed into his tunic to pull out a vial.

Ulan searched frantically for their own mageri. Or for Reynal, or anyone close enough to stop the new magic from forming, but their Torvus left such devastation in its wake, it was impossible to see. About to be trampled, still the Frizenzian mageri brought the vial to his lips, bit the cork, and tore it out with his teeth.

If the Torvus was bold, brutal life, the liquid in that vial was death. She could see it, imagine the scent of it. The acrid sting of corrosion, the taint of decomposition. The mageri flung the contents of the vial at the mist forming around his staff, and immediately it glittered green-black-gold, the iridescence of a raven's wing. It took on a long, ropelike shape, scaled on the bottom and spiked on top, as though armored. It unhinged its jaw to flash fangs dripping death, absorbed from the vial's poison.

A Sinuway! She'd only heard rumors of such a beast...she couldn't have imagined...

She quaked in fear for their troops as the scaled monstrosity coiled itself to strike. Before she could so much as gasp out a warning—as though anyone could hear her over the battle—it launched itself at the Torvus, which torqued aside, but not in time to avoid the Sinuway's fangs. They sank deeply into the chest of the Torvus, and caught, releasing a great gout of mist from the wound. The Torvus reared, lashing madly about with its razor hooves. They raked the body of the Sinuway, and the fangs retracted, leaving a gash in the Torvus's neck the size of a soldier.

The serpent-beast recoiled and prepared for another strike.

The Torvus bellowed, twisted as though it could bend itself in half, and took off away from the threat, back through its own army, spearing everything in its path with its giant scythe-like tusks and horns. The Sinuway sprang after it.

Men fell before them and regrouped behind, locked in battle.

The cries and blood were insanity. Ulan could no longer distinguish one army from another, they were locked so tightly together. Still, she searched once more for Reynal, knowing it was impossible, but hoping she'd somehow *feel* him as she could the magics. For a moment, she was sure that she could. She sensed him *there*, toward the center of the battle-field, guarding their banner and their commander, just before the Torvus, maddened by the snake's poisoned bite, thundered straight for the spot. And the banner toppled.

She cried out and fell, finally, beside Sofie, but something else cried out as well, something deep inside her that she hadn't even known she nurtured.

CHAPTER ONE

Cia

Cia stood inside the walled palace courtyard with the others, alone in the crowd, awaiting the return of the men from their months of battle. The portcullis stood open in welcome. She wouldn't be able to see a thing until the first riders came through, but she'd hear the hue and cry before then from the eager onlookers ahead of her.

She cocooned herself in her cloak, trying to wrap herself tightly enough to stop the trembling. She had no idea whether her husband lived or died. Garif had sent no message. If he thought of her at all, he preferred to leave her in suspense, balanced on the knife edge of hope. Every day she didn't hear was another she could convince herself that her fortunes had finally changed.

She'd known this day was coming. Winter had arrived early this year, and with a vengeance. Cutting winds screamed through shutters like banshees heralding icy-fingered death. But she hadn't heard even the faintest whisperings that the army and its mageri had been recalled until she'd been summoned.

No one had thought to advise her any earlier—not Cia, the handmaiden of the Poison Princess, suspected of acquiring the very poison that had killed the king and set off the Blood War. Oh no, Garif had *saved*

Cia when he married her, becoming responsible for her and for correcting her behavior rather than sending her off to be killed with her mistress. He took his responsibilities very seriously and schooled her regularly when he was home, never letting her forget that her life was his.

Being shunned by everyone at the palace, her embroidery skills prized but not her person, was bliss compared to her husband's attention.

Gasps and cheers presaged the Jucari men riding through the gates. Children broke away from their mothers, their wet nurses. Women raced after them or ran forward on their own account, the courtyard a sudden burst of chaos.

Cia was aware of it only peripherally. The noblemen in front leaned from their horses to lift children with laughter and hero-worship in their eyes or slid into the arms of waiting wives and lovers. Horses were handed off or held loosely while greetings were given.

She scanned those coming in. Waiting. Hoping she wouldn't find...

"Cia."

Her back stiffened. She hadn't realized she'd been hunched protectively around her heart until she heard that voice. He'd ridden up behind her while she'd been watching. "Come greet your returning hero."

She put away whatever flashed across her face, reached for the mask she prayed hadn't gone brittle with the passing months, and turned with enough speed that he couldn't interpret it as reluctance.

She gazed up at him.

Powerful. Protected. *Mageri.* Hardly a hero.

But she couldn't say any of that, and so she made her lips curl upward and forced her arms to unclench and open for him, praying that he'd interpret the tremors as excitement at his homecoming. Because sometimes it suited him to pretend, especially when others were around.

"Husband," she said, glad to be spitting the word up rather than choking it down.

Instead of accepting the invitation to walk into her arms, he grabbed her, snaking his arms around and crushing her against him. He mashed his lips down on hers so quickly she didn't have time to draw breath. When she went weak in the knees for lack of it, he finally let up with a look of satisfaction. As though anyone watching might think Cia was faint from being swept off her feet rather than biting back bile.

"I've missed you," he said loudly. "Let's not waste any more time."

He crushed her hand in his and led the way to their quarters, leaving the care of his horse and his baggage to the overworked stableboys rushing about.

Cia quailed, readying him for what he would find, though she knew it wouldn't matter in the end. "No one told me to expect you. I'd have stoked the fire, had a bath prepared."

On her own, they barely gave her enough fuel to keep her fingers thawed. If she'd been forewarned, she could have begged more wood at the least.

He didn't seem to hear her. As soon as the door closed behind them, he stalked toward the center of the room, gazing angrily down at the fire. He beckoned her over and she joined him, taking in great gasps this time rather than be caught out. He grabbed her roughly, even though she went to him willingly, and yanked away the head-scarf she'd worn to keep her hair from whipping in the wind so that he could spider his fingers through it. Then suddenly he clenched his fist, her hair twisted painfully in his fingers. With another man it might have been mistaken for passion. Not with Garif.

She let herself be pulled in, though she wanted to gag on his scent as her face pressed to his chest. He smelled of body odor allowed to ferment, of lathered horse and campfire and sickly-sweet death. It had to be her imagination that it clung to him like a miasma. She felt as though if she breathed too deeply, the creeping death would fill her up and waste her away. And so, she tried not to breathe at all, but stood there, forcing herself to stillness, creating embroidery patterns in her head so that she could be there but not there.

His fingers tightened further, pulling at the roots of her hair, as though he could sense her slipping away. She gasped as he yanked her head back so that she had to look at him, and then dove in for a brutal kiss, like a falcon diving for prey. He held on too tightly for her to move, even if she dared, and his grip had her on her toes, struggling to balance like a woman on the stool at the gallows.

He backed her toward their bed, knocking her into her sewing stand, sending it toppling. When she cried out, he reared back, as though he might strike her, but she distracted him by reaching for his belt.

She went away then, her thoughts on the floor with her embroidery, a wedding veil for someone with happier prospects.

She came back to herself sometime later, the weight of Garif's arm like a tree toppled over on her, pinning her down.

Or not like a tree—nothing so passive or so silent. He snored and snarled in his sleep, exhaling fumes that would have choked the cave bear he reminded her of, keeping its kill close as it slept to guard against other predators. She even bore scratches, as if from its claws, but the source was nothing so mundane. It wasn't just his rough nails. She'd swear the teeth braided into Garif's beard had been filed to points. Back in her home of Frizenze, people burned their lost teeth in the home hearth because of the bit of blood in the root. They offered that essence back to the anima and assured that no one could ever use it to gain control over them. Sheer superstition, since it was the open wound a mageri might tap into. But here in Jucar, people hid their teeth away or wore them around their necks in pouches so they might be reunited with them in death and go to the anima whole.

Except for the mageri, who guarded every bit of their being, and wove them like beads into their beards or hair, which they never cut. And since the war, some had started taking the enemy mageris' teeth as trophies. When the ani-mists swirled, the beads clacked together like chattering teeth or bone chimes, a cacophony of intimidation and sacrilege.

Despite Garif's snarling, she must have slept, because it was darker now. Much darker. And, aside from her husband, deathly quiet, as though even the wind had died out for the night.

She tried to be quiet as well, and immobile. Years of battles and forced marches had taught Garif to sleep soundly, but she knew from experience that if she so much as moved, he'd tighten up, going from bear to serpent, squeezing the life out of her. She desperately needed to use the garderobe. Her bowels screamed for release, but she couldn't risk escape unless it became truly desperate. And spirits forbid she actually wake him.

Garif snorted suddenly, explosively, and raised the arm clenched around her. She flinched instinctively, but he only brought his hand up to his face, rubbed so hard his nose might come off in his hand, and rolled over mumbling something. She didn't bother trying to catch the words, but moved as quickly as she could and not disturb him, rolling away before he could recapture her.

Free, she put a hand to her chest, willing her heart to stop pounding, afraid he would hear it. Forcing herself to slow her breaths.

She watched to be sure he hadn't sensed her fear, that his immobility wasn't some trick and that he wasn't about to lash out. After endless moments where her insides threatened to burst, she finally took the risk.

There was faint light behind the shutters when she returned. Dawn. He would wake soon, and expect breakfast laid out for him. Or he would sleep, lulled by softer accommodations than he was used to in the field. She'd have to time it just right. Too soon and he'd complain that the bread was stale or the cheese hard. Too late and he'd rail that she'd dawdled, probably accuse her, as he had in the past, of listening at doorways and being a traitor like her "bitch mistress" or lingering with lovers, like the slut she was.

She'd have to beg more rations for their fire as well, so that she could actually bring the water up to boiling for his chofee. And hers as well.

At least she'd have heat while Garif was in residence. Warmth for terror. It seemed a poor exchange.

Cia left, again closing the door behind her as silently as possible. She hurried to the kitchens. They, at least, were warm, a hive of activity as bread was kneaded and rolled, fruit and cheese were cut for distribution. Brinda, the mistress of the kitchen, was already drenched, her graying hair escaping her lopsided bun in spirals that stuck to her face. She had never forgiven that it had been her food supposedly poisoned by "that foreign *brula*" as she'd spoken of the Cia's mistress ever since King Cyril had been found dead following the private supper in his chambers with Queen Inaya. A supper *Cia* had taken from the kitchen maid at the chamber door. She'd seen to the serving out of the meal before she was dismissed. In Brinda's mind – in all of Jucar's minds – everything had been fine coming from the kitchen. No one there had anything to gain. So, the poison must have been introduced by the queen or her hand-maiden. Both from Frizenze, the land of potions and poisons. Also, spices and silks and so much else, but none of that mattered. They only saw their dead king and that Cia and Queen Inaya had the means and, apparently, the motive. The Queen carried his heir and so a foreign princess-turned-queen might think to control the Jucari throne through her son. The Jucari had made entirely sure this would never happen. Cia felt this in her heart, even if she couldn't prove it. After the king had been found dead, they'd thrown Inaya and Cia both in the frozen North Tower, but not together. Cia had been placed much lower – only close enough to hear Inaya's sobs. To know that their fates were tied, and should those cries ever cease... She'd tried to comfort her Queen by singing songs from their homeland, hoping her voice carried throughout the tower, so that

Inaya would know she was not alone. When Cia had received the baffling offer to marry Garif or die for her crimes, she'd thought that in agreeing to the marriage, escaping her captivity, she might plead for Inaya. She'd thought that a powerful mageri might hold some sway. She'd thought... a lot of foolish things. She'd been so young then.

But King Cyril's brother didn't want reason. Jannik wanted blood. He wanted war.

What he did *not* want was Cyril's heir, a possible boy-child who might someday supplant him. Cia was almost certain of it. Oh, women did lose babes, she knew that. But with medics and mageri on hand to protect her, Inaya should have been able to bring King Cyril's babe into the world. Unless... She would not think of the unless. But in her darkest days, she feared that in deserting Inaya, she'd hastened her demise. After Inaya lost the babe, she'd lost her will to live, and the Jucari moved up her execution, lest she die on her own and rob them of their sport.

Cia shut down those thoughts as they squeezed at her heart, threatened to show on her face. She couldn't afford to appear anything but serene and steady. And she could *never* step any further into Brinda's kitchen than necessary, lest she seem suspect. Even at the periphery she was watched like a hawk.

Brinda saw Cia the moment she arrived, but ignored her at first, except to watch through unsubtle side-glances until she could order one of her underlings to deal with her.

Maryllis, dark-haired, eyes the color of midnight, so petite she looked half her age, bustled up and dropped a curtsy. Cia was taken aback, but tried not to show it. While Maryllis's smile, like the sun, shone on everyone, the bob of respect was new.

"I hear that the men are back!" she said happily. "You'll be needing extra rations then, for Mager Garif?"

There was a note of hero-worship in her voice, and maybe that was what the curtsy had been about; Cia had suddenly gained stature with the reminder that she was Mager Garif's wife rather than just "the traitor's handmaiden." They had no idea she took more pride in the latter or how hard she worked not to hate them after all they'd done to her queen. She knew she couldn't blame everyone. Those in power told the people what to believe and tolerated no dissent. Not that any was offered when the salacious story involved a foreign princess to blame and her rich lands to invade, even if it hadn't gone as anticipated.

And so, she forced the smile she'd perfected over the years.

"Yes, thank you," she said, using precious energy to inject warmth into her words. "And the Mager requests that you send someone with more fuel for our fire."

Maryliss's lips compressed as though she wanted to scold Cia for not already having everything ready, as though she'd like to instruct Cia on the proper homecoming for a returning hero, only it wasn't her place. "I'll send one of the brindle boys up for the fire," Maryllis said instead, "and if you'll wait, I'll get you a tray. It will save sending one of the maids along on such a busy morning."

As Cia knew from experience, she might never see a maid on the quietest of days. Rumors ran rampant in the early days of the princess's imprisonment that Cia had acquired the poison for her. Or worse, poisoned the king herself! King Cyril was a known philanderer, and not well known to accept rejection. Perhaps Cia had meant only to strike out against him, discourage his amorous pursuits. It was more thrilling to speculate on possibilities than settle on a scenario. Whatever the degree, her guilt was apparently undeniable. Most treated her as though she'd ply her poison trade again at the least provocation. The fact that she'd never had such a trade didn't matter.

"I'll wait, thank you," Cia said. "And just ask the boy to leave the supplies outside our door when he comes." Garif didn't allow men or boys of any stripe inside their quarters—at least not when he was absent. She daren't change things now that he was back, for fear that he'd misinterpret a stray glance.

Maryliss curtsied again, then realized what she was doing on the way down. She popped up again and was off in an instant.

Cia shifted from foot to foot as she waited. She dreaded going back, but there was nowhere else for her to go. She'd been dead to her family and a traitor to Frizenze from the moment she'd married into the people who had killed her queen. Yet she prayed daily for the death and destruction of the war to end, and that the All forgive her secret wish that Garif not survive it. The mageri, with their constructs created from the energies ripped from the earth, were prime targets on the battlefields. So many had been lost already. Her people had found a way to subvert the will of the controlling mageri, to turn their creations against them using poison. Always poison. Her lands were known for their rich spices, their scents and oils that could soothe or enflame. Her people could heal or harm with equal artistry. When the Jucari framed her princess to start a war, they'd chosen a most likely lie.

11

So many lost, and yet Garif always returned.

Maryliss came back with the tray and handed it off with no further commentary, as though she was embarrassed by her earlier slip into deference. Cia was careful with each step back toward her quarters. More people were about now. A few even bobbed their heads in acknowledgement.

All was quiet when she reached their room. She listened first at the door, though what she expected to come through, she didn't know. The walls were solid stone, and the door a thick slab of wood that swelled and stuck in the warmer months. Maybe it was just a stalling tactic. She didn't let it last long. Instinct or mageri power, Garif always seemed to know what she was about.

She let herself in, balancing one end of the tray on her hip, and found Garif already up, staring into the embers of the fire.

"It's gone out," he said, not even turning to look at her.

If she said they didn't give her enough to keep it going when he was gone, he might use it as an excuse to call her ungrateful and show her how much worse she could have it.

"I've brought your food, and a boy will be coming with more fuel for the fire. The war has everything closely rationed." She prayed it sounded neutral enough.

He turned then, eyed her for falsehood or, she was sure, for any sign of dishevelment or excitement, as though anything about the marital state had left her wanting another man.

When he didn't immediately fly into a rage, she set the tray down on their table, which she'd long ago moved closer to the fire. He sat and let her serve him, eating as though he hadn't in a year. He didn't react when the knock came at the door, and she didn't linger taking up the armful of wood and straw-brick the boy had brought for the fire. She nursed the embers back to blazing life and set the kettle to heat.

"Strategy meeting this morning," Garif said, around a mouthful of bread and cheese. "I won't be back until mid-day, maybe later. Have a bath ready for me when I return."

He looked at her slyly out of the corner of his eye when he said it, waiting for the panic over the impossible task he'd set. She'd learned over the years to squirrel away bits of ribbon and lace to bribe certain maids to let her know when meetings adjourned. At least some had overcome their fear of her when years passed and no one came down dead. But if anyone played her false or didn't move swiftly enough or if it took the bath water too long to heat, Garif would take it out on her hide.

She did her best to beat back her rising fears as she would a fire that had leapt to her skirts. "As you will," she said passively, looking to rob him of his moment.

He grunted and continued eating. She readied the chofee, but he was gone before he could drink it, so she sat with it herself and eyed the dregs of the meal he had left to her.

CHAPTER TWO

Bess

Crown Princess Bessory V'Alban of Jucar curled her fingers into her palm tightly enough to draw blood. Her shiv-sharp nails sliced as cleanly into her own flesh as they had into her maid's where she'd tapped the girl to draw out her essence, her anima. The maid's discarded body was hidden back in her quarters, wilted and awaiting disposal via the secret passage to which only she held the key.

Her stolen energy raced through Bess's heart as she listened to her council lords and military men rant and rage, putting on a performance for the others present. The only thought they gave her was clear from their sidelong glances. Wouldn't this be too bloody and boring for her delicate sensibilities? She smiled inwardly, outwardly raising an imperious brow to which no one said a word. They barely noticed in the furor of casting blame upon each other—her generals and her mageri each certain they could have won the war by now if the other hadn't gotten in their way.

She allowed it to go on long enough to make her point, and then tugged on the tether she had to her Regent, the almighty man set over her when both male heirs of the V'Alban line had died too young – oh, not for her purposes, but certainly for theirs. Her second brother, Jannik was so fond of the war he'd declared that he'd ridden off to it himself. She knew what they all thought—so selfish of Jannik to take up the sword before assuring the succession, saddling them with this snip of a girl! If he was going to be inconsiderate enough to succumb to his war wounds, he could first have won them a decisive victory! King Grammond's youngest could not possibly assume control, all because she'd been born with the power to birth babies rather than beget them on others. Thus, they delayed the coronation while they scrambled to find her a husband, as her betrothed had died before fulfilling the role, preferably a relation to one of their lords. Or a male heir they could control in her stead. They didn't know her spymaster was under strict orders to assure that such schemes died aborning.

Regent Strego raised fists the size of mallets, and when he dropped them on the table, it sounded with a crack, as though it might split beneath them. Every man in the room froze. Lips stopped moving. Some hearts might have skipped a beat.

Princess Bessory stepped forward into the sudden silence. She used her strongest voice, but feared she still sounded like the child they saw her to be, "I will not belittle our achievements. We *have* gained ground. However, we have been fighting for six long years. I have lost a brother to this war, and you a king. Many of the people of Jucar have lost brothers, fathers, husbands. Too many to count. And while we've made inroads into Frizenze, we cannot yet see our way to victory. Now we fight Galitrüd as well, in need of undeadened, fertile lands. Unless something changes, the war might rage for another six years with nothing to show for it but more death, more scarcity, more unrest."

Immediately, General Bowstan and at least three others sought to interrupt her, and Regent Strego pounded the table again. He was built square and solid, like a guard tower, stone to the table's oak. There was no contest between them.

"You forget yourselves," Strego said, his voice like a lash. "You have all had your time to speak, and see what you've accomplished. Nothing. You tell us what we know. You offer problems with only the solutions you've brought time and again. We have something new to say, and *you will listen.*"

The Princess ground her teeth. The unquestioning respect he was afforded, the way all looked to him was the very reason she'd tapped into Strego, borrowed some of his strength and replaced it with her will, drawn him into her web. But the need for it stung like hornets.

"We are running out of resources," she continued. First, feed their own words back to them. "We are not outmatched, but if we don't recruit more and change our strategies, we may become outmanned. The Frizenzians have already had female mageri on their side. We know that there are women in Jucar who can perform workings as well." *But you must not look at me. It's been bred out of the royal line, as far as you know. As far as anyone knows.* "It was ever my father's policy and my brother's as well, that women were needed in the home, but there are clearly women who wield mageri powers. It is time to call them to service."

Everyone wanted to talk at once, but it was General Bowstan, a vein popping in his eye, flooding it with blood at the effort to rein in his anger, who shouted them all down. "Women? Who might come down pregnant? They have no place on the battlefield."

"You make it sound as though it is an ague–'come down pregnant'. If it is a sickness, we all know how it is passed. If you are concerned, keep the men away from them. Or do you fear your ability to do so?"

His face was now the color of hot iron fresh from the forge. "You insult all of us. The mageri. Me and my men. *All* of us who have fought so hard to win your war."

"*Our* war," Princess Bessory said dangerously. If his eyes were blood, hers were daggers. "Or have you misplaced your loyalties?"

"I am on the front lines of *our* war," he spat. "I see daily the death and sacrifice of your troops. To suggest that we are not enough, that you, sitting here in your castle and comfort, know better..." The General turned toward her Regent, appealed to him as the real power behind the throne. "Sir, you've been in the field. You know."

"What I *know*," Regent Strego said, not once looking to her for direction, "is that if you were enough, we would be winning."

General Bowstan reared back like he'd been slapped.

"This has been a war of attrition and it is coming at too high a cost," the Regent continued. "We need something bold. We need fresh blood."

"Even if women were suited for warfare—" Bowstan restarted, modulating his tone for the Regent.

But Strego cut in. "That female mageri, as I understand it, choked the better part of a battlefield, ramming the very air down their throats before she was taken down."

"But she *was* struck down."

"And how many died in that endeavor?"

"*Even* if women were suited for combat," Bowstan tried again, ignoring the gauntlet Strego had thrown down, "we couldn't spare the resources to train them. And defending them on the field would distract from the fight and get others killed."

"That's the very reason the Magery doesn't train women. Too easily distracted by thoughts of home and hearth, too vulnerable. Worrying over them makes others vulnerable," said a new man stepping forward—an imposing figure, tall and broad with a salt and pepper beard to his knees threaded with bone beads that fascinated her, though the man himself assuredly did not. Mager Garif, who'd been her brother Jannik's right hand on the battlefield. "By your leave, your Majesty, we have no female mageri to send."

"You misunderstand me," Princess Bessory said with a smile that showed teeth. If Bowstan and Garif wouldn't respect their elders, and Regent Strego was their elder by at least a decade, they would learn to respect their betters. It chafed that her actual coronation would not come until the thaw when most of her dukes could be gathered to witness, but she was their majesty with or without the crown. "I gave an order, not an opinion. Tell me again how you *won't*, and I'll find people who will. And then I'll have no further need of you."

She looked first to General Bowstan to be certain he understood her meaning. She could practically see him calculating whether or not she'd carry through. His was a face that could be best described in field maneuvers. His hair had most undeniably retreated, leaving the field to his brows, which were still skirmishing, as they certainly hadn't settled into formation. His lower jaw had gotten the jump on his upper, both over-shadowed by the hawkish nasal army of the north perched above them.

He didn't know enough to fear her yet, but he would. Bowstan, like most, saw her as a figurehead, a placeholder until she could bear a king.

"General?" Strego prompted.

Bowstan made a deep bow to the Princess and another nearly as deep to the Regent. "Your will is my command," he said, meeting the Princess's gaze before lowering his in deference. "I live to serve."

She would see to it. Or to the alternative.

Then she turned her head toward Mager Garif, his gaze practically burning into her. Most of the mageri who'd survived the Blood War remained in the field with the troops in their winter camps holding the territory they'd gained. In rare cases, they returned home for brief visits with family as it became too snow-swept for fighting, if that family was close enough for travel to be safe and return to be assured. It was her curse that Garif lived at the palace.

Gareth seethed, growing with each inhale, yet hardly seeming to diminish with his exhales. His eyes burned with the poisonous sort of hatred apt to corrode any vessel that contained it. *But not yet,* they promised. *You first.*

Erdain, their lead strategist, her brother Cyril's court mageri when he'd been king, was both older and wiser than Garif. He pressed his lips thin to keep from commenting at all. He didn't look happy, but neither did he look stupid enough to say so.

"You are dismissed," she said to the room at large, pointedly looking at Garif, letting him know who held the power.

In defiance, he flashed a glance at Strego, who nodded almost imperceptibly, making Bess bite her lip until it bled.

Then he was gone.

As soon as the room cleared, the Princess's spymaster appeared as though he'd formed from the shadows. He was a blade of a man, all sharp angles and no more flesh than it took to cover his bones. His hair was an ink stain pulled back into a queue, but at any given time it might be back or down, shaggy or slicked, parted to one side or another or not at all, his mustache overgrown or groomed and oiled, each change rendering him somehow unrecognizable. He could grow with menace or shrink with subservience, claim or avert attention. There was a reason Ruggerio had risen from such humble beginnings, a reason Jannik had elevated him after executing the previous spymaster for failing to stop Cyril's assassination.

Secrets swam in his eyes, but they were a pool of oil and tar, and wouldn't allow any to escape into the world.

She stifled a shiver that wanted to wrack her frame. There was something about Ruggerio that both intrigued and terrified her. Enough that she'd never tried her powers on him for fear that she would fail and he would take it very badly.

"He bears watching," Ruggerio said softly, flicking a glance at the Regent, but dismissing him to focus on the Princess. He had to look down to do it. She came barely to his chest, yet still she strove to find some modicum of height as she hadn't tried with Bowstan.

"Strego? Of all those present?" she whispered in disbelief.

"The others defy you openly."

She stared, then waved her hand dismissively. "If there's anything afoot, I'm sure you'll see to it. That's what I have you for."

He gave a small nod, his movements as economical as always. "But female mageri, Princess? Not that I question your directive, of course," he added swiftly. "My concern is how you'll recruit these women. It's unlikely they will step forward, even if you make it a decree. With so many lost to the war or the Rot, those remaining may have people to care for. Or they may follow the Church and be unwilling to use what power they have. They may go into hiding or seek sanctuary."

"If they won't come forward, we'll make it rewarding for people to report them. Offer a finder's fee," Regent Strego said, speaking her mind from his mouth.

She'd had to bring him along slowly at first so that when they began to work in concert it seemed that she'd finally accepted his guidance rather than the other way around. Deceptions were easy when they met people's expectations.

"Then my men will spend their time chasing down false leads on inconvenient women," Ruggerio said.

Bess narrowed her eyes at him. "Inconvenient women?"

He waved a hand like it was nothing. "Unmarriageable or barren, unforgiving of a man's affairs. Sickly or unmanageable."

The Regent held up a hand to stop the flow, which was probably wise, because Bess was seething, and Ruggerio was too dangerous a target for her rage, even if he merited it. But he wasn't giving his opinion, simply stating a truth as inconvenient as the women he imagined. Jucar didn't value women beyond their usefulness, and even then limited those uses.

Strego stroked his beard in thought, wiry gray hairs coming to mid-chest with stray raven strands here and there to show what once was. "Then we institute punishments for false reports. I would not be advocating along with the Princess if such desperate measures weren't in order. The war has come almost to a standstill. This is not the time for a gentle hand."

Ruggerio was shaking his head before Strego finished. "People would fear to come forward. It might drive people toward the Church or, worse, the Restoration, which is already against us."

"Well, then, what do you suggest?" Bess asked, her tone sharp enough to cut. The bloody Church taught that the anima was too precious to play with. Whether an individual's lifeforce or the collective spirit that flowed through all things, it was creative energy. Natural and necessary. Sacred. Not meant to be taken and twisted.

But it was like any other resource. What good was iron until drawn from the earth and tempered into a blade or a vessel? Or gold or silver until it was refined and fashioned into intricate works? And yet, the Restoration rebels thought that working the anima should be punishable by death.

"Discretion, my Princess," Ruggerio said. "We listen, we hunt down the prospects, we *impress* our need upon them."

As always. Women wouldn't be asked. They would be told. Her own plan, but it chafed from Ruggerio's lips.

"I have a prospect for you already," she said. "I've heard my servants speak of a widow who lives beside All Souls Cemetery who caters to the living but speaks with the dead."

Something shifted in his eyes, but it was gone so quickly she couldn't interpret what she'd seen.

"I will investigate whether she has any true skills that will contribute to the cause," he promised, but his voice was tinged with doubt. "Do you have a name?"

"Talk with my women," she said. "One of them will know it."

"I frighten them," he responded, but he smiled, as if that wasn't an entirely unpleasant prospect.

"They are wise to be frightened," she answered.

His lips stretched to show teeth, and it was the smile of a wolf, toothy and pointed. "Is that all, my Princess?"

Though it wasn't entirely proper, she felt an odd thrill at the possessive. She didn't like that at all. She'd had a childhood crush on the man who was now her spymaster. Growing up, she'd seen him as a shadow here, a suggestion there, flitting like a romantic figure through the castle. She'd done all she could to stifle it. She'd been betrothed from the time of her birth to the heir-apparent of Galitrüd, a sickly boy who hadn't made it to adulthood. Her father had died before he could arrange a new match, and her brothers had always been too busy, but she'd been meant for a noble and political marriage.

Ruggerio was beneath her, but it didn't stop the thrill she felt in his presence. Perhaps it would help if she thought of him as she should. Not Ruggerio, but the Crown Blade. Or simply, the Blade, as he was known by reputation rather than sight. A boogeyman to keep the nobility in line.

She forcibly stifled her reaction and inclined her head. She added before he could turn away. "You might bring Mager Garif with you when you go after the woman. Such an errand should be appropriately humbling, and he can help you convince her to come along if need be."

He bobbed his head and slipped silently from the room. Bess cursed herself at the realization that she'd phrased her order as a suggestion, and that, young as she was, he might take it that way. She had to do better.

Strego also glanced thoughtfully after the spymaster. "You are dismissed as well," she told him. "You have plans to set in motion."

When he took her hand to bow over it and graze his lips over her knuckles, she slit the skin of his palm with nails that were sharp enough to bite. She brought the hand to her mouth and sucked the blood away, tasting the jolt of fear like zest. It reminded her momentarily of the tang of the ginger candies he'd slipped her at court when she was small and trotted out for show at court functions she was supposed to stay at far too long without fidgeting. She wished she could whisk away her own memories as easily as she could tamper with his will and make him forget about her doing so.

But what choice had they left her. Pawn or player…it was no choice at all.

She'd known enough to hide her powers since she was a little girl. Since the time her mother had taken an interest in her and brought her to the gardens in the company of the courtier with the hair of autumn gold. There must have been ladies-in-waiting around as well. Or guards. But she didn't remember them. Only that she'd danced on ahead, feeling so much… something …in the wind that she struggled to put it into words. The collective breath of the world, the beating of wings, the rustling of leaves and living things, the energy and the spirit of it all. She bowed to flowers, breathing them in, touching their stems and feeling through them to the veins, and beyond them into the earth. Seeing a great tree blooming with white flowers, centers the pink of a lamb's tongue, and running ahead to throw her arms around it, her feet tangling with each other in her haste.

Her mother momentarily focusing back on her to laugh and ask, "My love, what are you doing?"

And Bess answering, "I can feel its blood run, Maman. Like when I put my head on your heart."

All laughter stopped then. All sound.

Her mother grabbed her arm. Hard. Bess cried out in pain as her mother yanked her away from the tree, pressed her against her skirts so that she could barely breathe. She was hurt, confused, bereft, asking her mother to stop, begging to know what she'd done. The skirts muffled her cries.

She cried all the way back to the palace. It was so rare that her mother touched her at all. When Maman was fed up with her cries, she shook her hard and told her to be silent. There was terror in her eyes. Then Maman swung her up into her arms and pressed Bess against her as she'd always wanted. Bess nuzzled into her neck, thinking finally to have the comfort, the soothing, the understanding. Only her mother's embrace was no comfort. The arm locked behind her was a steel bar that pressed Bess's face against her to keep any sounds from spilling out. Upon arrival at the palace, she locked herself and Bess in the nursery and made certain Bess knew she was an abomination. No one could ever know that Bess could sense the world as she did. No one. This wondrous thing was somehow not wondrous at all, but wrong. *She* was wrong. And she couldn't talk to anyone. Ever. Couldn't ask; couldn't tell.

She spent her childhood in pain and isolation, in fear of discovery, finally learning that what she'd touched was the anima. And that the power was forbidden to V'Albans, let alone *women* of royal lineage. It was too dangerous and potentially unstable. It had been bred out of the royal lines, ever since King Calestri had gone mad with power. Or so they said.

Which made her wonder whether she was truly her father's daughter, and if *that* was why her mother was so afraid. But she'd never seen her mother again except as a distant figure. She'd never taken Bess out again.

That would have been enough heartache, but she never even made eye contact. Her gaze would sweep over her daughter as though she was a tapestry, a mere furnishing. So Bess told herself lies—that her mother wasn't rejecting her, but working not to draw special attention to her. So that her daughter was safe. That it was love and not neglect. She never discovered the truth. Her mother died of a spring fever two years later, taking her secrets to the grave.

For years, she had tried to suppress her powers lest those secrets be discovered, until… But she wasn't going to think on that. She'd had years since to perfect her powers. To build up her protections. To come to her own understandings with no one to tell her where the lines were drawn. What she could or couldn't do.

She felt Strego's vitality trickle into her, but she could allow no more than a trickle. If he appeared too weak, if she took away too much of his will to reinforce her own, the court would see it. They wouldn't simply depose him in favor of another; they might depose *her*. Never mind that she'd been careful to assure there was no one left to take her place.

Bess whispered her will straight into Strego's veins as he stood there staring into nothingness, his mouth hanging slightly open. Her first command had been for him to be quiet and still, send his mind some-where far away, so that he could not fight her. She'd caught a glimpse of his quiet place once, and seen mountains in autumn, leaves in all their gemstone finery, a pristine lake glinting diamond facets. It seemed too serene for the man before her, whose power pulsed so temptingly. She had to force herself to stop when she thought it was enough.

But *enough* was a myth. The life force in his blood...the thrill of power that went through her...she wanted to drink it down, a flagon rather than a sip, a raging river rather than a stream.

She couldn't afford to. Not with someone as powerful as Strego. Not yet.

She continued her whisperings as she wiped her mouth and held her thumb against the wound to stop the bleeding, then she relinquished him, staring into his face to watch for the slightest sign of rebellion.

It didn't come.

Strego blinked twice, then smiled vaguely, as though he'd entered a room and forgotten why he'd come.

She smiled back at him, hoping his blood didn't show on her teeth.

"Thank you, Regent," she said, in her sweetest voice. "Would you send in my new maid on your way out?"

Irritation flashed over his face as he bowed. The errand was beneath him, but he would relay her wishes to someone who would tell someone else, and eventually her new girl would appear. Later, after the castle had gone quiet for the night, she would use some of her stolen power and the secret passage to dispose of the last girl.

CHAPTER THREE

Cia

Garif came back in a rage.

Despite the lace bribe, no warning had come. Maybe there hadn't been time. Not in the mood Garif was in. As heavy as the outer door was, he managed to slam it open, the wood cracking like bone against the wall.

Cia's needle slipped, stabbing into her finger, and she cried out as blood instantly stained the veil she'd been embroidering for months. Maybe she could save it if she soaked it right away, but Garif wasn't going to give her that chance. She quickly threw down her work and stuck her finger in her mouth to suck away the bleeding before Garif spotted it. So many things he could do with that blood. Use the excuse of her ruined work to beat her for clumsiness, tap into her with his power… That was what terrified her the most. He'd threatened it on any number of occasions, but he'd never done it. Yet.

She met Garif in the foyer, but the wild look in his eyes stopped her before she reached him.

"*You*," he spat, as though she'd done something to him. "Witches, all of you." He stepped forward with his staff, angling the weighted head forward. She knew the feel of it smashing into the soft core of her stomach, beating against her breasts. Anywhere he thought the bruises wouldn't show, wouldn't scar and diminish the prize he'd bought himself to abuse.

She stayed frozen, hoping that if she didn't move, she could maintain their tableau. She didn't know what he was angry about and so had no way to appease him.

She was terrified even to speak, to ask what had happened and how she could help. The idea that she might have any power to do so would incense him.

"Are you going to stand there as if I didn't give you very specific instructions before I left?" he roared. He hadn't even closed the door behind him. Anyone going by would hear what a terrible wife she was, how she'd failed in her duties. It so perfectly suited what they already believed of her.

"No, my lord," she said, the words no more than a breath. "I didn't know when you would return. I didn't want the bath to get cold. I'll go now."

Yet he still blocked the way, seething.

"Useless," he said, and it was even worse when he *did* step out of the way and close the door, because that was when the real hurt would begin. "Couldn't you just see yourself on a battlefield?"

She had no idea where this had come from or how to respond, and so she left it behind. "I'll see to the bath. The castle is in an uproar with the new influx. I'll have to go to the kitchens directly."

She started for the door, and Garif grabbed her painfully by one arm, hard enough to grind muscle against bone. "Use my name and don't dawdle. They'll do it now or you'll lug every jug of water from the pump to the tub yourself and heat it with your blood."

Cia swallowed hard, and he released her with a push that sent her into the door. She caught herself on her hands and was out into the hallway before he could grab her again. She didn't dare run through the hallways —always decorum for Mager Garif's suspect wife, lest anyone think he had her anything but perfectly trained. Cowed. But she walked with as much speed as her shaky legs would lend her.

It was one of the brindle boys, streaked with the soot from cleaning flues and tending fires, giving them the mottled appearance that led to their name, who saw her first and stopped to help, even with one arm laden with a brazier of hot coal to start a fire and a bag of tinder weighing down his other shoulder. She told him what she needed, and when he

25

started to respond that they'd have to wait their turn, Cia grabbed his free hand and held it to her heart.

If anyone saw... If anyone reported back to Garif...

"Please," she said, throwing all the desperation she felt into that one word, finally letting the fear show in her eyes. "Please. If he doesn't get what he wants, and fast…it won't go well for me."

The boy looked from his hand at her heart up into her face. His own eyes were huge in his pock-marked face. She'd never touched him before. Never touched anyone unless it was accidental and immediately withdrawn, but something in her manner must have reached him. Maybe on some level he understood.

"I'll see to it myself," he said, standing taller, as if this boy, younger than she'd been when she came to the castle, could save Cia himself.

Tears gathered in her eyes, and she thanked him, squeezing his hand and letting him go before hurrying off to the kitchen. She looked for Brinda or Maryliss or any of the kitchen maids, hoping to beg wine or ale that might take the edge off Garif's mood. Not too much. Just enough, whatever that might be.

She caught Brinda giving her the stink-eye and asked her for a bottle of Ridaldo red, invoking Garif's name. When Brinda huffed that she'd send someone up, Cia said she'd wait. Brinda almost chewed her lips off at that, as if she suspected Cia might poison their good wine on the way up.

"I'll bring it sealed then," she said meaningfully. "Mager Garif will have to open it himself."

Cia only nodded. Bringing the wine was a risk. The bottle was something he might fling at her or use to beat her. But there was plenty in their quarters that would do that job, and Garif might be loath to destroy a Ridaldo red. It might buy her time for him to cool down.

Brinda sent one of the maids off and distanced herself, but Cia had the wine before Garif could grow impatient. Though once she was back, she found herself standing outside her door, afraid to actually open it.

The brindle boy appeared at that moment along with another, carrying the tub between them. Cia sighed relief, and announced them before opening the door to allow them in. She followed after and saw Garif look from them to her to the bottle of red in her hand and stop. His gaze was no less wild or predatory, but she'd given him something to swoop down on, and witnesses to prevent it being her. For now.

Garif opened the red and sat with it, starting with a goblet, and then giving that up to swig directly from bottle as he watched with angry eyes the comings and goings of the boys. He growled in warning as the boy who'd helped her before poured the contents of one of his jars of water into her large cookpot for heating and offered to restoke the fire. The boy glanced at Cia for her reaction, but she didn't dare look back. Or even thank him. She only shook her head and went about her duties, feeling Garif's gaze shift to her, more heated than the fire that now blazed. She could almost feel it burning her where it touched.

As soon as the door closed behind the brindle boys, Garif flicked a finger at the poker she held and ordered, "Put that down and come here."

His voice was as hard as flint, and she feared any hesitation would spark the fire that seemed to be brewing in his belly. She looked to the poker in her hand. Barbed, tempered iron. For a moment, her fingers tightened around it. Perhaps his was not the only fire brewing.

But he saw. Of course, he saw.

Garif pounded the bottle down hard on the table and was on his feet in an instant, one hand wrapped around her throat and the other crushing her hand with the poker, squeezing so hard the pain had her gasping out the last of the air in her lungs. Panic tore at her. She tried to drop the poker, but Garif was gripping her too tightly. His fingers harder than iron, stronger than a vise, closing on her as though he could crush her hand and throat as completely as her spirit.

Please, she tried to say, but no sound came out. She didn't dare fight him with her one free hand, although instinct wanted her to claw, fight, pry his fingers away. Or jab for his eyes, tear at his genitals. All the things she'd ever imagined. Some of which she'd tried until she realized that he *wanted* her to fight to justify a bloodier beating. She'd given up when he'd bashed her so badly she had to have bones reset and reknit—thank the All a maid had been passing by and heard her that time, because Garif had gone back to the battlefront and not told anyone to look for her. And still it had taken her weeks to rise again. In her dreams, she still fought. In reality, dark spots were swimming in front of her eyes, coming together to blot out the world. Her head grew heavy, the world began to fade and for a second she thought she might finally have peace, slip away and deprive him of his favorite toy.

And then he threw her to the floor. The poker went flying, and he kicked it aside. Kicked her while she was down. She curled, knowing what was coming, protecting her soft bits as best she could while gasping in air. She tried to scuttle away from him before he could kick her again, but he pinned her with a foot to the top of her chest, toe of his boot pressing into her abused windpipe. Her air cut off again, then wheezed in as he eased up, only to shut off again as his weight shifted, as though he wanted to remind her that she lived or died at his pleasure.

"You forgot yourself while I was away. I guess I will have to reteach you."

She'd thought she was done fighting. Apparently, she was wrong. Instinct won out, and she pushed frantically at his foot, trying to dislodge it, desperate for air. He ground down instead, and her whole body seized before he let up. She coughed, but it shot agony through her, like she'd broken something that couldn't be fixed.

He lifted his foot again, but only so that he could kick her over onto her side. "Get up. Get my bathwater ready. I have another meeting ahead of me, and I won't smell as though I've been wallowing in filth." It was clear from his glower that she was the filth. As though she cared for his good opinion. As though his glare had the power to harm her when he had hands and feet and his staff.

Cia forced herself to rise, ignoring the pain in her side, and the gasp that threatened to tear open her throat. She had to stop halfway up to let the spots clear as her head went light and her vision swam again. She expected another kick, but it didn't come. Instead, Garif watched, taking it all in, the expression on his face warning that he had something else in mind.

She almost rose to her full height but couldn't quite straighten. Not all the way. She stood hunched and dizzy, but she couldn't wait for that to pass. She reached for the mitts that she used to handle the heated pots, but Garif slapped them away.

"Bare handed," he ordered.

She dared to look at him in disbelief. In horror. She couldn't. The hot metal would melt her flesh. She'd never again embroider or tat or lace. She'd never… She would be completely useless to him and to everyone. What would he do to her then? What was he about to do now?

His lips curled cruelly. He knew exactly what the burns would do to her. He didn't care. As bad as he'd ever been, she'd never seen him like *this*.

When she didn't instantly obey, Garif reached for his staff and held it like a cudgel. "If I bleed you, I end you," he threatened. "I can tap into your power, what little that may be, and take it into myself. Maybe some good would finally come of you."

It was her greatest fear. Not death, but that he might somehow consume her. She didn't know how his magic worked. Not really. But mageri staffs were cruelly tipped so they could stab into the land to tap the anima, to bleed its power and manipulate it into their battle constructs or do whatever they pleased with it. If Garif turned it on her...

No!

She was finished with this. He had taken everything else—her queen, her country, her dignity. Ending her was one thing, subsuming her was entirely another. *He would not use her.* Not anymore.

A fire started in her stomach and roared through her, as though a flue had been opened. It blew the pain back into the cobwebbed corners of her soul, straightening her to her full height. Maybe he was right, and she'd forgotten herself while he was away. Or maybe she'd just remembered.

Garif saw the answer in her eyes, and snarled as he swung the weighted end of his staff at her, aiming for her temple before she had time to seek a weapon of her own, the poker she'd lost or a hot log from the fire. She'd gladly burn herself up in his destruction.

But there was a weapon bearing down on her, and as it was about to strike, she reeled back and grabbed the staff at the bulbous, bashing end. Terror leant her preternatural strength, and she pulled hard, shocking them both by sliding the staff right out of his hands.

He lunged for it, arms outstretched to grab it back, and she gave it to him, the sharp end pointed right for his chest. His own momentum thrust him well onto it, and the tip stabbed deeply into his body.

For an instant, their eyes met—his wide in disbelief. Hers possibly just as wide, just as disbelieving. For once they were in perfect concert.

Then his knees started to buckle, and he faltered back, crashed into the edge of the soaking tub and toppled in, taking the staff with him. Cia watched in numb horror as the water turned red with his blood and she knew she had no more need to warm his bathwater.

CHAPTER FOUR

Cia

Cia collapsed to the floor, her legs suddenly refusing to support her. She was shaking, her teeth chattering, as though the cold of the grave had come for her instead of Garif. She'd always thought she'd be the one to die at *his* hand.

She'd done it now. Become what they'd always thought of her.

A killer.

A hard knock at the door scared her straight off the floor, and Cia found herself standing on quivering legs like a deer who'd been spotted by the hunters and couldn't make herself move. She stared at the door as though she could see through it, as though there could possibly be help on the other side. Her mind raced, coming up with and discarding a thousand plans. She could throw herself on the mercy of whoever had come, sink into the hysteria she felt at her situation and let them misread the cause as horror at the accident that had taken Garif from her. But even if she could be convincing, no one would care. She'd killed a mageri. The punishment was death.

She could blame an assassin or a terrible accident, Garif falling on his staff. Every explanation was more outlandish than the next, and in the end, they'd blame her as they had her princess. Because it was easy. Because she was the outsider. Because they hated her already.

Her only choice was to run.

"Mager Garif," a voice came through the door. A man's voice. Full of command. "I need to speak with you on an urgent matter."

Cia didn't recognize the voice, so she had no way to predict what would come next. Sooner or later, someone would come looking for Garif when he wasn't found for the important meeting he'd mentioned. There would be a master key for their room. Or the door would be broken down. She had to be gone by then.

The handle on their door rocked back and forth. Had Garif locked it? She couldn't remember.

Her heart pounded like it was going to beat right out of her chest.

Her embroidered veil was already ruined. She wouldn't be there to soak or finish it. Her quarters were on the second floor. Austerity had left her so thin she was certain she could squeeze through the window. The drop would likely break her legs if not kill her, but if she could anchor herself and let herself down with the veil...

The thing that flashed instantly to mind was Garif's staff, buried deep within his body. It would be long and sturdy enough to use as an anchor. But if she made a move, the man on the other side of the door would hear. He'd know there was someone within, and something wrong that no one was answering him back.

She didn't think twice. Better to make a mistake through action than inaction. At least she'd have tried.

She leapt at the staff and put everything she had into one great pull. Garif's body didn't want to give up the staff even in death, and at first rose with it. When the tip slipped free, the body splashed back into the bath with enough noise that the man on the other side of the door called again, "Mager Garif!"

There was great alarm now. Whether the door was unlocked or the man at the door possessed a key or had to send for one, she was out of time.

Cia grabbed the bloody veil off her table, tied one end around the middle of the staff and knotted it as best she could. She fled to the window and threw open the shutters. She twisted her skirts around herself so they wouldn't get caught and propped her hips up on the windowsill. She could hear the doorknob twisting violently as she tucked her legs through the narrow window, positioned the staff crosswise in the opening, and started to lower herself down using the veil.

She heard the door of the room burst open, and lost her grip, the

31

sudden fall shocking a scream out of her that had frigid air seizing her lungs. She fell two floors and hit the ground with a blow to her back that reverberated outward through her body. It took an instant for sense to return and to roll to her feet, thankful when she was able to do so. She looked quickly around. Their quarters were on the cliff side of the castle. She'd fallen mere steps from the rocky drop off. The wind blew her back against the walls and she followed its lead, pressing herself against the stone so that she couldn't be seen from above if someone leaned out the window looking for Garif's killer.

His killer.

She couldn't think like that. It still wasn't real.

Cia slid around the side of the castle, staying close, willing that the people who'd ignored her all this time would continue to do so. That she could remain invisible.

It was a futile hope. The yelling from above raised the alarm throughout the castle. A bell rang out from the ramparts, and an answering commotion went up from the gate. She couldn't hear words, only barked orders, and then the unmistakable rattle of the portcullis going down. She imagined it like the executioner's blade coming down on her neck. She gasped and had to spit out the hair the frigid wind had whipped in her face—her blue-black hair, the color of a grackle's wing. Common enough in Frizenze, but in Jucar there would be no mistaking her. The guards hastily mounting their horses would know just who they were after. The foreigner. And the only madwomen out in the crystalline cold without even a shawl running for the gates as though her life depended on it.

Think, think, think.

Behind her came cries to hold from the castle guards. Ahead there were horsemen about to ride her down. She had no power and no weapons and no time.

The first horseman was upon her, sword out, but he wasn't ready to use it, only to flash it menacingly. She dodged him, straight into the blade of another horseman. Her spine curved in a way she had no idea it could as she twisted out of the way of it and straight into the path of another swordsman. In these numbers, they didn't have to run her through on the spot. All they had to do was surround her, cage her in, and she'd be locked up in a tower until her execution, just like her princess.

And then she saw it. This one had mounted too quickly. Or a horse he didn't commonly use. The stirrups weren't set for him, and so he didn't have his feet though them. His seat wasn't secure.

She stopped for an instant, long enough for the swordsman to think she was frozen in place, so that he'd commit to grabbing for her. She was aware that someone could swing in from the other side and was prepared to dart away. If there was one skill she'd learned from Garif, it was knowing when to flinch. When the horseman before her moved, so did she, slipping under his reach, ducking under his horse, and coming up on the far side. She grabbed his foot and heaved him hard in the direction he was already overbalanced.

There was a moment where things could have gone either way. The swordsman flailed for a better grip on the reins, catching bits of the horse's mane in the attempt. The horse didn't like that at all, and thrashed his head, tearing the reins from the man's hand. The man went flying, crying out as he fell. Cia didn't waste any time in rucking up her skirts to an indecent level, grabbing the suddenly slack reins for herself, and sliding a foot into the closest stirrup to heft herself up on to the horse before the rider could rise again.

There were horsemen on the right and left of her, one reaching to tear her off her new mount, the other swinging for her head. Eyes wide, she lay low over the horse's neck, slid her other foot into the stirrup, which seemed to have been sized just for her, and kicked at the horse's side to drive him on. There was no way to turn him in the press. He bolted forward, straight into the royal guards who had poured out of the castle. He reared before them, hooves lashing out. It was only by hugging tightly to the horse's neck that she kept her seat. She'd ridden out with her princess on numerous occasions back in Frizenze, but nothing like this.

The royal guard fell back before the thrashing hooves, and it gave Cia the space she needed. When the horse fell back to all fours, she wheeled him around, spotted the narrow gap they'd left in the gatehouse formation and drove him hard through it.

The huge cry behind them added to the horse's burst of speed. He ran like the hounds of Ravenia were chasing him. Cia held on for dear life. Her haste and rucked up skirts meant that her seat was far from perfect. It was all she could do to cling low and hope her muscles held. Already her thighs were quivering from the clenching, and her hands felt as though her fingers had frozen in place and might never unclench.

The portcullis was nearly halfway down. It was going to be close, but she didn't dare stop. Crushed or caught, the result would be death.

As they hit the portcullis, she hugged even more tightly to the stallion, who was already head down, running full out. She felt the metal tip of the gate rake across her back, tearing fabric and scraping flesh, but it couldn't hold them, and in a searing instant they were through.

They galloped full bore toward the town, the road now unobstructed before them. Pursuit would come, but it would take time to reopen the portcullis and for those who'd poured out of the palace to mount up. In that time, she'd have to disappear into town, lose the horse, and find a place to hide.

How, she had no idea. She had no money, no protection from the elements and no one who would dare help her.

CHAPTER FIVE

Ulan

Ulan laughed with the crowd as she jumped back from the man in the flame-bright motley leaping for the lamp pole before her and swinging around it like a whirl-a-gig. She'd been prepared to walk around it, but not for a man to come flying, brandishing a wooden sword and yelling to his opponent, "Ho!" and "He!" and for a capering man dressed in scarves of purple and blue to holler back, "Have at it!" and "Be still, you swine!"

They swung and dodged and leapt and whirled with great pageantry, pulling faces. The capering man sometimes ducked behind a woman's skirts, only to have her beat at him, much to the amusement of the crowd. Ulan didn't have the time to watch. On the other hand, pushing through the crowd seemed near impossible.

Blue-motley ducked behind a young boy, making himself very small, and pressing a shushing finger to his lips, eyes gleaming with great mischief. But he was clearly the cad in the piece, and everyone was pointing, yelling, "Here! Here!"

With a great squeak, he popped up, threw his hands in the air, his play sword falling to the ground as he declared his opponent in Jucari red and gold the victor. The crowd cheered, and the hero produced two hats seemingly from thin air. He quickly brought them round to their audience, announcing that filling the one on the left was a vote for mercy and the right a vote to end the wretch.

Ulan didn't stay to see how the pageant wrapped. Something was wrong. She felt it as a pricking along the back of her neck. Not the icy awareness of something other. No, her ghosts hadn't followed her to market. But something had. She scanned the crowd, turned to look behind her, but there was nothing and no one glancing her way.

If it had been a ghost—well, there would be no reason for it to hide. Few stuck around rather than rejoin the All. When they did stay, they had an agenda. They didn't need to sleep or eat; they didn't have responsibilities to distract them. Their single-mindedness of purpose could drive those they haunted to the very edges of sanity. On occasion, they hunted Ulan down, knowing she could see them, hear them, insisting she provide them aid.

But this was no ghost. She pushed through the crowd to get to the apothecary, hoping to lose her follower in the crush and get back to her little one as quickly as possible. She hated these moments away, but she'd tried sending others for what she needed, and they never came back with the right stock or the quality, if they came back at all after she'd given them the coin to pay.

Ulan stopped quickly at a street vendor selling cookware, hoping to find something that gleamed enough to catch sight of her pursuer. A pickpocket, perhaps? If so, not a very good one, to be caught and to have chosen so poor a target. Maybe a shy customer, hoping to observe Ulan before approaching? She hoped not a client unhappy with her services. She offered stitches and salves, not miracles, as she was quick to point out. But that wasn't always good enough. When people were in pain, they sometimes needed to lash out. They couldn't fight an enemy they couldn't see, so some affixed her face.

She held up a pot as though examining it, angling it this way and that to study the walkway in all directions.

The sudden voice at her shoulder nearly made her drop the pot. "Ulanka, come with me."

Ruggerio.

She started to twist, to gauge how much trouble she was in, but he gripped her by the elbow, and she had just enough time to place the pot back on the table before he marched her away.

Ulan should be relieved it was only Ruggerio, but the tension with which he held her communicated itself. He might be her cousin, but he was first and foremost the Princess's Spymaster. Being family gained her nothing but his awareness of her existence in a way that was completely unhealthy for a woman with secrets. He had not, so far as she could determine, a scintilla of sentiment.

She didn't make a fuss but went docilely as he steered her into a small teashop, which was currently unattended. His doing, no doubt. He closed and locked the door behind him. They were in a kitchen hung with herbs, lined with glass jars holding an assortment of spices and loose leaves, bubbling cauldrons, steeping pots, and a platter of biscuits probably baked elsewhere. The warmth and scent of dueling herbs would have calmed her in any other company.

When Ruggerio released her, she whirled. She hated to have her back to him, but looking him in the eyes was hardly better. They sucked the light – glittering, but with the shine of venom.

"What do you want?" she asked, her voice coming out breathlessly rather than strong and annoyed, as she intended.

"A woman has escaped the castle after killing her husband. I need you to help me track her."

She was surprised nearly out of her fear. "What do you think *I* can do? I'm no tracker."

"You can talk with his ghost. I promise you, he'll be very motivated to find her, and so will you."

She blew a breath out through her nose. "Even if he's stuck around, I have no connection. He won't come to me. If he's recently dead, he probably hasn't even come back to himself yet."

"Ulanka," Ruggerio gripped her shoulders. Not hard, not punishing, but urgent. She could feel his tension straight through his fingers. "The Princess knows about you from her women. The war has taken its toll on her mageri. She'd already given the order to round up women of power, you included. With the murder of one of her most powerful mageri, she's stepped it up to an actual hexte hunt."

Ulan shuddered. Rumors had escaped the castle about what happened to women in Princess Bessory's circle. Rumors were, in fact, the only things to escape.

She swallowed hard. "So, you're bringing me to the Princess, to find this murdered man?"

"No." He squeezed a little harder, then released. "What she wants you for…I don't think you will suit her needs, and I can't say you'd fare well should you disappoint her." He let that sink in. "You are far more use to me free as you are. However, she wants you and she wants this woman who escaped. I can't fail her twice. So, you will help me, or I will have to bring you in. If you aid me, I can be sure that you get away."

"Get away where? You know why I can't leave," Ulan said quietly, thinking of her daughter Dazia.

"I don't think you have a choice."

She left that. There was always a choice, though not always a good one. "I'll see what I can do."

"There are soldiers and Crown guardsmen pouring through town. There will be other mageri. You should get off the streets. Get a message to me as soon as you have word."

"Other mageri?" she asked, her heart kicking up again. She hadn't even considered that.

"Oh, didn't I tell you? The man killed was *Mager Garif*. Run straight through and bled out in his own bathwater by his Frizenzian bride."

Ulan gasped. "His wife did this?"

"There is no doubt."

"Against a mageri?"

"You can see why she must be found. The Crown has put out that she may have been a hexte in hiding. There will be no safety anymore for witchy women. This is why I worry for you. *Someone* will turn you in. You need my help as much as I need yours right now."

"You're sure he's stuck around?"

"Mager Garif was not one to go quietly."

Ulan hurried back to her home. As soon as she was through the door, Dazia threw herself into her arms. She ended up half sunk into her mother, who closed her arms around her incorporeal daughter, wishing again that she could feel her, hold her, smell her hair, bury her face in it.

The slight chill where they touched was her only sensation, and she cherished it.

"Maman, you're back!" she said, trembling, and Ulan could tell only because she saw it. Instinctively, she tightened the hug that neither could feel.

"You're shaking," Ulan said. "You know I always come back to you."

"It's not that." She heard her daughter's voice like a whisper on the wind. While Ulan had the rare ability to see the anima, the power the mageri drew, she'd never seen ghosts until Dazia. Until she'd lost Dazia to the plague.

The Rot had come in the summer. Some said it began as a blight on the crops, something unseen like a worm in an apple or a sickness in the core that then ate people from the inside. Others said that death begot death flowing outward from the cemeteries, a foulness upon the air, or something seeping through the walls. It did seem to start with those too poor to live anywhere except abutting the filth and stench of the graveyard, without the means to move even once the bodies started to pile up and the strain broke through walls, spilling bones straight into cellars, poisoning the groundwater. But it quickly spread throughout the city.

Ulan blamed herself when Dazia got sick. She'd catered to others, caring for them as best she could with the skills learned on the battlefield, but poultices and potions didn't do anything against a disease where people coughed up blood and sometimes more, choking on their very substance.

She shut everyone out at Dazia's first cough, but by then it was too late. She tried everything she knew. Every tea and infusion, even sweating it out, hating herself more with every instant of her little one's pain. She said every prayer she knew, made up new ones as though she had the power to take the disease onto herself and spare her child. Nothing worked.

When Dazia shook with the chills, Ulan wrapped herself around her daughter, only to be pushed away because she burned Dazia with her warmth.

The night Dazia died, she'd gone so still. Her golden hair damp and tangled, her breathing shallow and wet, her round face so precious and so pale. Her dark lashes rested against cheeks sunken from days during which she could barely swallow enough water to stay alive.

Her chest rattled, but she didn't cough. Ulan rested gently beside her as she slept. She wanted to wrap an arm around Dazia but didn't dare add any weight for her to struggle against in the scarce rise and fall of her chest. She did stroke damp locks back from her face and kiss her forehead so softly she might have been a butterfly alighting. She didn't want to wake Dazia when she so needed sleep. She watched and listened for each breath, eventually lulled to sleep by the sound, exhausted from caring for her around the clock.

When she woke Dazia was cold.

She still couldn't... It hurt too much. Every time the memory surfaced, Ulan's heart stopped, and she hoped that it wouldn't restart. That she could follow Dazia into the grave.

Instead, Dazia followed her back from it.

She looked now into Dazia's little face—pointed chin, soft cheeks, eyes the blue-purple of twilight, faded with translucency, hair in flyaway curls. She was still in the nightshirt she'd died in. She was the child Ulan remembered before she had gotten sick.

Which was why when Dazia first appeared to her, she thought she was an apparition, Ulan's mind playing the cruelest and most beautiful trick on her. To see her Dazia again...

"What is it, baby?" she asked. "Why are you shaking?"

Almost six winters old, but still her baby.

"The bad man," Dazia said softly.

"Bad man?"

"He's so angry, Maman."

"Who is, baby?"

Dazia just lifted her shoulders and dropped them again. That was all Ulan ever got when she asked where Dazia went when she wasn't with her, a shrug and a vague look in her eyes, as though she wasn't able to form the words.

"*Him*. He's new. Not even making sense, but... I'm afraid he's going to hurt the lady."

It was a long speech for Dazia, and she seemed to fade almost to nothing, to the point where she was just a slight fogginess in the air. Ulan filled in the features from memory. But it wasn't enough. She needed to see her baby's face. She went to the table and picked up the knife there, checked it for cleanliness, and then nicked her thumb. She sat on the floor then, and held out her arms, waiting for Dazia to come to her. When the mist settled insubstantially in her lap, she put her arms around her daughter, and smoothed her thumb where she imagined her daughter's forehead to be, murmuring into her daughter's hair. She closed her eyes as she did it, remembering the texture, like spider silk, and the smell of the lavender she infused into her soaps. When she opened them again, she could see her daughter more clearly, imagine that she even felt her weight.

This was why Ruggerio came to her. Not for his niece herself, but because Dazia was Ulan's guide into the spirit world, and sometimes she could talk to other ghosts who had information important to Ruggerio's schemes. She'd become part of his spy network.

A new ghost. Angry. Vengeful. The timing was too coincidental to be any but Mager Garif. But did Ulan dare send Dazia to retrieve him? Could one ghost hurt another? Dazia's fear suggested the possibility.

She didn't want to send her daughter into danger. She'd already lost Dazia's father early in the Blood War, before he'd even known he was to become a father. She'd watched him fall as he'd defended their standard against a Sinuway, a horrible serpent-like construct formed of ani-mist and magic.

She continued stroking her daughter's forehead, renewing the blood, keeping her baby with her, but it couldn't last. Even borrowing Ulan's strength, Dazia could only stay so long, and if she didn't want Ruggerio to take her away, she had to act.

"Dazia," she said finally, "could you lead the bad man here?"

Dazia drew away instantly, turning to her mother and shaking her head violently. "He might hurt you!"

Her concern made Ulan's heart squeeze. "He won't hurt me, baby, but maybe I can help."

"Make him not so angry?"

"Maybe." She didn't like lying to her daughter, but she couldn't say that she might be trading another woman's life for her freedom. But, after all, the other woman was a murderess and a traitor. She was dangerous. There was "no doubt," Ruggerio had said. If Ulan could track a killer and put the victim's vengeful ghost to rest, she would be protecting her daughter in the end.

As long as she didn't get killed in the process. Would Dazia be watching and witness her murder? What would that do to her? Would it be worse if she didn't see what became of her mother and feared she'd been abandoned? But perhaps Dazia would feel Ulan joining the All and finally give herself over to it as well. Finally achieve the peace she deserved.

Ulan couldn't risk it, any more than she could move away and chance that Dazia was tied to her death place rather than to Ulan herself. She couldn't lose her daughter forever, not even at the risk of her own life.

"Okay, Maman, but he may not come," came her daughter's faint voice, no more than a sudden draft down the chimney, and gone as fast.

"Just do your best. And stay safe."

Dazia nodded and threw her arms around her mother, hugging her tight. Ulan closed her eyes and pretended she could feel it. Tears leaked out of her eyes, making Dazia's image waver when she opened them again, afraid to miss the last glimpse of her.

I love you, she mouthed as the girl faded away. And then the tears came in earnest.

CHAPTER SIX

Cia

Cia clung to the horse with every fiber of her being, her teeth crashing together with each hoof beat, the pain reverberating throughout her skull. Her thighs had gone from quivering to quaking and were threatening to give out entirely. She started to slide, and tightened her grip, trying to clench with her calves to give her upper legs a rest, but it only went so far.

People ran from the streets as she thundered into the town, the hoofbeats behind her a cruel counterpoint. It hadn't taken them long to raise the portcullis and spill out soldiers like pus erupting from a lanced boil. She slipped further as she turned the horse abruptly down a side street leading to the fabric bazaar she knew well, hoping that she could lose her pursuers there. No one would hide her, but it would be easier to disappear among the fabrics and tents, and the havoc a freed horse could wreak.

She felt a moment's pang for the wares that might be ruined, the merchants aggrieved. They'd been as kind to her as anyone. Kinder, because they wanted her coin. Everyone was kind when they wanted something. Or at least wore the veil of civility, like the wedding veils she embroidered for modesty. They were translucent, but served because everyone chose to believe the fiction of concealment. Ostentation was all in the adornments.

She slipped further, now hanging on to the side of the horse like a trick rider. Her mount sensed the precariousness of her perch, and faltered to the side, ready to crash her into the wagon unloading there, crush her between them. She forced her frozen hands to unclench, felt the joints crack as they released, and slid to the ground just as she would have been sheared from the horse's side. Freed, the horse ran on, kicking up his heels.

She was streets away from the safety of the fabric market. Her nose stung, and she made a quick decision to race toward the bitter bite of tannins and ammonia gasping out of the dyeing district. At best, the soldiers would have to divide up to hunt her along the narrow streets. Some might even pursue her runaway horse.

Hounds were a different matter, but the bite of the dyes that burned eyes and noses until they seeped should confound even them. And so, she ran toward rather than away. She wished she had one of her veils to tie over her face to protect it, but as she reached Tannery Street, her face began to burn as though it had been dipped in lye. She supposed others grew used to the scents, but her eyes watered until she was seeing the world through an unreliable lens. She ran straight into a woman who could have been in front of her all along or come from nowhere. The woman's curses trailed off into a wet cough as Cia dodged around her and ran on.

She couldn't hear anyone behind her. If Cia was caught, she would be killed, either struck down where she stood or after being made a public spectacle. She'd killed her husband, a mageri, a member of Bloody Bessory's court. There was no future for her.

She dodged off Tannery Street onto another she didn't know, the caustic scents reached around the corner, clung to her as she ran—until they were beaten back, chased away by something much more insidious. Her steps faltered, her trembling legs wanting to give out as she realized what it was. Death. The scent of decay, rot. The way Garif would smell in days or weeks. The way her queen had after they'd killed her and left her body hanging where it could be seen. Where commoners or even children could climb the scaffold and give her leg a tug, making her queen do a macabre dance for their amusement, regardless of the foulness soaking her dress from bowels released in death.

Garif had made her watch the execution, so she'd know what awaited her if she ever crossed him. If he ever even accused her of disloyalty. Her poor queen... She'd lingered for months in the tower while they'd waited for her to deliver, so that they could keep their King's get, and then murder his mother. When she lost the baby, they laid that at her door as well. As though the loss was her doing. As though the babe hadn't been the only thing keeping her alive, both spiritually and physically. As though her love didn't shine through the fragments of song she sang to the babe within that carried sometimes on the wind.

Cia's stomach heaved, and her throat, already burned from the tannins, wanted to erupt with the bile bubbling its way up. Hot lava melting everything in its path, eating her from the inside.

For a moment she let herself sink. What did it matter if they found her, killed her? She should never have outlived her queen. Marrying Garif had been sheer cowardice, self-preservation. She'd earned her punishment. And now? What did she deserve but her long-delayed death?

She had nothing, not even the dubious comfort she'd bought at the cost of her own self.

A sound locked her knees, stiffened her up in terror. A laugh carried on the wind. Sharp, biting, cruel, like the raking of bear claws down her back. She knew that bark, that bite. *Garif*. But it was impossible. Garif was dead.

That laugh again. Every hair on her arms and neck stood on end.

Did you think you could kill ME? That YOU were the stronger of us? She whirled around, but there was nothing. No one. Naught but a small girl peeking out of her mother's skirts as she hurried her away, staring at Cia as though she carried a contagion.

I will haunt you 'til the end of your days.

Cia ran on, desperate to outpace the voice, even if it was all in her head. Maybe the chemicals she'd inhaled were messing with her mind. Maybe Garif had finally broken her. But she wouldn't let him win. Wouldn't let *them* put her to death the way they had her queen. She wouldn't dance for their amusement on the end of a gallows.

Before her were the high stone walls of a churchyard, the quarried stone rough cut, the mortar crumbling enough for her to find hand and footholds, but that would only lead into the surrounding cemetery, and after the Rot... She'd heard tales of bodies piled to the top of the walls, spilling through the crumbling mortar. The idea of climbing the wall only to fall into an open grave with Garif's voice hounding her was too horrible.

She veered to the right, only to come up against ramshackle houses built against the cemetery walls, each bearing the mark of a plague house. She backed away, hands clutched against herself as though she might involuntarily touch something.

And then she heard the pounding of hooves behind her, people calling in the distance. She wondered whether the waggoneer had pointed her out or maybe the girl peeking from her mother's skirts. It didn't matter. She had to find a place to hide. Now. Somewhere they wouldn't look. Wouldn't dare.

A plague house.

Was it worth the risk? It had been nearly a year since the Rot had swept through the palace as well as the town, until it had been shut off and those infected thrown from the walls. Heartlessly. Their bodies dashed below, caught on spits of rock along the cliffs and left to the carrion birds or disappeared forever into the sea. She'd been warm enough *then*. They all had been, stoking the fires to burn out the fevers, sitting so close to the flames some still had raised marks, which they wore as signs of their survival. Even she'd been allowed extra fuel for fear she might not be cleansed and would poison them all with her sickness.

But it hadn't struck her. Did that mean she was safe? She'd heard stories of it, one in a household of ten ministering to the others as they died around her. A blessing or a curse to have survived.

The baying got louder, and one hound yipped excitedly, which set off a telling howl from the others.

She darted down the row and chose a deserted-looking house, hoping… So many things. That the Crown soldiers wouldn't dare follow. That the house would be empty of corpses. That she wouldn't become one of them.

The small awning that had once hung over the front of the house and perhaps been used to dry herbs had mostly collapsed. She ducked under it to find that if there ever had been a door, it was now nothing but debris. She tried not to disturb it as she stepped over the threshold, choking on the scent of dust and damp, mold and mildew. And something else… blood and piss. Yes, people had died here, and left something of themselves behind.

No light filtered through the collapsed awning and into the house. She tripped as she entered on something that rolled beneath her feet. She tried not to imagine that it was a skull or worse. What could be worse, she had no idea, but instantly the dark unknown became more terrifying to her than the pursuers outside. She could imagine that she heard skittering, chittering, scratching. Cia thought of the dead not truly dead, skeletons with meat and plague still clinging to them dragging themselves toward her. Or rats that had fed on the dead and could pass along the contagion if they nipped her. Instantly, her skin started to crawl as though she could feel them swarming her. She wanted to stomp, fling her arms, keep moving so that she'd throw off anything trying to latch onto her, but she couldn't risk knocking something over and making a noise. Or tripping on something beneath her feet and falling into a terror of teeth.

She heard a wicked laugh quite near and her heart quaked for fear that anyone might hear. Her blood was roaring in her ears now such that she had no idea how close pursuit was. They could be on the other side of the awning for all she knew.

And suddenly, it was as though she could feel them breathing down her neck. No, not *them*.

Him. Garif.

No, it wasn't possible. Killing him must have broken her. She was somehow keeping him alive to avoid facing the fact that she'd taken his life. She ignored the hairs standing up all over her body. The bone-breaking chill and paralyzing fear. It couldn't be. She kept repeating it to herself as though that would make it so.

I will kill you, Garif whispered in her ear.

A bolt of shock went through her, releasing the paralysis. She flinched away, stumbling over something at her feet. She swiveled in the direction of the voice, but there was nothing. Except maybe... Was there a faint glow? She'd never believed in *bosewights*. Could it be that she hadn't killed Garif after all, but had sentenced herself to an eternity of torment instead? If he could be with her anywhere, anytime, she'd never be free of him.

She felt phantom fingers pricking at her hair, pulling, scraping, but only with enough force to scare her, not to truly hurt. Not yet. But he was a mageri. If he could draw anima from things now as he had in life...

A cry escaped her lips, and she clapped her hands to them to keep it in. He'd get her discovered. Maybe he planned for the soldiers to do what he couldn't himself, tear her to shreds.

Or maybe she'd gone insane, her mind turning on itself.

She *could* see better now. It must be that her eyes had adjusted. She was in a one room home. Hearth in one corner, a pile of bedding and clothes in another. The rubble built up around the doorway seemed to be all the other household items—a stool bent as though to barricade a long-gone door, broken earthenware storage jars, dented metal pots, a broom handle, the bristles at the end scattered like chaff. It was as though the family had tried to blot out the world, either to protect themselves or others.

There were no bodies. Only the pile of bedding where one might once have lain. She wanted to drop. Too much fear for too long, too many long-unused muscles ready to give out. Her skin crawled at the thought of that bedding, but the rest of her didn't care. It was the only place to hide, and besides, she was so tired. She couldn't give herself away if she was asleep. And if she never woke…maybe that was for the best.

If only the plague let its victims slip away that easily. But it was gone, wasn't it? There hadn't been a new case in many months.

She swayed on her feet, weighing her options, realizing she had none. She could hear the Crown soldiers outside now that her blood surge had subsided. Calling for a search. She couldn't hear the response. Couldn't be sure there wouldn't be an uprising at the very thought. But she'd braved the plague house, and she wasn't under orders.

Cia approached the bedding, flicked aside the top layers to be sure nothing would jump out at her—snakes or rats or jumping spiders. Any kind of spiders. The emptiness seemed ominous in itself, as though even the scavengers wouldn't touch it. But if death clung, she couldn't scent it above the putrefaction of the graveyard on the other side of the wall.

Cia collapsed onto the pile of clothes and blankets and felt something solid beneath. Far too solid. Like a body.

CHAPTER SEVEN

Cia

Suddenly there was a knife to her throat and a growl in her ear. "Get gone."

Terror sent her heart lurching into her throat. She reeled away from the knife, hissing at the sting as the blade drew blood, fearing not just the physical threat but what Garif's ghost might do with a wound.

A body exploded up from the pallet, fighting off the top layers of bedding. The figure emerged raggedy, rumpled, and far smaller than she'd expected from the threat in that voice. He was only a boy, cheeks sunken and smeared with dirt, clothes hanging from a frame that was nearly skeletal. She'd have relaxed but for the knife that was nearly the size of his forearm and the blazing threat in his eyes. He held the blade as though he knew how to use it. Like he'd had to before.

"This is my house," he said, voice grinding out as if painful. "Go. Go or I'll cut you."

There was a call from outside, the scuff of feet as someone approached the awning. They'd be inside any second. Cia turned from the sound back to the boy, desperation bleeding off her.

"I can't go. They'll kill me," she said.

He looked from the doorway to her, his eyes wild, like he was a cornered animal with the baying hounds nearly at his throat. Her own feelings echoed.

Garif's ghost took that moment to manifest, maybe strengthened by the blood the boy had drawn, and she felt a sharp blow between her shoulder blades. Fear clawed a cry from her as she was thrown forward, straight toward the knife.

The boy leapt, whipping the weapon aside. "What the void, lady? Are you crazy?"

"Who's there?" came a shout from the doorway. "Hold in the name of the Regent."

Cia didn't answer but dove for the pallet and the bedding the boy had fought free of. She covered herself and sank into the thick layers beneath, thinking herself small, trying not to tremble with terror that the boy would give her away, that Garif wasn't done with her yet. That he would find her and finish her, somehow make her his corpse bride for all eternity, torturing her beyond death. She said silent prayers to all the spirits who'd never answered them before.

The stomp of heavy boots came to her through the muffled layers. She tried not to even breathe, but since that was impossible, she made her breaths as shallow and silent as possible, and listened with all her might. There was a curse, and a thud, as one of the soldiers caught himself on something, a lose floorboard or bit of detritus, and fell against the doorframe, and then a cry of "Don't hurt me!" from the boy.

Her heart squeezed. This was an entirely different voice than she'd heard before – smaller, younger. Either he was truly scared or playing it well. She'd brought this danger upon him. She hoped he still held the knife, although if the soldiers perceived him as a threat... No, better if he'd hidden it. Or dropped it somewhere she could make a play for it if he sounded truly endangered. Or if it seemed the soldiers were about to discover her.

"We're not after you," the soldier said, impatiently. "You seen anyone else around? A woman?"

"What kind of woman you looking for?" the boy asked. "You'd have better luck down by the wharves... so I hear."

"Mouthy one, eh?" the soldier said with a snort. "I'm talking about the kind of woman would kill her husband soon as look at him. Kind who probably wouldn't hesitate to kill a skin-and-bones boy."

"Sounds like a bad 'un. I'll keep an eye out."

There was a second of silence, where Cia was certain the boy was sending some silent signal. Any second now, a blade might come stabbing through the bedding and straight into her. It might almost be a relief.

And yet, she couldn't keep her mind from running through a million scenarios in which she could grab the knife or redirect the blade.

"Where are your people?" the soldier asked. "This is a plague house. It's been condemned. You shouldn't be here."

"You're here," the boy pointed out.

"And now I'm leaving. I'll see you out."

"I won't go," said the boy, voice veering back into the dangerous territory where it had started.

"Won't?" the soldier said, voice sharpening as well.

"Where else do I have to go? My family is dead, except for my sister, who works at the palace, but I haven't heard from her in nearly a turn. Maybe you know of her? Annalisa? She works as a maid."

Cia wished she could see what was going on, whether the soldier's gaze slid away or whether he truly didn't know or care what had become of this boy's sister. Her heart went out to him. She'd heard tales of missing maids, been told that this servant or that had run off. Flighty, unreliable, possibly in the family way. Or rumored to have been dismissed over this slight or that clumsiness. But then she'd heard darker rumblings— servants and others might whisper, but no one bothered to temper their tongues around her—that these women had been last seen in the company of Bloody Bess and then never again. It sounded like the boy was well and truly alone now. Like her.

"I'll tell you where you have to go," the soldier said, "the workhouse. Now, *out!*"

The boy gave an animalistic growl that Cia felt in the core of her being. She wondered if she'd made a similar noise when she'd run Garif through. Instantly, she was fighting the bedding. Without thought. Without a plan. She only knew that she'd brought this soldier on the boy and she couldn't let him fight her battle.

She got clear in time to see the soldier slap the boy away with the flat of his sword as the boy went at him with his knife. He cried out as he slid in debris and went down, but by then the soldier's attention was all for Cia. His eyes were wide, as though she were an apparition. Based on the position of his sword, it wouldn't be the flat side that he used on her. She didn't have a single weapon, so she wrapped the blanket she still held around her forearm the best she could and held it in front of her as though it was a shield and she could batter him aside with it. With no other choice, she went straight for him, hoping she could duck under his strike and bowl him over before he could recover.

But this was a trained soldier, and he slashed at her, his blade tearing straight through the meager protection around her arm, cutting in deeply. There was sharp, searing pain and then her arm went numb. Or maybe it was her brain, because she didn't think, couldn't think. Just reacted instinctively, reaching for the hilt with her good hand as though she could wrestle it from him.

The soldier had a death grip on the sword and was far stronger. He tore the hilt out of her hand and she whirled out of his way, hoping she could run around him, that at least terror would give her wings, but he reached out and grabbed a hank of hair, pulling her up painfully short. It reminded her too much of Garif's spidering of her hair. Her vision flashed red, and she couldn't see, couldn't think, could only fight and thrash and scream, raking with nails like tiny daggers, but to no avail.

Then suddenly, his hand spasmed and she was free. She whipped her head around to see what attack she'd have to ward off now, and saw the soldier, eyes wide with surprise, start to fall. He landed first on his knees and then toppled face down, a knife buried in his back.

Behind him, the boy, looking more shocked than the soldier, stared at the bloody wound.

"I'm sorry... I couldn't let him... Is he dead?"

She couldn't tell him the truth.

"We have to go," she said, looking around desperately. They hadn't been quiet, and reinforcements would be on them any second. "Is there another way out of here?" It seemed a crazy question. She could see the whole place from where she stood. This had all happened because the boy didn't want to leave. What would he do now?

But he nodded, stunned, toward the hearth at the back of the house, and she didn't ask, just headed toward it, grabbing shredded bedding as she went to wrap her badly bleeding arm. She hissed as she bound it so tightly she nearly cut off her blood flow altogether, that hiss redoubled by Garif's ghost, sounding his displeasure at seeing that lovely wound sealed away.

The hearth was soot-blackened and cold. Disused. There'd been a cave-in at some point. Though now that she was close, it appeared that some of the debris at the front of the house had come from there, because the collapse had been hollowed out, creating a small, moist tunnel. It smelled like putrefaction. Like death. But she nodded him to it. She'd cover his escape, then use the tunnel herself, if she could.

But first, she went back for the knife.

CHAPTER EIGHT

Ulan

Run!" Dazia said suddenly, her eyes large and luminous with fear before she winked out.

Ulan reached for her instinctively, but she was no longer there, and anyway was forever beyond her reach.

Suddenly her door frame shook with the pounding of fists. "Open up in the name of the Regent."

Ulan froze, even her thoughts icing over in utter incomprehension. Ruggerio said that if she did what he wanted, the Crown wouldn't come for her. Yet they were here. Even if he'd lied, he would have been sure he had what he wanted first. Which meant he couldn't protect her. Not now. Either he wasn't as powerful as he thought or they'd found her before he could misdirect them.

It didn't matter. She had only one way in and out of her house. Based on the strength of those fists, they'd batter the door down if she didn't open it, and then turn them on her for resisting. Unless they weren't looking for her specifically. Maybe this was just part of the Crown's door-to-door search for the missing murderess.

She couldn't take that chance.

Frantically, she looked for somewhere to hide, as though she didn't know her own home and that there was nowhere, as tiny as it was. And it abutted the other houses and the cemetery at the back. There were no windows, except those facing front where the soldiers awaited. No escape. The tiny house had always felt cave-like, but never like a tomb. Until now.

The blaze in her fireplace seemed to flare with her agitation. It gave her a sudden wild thought.

She was small-framed. Could she fit up the fireplace flue? Even if she could fit, would she burn up or choke to death on the smoke and ash? Facing the soldiers seemed a less frightening way to die. But she couldn't surrender. Dazia would be left alone.

As the door rattled again in its frame and the soldier outside issued his threat, her time ran out. Ulan fled to the fire and grabbed the bin she kept of old ash, hurling the contents into the fire to smother it. The flames died down, but didn't go out.

Wood cracked in her entryway. With a cry of terror, Ulan launched herself into the fire, instantly choking on the smoke, her skirt catching on the still smoldering embers. She could only pray the closeness in the flue would put it out. She had no other choice now. Her feet and skirts were aflame. She bit cracked lips to keep in her screams and reached up into the flue, finding handholds that branded themselves into her skin. She forced herself to keep hold to raise herself up.

She was going to die. Her lungs seized, and spasmed as though she'd cough, except they didn't have enough room to expand or air to expel. She kicked off the fire with her enflamed feet, the pain almost unbearable except that there was so much of it she didn't know where to focus. She shimmied herself up into the chimney. It was even tighter than she'd anticipated. She'd neglected everything after Dazia's death, and likely soot had built to a dangerous level, but it flaked off as she pushed, falling into her hair, her lashes, coating the air until she couldn't breathe. No doubt she was scattering soot in her wake as well. There'd be no way to hide which way she'd gone, but maybe she could get far enough ahead that it wouldn't matter.

It seemed a faint hope. Her progress was heartbreakingly slow. Spots swam in front of her eyes from the lack of air. She might suffocate before she cleared the flue.

Shouts came from some far-away place that might have been her very own home, and she felt something brush at her feet. It spurred her to keep going, clawing, wiggling, gaining height like an inchworm, twitch by twitch. But she was at least out of their reach. For now. Until they got a better angle or…

Pain stabbed through her, as a soldier below grabbed her fireplace poker and jabbed it straight up into her foot. She hitched an instinctive breath to howl, but choked on ash. Her lungs were betrayed by air that was all sharp, superheated edges. They cut until everything inside her was a molten devil of fury and mounting pressure.

In her pain she must have released a handhold. She felt herself slipping. Frantically, she kicked out, her good foot catching on an uneven spot in the chimney. She used it to push herself back up, increments until her hands gripped a ledge. Could it be…could she be *that* close? She fought for the strength to pull herself the rest of the way, and the poker came stabbing again. Same foot, same pain, only more distant now. Likely not a good sign.

She thought she heard Dazia's voice *Come on, Maman*, and it gave her the strength she needed to curl her fingers like hooks and pull herself up. The rest of her body twitched and wriggled as best it could to slither her way out of confinement, but then she heard another cry, distinct this time. No ghost voice. "There she is!"

The soldier must have called for backup, and when he discovered she'd escaped up the chimney, another soldier had climbed onto the roof to head her off.

She was half out of the chimney, choking and panting, coughing with such spasms she thought she'd fall back into the flue, when the soldier grabbed her and yanked her out the rest of the way.

He threw her down and stood over her triumphantly, something ugly in his eyes. She reached for his leg and grabbed it right out from under him. He started to go down, his other foot sliding due to the sudden loss of balance on the sharply pitched roof, and she released him before he could take her with him. He'd recover. She had to rally. She had to be gone.

Second to burying Dazia, getting herself up had to be the hardest thing she'd ever done. She used the chimney to help herself, putting all her weight on the unbloodied foot, though the pain of the burns had her near collapse. She couldn't spare a glance for the downed soldier. He had to be close. She looked to the churchyard. The graveyard wall was barely higher than her own roof, but she was hobbled. She thought again of

Dazia, and ignored the pain, stumbling the two steps that would allow her to leap for the wall.

There was an outcry behind her as she caught, her arms wrapped over the pointed stone at the top of the cemetery wall. She quickly pulled herself higher and swung her legs over. The ground was only slightly lower than the wall, and uneven with the barely buried bodies and the earth that had sunken in around them. Proper burials had gone away with the Rot, when bodies had been stacked wall high and covered over with dirt and lime. Her pierced foot wanted to give out under her weight, but she twisted it back to true and staggered into a run.

Rather than head for the churchyard exit, where soldiers were sure to be waiting, she aimed for the other end of the cemetery. She was sure that if she angled herself right, she'd hit roofs much like hers, not far below the cemetery wall. She should be able to jump over and slide down and lose herself among the other houses. She couldn't outrun the soldiers, not as she was, but maybe she could evade them. She knew the area better than they possibly could. She didn't dare look back and slow herself down. If they were going to catch her, there was nothing she could do about it. She didn't have an extra burst of speed in her; it was all she could do to keep her feet when every footfall was agony.

She must have lost more blood than she'd realized or more air to her brain, enough to cause hallucinations, because all of a sudden the dead started to rise. Something covered in grave muck rose near the wall of the cemetery in the direction she was running. Tiny and oh-so-thin, and for a second she had a flash of Dazia rising to meet her. Then a figure pulled itself free of the ground and turned to face her, alerted by her heavy breathing or unquiet run, and she saw that the eyes were quite haunted and alive.

A second figure started up from the ground, and Ulan froze. A shock went through her, as though she'd been struck by lightning, and she suddenly knew who this had to be. The woman's hair was loose and filthy, dirt clung to her in patterns that mimicked rivulets of blood. It could only be the lady they pursued, the one who'd started the hunt. *Mager Garif's killer.*

But if Ulan stopped now, the Crownsmen would take her too. She had to collect the woman for Ruggerio. Then maybe she could make things right again.

"You there!" came a voice from behind her. Too close.

Right there, in fact.

She whirled to face her pursuer, and the woman who had risen from the grave shot out, waving a blade as though prepared to use it. The Crownsman was so shocked by her sudden appearance, he didn't have time to stop or pivot, but ran himself right into the blade, the surprise of it registering at the same time as the pain, a moment before his mouth fell open, and then his body went slack, sliding straight off the blade.

It all happened so fast.

The horror that remained was on the face of the woman holding the knife. Blood ran down the blade to join the grave dirt already covering her hands, making it into a sticky paste as though to cement them together and memorialize the moment. Ulan's stomach threatened to rebel, but there were other calls now—shouts, threats.

"Follow me," said the skeletal boy. From the sound of his voice, he couldn't have seen too many summers past her own Dazia, and there was something familiar about it.

Probably he'd been talking to the murderess who'd risen with him, who Ulan now knew for certain had blood on her hands, but there was something about the look on her face. This woman wasn't a cold-blooded killer. Not yet. And if she was, Ulan had to protect that boy.

She stifled a scream as she stepped on something sharp enough to slice up into the open wound of her foot. Then a hand grabbed at Ulan's ankle and she pitched forward. Another sound escaped her as she went down, but it was cut off by the sharp blow to her chin as it hit the frozen ground and set off explosions of pain throughout her head. Ulan kicked out frantically to stop herself from being dragged into an early grave. She twisted her head nearly off trying to see the threat, only to spot the Crownsman she'd thought dead using her to try to claw himself upright. She kicked him again, smashing him in the face. Once, twice, and his hand fell away.

She forced her limbs under her and got to her feet, which cried out. Both had been burned by the fire, but the one opened by the poker back at home shot a lightning bolt of pain up her body from sole to center that momentarily blacked-out her vision. She forced the pain down deep where she walled it away as best she could and raced after the others. When the boy dodged behind a half-buried mausoleum, followed by the woman, Ulan did the same, only to be confronted with the knife.

The boy was nowhere in sight, but the woman guarded an open doorway. Or, not so much a doorway as a slab in the wall of a mausoleum that must have had a hidden catch, because it didn't look like the slab should have moved on its own. Maybe it was the kind of catch meant for care-takers, a sort of back-door entrance for turning or moving remains. Even families that could afford mausoleums often reused viewing shelves, sweeping their loved one's remains into an urn or a smaller burial chamber once they'd crumbled to dust to clear the niche for the next one to perish.

"Who are you?" the woman demanded, twitching the knife to bring home the consequences of failing to respond.

Ulan's gaze was drawn to the blade, already gleaming with blood and filth. "A friend," she lied. "There's no time to explain!"

The woman flicked the knife toward the opening in the mausoleum wall in invitation. As fearful as Ulan was to have the murderess at her back, she crawled inside and allowed herself to be closed off with her and the boy.

They were all three crowded on a low ledge, with their bodies bunched up beneath themselves, she and the boy with their heads and hands hanging over, looking out into the darkness of the sealed mausoleum, the woman still facing the hidden catch with no room to turn. If the shelf had held bones, the boy must have pushed them over the ledge when he entered. But there was certainly dust and debris. Ulan tried not to consider who it might once have been. There were no ghosts here. Not in the mausoleum. Ghosts were a rarity, and those that existed gravitated toward the living, not the dead.

"Who are you?" the mager's killer repeated again in a hush.

She'd pulled the slab in behind them, cutting off the howling wind and the cries of the Crownsmen chasing them down. They wouldn't have any warning. If the soldiers discovered their hidey hole, there would be no way out. But the woman and her knife were a more immediate worry.

"My name is Ulan. The boy knows me." She'd realized why his voice had sounded familiar. But whether her eyes had adjusted or his burned hot enough to glow in the darkness, she knew instantly that she'd made a mistake calling on that recognition.

"I came to you for help." He practically spat the words. "You refused. My family is dead."

Ruggerio was right—whatever Bloody Bess wanted from her, she did not have the power, and the cost of failure was always too high.

"I couldn't. My daughter—" Ulan's voice broke, and she stopped, swallowing back the tears she thought she'd exhausted.

"Your daughter what?" the woman asked, voice hard and hushed. The stone of the mausoleum and the pounding of the soldiers' boots should protect their conversation from being overheard, but she wasn't taking any chances. None of them were.

"My little Dazia had the Rot herself. I couldn't leave her. And I couldn't cure her. I couldn't cure anyone. There was nothing I could do. There was nothing anyone could do against the Rot."

"You could have tried," the boy said, at the same time the woman asked, "You're a healer?"

"Battlefield trained," she said. "Bandaging wounds, taking down fevers. Nothing like…nothing like the Rot."

"Why were the Crownsmen chasing you?" the woman asked Ulan.

"Because I ran."

She huffed. *"And why did you run?"*

It could have been Ulan's imagination, but she thought she felt the point of that knife. She was going to have to do better, and quickly. "Bloody Bess is after me, and I didn't want to be taken."

"Why?" It was the boy who asked this time, a strange note to his voice.

"The Princess is running short on mageri. She's now looking for anyone with power."

"You have power?" His voice was half question, half accusation. "And still you wouldn't help?"

"Couldn't," she repeated, heart twisting itself in knots. "And not that kind of power. The most useless power there is," she said, mostly to herself, though she realized as she said it that was a lie. It wasn't useless. She still had her daughter, even if she couldn't hold her.

"What?" the woman asked in a way that said she wouldn't be put off.

"I see ghosts," she said softly. "Only that."

The woman was silent. They all were, until the boy broke it. "Can you find my family?"

There was a flat, dead tone from the other end of the mausoleum, as though someone had tested the solidity of the door, and then all went quiet again. Quiet enough that she thought she could hear her own too-rapid heartbeat. She could hear the other woman breathing too quickly and shallowly, and wanted to say something but didn't dare. The boy might not have breathed at all.

When she could finally convince herself the soldiers must have moved on, she couldn't at first remember the question. Ah yes, his family. "Most people go to their rest. Bosewights are generally very unquiet spirits."

"Would you try?" he asked. "Like you didn't before?"

Ulan might have walled off her earlier pain, but the boy had just blown the walls down. There was such a depth of need in his voice that there was only one answer she could give. "Yes, but not here."

And not now, while they were with the woman and her bloodied knife. She might kill to conceal the kind of secrets a spirit might reveal in her presence.

CHAPTER NINE

Bess

Bess clenched the chair hard to keep from throwing it across the courtyard. It was a garden chair. Heavy. Wrought iron, the edges of the decorative vinework dug into her fingers, into her palms. She'd been walking the winter-bare gardens, her guards trailing behind her, using the peace to formulate her plans when the Regent accompanied the messenger into her presence. The messenger now bowed before her, one knee to the ground, forehead almost to the other knee, delivering the news to the cobblestones as though she couldn't take his head off if he didn't make eye contact.

"She did *what?*" she thundered.

She lifted the chair and dropped it down again, hard, the sound echoing through the silent gardens, causing the messenger to look up, at which point she speared his gaze with her own and didn't let him loose. It was like watching a man squirm on the end of a pike, only less satisfying.

He swallowed hard, "She's… escaped. For now. But they're conducting a house-to-house search. She has nothing but the clothes on her back. No one will help her. Ruggerio anticipates that we'll have her by nightfall."

"He should have her already."

The messenger had nothing to say to that. When Bess looked to

Strego, the boy let go a sigh of relief as though released from captivity. His chin fell back to his chest.

"What do you think?" she asked, because it was expected.

"The traitor has nowhere to go, and they're on her trail. It's only a matter of time."

"And if it isn't?"

More silence.

Bess shook with rage. She'd been robbed of one of her mageri *and* the capture of his killer. This was not to be borne.

"Take me to Ceramor."

"Princess?" Strego said, as though he couldn't possibly have heard her.

"*Ceramor*," she repeated. "*Now.*"

"But he's insane. And dangerous," he said, somehow resisting the command in her voice. That shouldn't have been possible. Clearly, she'd held back too much in her working with him. Either she hadn't siphoned enough of his will or brought him sufficiently under her thrall.

"And behind bars," she reminded him. "Or are you going to tell me that you consider your precautions against his escape inadequate."

"Not at all, but…the oubliette is no place for a lady."

"Well, then, I shall attend not as a lady, but as your future queen."

"As you wish," he said.

"Finally."

He turned toward one of the guards and snapped. "You heard the Princess. Please run ahead and let the guard captain know to prepare for her visit, then return here to escort her."

He bowed and was off, wisely keeping any thoughts to himself. For all she could tell, he had no opinion at all.

"Wouldn't it have been faster to have him summon a messenger to announce us so that we could start right out?"

Strego looked down toward her feet, drawing Bess's gaze there as well. "I thought you might want to change your footwear. And perhaps your gown. I can't vouch for the conditions down below."

She snorted inelegantly through her nose. "I am not so precious as all that, though I suppose a maid can be sent out for more appropriate clothing."

Strego saw to it himself rather than send the other guard for a maid. She wondered whether some part of him was fighting her control, reasserting himself. Assuring that he wouldn't be left alone with her. For a moment, her heart fluttered in her chest, and it was such a strange feeling. But it settled as she remembered that a mageri, *her* mageri, had been killed right there in her palace. Strego's behavior was a reasonable precaution. After all, someone had gotten to her eldest brother years ago —the poisoning that had started the Blood War—and she didn't believe for an instant it was that foreign princess they'd executed for the crime. She suspected the poisoner had been much closer to home, probably her second brother Jannik, who had assumed Cyril's throne. Now, it was possible Jannik's adherents weren't terribly happy that their man had died. They might be scheming to pass the crown to someone more to their liking. And so, it made sense for her to go guarded at all times.

She chafed with the wait, and especially with the boots and cloak her maid appeared with. Her most serviceable set. She wondered what they thought she'd be walking through or brushing against, but refused to quail when she realized she'd find out soon enough. Instead, she tugged the heavy wool around herself and brought the ermine-edged hood up over her hair to protect it. Just in case. She wasn't afraid of much that she could see, but mites, ticks, lice, spiders, small things that might creep and crawl, burrow and bite before she had the chance to bite back…those she couldn't stand.

At the very thought, Bess's scalp itched, as though she could feel prickly little phantom legs, as though she couldn't smell the lavender her maid crushed into her clothes to keep the insects away. She didn't give in to the urge to itch or show any sign of weakness. She only flung one end of her cloak over the opposite shoulder and started for the door as soon as she was ready, leaving the others to follow or not. The guard who'd returned stood between her and the door and quickly opened it for her. Outside her quarters stood two more guards to surround her on all sides.

She almost choked with the memory of… but she fought that down. She was not closed in. No one would touch her or trap her. She was all they had for now. Her brothers were dead. The father who defended them long gone. She was safe. Protected. At least until she bore an heir or her opponents could find someone else to place on the throne. Safe as long as she was expedient.

Panic under control, she nodded regally to the guard holding the door, cleared her throat loudly for the others to make way before her in the hall, and allowed Strego to fall into step beside her as the other two guards closed in behind. There was the itching again on her scalp. This time she gave in, digging both hands into her hair and scratching her way through, denting her own skin. It gave her another focus, and the pain relieved the itching, in and outside of her head.

The hallway itself was colder than her chambers with the roaring fires, perhaps because her wing was empty, other than the rooms she used, as she willed it. They met no one in the passages, not even as they descended. She had her own staircase down to the more formal audience chambers, ballrooms and other stately areas, but as they descended, a damp chill became more pronounced. There was one passageway with slanted walkways leading from the larders to the base of the cliff, where skiffs that rowed in from larger ships could dock to offload supplies, but that didn't lead anywhere near the cells. She had no idea where the moisture originated, but the damp and the smell of mold and mildew, of urine and feces barely battered down by whatever cleansing was done here, was nearly overwhelming.

"Perhaps this will help," said the guard from behind her, the one who'd gone on the errand.

A linen cloth appeared at her elbow, and she took it in hand. The lavender essence within, stronger than the dried flowers pressed into her cloak, masked the odors somewhat. But it was like gilding a swine. You knew the thing was still there; the covering only made it slightly more palatable.

But she was grateful for that much. She pressed the cloth to her nose and nodded her thanks. Perhaps Strego had been right to question her readiness for the oubliette. At least with the cloth, she could cover her face and prevent anyone from seeing something they shouldn't. As for Ceramor... He'd been more than a bit intimidating when he was just a man, but his misuse of mageri powers had driven him feral. Would he be able to smell her fear? Could he smell anything at all over this morass of death and decay?

They quickly came to a heavy wooden door reinforced with strips of iron studded with spikes. There was a knocker in the center, unadorned. Merely a ball and catch plate. One of the guards raised the knocker, banged it back down three times.

They heard nothing from the other side. Not footsteps or the jangle of keys. But once the door was opened, the sounds and scents were overpowering She breathed as shallowly as possible, and then through the lavender cloth as bodily odors and the even stronger scent of released bowels clawed at her. The corridor had been vermin and rot; the prison was all human misery.

Bess stepped from behind the guard blocking her view to see what she was getting into before going further. The lanterns hung high at intervals along the stone walls showed two men waiting for them on the other side of the door. One stoop-shouldered, straightening at the sight of her, but only so far, as though it was all his body would allow. She'd never had cause to know, but it appeared that the prison guards wore clothing of their own, only a quilted vest in the house colors of red and gold to separate them from their charges. Well, that and their level of filth. This guard had rags tied around his boots for warmth. The other, in contrast, was ramrod straight, and his vest had sleeves, though it seemed someone had sewn them on as an afterthought, as the fabric was cheaper. Dingier. More than that, he wore the air of authority.

"Princess Bessory," he said, sweeping a deep bow that the other guard did his best to emulate, though he couldn't dip nearly as far. "You grace us with your presence. I fear that conditions here will not be what you're accustomed to."

She eyed him above her sachet, which she lowered momentarily to be heard. "Your fears are misplaced. As is your estimation of my intelligence. I don't expect a prison to be a palace. I'm here to see Mager Ceramor. If you have a fear, it should be of standing in my way," she snapped.

His shoulder blades twitched, as though he'd felt the blow of her words physically. "My humblest apologies," he said to the floor.

When he raised himself up to lead the way, he didn't glance at her, or even over at Regent Strego, as so many did to take their cues from him. He simply ordered the other guard to relock the door behind them, took a lantern from the wall, and started off down the corridor. They passed a cacophony of racking coughs, sniffling, moaning, pleas and curses. Bess ignored them all. She didn't look to the cells that flanked them to the left or the right, but watched her footing, lest anything move in the rushes beneath their feet, soaking up the moisture she'd sensed from the moment they'd arrived. She was glad for the boots now. Anything could have seeped in through her slippers.

There was another door at the far end of the corridor. No wood this time, but metal rods, woven together tightly enough that only a small child's hand could fit through. The guard commander took a key from around his neck to turn in the lock, and then held the lantern up and the door open for the rest to pass.

The lantern light reflected off rough-hewn walls, cut right out of the bedrock on which the castle was built. It showed a room small and cave-like...and hollow in the center. The smell emanating from the oubliette, the forgetting place, was like a physical thing, pressing them back against the stone walls, as though it couldn't touch them if they didn't get too close. Body odor and excrement, but also something so acidic it bit at the nose and wanted to force its way in and take up residence. Bess pressed the lavender cloth more closely against her nose, but it did no good. Taking in one scent meant taking in all.

The sounds from below sent an instinctive fear through her, as though she were prey reacting to the proximity of a predator. Even she wanted to look to Strego for reassurance, or to the guard commander, but she didn't. She'd ordered this and she was going to see it through. She'd kept Ceramor alive for a reason, even after all her brother Jannik's hounds had been found dead, after Ceramor had been discovered snapping at people with teeth grown too long and sharp so that it was clear who the culprit was. She hadn't known just what, but it would have been foolish to waste such a resource.

Reluctantly, she stepped to the edge of the oubliette, careful to get close enough to see over but not so close that she could be grabbed from below. She knew the hole was too deep for that, but her instincts screamed that she still wasn't safe. Not even a bit. That she should go, and go *now*.

When she bent over, motioning for the commander to hold his lantern out over the hole, what she witnessed was no longer recognizably human. Eyes flashed in the light, like cat's eyes or wolf's, orbs seen in the dark just before the teeth and the terror. Ceramor's hair was so overgrown and so matted with filth, it was more pelt than anything, and it was too dark to see where his pelt left off and his clothes began, if, in fact, he was wearing any. At the light, he snarled and leapt for the walls of the oubliette as if he might catch with claws and climb his way out. From the gouges in the stone, it wasn't his first attempt.

She recoiled instinctively.

Gouges in the stone. She let that sink in as she tried to process what she was seeing and whether she'd made a grand mistake. Not too late to turn back.

There was a good reason mageri were feared as much as revered. But perhaps it had been a mistake to keep Ceramor around as a living reminder, especially when she had secrets of her own. If anyone learned of her powers, they'd probably kill her instantly to avoid any questions of succession. Either her mother had played on the wrong side of the sheets or a freak talent had risen up. Neither made for a long life.

Mageri channeled the lifeforce all around them into their workings. Whatever was left, they returned...except when they didn't. Except when the power became too seductive, and they became addicted to the quickening. Bess knew the feeling. The first time she'd tapped into the anima, it was as though she was fully alive for the first time. Lungs truly expanding, air inrushing as though filling a vast void, heart racing and her body tingling and hypersensitive, as though the barrier between her and the All was whisper thin, and she might dissolve into it. It was addictive. Mageri could use the power of the anima to build their constructs and spells, or they could keep some of that power for themselves.

The problem was that drawing from the anima depleted it. Too much, and it was like a mine worked until it collapsed in on itself or earth that was salted. Mageri who didn't release the power *changed*, mind, body and spirit, until they were *ankari*. Wild. Unfettered. Mad. They could not throw down their barriers, invite in something so vast, so other, without losing too much of themselves.

Ceramor was no longer mageri, but ankari. Anathema. He'd drawn not from the universal anima, but from the lifeforce in her brothers' hunting hounds, but it was enough. It had made him feral.

Something prodded at her consciousness—a knowledge, a thought, a concern—but she crushed it like dried lavender and let it blow away.

As she gazed down at the ankari, he launched himself at her so suddenly that she leapt back. She glanced quickly to either side, but could see by the jerkiness of the lantern light that the guard captain himself hadn't been unmoved—though Ceramor was too far down to reach them. Further, he was caught in his own filth as though it was quicksand, sucking him back as he tried to escape. The scent was almost overwhelming, but it was his eyes that she stuck on. They flashed again in the lantern light, and then latched onto hers disconcertingly. More disconcertingly than when he'd leapt at her, he calmed as he stared into her eyes, as though he sensed a kinship.

That insistent barb in her conscience tried to lodge itself again, and she shook it loose. Then something else tried to take hold. There'd been no bloodletting. No tap into her where he could insinuate himself, but she felt him prodding, as though he could bleed her out through her pores.

Ceramor was strong. Freakishly strong. And his thirst was a match for hers.

"Knock him out, clean him off and put him in a cell," Bess ordered, her voice echoing off the cave-like walls, and she was glad to hear that it was strong. She hadn't been at all certain of it.

Even Strego, bespelled to support her, gasped at the order. "Princess—"

"Do it," she said. She met his gaze and spoke only to him. She counted on all of the men hearing, but would not explain herself to them. They wouldn't dare stand in her way...unless Strego gave the wrong cues. They would consider him to overrule her, and she wasn't yet ready to make her move. "He drew power by draining my brother's hounds." After her brother had died and he didn't think anyone would discover or challenge him. "Hounds can be brought to heel. Our forays into Frizenze have yielded more than territory. We have intriguing new resources. It is, perhaps, time to test them out."

She had to be very careful here. Frizenze was well known for their potions and philtres. It could easily be believed that they'd encountered something during their invasion that would tame Ceramor, but she had to remain vague. She couldn't tell them that she had the means to control a man. Let them think she had a balm to soothe him or a medicinal to drive back the mists of madness. They could think whatever they liked. Rumors could be spread, thoughts could be influenced. Evidence was trickier. But witnesses could always be produced or disappeared.

Strego gave her a sidelong look. She knew he was aware of no such resource. But he gave a nod to the guards, letting her play things out, as she counted on. She knew what he told himself about his capitulations to her, because she'd used his own preconceptions to form her suggestions. So much easier that way. When he looked at her, he still saw the little girl she'd been. The one painfully grateful for any attention. A wink, a snip of candy. A bib or bob. He enjoyed seeing those fey eyes light up for an instant. Humoring her now was like that. After all, she was just a snip of a girl. There was little harm she could do and nothing he couldn't counteract if it came to it; best they present a united front before others. Sooner or later, a husband would come to take her in hand.

The guards exchanged looks, but the commander had eyes only for her and Strego. He looked between them, clearly disconcerted. Maybe even afraid that he would fail to properly subdue the prisoner and thus endanger the Regent and his charge. Or that someone would become overzealous in subduing the prisoner and thus fail to satisfy their demands…

"It may take some time to prepare him," the commander said.

"See that it doesn't," she said. "We'll wait."

She could see him about to object, but then he snapped at the closest guard. "You heard the Princess."

CHAPTER TEN

Ceramor

Ceramor snapped at the water being flung at him, lips cracking as they peeled back from his teeth. The water bit back. Stinging. Not good. Not to drink. It stung chapped lips, open sores. It burned everywhere. Hot, itchy, unbearable. He crouched, made himself small, less for the water to hit. It put him in a bad position when the first rope came flying, too slow to knock the loop away before it started to tighten around him. He was already so slow, and weak from no food or light or prey. The second loop landed as he fought the first and together they squeezed him like a constrictor, arms to ribs, elbows to sides. So tight. He couldn't breathe.

His vision went black with terror, and then he became a…a something…there used to be a word, but it didn't matter. A spinning, dangerous thing made of sharpness and power. He strained and lashed, snarled and strained. If he could twist enough to gnaw through the ropes or slash them with his claws…

He reached instinctively for the brutes with his power. Hoping they were flawed, bloody, raw, something he could grab onto. Got nothing back. He would change that.

He twisted and twisted and twisted, until he tightened the ropes around himself, almost unbearably. Win or die, but his choice.

A panicked shout, as the rope ripped through the brutes' hands. He felt it when the rope burned through the skin of one's palm, raising blood to the surface. He reached for it. Starving. Desperate. Famished.

There was a flash of darker darkness coming for him. He saw it suddenly at the edge of his vision, and then the blow fell. Agony flared, and he was falling away.

His cheek felt frozen to the floor, and instantly that was wrong. The ground was solid. Dry. Arctic. Cold stone rather than moist filth. And then the throbbing. Throbbing. Bobbing. As though he was surfacing and laid low again. There, and then poked down by pain. Up. Stab. Away.

Away was good. Away was floaty.

And then the moisture. Wet, familiar, flung over him in a way that shocked and burned. So cold his body jolted upright as though he really would freeze to the stone otherwise.

Light was unfamiliar, but stabbed like the pain, an ice pick through his eyes. He closed them, but not before he saw that he was surrounded. And bound.

He sniffed instead. His nose still burned with whatever the water had been laced with, but he put that down, breathed past it. Took in piss and filth, and something sweeter.

Lavender. And cloves.

He sighed, and it hurt. Everything hurt.

He remembered lavender and cloves.

Slowly, he opened his eyes again. A sliver, at first, adjusting to the pain. More, until he could focus on her. The lady. Shining like a beacon with power. If he could draw her force, he could be free.

She had a name. He was sure he'd known it. He had a name too, but names were for one thing. *Me. You.* They were limited, vessels for perception. They didn't encompass multitudes.

Her power tasted tart on his tongue. She would sting. She would fight going down.

"Ceramor," she said. Her voice was like her taste. Tart. "You like to hunt, yes?"

Ceramor. His label. No longer defining. But his mouth flooded at the word *hunt*. His chin jerked upward as he scented for prey.

"Does he speak?" she asked…someone.

"He did when he was taken," came the response.

Ceramor glared at her through eyes that felt swollen, dry despite everything that had been thrown at him. He could speak for himself if it would set him free. He just had to remember…

"Yes," he snarled.

"Good," she said. "Muzzle him. Get him ready."

"How is he better than the dogs already on the scent?" Strego asked her.

"He is more."

"Is he?"

"He just needs to remember himself."

Strego snorted. "And if he doesn't? If he attacks and manages to bleed someone? He could get loose. We could be expanding rather than containing our problems."

The Princess turned to him, stared him down, then turned that gaze on Ceramor, willing him to hear her as well. "The handmaiden killed a mageri. If she has power, and that's how she was able to kill her mageri husband, Ceramor may be uniquely able to hunt her. I promise you, if he behaves like a rabid dog, we will put him down like one."

Ceramor's lips peeled back from his teeth, but he kept the rumble quiet.

CHAPTER ELEVEN

Ulan

Ulan breathed a sigh of relief, only to have the air blown out of her again as the murderess beside her became more wildcat than woman.

"Liar!" the woman yelled, pitching from side to side, fighting against some force as though for her life in the tight space of the mausoleum shelf.

The boy shot out of their hidey hole to get away from her lashing limbs and dropped to the floor. He managed to twist in mid-air, but not to land on his feet. Instead, he fell onto hands and knees and cried out. Probably bruised, hopefully not broken. At least he hadn't fallen on his head.

Ulan could now see a faint glow in the mausoleum, and it surrounded the other woman. Dazia had said she was being haunted, and here was the proof.

"Lady, are you crazy?" the boy hissed, getting to his feet. "You could have killed me. And if you don't stay quiet, the guards will come for us all."

"No!" the woman cried out, but it wasn't in answer to the boy. She was locked in her own private terror. The glow was all Ulan could see of the bosewight, but it was unmistakable. Even during her time on the battle-

74

fields, Ulan had been able to sense anima in action. She knew that Sofie and the others couldn't see the ani-mists called to create the Torvuses and Sinuways, Monstrates and other constructs the way that she could, but this haunt must be focusing all of its residual power on tormenting this woman. His killer. His wife. She'd never heard of a spirit regaining a sense of self so quickly after death, but perhaps he was running on sheer vengeance. Maybe that or hatred or violence had been at his core all along.

Ulan slid to the edge of the ledge and lowered herself down more carefully than had the boy. She dropped to her feet, cursing at the pain that shot through her, momentarily dizzy with it.

"Not crazy," Ulan said when she could, breathing through the pain and the effort it took to stay upright and back away from the ledge. The boy followed her lead. "Haunted."

His mouth fell open. "Can you stop it?"

"No!" the woman cried out again, more violently this time, as though she could repel her tormentor by will alone. Then she suddenly dove out from the ledge, as though stabbed or pushed, and Ulan lurched forward instinctively to catch her. The woman fell heavily against her chest, her arms coming round Ulan's body, holding on for dear life.

Her eyes were wide, all the white swallowed by dark, and there was no recognition there. No awareness.

"Shhh," Ulan soothed, as though anyone had ever been soothed by that sound. "It's okay. He's just a spirit."

"He should be *dead*," she gasped.

"He is dead. But not at rest."

The woman quivered in her arms. She was ice cold. Deathly cold. If they didn't get her warmed, the ghost would be the least of her worries. And…it wasn't Ulan's problem. She was to turn the woman over to Ruggerio. Nothing more. It was her only chance of going home again, back to where Dazia knew to find her.

But was it the only place? This woman's haunting sent her mind reeling. Was her tormentor tied to his killer or could he go anywhere he had the power to reach? Ulan had never called to Dazia outside their home. She'd never considered why. Maybe she didn't want to share her daughter with the world, having lost her to it once. Maybe it was bad enough that the only person who knew of Dazia's spirit wanted to use her for his own ends. She'd always assumed Dazia *couldn't* come to her anywhere else.

Maybe when she was safe, she could find out for certain. If she and Dazia could go away, start fresh...

She hastily swiped tears from her eyes and worked on rubbing warmth back into the woman's arms—until she came to the fabric wrapped around one forearm, tacky with blood. Ulan pulled back the sleeve to examine the wound and found a makeshift bandage entirely bled through.

"You need care," Ulan said, looking into the woman's eyes for the first time. They were dark and flecked, like choffee spiced with cinnamon, still wild, but with sense starting to seep back into them.

The woman shrugged off Ulan's concern, pulling her arm back, as though uncomfortable with the contact. "Thank you," she said. "He...he seemed to retreat at your touch. I don't understand it."

"He's still here?" the boy asked, looking frantically around. He backed into Ulan's side, as though he was used to doing that for a mother's comfort. Her heart broke, and she tried not to imagine it was Dazia at her side. She reached an arm down to rest on his shoulder, and he let it stay.

"He won't hurt you," Ulan assured him. "He's after the lady."

"Why?" The boy looked up to her for answers, and his eyes nearly glowed even in the dim light, pale and luminous. So much like Dazia's.

"Yes, why? What's he to you?" She asked, because she wasn't supposed to know, and because she needed to remind herself that this poor woman *was* a killer. Not only of her husband, but of a soldier as well. She still had his blood on her hands.

Right now, she was a danger to them all, but as long as Ulan was here, she might as well gather information while she waited on her chance to contact Ruggerio. While she decided...

There was nothing to decide.

"He was my husband," the woman said, her voice a whisper, as though she was the ghost.

"And?" Ulan asked.

"I killed him in self-defense."

Her legs gave out without warning, and she sat down before she fell. The boy lowered himself as well, putting a hand over one of hers, tentatively, as if hers might bite. Ulan tried not to think about where dust ended and ashes began, about sitting on the remains of people who had once been. She knew their spirits would be elsewhere. Returned to the earth. It didn't help. She was going to be filthy. They all were. It would make them conspicuous.

"Tell us about it. Start with who you are. We need to know what kind of danger we're in."

Ulan again told herself she was gathering information for Ruggerio. And she was. Of course she was. She wouldn't be taken in by what she'd seen and felt. Because the woman *had* to have power to have defeated a mageri. There had to be something more to the story. It couldn't just be...

"You could leave now," the woman said. "Call out to the guards. Turn me in. Save yourselves. They can't torture me any more than I'm already tortured."

She twitched then, as though something new had befallen her, but her lips snapped together, biting off any sound she might have made.

"We're not going to do that," said the boy, looking to Ulan for confirmation.

She only nodded. He was right. She wasn't going to call out for the guards, who had chased her as readily as the others.

The woman looked beaten. Defeated. Her lips stayed in their tight line, as though there was danger in opening them.

Ulan was about to give up, go her own way, risk that the guards had gone and that Ruggerio could protect her and she could be done with the whole mess, when the woman spoke.

"I suppose you'll find out soon enough. They'll probably have my likeness all about town when they realize I've escaped them." She swallowed hard, closed her eyes and gathered strength before opening them and meeting the boy's gaze and then Ulan's. "I'm Cia. My husband was Mager Garif. But he wasn't a hero, like they say. He was a horror. Yes, he saved my life, but only so that he could make me regret every moment of it thereafter. When he was away, I was loathed and distrusted by those at the palace. When he was in residence, I was in fear that he would take the life he felt I owed him. He would have today. Only this time I fought back. This time...well, one of us was going to die. But even in death, he wins."

Sickness washed throughout Ulan, making her hot and cold and so angry she wanted Cia's husband's spirit to manifest in such a way that she could destroy him herself. "I'm so sorry," Ulan breathed, and a part of the churning was for the worry that she believed too easily, followed by the horror at herself for her doubts. She'd seen what Garif's ghost could do – or his bosewight, because surely his was the sort of evil spirit that would drain the life from those left behind.

"You came from the palace?" the boy asked, after a moment of silence, and a squeeze of support. "Do you know my sister, Annalisa? Can...do you know why I haven't heard from her?"

Cia's startled gaze went to Ulan's, and they exchanged a meaningful look. There were rumors from the castle, none of them good.

"I'm sorry, I don't know your sister," Cia said. "I was very... sheltered."

There was a world of meaning in that sentence, and Ulan realized why she knew those names—Cia, Mager Garif. Cia was the Frizenzian woman who'd come with the Poison Princess. It had been a huge scandal when her sentence had been commuted, when she'd married a mageri and been allowed to live freely. And look how the Mager had been rewarded. Maybe the woman before her had planned to take him down all along, to weaken Jucar. But if so, why wait so long? On the other hand, if she'd never truly been free—if her life with Mager Garif hadn't been the reward it had seemed—then Ulan would have to rethink everything.

She tried to ignore the voice that reminded her that Dazia had said *he* would hurt the woman, lending credence to Cia's story. *She was a killer. She had killed.* It was as simple as that. Because if it wasn't, she wouldn't be able to turn Cia in, and if she didn't do that, Ruggerio wouldn't be able to protect her. She couldn't stay in her home with her little ghost girl. It was as simple as choosing Dazia over a murderess. Wasn't it?

The boy sighed so hard he deflated. "Still, if you know the palace, I have someone who might help you."

"Who?" Cia asked dubiously.

The boy, who still hadn't given his own name, slid a sidewise glance at Ulan, as though *she* was the one not to be trusted.

"I can't say. I can't even take you to meet him unless he says it's okay, but if you're willing to use your knowledge for a cause..."

"What cause?" she asked, and Ulan listened with interest. There was something more here than murder and escape, maybe enough to buy her eternal safety with Ruggerio.

He looked left and right, as though the bodies might give them away, as though the Mager's ghost might hear. "A good one," was all he would say, even after all that.

Cia chewed her already bloody lip. "This man would help me escape?"

"For a price."

"And me?" Ulan asked. She knew the cause he had to be talking about, the one that would find knowledge of the castle and the inner workings useful—the Restoration. As the Church had grown more fearfully quiet on the Crown's magical depletion of the anima, the Restoration had grown ever louder and more revolutionary with their street-corner sermons about the mageri stealing the collective energy of creation for their workings. They insisted that desperate times called for desperate measures——the death of all mageri to counteract the death of the land. With the deadlands left behind in the wake of battles, the drought and famine and deprivation that followed, the recent Rot and the mass buri-als, their brand of zealotry was gaining ground. Ruggerio would desper-ately want any information she could gather.

"You'll try to contact my sister?" he asked Ulan.

"I will."

"And you'll use your skills for the cause. You won't keep them all to yourself?"

"I have nothing else to lose." It would be true enough without Dazia.

"Then I'll see. Stay here," he ordered, ready to dash off.

"Wait," Ulan called. "What is your name? In case we need to ask after you."

"Hostill," he said. "Grammy said it wasn't always, but that I was such a squiggler she had to tell me to 'hold still' so often it took."

And then he was off, and the two women were left alone with nothing but the faint glow and Cia's twitches and stifled cries to indicate they were not alone.

Cia almost immediately toppled. It was slow, controlled, but as though she could no longer hold herself even that much upright. Death, torment, escape and pursuit. She'd had as much as she could handle, and her body was shutting down. Ulan had done that after Dazia's death. She understood.

"I'm Ulan." It came out of her unplanned, unintended, like the offering that came next. "Why don't you lay your head in my lap?" As though she was afraid that if Cia lay down with the dead, she might give up her own ghost and Ulan had to offer herself as a buffer.

Cia must have had her own reservations, because as exhausted as she was, she hadn't yet rested her head. She now shifted to put it on Ulan's leg, though not quite in her lap. Ulan had a feeling that Cia wasn't much for touch. She'd seen it in others who'd been abused. For a moment, she was overwhelmed by the trust, even if it was inspired by exhaustion.

Ulan tried to find somewhere for her hands, which she'd moved to make way for Cia to rest her head, but she eventually wearied of holding them apart and ended up resting them on the woman's shoulder as feather-lightly as possible. She thought of Dazia, the times she'd rubbed her daughter's back or brushed hair back from her face as she lay in Ulan's lap. The memories pained her worse than her wounds. She wanted to lie down herself and sleep to escape the pain of existence, as she'd done so many times.

Despite her history, Cia breathed an unconscious sigh at the light touch, as though a part of her remembered some gentleness. She seemed at once to sink into the floor, grow heavy. Ulan pushed away the thought of *dead weight*, and was relieved to hear the faint snore a second later. So soft it was almost a kitten's purr.

The faint glow of Garif's ghost faded, leaving Ulan in total darkness and Cia in peace…or so she thought until she started jerking and crying out in her sleep. But were they nightmares or something worse? She had nothing to do but try to make sense of the sounds and listen intently for signs of the boy or the soldiers returning.

But there was nothing, and for a time, Ulan thought she might go mad with the waiting. Her brain wanted to eat her up, thinking about everything. What she had to do to survive and the fear that it wouldn't be enough. If the Princess knew about her, would Ulan ever be safe? Could Ruggerio actually protect her or would he use Ulan to cement his position once he had what he wanted?

Was there any choice but take the chance that he would keep his word if she could give him Cia, who Bloody Bess wanted more than Ulan herself? Because while Dazia *might* not be tied to where she'd lived and died – now that Ulan thought about it, other ghosts had come to her for help, after all – she didn't know whether Dazia would grow weaker the further away she went. Or whether there was a range beyond which she'd disappear altogether. Ulan couldn't experiment with her daughter's life… afterlife.

But guilt at the thought of what she was considering ate at her nearly as badly as Cia's bosewight harried her. Exchanging another life for her own was easier when she could believe Cia a monster. Nearly impossible when the woman lay slumped in exhausted sleep in her lap.

Cia

Over and over, Cia saw the sharp end of Garif's staff coming for her. No, that's wrong! her mind screamed, but it didn't matter. It was Cia standing by the bath. Cia whose chest was pierced, who cried out with shock and betrayal. The pain took an instant longer, and then was her whole being.

Her gaze flew from the staff piercing her chest to meet Garif's eyes. There was triumph there, a sick elation. Maybe even a hunger.

Her body convulsed as the blood began to twine around the staff, to race toward Garif as though he called it, which she knew he did. Garif was doing what he'd always threatened. He was stealing her lifeforce, and she was powerless to stop him. She tried to grab at the staff with hands gone numb, but they wouldn't obey her. Frantically, she tried to pull herself off the staff that impaled her, but it only made the blood flow faster. Streams meeting and mingling and racing like a river overflowing its banks.

She was dying, and it was all going to empower Garif. He could tell whatever story he liked. That she'd attacked him. That the Poison Princess's handmaiden had shown her true colors. That they were all alike and Jucar had been justified in going to war, wiping the Frizenzians off the face of the earth like vermin.

No!

She came to screaming it, madly grabbing for the staff she was sure stabbed her through, but though her hands worked, her eyes didn't. She couldn't see a thing, couldn't grab it. Couldn't…

There was a hissing sound, and she thrashed like a madwoman, lashing out with hands and feet, trying to strike it away. Had Garif transformed himself into a giant snake with her lifeblood? Become his true self? But what she struck was softer than that. Flesh.

"Cia!"

It was a woman's voice. A woman?

A trick. She fought that much harder, the blackness terrifying. If only she could see what she faced…but it was Garif. It had to be. She wouldn't be able to trust her eyes any more than her other senses.

"Hostill, help me!"

It was the woman's voice again, and it made no sense.

Suddenly Cia's arms were crushed to her, and she was helpless again. She thrashed out with her legs, but something grabbed them. Weight pressed down on them. Trapping her. Her heart raced, pumping out the blood she knew she was losing. It wouldn't be long now. She'd lost.

"Cia!" the voice came again. "Cia, it was a nightmare. A dream. You're safe. You're here with us. Me and Hostill. Remember us?"

Me? She didn't know a 'me.' Hostill... Did she...?

She let her muscles relax. They weren't doing her any good anyway, and maybe they'd lure her tormentor into a false sense of security. If she could gather her strength...

But then, *Hostill*. Her brain started to quiet with her body, and she remembered. The boy, the escape, the cemetery. And the woman.

"Ulan?" she asked, her voice high with terror. It could be a trick, but she was already helpless.

"I'm here. Hostill's here. If we let you go, will you promise not to hurt us?"

The flesh she had hit—had it been theirs?

She nodded, then realized they couldn't see her either. The mausoleum hadn't been all dark before. There'd been a glow about it. But maybe that had been Garif's ghost, and maybe he'd worn himself out entering her dreams.

"I promise," she said.

The pressure on and around her eased, and she could move again. She shook with reaction, and realized her face was wet with tears. Her wounded arm pulsed with pain.

Someone brushed her hair back from her face. It went reluctantly, wet and salty and sticking. Her tears came faster.

"Shhh," the woman said, and Cia realized that was probably the hissing she'd heard earlier.

"I'm sorry," Cia said, tasting the tears now as she spoke. "I thought I was fighting Garif."

"He's gone for now," Ulan said.

Small hands patted one shoulder, and then there was a weight nestling up to her side, a warmth. Hostill. Comforting the crazy lady, as he called her. Not wrong. She *felt* crazy. Fractured. As though one more thing might break her into a million pieces. Everything she'd been through, only to end up *here*.

"He'll see you," Hostill said after a second of silence. "He says to bring you to him. He can't come to us. The soldiers lost you here. They may be back to recapture the trail."

Cia shivered. So cold. As though she really had lost all the blood she imagined.

"Well then, let's go," Ulan said. "As long as Cia can walk."

"Oh, I brought you this." Hostill's weight left her, and a second later she was enveloped in a hug. No, a cloak. It smelled of goat, but it took some of the chill away almost instantly. Cia hugged it around herself.

"Thank you." The tears were still there. Choking her. She'd known more kindness from this boy in the short time of their acquaintance than she had in years at the palace.

Cia checked her legs, found them working. She couldn't help checking her chest as well, though she knew now it had been a nightmare, that she hadn't been killed. It had been so real her breastbone ached.

"Let's go."

She couldn't wait to get out of this place of darkness and death. She needed the light. She needed to *see* her reality.

She could hear Hostill moving around, and turned in that direction, aided by a gentle push from Ulan. She wondered how badly she'd hurt them and why they were still being so nice to her. The last person to "save" her had eaten away at her soul.

There was the sound of stone sliding on stone, and then...light. Not much of it. The sky was already darkening toward night, but there was enough. Cia stepped toward it, but had to be helped onto the ledge by Ulan. She'd exhausted herself, and her limbs felt heavy and awkward. She nearly sobbed as she crawled out into the gloaming with the effort and with the ridiculous relief of the fading light.

She wanted to collapse onto the sacred ground that felt anything but holy, riddled as it was with bodies, but Ulan was behind her, and she feared the falling darkness. She moved out of the way, sheer will keeping her upright.

"They've probably left guards on our houses," Hostill said, turning to them after scanning the graveyard to be sure nothing had changed since his reappearance. "I saw guards at the exit. There's only one safe way out."

"How's that?" Ulan asked.

"Follow me." Hostill moved swiftly and silently, as though his gristle-and-bone body was too light to leave a trace. Ulan reached out to help her keep up, and she flinched on contact, but let Ulan's arm stay beneath hers, hand clasped to her wrist, steadying her and urging her on.

Hostill stopped at a ramshackle wooden outbuilding at the rear of the church. It was so weathered and sooted from the detritus of chimneys all around that it was more black than brown, but for the rusted metal of the latch and lock. Hostill produced a key from around his neck and made short work of the lock. Cia expected the door to creak as he opened it, but it didn't make a sound, as though respecting the eternal rest of the graveyard's occupants. Inside there were hoes and rakes, claws and clippers, clay pots and soil, shovels and the stink of feces. Rats, mice, fertilizer? She had no idea, but it nipped at her nose.

"The caretaker's shed?" Ulan asked. "How is this going to help?"

Hostill didn't answer, but went to the back wall where the light barely reached, and tugged at something. Slowly, the whole wall pulled toward them, tools and all. It was dead darkness beyond.

"How? Why?" Cia asked, her power of speech gone with her coordination.

"Priests' bolt hole with entrances from the grounds and from the church. I've heard two tales—one that the passage dates back to the troubles, when old King Calestri declared himself the head of the Church and stole the souls of the pious trying to deify himself."

That was a centuries old story, a bloody, horrible point in their history and the reason that no mageri blood was allowed in the royal line. It was too dangerous. Too unstable. Too powerful to have mageri and majesty vested in a single individual.

"The other story," Hostill continued, "is that the Animist presiding over the church's reconstruction had it built to sneak mistresses in and out. Either way, it's useful."

"And you know about this how?" Cia asked. He could be leading them into a trap. There could be someone waiting to take them hostage for a trade—Cia for Hostill's missing sister.

Hostill was fussing with something still mounted to the wall he'd pulled back, and a moment later they had light. A small lantern hung from a metal ring held in Hostill's hand. She used it to study his face.

"I just do." He said with a shrug. He tucked the key back into his raggedy shirt and stepped into the darkness, repelling the shadows with his light, and Cia had to make a decision. Stay or follow.

"I need more than that," she said. As though she'd be doing him a favor to follow. But she couldn't make her feet move. She couldn't trust.

Hostill glanced up at her, startled. "That's all I've got. I know because I know. Because people have shown me. Those people are taking a huge risk meeting you. I mean, you're a killer, right? Unless all of this is some big ruse. I didn't find you. You came crashing in on me, bringing soldiers and driving me out of my home. If it weren't for Annalisa…"

Pain knifed through her, and she rubbed at her breastbone as though she could feel it lodged there. Or as though the tip of Garif's dream staff still pierced her.

You're a killer, right?

She had killed. There was no denying it. She couldn't shed a tear for Garif. He was no loss to anyone, except Bloody Bess and her war, but that soldier from the graveyard... He'd only been following orders. Who knew what he was to somebody?

Perhaps Hostill was right to fear her.

What had she ever brought those around her but misfortune? She should never have survived her princess; she knew that. She'd been raised to serve at court from the time she was very young, to find a good match. She'd been chosen as a lady-in waiting at just twelve, been the princess's only courtier to travel with her for her marriage at fifteen... Her life had never been her own. The only real choice she'd ever been given was to marry Garif and avert her own execution – and look how that had turned out.

Oh, Garif had been a master of manipulation, making it seem during their marriage as though Cia had choices when he was giving her none at all so that he could call her complicit in her fate—you *chose* this, you *drove* me to it, what did you *think* would happen. The real choice was not to play his game. To get out. She should have done it before it had come down to one life or another. Even if it meant imprisonment and death with her princess. Or escape and starvation on her own. Sometimes 'care' was a cage.

But here was another chance to make a decision with no one whispering in her ear. Did she trust this boy?

No more than he trusted her. But she didn't have to go on faith. She wouldn't fall into the same trap again. She would be ready this time to move at a moment's notice if anything felt off. If these people could help her, and if she had the chance to strike a blow against the family who'd put her princess to death and gone to war with her people, she had to take it, no matter how terrifying it might be.

"I'm sorry," she said to Hostill, and cringed. She hadn't meant to bring the soldiers crashing down on him or his house. She'd been the cause, but she didn't feel it had been her fault, and taking the blame felt like echoes of Garif and all the times she'd said these same words in a desperate, futile, *don't-hurt-me* way, trying to head off a blow that came anyway.

She was full up and fractured with the pain, cradling her damaged arm against her heart as though they might protect each other.

She followed Hostill, and felt Ulan do the same behind her. There was only room for them to go singly and not even straight on. Hostill was fine, as small as he was, but Cia had to go through sideways, even her slight shoulders too broad for the passageway.

She was relieved when they reached the end, and Hostill pulled and twisted something she couldn't see in order to open another wall for them. He gave a whistle, and when one came back, two notes to his one, he stepped into whatever was before them and motioned with the lantern for Cia and Ulan to do the same.

"Put out that lantern before you burn us down," a woman said. She had her head wrapped in a faded blue headscarf, from which a few thin white hairs escaped to fly this way and that. Her eyes were the same washed-out blue as the fabric, lighter than the veins that stood out on her pale neck. Her hands fluttered as she waved them at the lantern, looking like giant moths drawn to the light after feasting on the swatches of cloth and lace all about them. Interspersed were cases of icons and medallions, pendants and prayer books. They'd come out in a shop for the faithful who needed offerings or head-coverings or other shows of piety.

Hostill put the lantern out right away but didn't introduce them to the elderly shopkeeper.

"Take Tallow Way," she said. "The guards have cleared that already."

Hostill nodded and slipped between Cia and Ulan to place the lantern inside the passageway before closing the door. The shopkeeper bent toward him as he passed her, ready to lead the way again, and he gave a kiss to her parchment cheek as he passed by.

"Safé vienu," she whispered to him, making a sign to go with it, probably some sort of blessing or warding, and then they were out on the street and into the now-dark night. They heard the snick of a lock as she closed up behind them.

"This way," Hostill said.

Cia shrank into the cloak he'd given her to avoid recognition—no one outside the castle or the market would know her, but surely the guards flooding the streets would have described the murderess for whom they were searching. By now, it was even possible a rendering of her had been commissioned and copies were being posted around the city. Ulan crept silently beside her, nearby in case she needed help, though she herself was barefoot and hobbling on the outsides of her feet.

They turned when Hostill did, the scent of smoke and animal fat grew from faint to unmistakable to almost unbreathable. Cia's chest tightened, and it still seemed as though she could feel something piercing it. If Garif had found a way to tap into her from the grave, he could be slowly dragging her down with him. She might only have so long. If through Hostill she'd have the chance to strike a blow, she would take it, especially against the Jucari monarchy, the mageri like Garif and others at the palace who'd looked the other way at her torment. Let Garif but watch.

Hostill stopped in front of a door that looked like any other, except for the plague marker riddled with dents and discolorations, as though kids had used it for target practice. He gave a rhythmic knock. There was an answering one from inside, and Hostill gave another response, verbal this time, at which the door opened.

A boy looked out. Cleaner than Hostill by a good deal, but also more solemn, as though someone had mistakenly put an old soul into a young body. He stepped aside without saying anything, ushering them inside. He closed the door directly behind them, quickly enough that Ulan had to sweep her skirt out of the way. The closing of the door cut off the wind, but there was no warmth to be found inside. No candles, no fire.

As soon as they were in, Cia's arms were grabbed, yanked behind her. Panic blinded her despite a light that suddenly flared, and she fought, but the hold was too tight to break. At a curse when her elbows connected with someone's center, a hand came up in front of her face with a cloth. Either her captor had three arms or there was someone else. The cloth was clamped over her nose and mouth, and she smelled something funny. She thrashed, whipped her head to the side, and caught a flash of Ulan getting the same treatment. Ulan's eyes were wide, wild, spooked. And then drooping, as Cia's were.

They'd been betrayed. It was her last thought.

CHAPTER TWELVE

Ulan

Ulan's stomach lurched, and only the fact that there was nothing in it kept her from getting sick all over herself. She rolled to get out of bed and to the chamber pot, or at least position herself so that she'd only have to clean the floor, but found she was already there —on a cold, hard dirt floor.

Her brain felt…drifty, and as soon as she became aware of it, it started to pound as well.

Thoughts came sluggishly, but they came, and she remembered. The rebels. The attack.

But why? Had she given herself away somehow? Been seen with Ruggerio? He was always so careful that no one could ever connect them. She'd not been anxious for anyone to see them either, in case someone knew him for who he was. It wasn't likely. Hardly anyone could describe the Crown Spymaster, if they gave him even a moment's thought in times more focused on survival than subterfuge.

But something had happened for the rebels to take them the way they had. Or maybe rebellions simply didn't run on trust.

The room she was in was dark. Much like the mausoleum. And that reminded her of Cia. The thick clouds obscuring thoughts and memories started to peel back, and she flashed on Cia's terrified face as the cloth went over her mouth.

Had they locked them up together or separately? One way to find out. She'd rolled in one direction on awakening and hadn't encountered anyone, so she rolled in the other direction and quickly came upon another body. Her arms were tied behind her, which really should have been her first indication that things were horribly wrong. It meant she couldn't reach out and check on Cia. Instead, she hooked her chin over what she thought was Cia's upper arm and gently called her name, in case her head was pounding as well. She called more and more loudly as no response came and then shut herself up so that she could listen for breathing. It was difficult over her own pounding heart, and ridiculous that she should fear for the woman she meant to turn in. The *Frizenzian* woman, she reminded herself. Still, she sagged with relief when she heard Cia's breath. It was coming too quickly. Breathed in shakily and let out in gasps, as though she was locked in with her fears. But it was coming. She was alive.

Ulan was alive.

Both of them survivors.

She put the thought away the second it arose. They had nothing in common but their current circumstances. For now and now only their fates were tied.

There was a distant *thunk*, and a closer *clank*, and the sound of a door too tight in its frame being yanked open, and then Ulan was blinking back against the light flooding what she could now see was a small cell. Almost a root cellar. Or not almost—a simple root cellar storing nothing but captured women.

Two hulking figures ducked into the hole, one headed straight for Ulan. She flinched back, as though there was anywhere to which she could escape, but one figure grabbed her by the shoulders and hoisted her up until he could get her on her feet. She gasped and started to go down, her feet screaming in pain, whatever shock or survival instinct had driven her flight previously no longer shielding her from the worst of it. The man growled and grabbed her by the back of her gown, the neck of it nearly choking her, and held her up by it, propelling her up the narrow stairs on her toes. Nothing about her churning stomach, bound hands or throbbing head helped with her balance, but if she fell it would only have been into her captor, and she had no choice but to keep moving.

At the top of the stairs, her captor thrust her into the glare of the lantern held by the boy squatting in the hatchway to provide light for his companions. He quickly set it aside to catch her and just barely managed to keep them both from going down. It was the same boy with the ancient eyes who led them into the trap. His face showed no apology now. He pushed her aside as soon as she was standing to make way for her captor to alight, and she managed to keep her feet, but it was a tricky thing.

"She won't wake," said the man still down with Cia, yelling up through the open hatch.

"Have you tried slapping her?" Ulan's guard called back, taking his last step up to recapture Ulan's bound hands.

There was a sound of flesh against flesh that made Ulan flinch. Then there was a moan, but it didn't sound like one of awareness.

The guard holding Ulan must have reached the same conclusion. "Just carry her then."

"You carry her," the other guard grumbled.

But a moment later he was coming up the stairs, grunting as though Cia wasn't just a wisp of a woman.

"What's going on?" Ulan asked.

But no one answered her. After Cia's slapping she expected to be manhandled, but her guard wasn't rough, just implacable and incredibly strong. *He'd* have had no trouble carrying Cia up the stairs. And he had no trouble getting Ulan through the door at the end of a hallway and into a room with only the center illuminated by low-lit candles, as though to intentionally obscure the rest. In that center was a single table with a man at it, the flickering of the candles casting his face in odd shadows that made him look like something unnatural. She would have thought it more theatrical than ominous if she weren't facing it bound, her feet crying out in pain and about to give out from under her.

The guard stopped her in front of the table, and the other set Cia on the ground, her torso leaned up against him so that she stayed upright. Her eyes suddenly flew open, and she jerked as if pinched, crying out and looking around wildly for the source. At the sight of her guard, she stumbled away, wrenching her shoulders as she tried to throw her arms forward and discovered her bindings, throwing herself off-balance. Her guard reached for her as she started to fall, but at his first contact, she dropped to the ground rather than let herself be gripped.

The guard cursed and let her stay there staring up at them as though they might all be mageri constructs about to pounce.

Ulan shook her guard off and found herself squatting next to Cia, mumbling nonsense like that they were safe and it would all be all right. The same things she used to mouth to wounded soldiers, knowing in some cases she was lying through her teeth. Kind lies, gentle lies. Some even believed her.

"We mean you no harm," said the man behind the desk. He had an orator's voice, and it bounced back at them from the shadows, giving her at least a sense of the size of the room.

Ulan rose in a fury. Despite everything, seeing Cia on the ground brought out all of her protective instincts.

"No harm? You've bound us, kidnapped us, terrified my friend..."

"Word is that you are a mageri and that your 'friend' here killed one— a man to whom she was married, no less. Between the two of you and all of us, who do you think is the bigger threat? We are just leveling the field."

Ulan's mouth fell open. She had no idea what to respond to first, the fact that he'd called her a *mageri* or that she *knew* that voice. He was more than just an orator. The way that he'd said *mageri*—as though it meant something most foul—she'd heard it before, heard *him* preaching in the market squares, and always gone quickly past, uncomfortable with his zealotry and the danger in his rhetoric. This was Vizi, the Restoration's main mouthpiece. She'd always been stunned and amazed by his audacity, challenging the Crown right there in the public squares, risking his life and the lives of those who might listen. But then, how else to recruit? Ruggerio would give his eye teeth to catch this man, who seemed fully able to vanish almost into thin air at the very appearance of the guard, as though he had a magic all his own.

But magic went against everything Vizi stood for. The land was sick, he railed, and the mageri, and the Crown that employed them, were to blame. They were not only killing people, they were destroying the anima from which they stole their power. The plagues, the starvation all stemmed from this. It wasn't a new idea. The Church taught that life needed to return to the collective energies of creation, to renew, refresh, provide the substance for new life, and she believed this, though surely her one little ghost girl wouldn't be missed... Manipulating, stealing these energies weakened the All, took something from the world that couldn't be replaced.

The Crown's employ of mageri to do this very thing – rip away the anima to fuel their constructs – was what put them at odds with the

Church. Then a century ago, Mad King Calestri went so far as all-out war with the Church and had shaken it down to its foundations.

Eventually its sovereignty was restored. Worshippers returned to the Church, but leaders who preached anything but love and acceptance, people bettering themselves to better the whole when they returned to it, tended to die mysterious deaths, rendering them back to the land they loved. Or they encountered emergencies that took them outside the city to which they never returned. At least, so it was said. Maybe people made conspiracies out of coincidence, brutalities out of bad luck.

The Restoration's approach was not nearly so constrained as that of the Church. Anyone who drew life force from the anima was required to pay it back in full. If they believed Ulan to be a mageri, she was in great danger.

"I'm no mageri," she said, her voice as steady as she could make it.

"You commune with the dead who refuse to go to their rest."

"I don't commune. They come to me, and I deliver their messages, hoping that they can go to their rest after their business is completed. I *help.*"

The first time had been a mistake. She hadn't told anyone about Dazia. She knew she should encourage her daughter to move on, but she couldn't bear to do it. She'd already lost Reynal. She couldn't bear to lose Dazia as well. They were a pair, their bond so strong she'd almost followed Dazia into death. Losing her again…it would kill Ulan, and wasn't self-destruction wrong? She wasn't devout, but doctrine said it polluted the whole, brought with it a taint, and that suited her denial, justified her position. She couldn't send Dazia along without dying before her time. Dazia would pass eventually, would add to the energies. It would just perhaps take Ulan's entire lifetime, but what was that in the face of forever?

She'd thought it was just Dazia, her own ghost girl, until a young woman came to her, almost the age she was when she had Dazia, seeking medicine for the younger siblings she cared for. A spirit hovered around her, older but looking so much like her that Ulan knew who she had to be. The girl's mother, clinging to her like a shawl, her face drawn with worry. The girl was bent over, young as she was, as though she could feel the ghost like a physical weight, though Ulan realized it was the chill, and the girl hunched to protect her core, keep what heat she could.

The words escaped Ulan before she could think twice about them. "You're killing her."

The girl started, her face a mask of horror. "Killing who? I only mean to help. I've tried willow bark and dandelion root, but she coughs it back up. She can't keep anything down. And the baby...he cries until he has nothing left. You must help me. We lost our mother and father. I can't lose them too."

She sobbed, and Ulan was sure tears would have fallen if she had any left. The girl looked exhausted, her skin like paper, as though she'd cared so much for others she'd forgotten to care for herself. Did she drink any of the teas herself? When was the last time she'd eaten?

"Shh, child, not you. You're doing all you can, and I will help."

Ulan had just made some tea for herself and had dark bread and a bit of soft cheese that someone had traded for one of her remedies. She pushed all of it at the girl. "But you have to take care of yourself so that you have the strength to care for others."

The girl was shaking her head. "I'll care for myself when they're well. We must hurry."

"It will take me time to gather my things. Right now, you will eat and unburden yourself."

She said the last two words to the ghost, who was staring at her in shock at being seen. Her eyes widened. She flickered as though she might go out, but then slowly unwound from her daughter, taking the unburdening to heart, though she moved only far enough away that she could stare at her child, lovingly, sadly, her mouth opening as though she had things to say, but no sound came out.

Ulan was slow gathering her things to be sure that the girl had time to finish her tea and bread. Really, she had about everything ready. She kept a bag packed with all she might need. She only checked it to be sure and grabbed her small knife in case there were any infections to be lanced. She wrapped it in its stiff cloth covering and turned with everything in place, only to see the mother with her hand out to her daughter's cheek, and the daughter slumped over her food.

"Don't!" Ulan cried.

The girl had come in half frozen to death already from the chill of her mother's mantle. If the woman drew any more from her daughter... The ghost's hand fell away as her daughter jerked upright in her chair.

"What—" she started, but Ulan held up a hand to stop her. The ghost had turned to Ulan, knowing that her daughter couldn't see or hear her. She was speaking, but her voice was no more than a sigh, and if Ulan wasn't careful, she would miss the words.

"Tell her," the ghost begged, and Ulan put the words together as much by the movement of her lips as by the sighing. "Swaddle the baby against her chest next to her heart, and soak a cloth in goat's milk for him to suckle."

93

Ulan started to speak, but the ghost wasn't finished, and so she leaned in, watching and listening. "Tell her, money in the mattress. No more willow bark."

She waited, but there was nothing more. Just the ghost watching her, waiting for her to deliver the message. What would happen then? How could she pass it along without revealing herself? The first part she might know as a healer, but the last... Souls who stayed behind were a sacrilege known as bosewights, evil spirits, because they haunted and sucked the life out of the living, as this woman was unwittingly doing to her daughter. A woman who would truck with them... there was no telling what she would face.

"What?" the girl asked again, following Ulan's gaze, aware that something was wrong. "Is...is someone there?"

It seemed she'd already given herself away. She could do the right thing, or the safe thing. But surely the risk was low. The girl wouldn't want to talk about her mother's unnatural spirit any more than Ulan ever talked about Dazia. And anyway, if the right thing meant saving a life, maybe more than one...

"It's your mother," she said gently. "Her spirit. She's too worried about you all to pass on. Still looking after you." She relayed what the girl's mother had told her, and then turned back to the ghost. Her face no longer looked quite so pinched, but neither had she faded out, her job done.

"You can't stay," Ulan said. Words she'd never spoken to Dazia. "You only draw energy from the living, and they need all that they have. You need your rest. I'll look after them."

The ghost stared at her, her eyes glistening like she might be able to shed tears. She closed her eyes against the overwhelming emotion that twitched across her phantom face. Then she reached out for her daughter one last time, just to smooth her hair, and her daughter seemed to feel her for a moment, closed her eyes and leaned into the touch. And sobbed when it faded away.

Ulan found her cheeks wet as well.

"She's gone," Ulan said, choking on the words. "We should go to your family."

"Thank you," the girl whispered. She reached out a hand to take Ulan's, her own still chilled from her brush with the spirit world. "Thank you."

The girl hadn't stayed quiet, but let it be known who she was grateful to when her baby brother calmed and thrived and her sister did better with ginger, mint and other remedies than she had with the willow bark. It might have begun with a single telling, and a single telling beyond that, but word spread, and before long she had families coming to her, asking whether their loved one had stuck around, particularly in the case of sudden, unexpected death. Almost always the spirits had moved on.

Enough people had been disappointed that the appeals dropped off, but they didn't end entirely. Sometimes – rarely – she was able to help.

She'd never thought the word of mouth would reach all the way to the palace. Or that the tales would be credited. She'd never even considered that she might draw the attention of the zealots. But she should have. Of course, they would consider her dangerous. She could explain that thanks to her, some spirits had gone on to the All, but she didn't know whether it would move them. And what if they found out about Dazia? The fear chilled her bones.

"Hostill says you've agreed to help him. To see if you can find his sister," Vizi said, and it took her a moment to hear him, lost as she was in her own fears

Even then, she wasn't certain she'd heard him correctly. "I – yes. She may still be alive. If not, it's more than likely that she's moved on. There's only a very small chance she's still around, but I'll do what I can."

"And if you locate her, if you're able to shed some light on what's happened, you would be able to send her on toward the anima?"

It was not a certain thing. She didn't have any actual power of her own. She couldn't *make* the spirits do anything. Not that she would. She wasn't like the rebels. She didn't believe in enforcing her will on others.

But she knew the answer she had to give. She didn't know exactly what Vizi would do if she answered incorrectly. Only that she was a prisoner. Her freedom and maybe her life depended on his goodwill.

Vizi's attention snapped away then and toward Cia, who he pierced with eyes like arrows. "You killed a mageri."

"I killed my husband," she answered, her voice was hard and her chin jutted, defiant.

"Why?" he asked.

Cia

There was no way to hide her vulnerability. The man had her bound, in his lair, controlling the environment and what could be seen, plotted, planned. But she didn't have to show fear. Some liked that, as she'd learned well enough from Garif. Drank it like fine wine. Cia wouldn't give him the satisfaction. Instead, she studied the eyes of the man before her, trying to learn what she could so she'd know how to act...react. They were dark like deepest night when secrets might be spilled like blood. His hair was equally dark, though his beard—pointed, trimmed, better kempt than a mageri's, who never cut away any of his substance—had silver threads sprinkled throughout. He seemed too narrow for his size, like the tall trees that grew in the forests of her home, straight up because it was too crowded to grow out. He didn't look any less solid for that. Or less threatening.

She resented everything—being bound, terrified, interrogated as though he had a right. Most of all, she resented exchanging one prison for another.

She felt a flare of cold on her neck, as though Garif's ghostly hand suddenly rested there and squeezed. For a moment, words were locked in her throat, as though blocked by ice floes, but she forced them out, "Because he would have killed me otherwise."

That ghostly hand squeezed tighter, seemed to sink straight into her, squeezing everything inside.

She started to choke.

Vizi rose from the table quickly enough that it quaked. The candles spilled wax, the flames sputtered and threatened to go out. Or maybe that was her vision.

She tried to claw at her neck, to fight the ghost hands, but her arms were bound behind her, the wounded one gone cold and numb. Terror stole her breath more effectively than the ghost.

There was a sound, a bark of words, and her throat ignited, burning away the chill. It crackled and popped like a thing caught in a fire, leaving her scorched but whole.

She blinked tear-gummed eyes open, looking around wildly for the new threat, and met Vizi's dark eyes. Aside from whatever he'd done, he didn't touch her, just watched her intently.

"What did you do?" Ulan asked, and Cia was grateful. She wasn't sure she could have spoken or that she would have. She didn't know this man and whether questioning would anger him. Or what form that anger would take. Weak and bound as she was, she'd have no chance to defend herself.

But Ulan didn't flinch as he turned those lightless eyes to her.

"She is haunted?" he asked, rather than answer her question.

"By her husband," Ulan said. "He hounds her even in death."

"If anyone would defy the natural laws, it would be a mageri," he spat.

Ulan didn't say anything. Cia knew the ploy. She waited, hoping the man would answer if she didn't ask so that it was his own decision to do so.

"I impressed a protection upon her," he said finally. "She will be safe as long as she doesn't disrupt it."

"But isn't that a mageri power?"

No, no, no! Cia called out in her head as Vizi bristled and seemed to grow in size, towering over Ulan. She knew he hadn't really grown, but it was the body language, the threat, the contained energy, the restrained violence. She waited for the blow, already cringing against it in sympathy.

She opened her eyes when no slap sounded.

Vizi was seething but still. Almost unnaturally, as though the accusation had turned him to stone.

"No," he answered, voice as hard as that stone. "It's the disruption of it. The antithesis."

Ulan had struck a nerve, and Cia wondered. It took power to fight power, didn't it? But mageri workings were against everything the Restoration believed, and they were willing to kill for those beliefs. She would have to be watchful. She couldn't trust them, but she agreed with them on one point: She was against mageri powers. She was against anyone having so much power over another, particularly the kind that could drain someone dry, even after death.

A door slammed open from the darkness beyond the flickering candle flames, startling them all.

Vizi whirled and caught the ball of motion barreling toward him. It was Hostill, out of breath, his pinched face spooked.

"They arrested Silgar," he panted. "Roha said to tell you. The guards, they came for her, captured her before she could get word out."

Vizi took Hostill's words like a physical blow. "Silgar will never tell them a thing. She'd never— " He shook his head as though to dispel whatever he'd been thinking. "No, she'd die first."

"Die?" Hostill said, squirming out of Vizi's hold to fix him with a look. "Then we have to save her. Go in before they can do anything. For my sister. For the lost girls."

Vizi reached for Hostill, who jumped away from him. "We're not ready."

"If they keep taking your people, you'll never be ready," Hostill fired back.

"This is a war. There will be casualties," Vizi said.

"You're supposed to be ending the war. You're supposed to be *different*."

"We are different," Vizi said, voice still rock hard. Then to the room at large, he ordered, "Scorched earth protocol."

Hostill's gaze flew toward Cia's, and what she saw there made her tremble.

CHAPTER THIRTEEN

Ceramor

Ceramor strained at the harness. A *dog's* harness, like for the hunting dogs whose life force he'd drawn into himself after his king, Jannik, had died. But Jannik was no longer using them, and Ceramor needed their power, their strength after his dear Reina had come down with the Rot. If only he hadn't been too late…

But now Princess Bessory's people had *him* harnessed. Leashed. Using him like a dog to track her adversary.

He snuffled at the scents coming from above. Pulled them through his nose, over the back of his tongue, up into his head until they took it over. Meat, blood, juices. What little moisture he had left coated his mouth, and his tongue came out to taste the air. Meat. He remembered meat. The kitchens. He lunged toward the scent and was yanked back so hard he overbalanced, fell into the man behind him, the one holding his leash.

He snapped backward, over his shoulder, but his neck wasn't long enough, and the man punched him in the face, the blow coming so quickly he couldn't dodge it.

Then the only blood he could smell, taste, came from his own nose. Dripping down his face and the back of his throat.

He spat, and blood spattered the guard's face. He snarled, and Ceramor surged forward, hoping to catch him off guard, but the leash snapped taut, and Ceramor's air was choked out at the sudden pull of harness against ribs, the straps digging into his chest.

He choked, hacked, pulled up short, ready to spin and attack, go for the jugular. He was *so* hungry. If he couldn't get to the kitchen, he'd get his meat fresh from the bone.

But another guard stepped in, rapped him on the nose, and he yelped and went down to the ground, cringing as the sting from his nose swarmed through his head like a storm of bees. He had to be satisfied choking down his own blood.

He glared up at his captors. Committing their sights and smells to memory. He would escape, and then he would hunt *them*.

The second guard stood over him, daring him to misbehave again, and then nodded to the first, who yanked him back to his feet. His lips peeled back from his teeth, and he growled, but he did it quietly. For himself. He had no need to warn them. When he came for them, he would be silent. But he'd make sure they knew what hit them before they died. He wanted the last thing they saw to be his teeth.

They seemed to lengthen as he considered it, as the taste of his own blood made him that much hungrier. He licked at his teeth and considered their length and sharpness, considered his reach. He'd know his moment when it came.

In the meantime, they went up stairs and more stairs, the scents of the kitchen now fading below them. Other scents criss-crossing. Body odor. Sickness. Unemptied chamber pots. Uncleaned garderobes. Lye. But beneath those, softer scents——amber, heather, sandalwood. He distracted himself chasing them until they stopped in front of a chamber, and the guard who didn't hold his leash opened the door. He was hit by the smell of smoke, sweat, blood and...bowels.

He tried to back away, but ended up against the guard, who pushed him forward roughly.

"One of you died here," the guard said. "Killed by his very own wife. You want your freedom. You want to hunt someone. Hunt her."

Hunt.

"You understand, don't you, boy," said the other guard with a smile that stretched aside to show his teeth.

Ceramor pulled back his lips to reveal his much sharper teeth. *Boy.* He'd rip the guard's throat out for the disrespect. He'd show the pup who had the power. One second's inattention...

Ceramor licked his canine teeth with his tongue, staring at the guard as he did. His teeth had grown. And his nails bit sharply into his hands as he curled them into fists. They were rough from clawing at the sides of his prison pit, trying to escape. Probably crawling with all kinds of filth as well, despite his bath. Deadly weapons. His magic and the life forces he'd taken had transformed him into something more than the pups who thought they had him under control.

The guard stepped further into the room, out of range of Ceramor on his tether, but he eyed the man just the same, waiting for an opening.

When he bent over to retrieve something, Ceramor had to contain himself. If he was free, he could have jumped on the man's back. It would all have been over in an instant. The guard behind him moved forward as well, pushing Ceramor ahead of him into the room. There was some slack in the leash in that moment. But not enough. He huffed frustration, but stepped forward, processing the smells, trying to focus on some and ignore others, but the scents swamped him, flooding his brain.

Then he focused on the fabric in the other guard's hand. "Whose blood?" the guard asked him.

Ceramor stepped nearer, not because the guard asked, but because he was drawn to the scent. It was purer than in the rest of the room, and he narrowed in on it, trying to cut out the cacophonous death-scents that wanted to choke him. The blood on the lace wasn't fresh, and so not as potent as that in the rest of the room, but sweeter. So small a sample, and yet... He stepped closer. The guard stepped back, taking the fabric with him. Ceramor snarled, and the harness snapped, pulling him up short, but he didn't give the guard behind him the least look.

He extended his neck, his nostrils flaring. The guard before him stretched out his hand, moving the lace close again. But not so close he could rip the man's hand off with his teeth. More's the pity.

Anyway, spilling the man's blood would override this wonderful scent.

And what was it? Not just blood, but beeswax and bergamot, as though the woman who'd worked the lace did so too close to a candle, one scented to overcome other odors, but it wasn't up to what had happened here. The sharper, citrussy scent of the bergamot tickled his nose, and he flinched aside to sneeze, before going back to the fabric and taking in one more sniff. To be sure. Too lock it into his mind.

"Well?" the first guard said, tucking the fabric into his pocket.

"A woman," Ceramor said. What did they expect? Did they think he could name her? As if blood came with an introduction. He cough-laughed at that. His guard yanked his harness at the sound, as though he was a dog who'd misbehaved. He snarled, but he kept it largely to himself. He wasn't out of the castle yet. His best chance at escape was yet to come.

"Can you track her?" the first said impatiently.

He sniffed the air experimentally, pulled at his harness, followed his nose to the window, where the shutters had been knocked aside. The guard behind him allowed it, but kept the leash taut.

Wind whipped through the window like a child chasing a ball, heedless of what might be in its way. It packed the punch of ice, of cold and wet and winter. There would be snow by morning. He could sense it.

But it was fresh and pure, and he held his face to it, letting it lash him, hoping to drive away the oubliette stench that had gotten up into his head and made a home. There were times he imagined the dirt and grime and worminess of things that thrived in the dark had slithered and oozed into his brain and settled there, decomposing him as he lived and breathed. Times he could *feel* it, tried to dig it out, scratching like a dog at an itch that was internal, stopping only for fear that opening a gash would accelerate his decomposition, knowing that either he ruled himself or ceded control to the fear.

But instinct was sometimes stronger than reason. More primal.

He shook his head hard, sending those thoughts away. There was something he had to do. Something... "She went this way," he said, as he remembered. "Out the window."

He started to reach for the frame, ready to jump though, but his guard yanked him back. "We'll start in the courtyard," he said harshly.

Would they? It seemed a waste of time, but maybe not. He'd lost track of the corridors and stairs. For all he knew, they were in the tower, and he would have jumped to his death. But she hadn't. She'd killed a mageri and done something the guards wouldn't do.

This was no normal prey.

Three other guards joined them in the courtyard, and he led them on the hunt—to a falling-down house and then a church boneyard, where he lost the scent at a gardener's shed, but picked it up again while circling the outside walls, through a riot of scents that threatened to burn out his nose. The dogs had gotten them this far. "The other dogs," his handler had said, and Ceramor almost turned and bit his hand off. He knew on some level that most men wouldn't do that, but he didn't care. It would be so satisfying, and the man's blood could help restore some of what he'd lost.

But he waited, scented the air. It was a tingle, a feeling, mageri-sense rather than scent, that led him down a side street, the men on his heels. That meant something. There was power here. Hers or...maybe she was with someone. And something else he'd sensed. Another scent, another person traveling with her who smelled familiar. So familiar. Yet he couldn't place it. Not yet. But he would.

The path he'd led them down smelled and burned like rendered fat. His nose and eyes ran, and he had no way to stop them but with the back of his hand. He led them straight up to a door that looked like any other, bashing his body into it, wanting in, wanting to solve the mystery and taste the tingling.

The guard holding him yanked him back, and this time he did snap, but the guard was ready for it, and wrapped the slack of his leash around his neck, tightening. Ceramor stopped cold, quivering with rage and a little fear. If he pulled, if he fought, his air would be cut off, maybe or maybe not before he could kill the guard. But there were four others. This wasn't his moment.

He watched as two of the other guards rammed the door together. It bucked in its frame but didn't give. Not until the second try, when it slammed inward, leaving the bolt and part of the door in the frame while the rest shattered away from it. They burst into the place, and his guard let out some slack. Ceramor untangled himself from the leash and rushed in after them, but the place was deserted.

He scented the air as the other guards fanned out to search the place. His prey had been here, and not long ago. There was the piss-odor of fear sweat, the smoke and burn of snuffed candles.

And...

He strained at the leash, and his guard let him move forward until he stood in a particular spot, pulling air through his nose, trying to relax into the memory that teased at him.

In addition to the mageri-killer, there'd been other people in the room, but one most significantly—the familiar scent he'd sensed earlier. It was clearer here, walled off from the street scents.

A boy.

A boy who smelled like his former master.

He started to do a twirl, but stopped himself, remembering the leash.

"What is it?" the guard asked. He'd given something away.

Ceramor shook his head to deny anything and everything. "They were just here," he said to cover. "They can't have gotten far."

He sniffed again, and there was something else. The burn smell was getting stronger, and… he froze. There was a hissing.

Burn powder? A fuse?

He opened his mouth to speak as one of the guards opened a door and the entire place erupted. A flash and a bang and fire blew them all off their feet. He flew into the guard behind him, knocking them both to the ground. His head rang like a bell that had been cracked by the striker, but he realized that he was free, and scrambled to his feet, only to hear a crack above his head and look up to see the ceiling crashing down on him. A beam struck him in the face, and he hit the floor. Another came on top of it, crushing the last of the fresh air out of his lungs. He tried to gasp in more, but his lungs were being pressed, and the only air to be had was hot and polluted with smoke. He coughed, and he thought he felt a rib break, coughed again and felt a searing pain like it had punctured something.

More weight fell. More pain and searing and smoke. He tried to howl for help, but couldn't gasp in enough air.

CHAPTER FOURTEEN

Bess

Bess held her head as though she could keep it from splitting.

Ho' still, a voice kept wailing. *Ho' still. Ho' still. Ho' still.*

But she was already holding as still as she could in the dark quiet of the anteroom. If she leaned forward, moved in the slightest, it felt like her brain was wrecking itself on the jagged edges of her skull, like a storm-tossed ship tearing itself apart on a reef. The pressure...part of her wanted to bash something into her own skull to release some of the pressure. But most of her wanted to lie down with a cold cloth over her eyes in a warm, dark, silent room everyone was forbidden to enter.

What she did *not* want was to address her council. As Princess, as Queen-to-be, what she wanted should matter. It should be everything. It wasn't. Not yet. But it would be.

Murderer.

Killer.

Monster.

The voices in her head swirled, whipping up and up. Blowing the pieces of herself to bits, tearing through her like she was nothing but steam blown away by this gale of memory, that waft of will. Not her own. She had to collect enough of herself to present to the council.

She had to get control. That's what this had all been about. Power.

Control. And she could keep it, usually. Except for times like this, when her head threatened to crack. And then what? If she really did open a release, would the power escape with the pressure?

It was the voices talking. All the women whose anima she'd ever drunk down trying to sabotage her. To bleed her as she'd once bled them. To escape.

The knock at the door drove her almost to her knees. If she could control the descent, lying down seemed a wonderful idea. She'd never make it to her chambers. The floor of the council antechamber would have to do. But someone would catch her in that position. She'd be vulnerable.

And there had been a knock.

She kept one hand to her head, holding it together. The other clenched the arm of her chair, keeping her upright.

"Come," she said as loudly as she dared.

"Princess?" It was Ruggerio. Why would it be Ruggerio? Strego, she knew, was already in with the council. She'd asked for a moment. She expected he'd send a page or come himself when they were ready for her. Ruggerio should be on the hunt. He saw too much. That focus needed to be directed elsewhere.

"Why are you here?" she asked.

"I thought you would want to hear this first, privately." His voice was soothing darkness. Cool like the cloth she wanted over her eyes. The voices in her head grew in volume, as though he might hear them, shouting over each other, wailing, clashing.

She couldn't control the wince, the eyes clenched shut against the pain. Her stomach joined the rebellion of her head. Nausea and dizziness swamped her like she was that boat in the storm, taking on water that sloshed about.

She swallowed down the bile that burned her throat.

"Hear what?" she croaked, her throat raw. She forced her eyes opened, met his too-sharp gaze. It pierced her, but didn't relieve any pressure.

"Cia—Garif's wife—she's with the Restoration."

And suddenly the voices went quiet. Or Bess's own thoughts finally burst through.

Cia? Everyone had watched Cia after her mistress's imprisonment and execution. She couldn't go anywhere, do anything without it being discussed, analyzed, reported.

"She can't have been with them all along. We'd have known. *You* would have known." She watched Ruggerio for any sign that he *had* known and kept it to himself, but as usual, he was impossible to read.

"No, but she's with them now," he said.

"Willingly?"

"Does it matter?"

She bit her lip, thinking. Tasted her own blood. The voices started murmuring again, but Bess focused on her own, tuning out even Ruggerio's face before her as she considered how this fit into her plans. This woman, this *nothing*, had robbed her of one of her most powerful mageri. But she'd also provided her with an opportunity, the perfect excuse to give her council to start the search for female mageri. Perhaps the All had finally smiled upon her.

"No, it's perfect," she said. "The council has been against a city-wide sweep, a full-scale cleansing of the Restoration zealots, afraid it would turn the people against us, and give any of them we missed a rallying point for recruitment. But now they are harboring a murderess."

Ruggerio allowed his eyes to gleam. "My thoughts exactly, though there's still the Church to consider."

"The Church supports the Restoration's message, not their methods. They won't dare stand with them."

"Yes, but will they stand aside?"

There was another knock, this one at the door leading to the council chamber. If her head hadn't been splitting, she'd have realized earlier that the other knock had come from the outer door. It didn't matter now.

"Tell them what you told me," she said. "The rest will follow."

She'd see to it. She'd had plans for some time, but couldn't see how to execute them, especially with the troops and the mageri off at war, and the people already up in arms over shortages and sickness. But now... Cia had been a catalyst. Bess would turn a loss into an opportunity. Everything was coming together.

All except her head, which was still threatening to come apart. The voices rose again in volume, shouting, fracturing, desperate to break through and be heard, fighting for control. Ruggerio looked at her oddly, as though he could see the struggle on her face. Maybe the pressure in her head had bled through to her eyes. It had happened before, shooting them through with bolts of red. It was what had earned her the nickname Bloody Bess. Or so she thought. She wasn't supposed to have heard the name-calling, whispered when it was assumed she couldn't hear. Or maybe she was meant to hear, but not clearly enough to pinpoint and punish the source.

She wished she'd never drained Galina, swallowed her spirit. She'd been the first, an act of desperation after her brothers had hurt her. When she'd needed the strength. But she'd needed Galina's council so many times since, missed her desperately, the one person in whom she'd been able to confide.

The one voice that stayed horribly silent in her head.

She stared Ruggerio down, daring him to say anything, as a page entered quietly, eyes downcast, to say that Regent Strego conveyed his best wishes and asked whether she was well enough to join them.

She could be on her deathbed and be well enough. She would not let Strego rule what was hers.

Ruggerio broke contact first, as he should, bowing low and indicating that she should precede him.

She battled back the voices, held her head at a very precise angle as she rose from her chair, trying hard not to jostle it in any way, and swept into the council room.

Ceramor

Ceramor's eyes ran, gunked with soot. He closed them against the burning, stinging air. His nose was stopped up with snot. His lungs struggled to expand, compressed by the weight of everything atop him. But he could feel the blood in the air. The explosion must have ripped through the guards. Or their blood had spilled when they hit the ground.

It called to him. He reached out with his powers, blood like a tingle in the air, like a beacon. He tapped into the guard closest to him and felt his life force. It was fluttering like a bird caught in a cage, trapped but dashing itself against the bars, sensing escape. He set it free, pulling it toward him, feeling the flapping force of it. Wanting. Needing. There was an emptiness inside him he needed the force to fill. He'd felt it when he'd reached for his master's hounds. He felt it now.

But…

This was a person. A human being. Like him. The dogs…they'd been hunters. They understood predator and prey, and they hadn't been let out to hunt since King Jannik had died. Their purpose ripped away. He gave them new purpose.

But this was a man, also a hunter of a sort. Now being crushed beneath the weight of the collapsed building with no more meaning than Ceramor could give him. Ceramor could repurpose the life force he had left, use it to save himself. With it, one would live. Without it, they all died. The Church said that was the way it was meant to be. They were meant to live on in communion with all things. The very thought terrified Ceramor. To be swallowed up...to lose himself... He didn't know if he believed, but he feared it.

And how did the hounds feel? How would the guard feel, to be swallowed up by you?

He ignored the voice. The hounds sometimes bayed in his head. They lived on. Through him. He honored them with the hunt, would feed them through the blood of this dying man. *These* dying men.

He, *they,* were so hungry. So, so hungry, a weakness creeping over them with every breath he couldn't take, the tiny bit of tainted air that got through not enough to sustain them.

He swallowed the force, pulling it into himself, absorbing it through his very being. It stung at first, like hail on bare skin, but on the inside. It snapped and sizzled like air after a lightning storm. He felt alive. Hyper-alive. Too big for his skin. Like a swarm of bees ready to bust out. Buzzing, stinging, flitting.

He started to shift, pushing against the floor, trying to rise, but there was too much weight.

He reached out for the other blood, the other life forces. One had already fled. He had no idea if it went to the earth and the air, as the teachings went. He couldn't tap into the energy of the land through the floorboards he had no means to pierce. But the other flowed, thick and lush and vibrant. Pulsing out.

He used the open wound to reach into the man, the guard. His vitality seemed to ambush Ceramor. Unlike the other, he was bleeding but conscious, fighting to live. To free himself from Ceramor's intrusion. Ceramor tried to slip an anchor into him, to pull his lifeforce in, but the man slipped the hook, throwing it off. Fear and desperation giving him a desperate strength.

All that blood... Ceramor had no idea if the man could survive. If Ceramor didn't take his life, would he die in vain? He didn't know, but he understood that desperation. He'd felt it, trying to claw and climb his way out of the oubliette. He felt it now, frantic to escape the burning, choking rubble.

He drew back his anchor. He couldn't take this life. Take one, leave another. It was a form of balance maybe. Or folly. Sentimentality.

But it had given him an idea. If force could escape into the air, he could draw from it. He'd never done it. It was too diffuse, too hard to capture. But here it was trapped and superheated. So much energy. So much strength. The small shift he'd managed allowed him to draw more air. He now pushed with everything he had, gaining himself a few increments of space, enough for a strong gasp, pulling everything in, not just into his chest, but into his being. He ignored the urge to cough it out again, swallowed the pain, choked on the foulness. And then it sank into him, the heat forging him, fortifying his muscles and bones. The guard's lifeforce rushed through him, giving him strength that was almost sentient. *Wanted* to be used. And now, before it could sink and settle.

He gave a great heave, and the beams shifted on top of him. Another, and they started to slide to the sides. He took the first full breath since the explosion, and it was pollution, but it sank into him and gave him the strength to throw off the last of the debris. He stood, mighty. Sooted and bloodied, but alive.

The air wasn't so superheated. He'd drawn in the heat and the power, taken for himself the fuel for the flames.

Maybe the remaining guard would breathe the cooler air and live. Maybe he would be found. He had a chance, anyway.

And Ceramor was free.

He blew the snot from his nose as best he could, trying to clear it, to scent for a way out, but it was no good.

He blinked soot out of his eyes, but everything remained hazy, indistinct. He stumbled for the area of brightest light, where the collapsed ceiling let in the reds and ambers of twilight, and clambered over the debris to escape into the falling night.

CHAPTER FIFTEEN

Ulan

Ulan sank to the hard dirt floor. She'd tried calling to Dazia again and again, but she hadn't come. What if her daughter couldn't find her? What if Ulan's lifeforce was all that was keeping Dazia "alive" and without her she faded away?

That's how it's supposed to be, part of her said. *You're not supposed to keep her here*. But staying behind had been Dazia's choice. What if she thought Ulan had abandoned her? Her heart broke, and a breath shuddered out of her, feeling like her last.

A body bumped hers in the dark, and she gasped in a new breath of surprise.

"Are you okay?" Cia asked.

The woman she was supposed to betray. But for what? If Dazia was gone...

Still a murderess. Still...

"I'm fine."

"You're not," Cia said. "Maybe you could hide it from me if I hadn't spent my life for others and gone years wondering whether anyone would notice my pain. I know it like an old adversary."

"My daughter," she said finally. Maybe talking about her would bring her close. "I can't call her to me."

Cia paused before saying in what was probably supposed to be a gentle tone, "I thought your daughter was dead."

"She is."

Cia didn't have an answer to that, and Ulan let her head fall forward, feeling as though she'd never lift it again.

She was wrong. The door above them opened, and involuntarily she lifted her head to look, blinking against the light, as faint as it was. They were again in a root cellar, crates jammed against one wall, jars and jams stacked against another. Dust motes hung suspended in the air, catching the light. Ironically beautiful. Through them, she saw a small figure descending the stairs, a large wooden cup in hand.

The way Hostill peered over his shoulder back the way he'd come made Ulan think that he wasn't supposed to be there.

"I brought you water," he said. "I don't know how long we're going to be here, and I don't know if anyone's thought of it. They're pretty stirred up."

"What's going on?" Cia asked, her voice curiously uninflected, as though she'd expected to be betrayed and she had been, and that was that.

Ulan wanted to launch herself at him, bowl him over and blow past him, get back to her house and her daughter and her *life*. Only she knew none of those things were possible. Not while bound. Not while Bloody Bess's soldiers roamed the streets.

"All they know is that you're not the only one the guards are looking for. You might be the excuse for the patrols, but others have been taken, like Silgar."

"Who's Silgar?" Cia asked.

Hostill looked back toward the light, as though the answer might be found there, and then turned toward them, leaning in with a whisper. "She's one of them."

Cia huffed. "That's clear enough, but *why* would the Crown want her? Because she's part of the Restoration?" *Or maybe she's not as resigned as all that.* Easier to get answers if people thought you too docile to do anything with them.

"I don't think so. She's very discreet."

Ulan slipped in a question of her own. "Does she have powers?"

"Not that she'd ever use." Hostill's eyes grew big, and he looked over his shoulder again like he expected to be discovered and locked in with them.

A shock ran through Ulan. She'd known from Ruggerio that the

112

Crown was rounding up women with power but had no idea any could be found among the Restoration. What use would they have for someone like Silgar? Would they trust her to renounce her power? If she never gave herself away by using it, how would the Crown have discovered her?

But if Hostill didn't know Bloody Bess's sweep related to mageri magic, Ulan couldn't give it away. She couldn't let him pass such dangerous information back to the Restoration. It would label anyone who went missing as mageri and put them in the Restoration's sights. So far the rebels had given the Magery a great deal of trouble, causing them to consolidate from two schools down to one, but they hadn't been active within the royal city, hadn't made any direct attacks on the Crown. But their rhetoric was dangerous, and the fact that they were so present here...they had to be building toward something. They were clearly mobilized if they had safeguards and scorched earth protocols.

Secret sweeps might be just the spark they needed to ignite the flames of all-out revolution against the Crown. King Cyril had been bad – raising taxes and tariffs to the point where people squeezed their crona until they bled. Jannik was worse with his forced conscriptions for his war—men, mounts and metals. Then his mageri stole the very soul of their land for their war constructs, slowly draining it to death. Jucar and the Crown were the weakest they'd ever been—a young girl on the throne, a Regent having to work with a council who couldn't agree on anything that would sway them from the current path of destruction. The Restoration could easily decide that now was the time to make their move. And they wouldn't be wrong.

It was a seditious thought. Maybe Ulan had more rebellion in her than she thought. But she'd seen firsthand the brutality of battle and the after-math. Neither side won. Six years later, they were still fighting the same war, the original declarants all dead, their descendants left to carry on. But she didn't believe in outright revolution. If the Restoration did take power and assert their will, wiping out the mageri... Well then, that would leave Jucar completely vulnerable. Their opponent, Frizenze, would overtake them with what was left of their mageri. Or Galitrüd or Markens or some country further afield would decide that Jucar would be easily overrun without its magics to protect it.

As bad as the Crown was, at least Ruggerio was in a position to protect her. As long as she gave him something of equal value. Her cousin was nothing if not pragmatic. With the Restoration, she and Dazia were abominations. Renouncing her meager powers would mean renouncing her girl, and that she would never do.

She ignored the voice that said that Ruggerio *hadn't* protected her, that the Crown guards had come for her anyway. Ruggerio would have taken care of things if she'd been captured. She'd have found a way to stay with Dazia. *Would* find a way, as soon as she could get free and report back.

"When we were in with Vizi, he told someone 'Silgar would die first'," Ulan said to Hostill, ignoring the question about how she'd guessed about Silgar's powers. "What did he mean by that?"

His gaze shifted away again, "Here, have some water."

Ulan clearly wasn't the only one who could ignore inconvenient questions.

He lifted the cup to her lips before she could ask any more of them, and she had to drink or drown in it. She gulped the water thirstily, and just as she felt a burning need for a breath, he lifted the cup and brought it to Cia.

"This would be easier if you untied us," Cia said before he lifted the cup to her lips and she, like Ulan, was forced to drink.

"I can't," he said as he poured. "If you escaped..."

He pulled the cup back, and Cia licked an escaped drop from her lips before saying, "Where would I go? Certainly not back there." She nodded her head as though she knew which direction the palace might be.

Hostill studied her. "You'd join us?"

"I'd consider it."

Ulan flashed her a look. If what Cia said about her husband was true, she couldn't like going from one captivity to another. Maybe she was trying to save herself, like she had once before... But Ulan didn't know her well enough to read her intent.

"I'll talk to them. I'll tell Vizi."

And he was gone, up the stairs again in a flash and the women left behind in the darkness.

"Would you really join them?" Ulan asked.

"I've seen what mageri power can do. I want no part of it."

"But would you fight and kill to end it?"

"I already have," Cia said quietly.

Ulan couldn't see her, but heard a rustle, as though Cia was turning away, and then she seemed to slide to the floor, maybe to rest her head. She'd been through so much.

It made Ulan think of whatever Vizi had done to knock out Cia's ghost. Maybe that was why Cia was so willing to join. And why Dazia couldn't come to her here. But was it permanent?

She had to get away and find out, as soon as possible. She'd never been away from Dazia for so long except in the hours right after her death. It had taken Dazia some time to collect herself and come back to Ulan, and in that time, she was sure she'd lost her like she had her father. That everything that mattered to her had gone and with it, all light had been snuffed from the world. Her well of grief was endless. A dark, sucking mire that held her fast and wanted to drag her down, down, down until the earth closed over her head. She felt as though she was breathing muck for air.

Maybe Dazia had sensed her need. Returned to pull her back into light and life. She'd struggled with that guilt, but not hard. Not when she wanted Dazia with her so very, very badly, and she couldn't let her sensitive daughter feel any ambivalence about her happiness at her return. And not when Dazia herself seemed so happy to be reunited with Ulan.

She struggled with her bonds, but they were too tight. There was no give, and the rope was rough, her wrists already raw. She didn't want to go at them until they bled. Her feet had scabbed over—at least, so she thought. But they alternated between a screaming pain and mid-level throbbing she could clench her teeth against. They needed a good cleaning, and soon, or they would become infected, if they hadn't already. But as soon as she could accomplish it. Also, a poultice and bandaging. But at least for now, they were stopped rather than seeping. The Restoration wouldn't use her blood, couldn't tap into her, but there were no such limitations for the Crown unless whatever protection Vizi had impressed on Cia extended to her. Ulan didn't know who had been set on their trail or whether they were after her in particular at this point, but she thought it near certain. She'd run, and why do that if there was nothing to fear? And when she'd run, she'd left more than a bit of her blood behind. Enough for the hounds to catch a scent. Enough to make clear that she'd have open wounds if any mageri got close enough and needed to tap in to take her down.

Her mental struggles were as fruitless as those against her bonds. The only plan she could come up with involved waiting until Hostill returned and she could work on his sympathies, convince him to free her; until someone came with food, hopefully releasing their hands so they could eat on their own. Either way, there'd doubtlessly be someone guarding, prepared to stop her. She'd need to fight her way out. The very thought made her cringe. She was a healer. She didn't want to hurt anyone, not even to save herself.

Won't turning them in to the Crown hurt them? Do you think they'll be given luxurious chambers and treated like royalty?

She pushed down her hypocrisy. She'd already been to war. She'd seen what it could do. She didn't want to live through a revolution. See the city burn, the streets running red with blood. The mageri... She only had to imagine a Torvus or Sinuway, a Monstrate or Drayven tearing through the city and the devastation left behind to steel her resolve. If not their mageri, then it would be Frizenze's or Galitrüd's or Markens' with no one in Jucar to counter them.

But what if the Restoration had a way to shut them all down like they did Garif's ghost?

She couldn't know. And anyway, dead was dead, whether by magic or blade.

She became aware of the pounding of boots on the floor above when dirt sifted through the floorboards down onto her head, and into her eyes. She couldn't wipe her eyes, only swipe them ineffectually against her shoulder. She blinked harder, faster, too dry for natural tears to form and wash the debris away. There were cries now, and a thump like someone or something thrown to the floor.

"Cia!" she said in a sharp whisper. "Cia, wake up, something's happening!"

She felt around behind her with her bound hands until she hit Cia's body, and she shook her until she stirred.

"Wake up!" she hissed.

She felt Cia start to rise, and left her, scooting backwards until she hit a wall, feeling around for something, anything she might use as a weapon, but it was futile. Her hands were trapped behind her back, and even if she could find something, she didn't have the means to wield it.

"What's happening?" Cia asked.

There was another huge thud, and a crack. It nearly sounded like the ceiling would come down on top of them.

"I don't know. Nothing good. Do you have any powers at all? Anything you're holding back?"

It wasn't lost on her that in her moment of desperation, mageri powers didn't seem so bad. But for a little thing, like escape... Maybe that was how it started.

"No, nothing. Do you think—"

The door to the cellar was yanked open before she could finish, and Cia fell silent as though they could avoid attention.

Between the grit in her eyes and that sifting from the ceiling, Ulan couldn't see very well, but she could tell from the size of the boots and the legs in them that the person coming down the stairs wasn't Hostill. Wasn't anyone they'd met.

Fear made her breath catch, and she held it as though it might save her.

The man who ducked down to look into their small space was practically a giant, his beard as thick as a bramble. But that wasn't what held her attention. *That* was saved for the red and black of his tunic. A Crown soldier. It was too late. Her caught breath quaked out. Here was no more need for silence. They'd been discovered, and there would be no escape.

"Two more down here!" he called up.

Ulan crushed herself against the wall as he approached, trying desperately to push herself into a standing position using just her legs and her bound hands behind to climb herself up the wall so that she could push off, have some leverage, but it was no good. All she did was plaster herself against it.

As the giant came closer, bent nearly double, she could see his eyes widen as he spotted Cia. "I've got her!" he called triumphantly.

Ulan cried out as he grabbed for Cia's feet and yanked, crashing her to the ground, so that her head bounced off the packed dirt floor, her back arched over the hands bound behind her back.

He said nastily, "I'll be back for you."

Cia craned her neck to look back at Ulan, as though pleading with her to do something. Ulan wished Cia could communicate exactly what, because her mind was frozen. She hadn't had the chance to alert Ruggerio about anything. Would there be a way to get word to him of her capture? Would he visit the Princess's prisoners? Would it be too late for Ulan once she was in Crown custody?

And what would they do to Cia? To Hostill?

At the ladder, the giant dropped Cia's feet, letting them fall against a higher rung so that her dress fell to her knees, revealing woolen stockings. He refitted his hands under her knees, hauling her up and handing her feet first to someone above. She dangled for a moment like a side of meat, something falling from her bodice, which Ulan would have taken for debris if it didn't roll away. The giant ignored or didn't see it. Whoever was above hoisted her up, and she was gone, taken.

Ulan was left alone with the giant.

She started to kick out, but he grabbed her foot and yanked like he had Cia, knocking her just as easily to the ground. She twisted and snapped with teeth and continued desperately trying to kick, anything to make it difficult for him to get a hold on her. He cried out when she got a foot loose and connected with something soft. She knew a moment of freedom before he towered over her and brought a boot down on her head.

CHAPTER SIXTEEN

Cia

Cia's teeth clacked together nearly hard enough to shatter as she was spun upright again and dropped feet-first to the ground. She landed awkwardly and started to fall, but the guard holding her brought her back around to face him, grabbed her around the waist and lifted her onto his shoulder like she was a sack of potatoes. Her shoulders strained and her arm wound screamed again, bleeding down his back as she hung awkwardly, her backside straight up in the air. The guard held her by it as he strode out a door, and when she kicked and tried to throw herself to the side to overbalance him, he swatted her so hard it shocked her momentarily still, stinging along with her other pains a second later when the shock wore off.

And then the pins and needles turned to icicles, or ice blades, as the cold seemed to stab through Cia. The guard who held her stumbled, as though he felt it too.

He approached one of the horses, who threw his head, yanking the reins out of the hand of the startled man who held the reins of several. The horse danced backwards, his eyes rolling in fear, lips pulled back from his teeth and his ears laid back against his head.

"Shht," said the man, "Shht, it's okay, Duncor."

But it clearly wasn't okay. Not for the horse.

The bladed wind kicked up again, whipping through the courtyard, and the other horses shifted their weight, threw their heads back, and blew their stress through their noses in great plumes that misted the night air. And in one of those plumes a face formed.

Garif.

Of course, Garif. Panic filled her, kicking her heart so hard her captor must have felt it straight through her chest. She renewed her thrashing. She could *not* let him get her. Especially not when she was a captive.

"What is it?" asked the man who'd been keeping the horses, responding to the horses and the unnatural night. He couldn't see Garif, but his voice trembled just the same.

Her guard shrugged, jostling her hard to warn her again to settle. "Word is one woman is a murderess and the other a *hexte*, a witchy woman. Nothing is right here. The sooner we get them out of our custody the better."

The giant who'd hauled her up entered the courtyard then, carrying Ulan, also flung over one shoulder, but something had happened to knock the fight out of her. She hung like a ragdoll, flopping with each monumental step, head banging against the monster's ribs.

He grabbed the reins of one of the shying horses, wrenched the horse's head around, and threw Ulan over the front of his saddle so that the pommel likely dug into her stomach. Not that she would notice.

Cia lurched, throwing herself forward, as though she could dive off her captor's shoulders, and he knocked her so hard on the head he saw stars. "Need help with yours?" the giant laughed at him.

The bastard who held her spat something back and grabbed for his horse's reins, but the horse suddenly reared back, lashing out with his hooves. One foot caught her guard in the shoulder, and he staggered away from the flashing hooves and the pain. Cia started to fall, but he tightened his grip where it had no business being, and barely managed to hold on.

"What in the void's gotten into you, stupid horse?" he snarled, looking like he'd like to land a fist on the horse as he had on Cia.

The giant spat an obscenity and reached for this horse as well, grabbing the reins in an iron grip before it could rear again. He stared it in the eyes and blew straight into its face in a sort of challenge. The horse's nostrils flared, and it stomped, but it stayed in place long enough for the giant to take Cia from her guard and throw her over Duncor's saddle. He made a mocking gesture to her guard to mount up, and the looks that flashed between them were severely unfriendly.

Then they were off, the saddle driving into her stomach with every hoof fall, pain screaming up and down her body. She could hear Garif's laughter trailing her, but never falling behind. He must be loving this. If he couldn't beat her himself, at least it was being done by proxy. Or would he punish her for that too—that another man's hands had been on her, nevermind that it was abusive? She'd brought it on herself, he'd say, by running away. She'd known what would happen, that they'd drag her back. Maybe, Garif would suggest, he'd even given her a taste for the rough... She shuddered and tried not to wish for death.

There were wards on the prison, that's what they'd said. Maybe she'd finally be free of Garif. At least for whatever time she had left.

Their horses slowed as they ascended the hill toward the palace and passed through the portcullis. It gave the wind the chance to settle upon them rather than blow past, and Cia shivered and cried out as it fell on her like an icy cape of thorns, a thousand stinging slivers stabbing into her, bringing with them the spreading, seeping cold of death.

Her lungs started to seize, and she heard Garif's voice on the wind, "You won't escape me that easily." And it hit her. That cold, the iciness of death—it wasn't all the weather. It was Garif. Stealing her breath. Whatever protection the Restoration had laid on her had been temporary. It was gone. He could get to her again—not just with his mocking laughter or his image, but with everything he had. He could hurt her. And he'd been ready to pounce. Before she could be stolen away again.

She would never be free, could never count on any protection not to be imperfect, transitory. But none of it would matter if she couldn't save herself. She gasped, trying to suck in air, starting to shake. But no one noticed her tremors, the horrible sucking sound among the commotion of reaching the courtyard, tossing captives from their horses, carrying or marching them into the castle.

The guard who rode behind her yelled at her to stop and slapped an iron hand down on her back, thinking that she was pulling something. He retracted the hand instantly, as though burned, or maybe stung by the deep freeze that had overtaken her. Beneath them, the horse twitched in panic.

She was desperate now. Vision blacking, world going dark, everything lurching, trembling, and shutting down.

Maybe she thrashed. Or her trembling set the horse off. Or he sensed Garif. But Ducor reared, head tossing.

The guard yelled.

Cia began to slip.

There was nothing she could do to stop it. Her vision was sliding in and out as the stabbing paralysis spread. Yet her heart beat like a winged thing trying to escape a jar. She panicked as she couldn't catch a breath— Garif's favorite form of torture. She hardly felt the ground as she hit it, too numb, too frozen.

But she felt the sharp sting of the horse's hoof as it came down right beside her head, nicking her ear and drawing blood. He seemed to have dissipated Garif's ghost, at least for an instant, and she gasped in a hard breath that hurt going down, as though her lungs were so cold they'd lost their elasticity and might shatter with the expansion. She gasped and choked, and when the horse reared again, she rolled away before she could get trampled.

She blinked away the blinding prisms of her vision, tried to clear eyes that were icing over, and spotted Garif again in the vapor of her breath. His face was twisted with hatred, his frost-white eyes going immediately to her ear. Fear stopped her remaining breath. The horse had bloodied her, which meant that Garif had a way in. He could get to her. If he could steal enough of her lifeforce to regain his own... No, surely it wasn't possible. His body was dead and gone. Unrecoverable. But then, *he* should be dead and gone.

Whatever he thought he had to gain, he couldn't have her. There must be something she could do against him. But she was no mageri, and this time he had no body and she had no weapon to plunge through it.

She flinched at the icy-feverish feel of his touch as he reached for her, as his foulness started to seep into her. Heat began fading from the extremes of her body, as though it had shut down power from all but the killing fields where they fought for supremacy, all that was nonessential dying a slow, frozen death. Her left foot and fingers felt insubstantial, but then, so did the rope that bound her. Brittle from the cold that enveloped her. She pulled, hoping her body would still respond, and her bonds broke, her hands floating apart as though they were mist. It was Garif who brightened in the night as her light seemed to dim.

She heard another voice cry out and thought it might be Ulan's. *She*, at least, would be able to see Garif. Would understand Cia's sudden death...

No! She would not allow it.

Garif wouldn't win.

He was tied to death, *she* to life. That had to give Cia a better hold on it.

A figure staggered toward them, and Garif pulled at the power within her, torquing her head around so that he could see, aiming her good hand toward the interloper.

Hostill! Hands bound behind him, he'd nonetheless dodged his captor to try to save her. A guard was yelling close behind him, and she felt more than saw others closing in as well, but it was Hostill that Garif aimed for, using her hand as his weapon. When she felt power flare, she yanked back hard on the poisonous, chilling tendrils of his influence. They writhed like eels or those worms that grew inside you and fed their growth on your substance until they killed you entirely. That was Garif, using his power, her strength to send lashes of heart-stopping chill through her body, as though it was his to do with as he pleased. As it had always been.

She yanked, and the power went wild, missing Hostill and hitting the guard behind him instead. He cried out and crumpled to the ground. Garif tried to regain control, swinging her arm back toward Hostill. She clenched her teeth together and fought him with everything she had. Bad enough what he'd done to her. He would *not* have this boy. She grabbed the eely ends of his power and *squeezed.* They wrapped around her phantom fist, covering it, seething and squirming. She was icing over, and his voice said, "You can't fight me." The sickness of it right in her head started a fire in her belly, and she fanned it into a blaze.

When he released another bout of icy power, she opened the blast furnace of her rage. It incinerated the draft of his cold, empty infiltration, and she pulled his aim once again, blasting the nearby guards. There was screaming and falling, and she could only hope she hadn't hit anyone she hadn't intended, because her eyes had filmed over like smoked glass.

And now her gaze was all internal. She chased down the shards of ice stabbing through her, melting them and reclaiming what remained, burning it up in the fire of her will. She felt Garif scream with rage and... yes, with fear. It felt powerful, adding fuel to her fire. She devoured him with it, ate him up until there was almost nothing left. Just a nugget of eternal ice, the kind that never saw sun, which she kicked embers over and left to smolder and melt.

She fought her way back to the surface. To her body, to the courtyard, raising hands to her face to rub her eyes clean. Her hands were free, but not just that. Insubstantial as they'd felt before, but not like mist now. Like smoke.

She looked around, and there were bodies on the ground, others staring at the place where she was, but not at *her.* Only Ulan, down on the ground, hands still bound and a guard bleeding at her back, met her gaze. The look in her eyes was sheer terror.

Cia turned her back, and it wasn't a physical turn. It was a whip, the gust of a fire in a new direction when the wind flared up. Was it possible that she'd turned the tables on Garif, taken his remaining lifeforce where he'd meant to steal hers? Did that mean he was part of her now?

She shuddered at the thought, and it blew her a bit away. She didn't know how long the power would last. She hoped it would be long enough to get away, but only just. She didn't want Garif, not any part of him.

She tried to run, though it was more like a bounding, her feet never hit the ground, but each footfall propelled her farther than it would have on its own. No one stopped her. If she was right, only Ulan could even see her. To the rest, she must have gone up in smoke.

CHAPTER SEVENTEEN

Cia

Cia was well into the town when her steps started to actually fall. The first time she was startled, the second she nearly stumbled. By the third she was conscious of the weight and her exhaustion and how utterly horrified she was with herself.

When she glanced around to get her bearings, she was no longer seeing through a smoky haze. She was lucky enough that it was dark, and there weren't many people clogging the streets, but those who were cast warding signs and or hurried inside as she came into view.

She'd become an object of terror. As far as anyone knew, a mageri—or a hexte, because after all, she was only a woman—had appeared in their midst. They would remember, and when the guards came after her, they would point out the direction she'd gone without a second thought.

Despite the exhaustion and the desperate need to collapse and process all she'd done, she forced herself to continue on, zigzagging through streets and alleys to confuse any trail. She'd no longer merely killed; *she was a killer*. People were dead because of her.

But not Hostill. Not Ulan. Not yet. Maybe she could balance the lives she'd taken with those she could save.

She ran until she couldn't anymore, and then dodged into an alley, ignoring the horrible smell of rotting fish—maybe it would help obscure her scent from any hounds. Maybe subconsciously she'd chosen it to punish herself. She didn't know anymore. She was so tired. She'd been on fire, and the fire had gone out, leaving her in ashes.

But her arm—wounded before, gone numb and useless—had re-formed perfectly. No longer cold or cut to the bone.

What had she done? The Crown would never leave off looking for her now. The surviving guards wouldn't know what they'd seen. Just that she'd manifested power. And the Restoration... She sank to the ground, her back to a wall, knees drawn up in front of her. She hugged them, unaware she was keening until she frightened away a rat who'd come to investigate. She forced herself to quiet. For so long, she hadn't been able to allow herself anything; she'd become skilled at self-deprivation. Silent suffering was a particular talent.

But the keening still sounded in her head. For one shining moment, she thought she might have purpose, that she could join the Restoration, once she convinced them of her sincerity. She could be part of something and take down others like Garif. But now...they'd see her as one of those others. Dangerous. Destructive. The evidence was overwhelming. How could she convince them that they were wrong?

Those guards she'd killed—they worked for the power she hated, the royal family who had blamed Queen Inaya and killed her for a crime Cia suspected one of them had committed. But in a sense Cia had toiled in silence for them as well, keeping her head down after her queen's execution, feeling *grateful* to Garif at first for taking her in. She'd embroidered lace for the nobility, attended their events when Garif insisted. Maybe the guards had only been doing their jobs, putting food on their tables when there was little enough to be had outside the castle. And tonight she'd taken someone's father or son or best hope for survival.

Who and what was she now? She'd done to Garif what he'd always threatened to do to her. She couldn't help thinking of that icy ember she'd buried inside herself. She hoped to smother it, melt it to nothing, but... she was afraid to go looking. The Church said that nothing ever died, just transformed. Mageri went mad, became ankari, when they took power for themselves without releasing it into a spell or a construct because it transformed *them*, modified their essential essence. If that power was another person or being, it fractured them. It had happened with the last court mageri. Ceramor was the reason all the mageri were sent to the battle fronts now with no new court mageri appointed. It was decided that their powers were best when used, exercised—more suited to times of war than peace. They were too dangerous, and too potentially unstable.

It was the first time she gave a moment's thought to Garif's position. He'd been needed, valued, but also distrusted, feared, ever watched for signs of fracture. But Garif had always reveled in the fear. Maybe he felt the scars his wife bore, physically and spiritually, *enhanced* his position. And everyone took his behavior as his right and her due. A healthy way for a powerful man to vent his spleen.

A plague on them all.

She'd met two good people since leaving the poisoned palace. Hostill and Ulan. And they'd been captured because of her. She had to find a way to rescue them. She couldn't do it on her own. Even if Garif's power stayed with her—and she didn't want to think about that or what it would mean—she didn't think she could bring herself to use it again. Besides, the guard had mentioned the prison was warded, which meant the power would be no good.

She needed allies, and she didn't have them. Not of her own, but she knew one person who might be able to help, if she could get there ahead of the story of what had happened back at the palace—the woman at the curio shop beside the churchyard, the one who'd helped them when escaping the cemetery.

She forced herself to her feet again, though she had to steady herself on the wall when the dizziness threatened to overwhelm her. She couldn't remember the last time she'd eaten, and she'd only had the bit of water Hostill had given her to drink.

The icy wind ripped through her the second she stepped out of the alley into a wider street, but it wasn't the stabbing cold of Garif's ghost, so she thought she would survive. That was the new chill by which all others would be measured.

Ceramor

Once out in the streets, Ceramor didn't know where to go. At first he just ran, away from the burning building and those who'd come looking. He'd been so long in that pit, he had no stamina. Even his stolen strength couldn't take him far. He'd needed it for healing, lifting, getting free. It had practically brought him back from the brink of death.

He had no home. No place to go. No idea how to begin or what to do with his freedom.

Food first, his instincts said. They'd given him something before sending him off, but it was long gone. He had no money, and nothing to trade but the clothes he wore, which were not fine. If it were warm, he might still have been tempted to give them up for whatever they would bring and beg or steal new, but not now, and not with night fallen and the promise of snow in the air. He could practically smell it.

He'd go toward the cemetery. There were plague houses up against it. Possibly long looted, though people tended to avoid them—making useless, superstitious warding signs when they passed—but there were no guarantees. Some survivors even lived where their families had died; they had nowhere else to go.

Ceramor no longer feared the plague. It had already taken from him all it could. It started with Reina. Her spark, her laughter, her kindness dying before him as she was racked with pain, as she started to bleed from… He closed his eyes against the memories, but they were in his head and all he did was lock himself inside with them. When he opened his eyes again, it was to let the tears out. The sickness passed to him next, and he'd had to go for the hounds before he became too sick to move. He could have drawn power from the land, but the anima didn't work like that. It took a life for a life, the darker, forbidden magics. He'd gone for the hounds, thinking he wouldn't be discovered. The sudden death of the hounds would be remarked on, but not investigated. Not the way a person's would be.

Anyway, he couldn't bring himself to kill another man. The dogs would be hard enough, but he'd seen them rip prey to shreds when the master allowed it during a hunt. They were only doing what came naturally, obeying instinct, taking life so they could hold on to their own. Nothing more or less than he was. If he could explain it to them, they would understand.

He hadn't meant to keep their lifeforce for himself. He hadn't ever intended Reina to be dead by the time he got back. Never that—alone as though unloved. He'd whispered to her that he'd be back, that he was going to get help, but she'd been nearly unconscious, delirious with pain. He had no idea if she'd heard him or if she'd come back to herself in her final moments. If she thought he'd deserted her.

The pain drove him to his knees at her bedside, and he laid his head down on her chest. He'd used only enough of the hounds' strength to get himself back home, saving the rest for her, and now it was no use. He waited to die, and when it took too long, he climbed into bed beside her, balancing on the very edge to avoid disrupting her, even in death. And besides, she hadn't gone cleanly. He couldn't think of that. His nose was stopped up with tears, but still…it was a smell he would remember for as long as he lived. He didn't intend for that to be long. He waited and he waited. Too heartsick to move. It was only, finally, his body's needs that drove him from the bed.

He'd taken in enough power that he healed despite himself, growing better as Reina grew colder, going slowly mad until he had no idea whether the baying inside his head came from his own grief or the hounds'. He hadn't meant to keep their lifeforces for himself. He knew the consequences. He just couldn't bring himself to care. Or to alert anyone to Reina's death. But Bloody Bess's people cleansed the castle; they came to check on Reina, on him. He defended her with everything in his arsenal. When his power didn't work due to their wards, he came at them with hands hooked into claws, with lips pulled back from his teeth, showing them in threat. He stood between them and Reina, and when they didn't back down, he went for their jugulars.

And ended up in the oubliette.

Nothing to live for but vengeance. On one level, he knew it was the Rot that had taken his beloved. But he couldn't fight the plague. On a more instinctual level that didn't allow for logic, only deeper, more personal truths, he felt it was Bloody Bess who'd taken her away, who'd thrown her body into the sea like something to be discarded. It didn't matter that the alternative was a mass grave or a cleansing fire. The only thing that mattered was that if he couldn't die, he'd have something to live for, something he could still do for Reina, even if it was only to avenge her.

And now that he was free…

He did have a purpose after all.

He'd been so lost in his memories, he'd forgotten to search out food, and now he was nearly at the churchyard. He slowed, sniffing out nourishment, and catching whiffs here and there, but always behind closed doors.

Then he caught the scent of something else. He froze, quivering. It couldn't be… This scent was fresher than earlier, but cutting back on itself.

The woman. The one he'd been sent to track. The one who'd killed her husband. The man she should have loved most in all the world. Obeyed. Cherished like he'd cherished Reina. All that anger at Bloody Bess transferred itself to her. He could thwart Bloody Bess by taking out her quarry and at the same time right a wrongful death. It wouldn't bring the mageri husband back. Or Reina, but it would satisfy the howling inside for the hunt. For vengeance.

At least temporarily, like food or water would only satisfy for a time.

He changed directions, following his nose. Yes, it was her scent. The same, but…different. There was something else to it, as though she'd rolled around with someone else, their scents intertwined. The second a lot less pleasant. It tingled the nose like dust or smoke. Made him want to sneeze it out.

It was late, but still there were some people about. Odd stares and quick scurrying out of his way as he was too focused to worry about who might be in his path. And then he saw the killer-woman and stopped in his tracks. She was looking around, frightened, watchful for anyone paying too much attention. He forced himself to drop his gaze, but he worried that she'd disappear, and he didn't drop it for long.

She was huddled in the doorway of one of the buildings abutting the churchyard, trying to make herself small and unnoticeable, not realizing that her body language compelled attention rather than sending it on its way. She knocked, looked around again as she waited for an answer. Knocked harder.

Ceramor crossed the street, out in the open, walking as though he had nothing to hide. He wanted to run, to pounce, but he didn't want her to bolt. If he could get close, he could wrap a hand over her mouth, carry her off before she could so much as scream.

Her weight shifted with impatience, and he was sure he'd have a chance. The place was closed up tight for the night. There was too much fear and need in the world to open the doors in the dark.

But then the door opened, and the woman framed in the entrance said something too low for him to hear. He sped up, his heart pounding, his lips peeled back and teeth out. He could practically taste his quarry's blood. He recoiled at the thought but didn't stop himself. He sprang for her, but the woman reached out, grabbed her and pulled her in. She never looked back to see the danger she'd been in. How close she'd come to death.

He seethed, staring at the doorway, debated breaking in versus waiting and watching. He knew which was the smarter move. Right now it was at least two against his one, and he was still weak from healing and hunger. He needed to eat and rest. His throat was so dry even the air hurt going down.

Now that the initial excitement had passed and instinct was urging him to caution, he could think again, analyze. Earlier she'd been with the boy, the one who smelled like his former master. If he stalked and surveyed instead of attacked, maybe she could lead him to the boy. He didn't know quite what he'd do, but there was a lot of unrest. There'd always been rumors of by-blows—the V'Alban princes had certainly bedded enough women, willing and unwilling—but none had been found. Given their death rate and rumored chances of survival should Bloody Bess discover them, it was possible none were willing to come forward.

But if he could capture the boy, then he'd figure out what next. If he could get the bastard onto the throne, it would be the ultimate end for Bloody Bess. And maybe he could return to his former position at court. He didn't even know if he wanted that, but his urge to see the boy, sniff him, be certain, was almost as strong as his urge to overtake the woman. If he could hold on to himself, play things right, perhaps he could do both.

Ceramor pulled back before someone could remark on him standing in the street, staring at this place. He had to find food, but he wouldn't go far. He'd be back to watch and wait.

CHAPTER EIGHTEEN

Ulan

Ulan lay on the ground, stunned. Cia had vanished before their eyes, turned to smoke and faded away. But not before she'd killed again, actual bolts of concentrated fire, almost like lightning, shooting out of her hands.

Cia's husband was the mageri, which meant…was it possible she'd swallowed up what remained of his lifeforce? She'd never heard of anything like it. Wouldn't have believed it if she hadn't seen it with her own eyes.

She'd left chaos behind. Bodies, guards tending to the wounded, calling for a medic. Ulan could have told them she could help. They wouldn't have believed her. Certainly wouldn't have freed her. Not after seeing the woman she'd been found with do…that.

There was a flicker before her, and she flinched, afraid Cia was back. Afraid she'd rage out of control. She'd seen her miss Hostill. It looked intentional, but if she'd really just eaten up her husband, she wouldn't be in her right mind. They might still be in a battle for control or…could a normal person become ankari? Would this drive Cia mad? With everything she'd been through, it was a wonder if she wasn't there already.

But the flicker steadied and grew in brightness as she focused on it, and there in the courtyard amidst the chaos was Dazia. Ulan cried out and came up against her bonds as she tried to open her arms. Her ghost girl cried as well and threw herself against her mother's body, backing off as she fell half into it, her tears coming even harder, racking her small, insubstantial contours. She wished with everything she had that she could feel her daughter, stroke her back, comfort her.

"I thought I'd lost you," she said into her ghost girl's hair. "I was so afraid."

You'll never lose me, Maman. I'll always find you.

She didn't know if that was true, but she knew more than she had before. Dazia wasn't tied to their home. She could come to Ulan at least as far as the castle. Maybe, if Ulan could escape, there was hope for a new life.

A guard came and grabbed Ulan roughly to her feet. She cried out more at the loss of her daughter than the harsh handling. The other guards were rallying, anxious to get the rest of their captives locked safely away in the warded dungeon. She tried to fight, but he cuffed her hard enough for spots to appear in her vision. She fought them back for Dazia, anxious for every last sight of her. She searched for and found her daughter's eyes, saw the horror in them.

"The dungeon will be warded," she warned Dazia. She didn't want her afraid when she couldn't find Ulan. "I'll...I'll find a way out."

She hoped she hadn't just lied to her daughter.

The guard cuffed her again, and she nearly blacked out. "Who are you talking to?" he demanded.

She couldn't see him, but she could hear the fear in his voice, thinking she might be like Cia. He had no idea.

"You," she told him, her tongue thick in her mouth. Her words slurring. "You can't keep us down."

"We'll see about that." He manhandled her through a doorway around the side of the castle, where he force-marched her behind the others. There was a guard between her and Hostill, pushing him from behind, but she'd caught a glimpse of him as he'd looked back, checking on her as though he didn't have problems of his own.

The icy wind had cut off as they entered the castle, but the air got progressively colder as they were taken down, down, down, and by the time they were shown to their cells Ulan was shivering, either with reaction to all she'd seen or with the cold. She would have hugged herself if she could, but her arms were still tied behind her. They had to be, though she could no longer feel them.

Her guard pushed her into a cell with Hostill and slammed the door. They were the last two in a long row of cells with stone wall partitions and metal barred doors between them and the corridor now holding only guards, watching them, some with calculation, as though they'd take out the killing of their fellow guards on their captives. But there was a call from down the line, a command, and the guards fell to order, some mumbling angrily under their breath. She was afraid retribution had only been postponed.

But the guards filed out, and in relief, she dropped to her knees, which stung at the hard floor, softened only by rushes that smelled of moisture and mildew. The wetness immediately seeped through her gown. She didn't care. From her knees, she went down on her backside, then pushed back until she could lay her head against the wall. Hostill followed, and sat on one side of her, huddled close. She hadn't meant to lean on him, but it was that or fall over. The wall, as it turned out, was not enough support. She wanted to curl up into a little ball and wake to find that this was all a nightmare and that she was warm at home with Dazia.

"We'll get out," Hostill whispered to her. "They haven't gotten everyone."

Everyone who? She didn't think being knocked around as she had in the last day had done good things for her head.

She started to nod in response but stopped when it made her so dizzy she thought she'd vomit. She did lay down then. Upright hurt. Down hurt too, but it was less work.

Hostill curled up against her back, and she tried to pretend it was Dazia, that her little girl was with her. But then she realized he wasn't curled. He must have gone back to back with her, his fingers working on her ropes.

Her stomach roiled, and she felt sick, but she had to fight it down. The rushes were foul enough. No one would change them if she soiled them further.

She should have been working on Hostill's ropes. She should have been finding their way. She tried to shift and ended up swallowing down bile.

Soon, she thought. *Soon I'll take care of him, I'll look for an escape. I just need to sleep first.* And she went out, unaware of the moment the pressure on her shoulders eased and her hands flopped uselessly to the floor.

She woke sometime later with the slamming open of a door and Hostill hissing, "Hide your hands."

Her whole body protested, but she managed it, opening her eyes into the dim light of a lantern nowhere near their cell. But they were at the end of the row, and there was nothing to see.

The stomp of boots echoed through the dungeon, shooting pain through her head with every footfall. It stopped just before reaching their cell. Ulan forced herself to sit up, her head spinning, and Hostill pressed up against her side, his warmth giving her something to focus on. She didn't know if he was shaking or she was, but she knew children. If it was Hostill, he wouldn't thank her for mentioning it. Anyway, her stomach still rolled like a storm-tossed sea, and she was afraid of what might come out of her mouth if she opened it. Then the footsteps continued. She made doubly sure that her hands were behind her, out of sight, and was glad of it when she saw who it was.

The Blood Princess. Bloody Bess. She'd seen her only twice, once when she was just a child, around Hostill's age, a tiny slip of a thing, veiled, but with her head held high rather than hung in grief at her father's death. She'd walked in a royal procession at the side of Prince Jannik, who would later succeed King Cyril, but she never looked at him. Never took his arm or huddled against him for comfort. Maybe that was not how princesses behaved, but Ulan had thought then how alone she seemed, but also how brave. She'd seen her years later, after Ulan had been to war and back, after she'd had and lost a daughter. Watched the princess address the people upon the death of her second brother in the war set off by the death of the first. She was not so much bigger then or now. She still looked like a child dressed up in her mother's finery, but for her eyes, which were almost antiques, too cold and knowing for the pink blush of her cheeks. Her hair was gleaming rose gold contained by twists and pearls and a simple gold circlet. A perfect doll-baby of a princess, but one too precious for play.

Now she was flanked by two men, the nearest, largest of them she recognized as Regent Strego. His gaze barely grazed the captives, scraping along, sampling, finding them wanting. But the other man...she realized he was staring, straining to see in the faint light, and when her own eyes adjusted that far, she knew why.

It was Ruggerio. As soon as he saw her looking, he pressed his lips together hard and glanced away again, as if she was of no particular interest to him. She got the message. She was to keep her mouth shut. They didn't know each other. She couldn't appeal to him. At least not now. She didn't know whether it was for his good or hers or both. The first she could be certain of. The rest... She didn't know what would happen if he decided the risk that their relationship would be revealed was too great and that she was of no further use to him. She looked away, shrank into the shadows to avoid further notice.

The party turned back the way they'd come, footsteps stopping again before one of the other cells.

"That one." It was Ruggerio's voice, and she could imagine him pointing as well, targeting their prey.

An outcry started up immediately, nearly drowning out the sound of the creaking cell door opening, a scuffle going on inside, what sounded like a body hitting the wall and then the floor.

"Enough," came a voice, and it took her a second to realize that it was Vizi's. It had such command she would have expected it from one of the people in power *outside* the bars, but there was no mistaking it. Vizi had an orator's voice. It carried, bouncing off the stone walls, sending shockwaves through her aching head, but also an odd jump to her heart.

It was followed immediately by the sound of a blow sharp enough that even from several cells away, Hostill flinched with it. But Vizi's voice rose again, mushy this time, as though his mouth was filled with blood, "Take heart," he cried. "A reckoning is coming! The Restoration will rise."

There were cheers and calls from the other cells, but in the midst of them, another blow and no more proclamations from Vizi. Ulan thought she could hear the sound of dragging feet, Vizi being carried off.

To interrogation? Torture?

She didn't think he would betray his cause, but that didn't mean Ruggerio and the Blood Princess wouldn't destroy him in the attempt.

Or were there other methods? There was no current court mageri, but Cia's husband hadn't been the only one to return to the castle from the front. She knew that mageri could tap people as well as the earth, but could they do it with enough precision to extract specific information? Could they do it without rifling through and leaving the rest of the mind in disarray?

She questioned which side she was on. What would Dazia say if she knew the sacrifices her mother made for her? Ulan cringed at her own thinking. She wasn't sacrificing herself. She was sacrificing others. But was it for the good of all? The good of the kingdom? Was it truly about the horrors of revolution or her own unwillingness to give up her daughter?

As soon as the guards and all were gone again, Ulan looked to Hostill.

"Turn around," she said. "I need to work on your bonds as well. We need to find a way out of here."

Then she wouldn't have to decide. They could all be free and if they were rounded up and recaptured afterward, it wouldn't be her fault. Now that she knew Dazia wasn't tied to their horrible little house, she could flee. Maybe not out of the city, that might test the limits, but disappear somewhere Ruggerio would never find her, if there was any such place. At least, live or die, it would only be her own life at stake.

Cia

"You shouldn't have come, and you can't stay," the old woman said, hurrying Cia along with a hand that fell just shy of her back. She'd touched Cia once, and she'd flinched so hard the woman had immediately let up, but Cia could practically feel the heat of the woman's hand hovering between her shoulder blades, ready to give her a push if needed. Her other hand held a swinging lantern that sent odd shadows along the walls, giving Cia only faint impressions of dirt and stone and things that skittered away from the light. They were pressing through the tunnels back to the churchyard, the way that Hostill had led them to escape and then capture by the Restoration. Only desperation could have brought her to return.

"Where are you taking me?" Cia asked over her shoulder. Not that she had any option but to go forward, or turn back and run over the old woman on her way.

"I'd think that would be clear enough."

"I mean from here."

"Shht," the woman said, which must mean they were near enough an exit to chance someone overhearing, even at this hour. "Stop here."

Again, Cia couldn't see that she had any choice. The passage came to an abrupt stop ahead.

The woman performed a complicated knock on the wall at approximately chest level, facing toward the interior of the church rather than the gardener's shed.

Cia backed up, started feeling along the opposite wall with her hands behind her, looking for a latch or a catch or something that would open outward in case she needed to escape. She didn't understand. Was the woman turning her over to the Church? Would they offer sanctuary to a murderess, one who'd taken in the essence of her mageri husband? Even if they would—and she couldn't imagine it—would they risk an outright rift with the Crown after what had happened the last time? The Church lived on the Crown's sufferance, and only because they preached peace and mollified the people and disposed of the dead. In the same way that Cia had held her tongue, the Church largely held theirs. Cia knew their rationalizations as she knew her own—striking out brought nothing but pain and punishment and no sign of change. But on their end, they could also believe they did some good. That they served the people. Cia had finally struck her blow, and it had been fatal.

She couldn't find an escape latch of any kind before someone on the other side of the wall returned a complicated code, and suddenly the wall slid back as though it had been a panel all along and never solid at all.

The figure standing where the panel had been was backlit. Cia blinked to adjust her eyes, but she got only an impression of a tall person standing so erect as to seem almost a statue. The head turned, looking from the old woman, who received a nod, to Cia, who felt she was being evaluated. She felt hollow, exposed, wondering what she'd ever done that might deem her worthy, turning already when the figure suddenly stepped out of the way to invite them in. Something gave way in Cia's chest, and she tried to let the air out slowly rather than in a gust that might give away that she had expected another outcome.

The old woman waited for Cia to go before coming through herself and closing the door behind.

In the meantime, the statuesque figure had bent over a lantern and turned it up. When the figure straightened, Cia swallowed a gasp. The face might as well have been carved of some warm wood, because it was the face of an anima incarnate. Icons, altar figures and paintings were commissioned to represent the collective spirit of humanity, but she'd never seen one that captured the perfection as well as the figure before them. She couldn't say whether the face was masculine or feminine. It held the balanced beauty of both. Jet hair as textured as raw silk, oiled and glistening pulled back into an acolyte's topknot revealing a high forehead. Brows arched above eyes a gold that gleamed in the lamplight, a shade lighter than the deep alderwood from which the face might have been carved. The cheekbones stood in stark relief, and the lips were ridiculous, perfect. A shade darker on the bottom than on top, which made them arresting.

Cia realized she was staring and looked away, only then noting that they were in a small vestibule, a robing chamber, based on the hanging robes and vestments. There was open cabinetry with folded fabric Cia guessed to be altar cloths, some shot through with threads of silver or gold.

"I brought her," the old woman said.

When Cia turned back to study the person who seemed an anima incarnate, she caught a glint in their eyes and a challenge in their stare. She strongly suspected she was in the presence of the person now in charge of her fate.

"So, I see." The voice was deep, melodious, but also quiet, as though there was a peace not to be disturbed in the church. "I am Roha."

Cia racked her brain. She'd heard that name before somewhere.

Roha. It might stand for Rohan or Rohanna or...

No, it had been Roha. She heard the name now in Hostill's voice. *They arrested Silgar. Roha said to tell you...* Back when they'd faced off with Vizi at the Restoration safe house. Did that mean that Roha was one of them and Cia wasn't being turned over to the Church after all?

"I am Cia," she responded. "But I suppose you already know that."

"Come with me," Roha said, turning.

Cia looked to the old woman, but her face gave nothing away as Roha opened a door deeper into the church and preceded them through it. Cia took a deep breath and followed Roha into the pulpit area of the church. What she thought of cynically as the performance area. Back in Frizenze, they had more personal altars for incense and offerings to the spirits of the land, tiled pools for meditating and giving up the sense of self, time and place, and letting stresses and concerns flow out rather than bottle them up until they poisoned the spirit. At least in the wealthier houses.

She'd never been to the communal pools, and the one behind the altar didn't encourage lingering. The water wasn't clear and inviting, but clouded. In need of purification. She hadn't given herself up to the anima in so long. Maybe if she had, she could have released some of her anger and fear. Maybe Garif would still be alive... No, she couldn't wish that. Dead by someone else's hand, yes, but she would do it all again if faced with the same choice. The Church would condemn her, but the Restoration would wish Garif dead for his crimes, if not against her then the land. She had to know which she was dealing with here—institution or rebellion. Repudiation or recognition.

Her steps slowed until she stopped altogether, as she realized that Roha was approaching the altar.

Cia was still several steps away when Roha turned to her. Rather than encourage her closer, the acolyte asked, "Do you know the story of Lehren Gelerte?"

"Everyone knows of Gelerte. He was Lehren nearly seventy years ago when the Church went to battle with King Calestri. He was a scholar and an outspoken advocate for maintaining the natural order of the anima. I think his main teaching was that power was pure, but man was fallible? No matter how righteous man might feel in his motivations, he would be shortsighted, there would be unforeseen costs. He would try, sometimes fail, often destroy. Men could not be trusted with power, especially not as much as King Calestri wanted to wield."

Roha nodded but said nothing, and Cia got the sense that more was expected, so she continued.

"Lehren Gelerte battled Mad King Calestri. The King started stealing the souls of the devout to feed his power, then tried to declare himself a walking manifestation of the anima. Essentially a god. When Lehren Gelerte and the leader of the Church, the Animist, stood against him, King Calestri declared himself head of the Church itself and sent his forces to take them down. The congregation rose up. The people grabbed whatever weapons they had at hand to defend against the King's forces. It didn't end well for them. Churches were razed to the ground with only Calestri's side alive to tell the tale. It's said they doubled the bodies in the burial yards in a single day."

"All true, as far as it goes."

Cia studied Roha, but—*he, she?*— didn't give anything away. And then it struck her. Could Roha be *Nim?* At first sight, Cia had thought Roha one of the anima come to life, and maybe that wasn't far off. She'd heard of the *Nim*, though distantly, almost as something mythical—people born both male and female. She had no idea…

Roha turned to the altar, ran fingertips along the bottom, and pressed some hidden button. The top of the altar swiveled away, and at first Cia couldn't see what it revealed for the flare of light that nearly blinded her. She threw her hands up in front of her face to protect her eyes. When the flare died down, she peeked between her fingers to see that what rested in the crevice revealed was the top of a mageri staff, thin bands of metal twisted into a cage that came to a point that would pierce if used as a lance. In the center of the cage, the glow dimming now, was a smooth stone the size of a child's fist, white with flecks of every color imaginable. She would have thought it the largest opal she'd ever seen, except this seemed to have its own inner light.

It was the most beautiful thing she had ever seen, but there was something ominous in Roha's tone, and Cia was afraid of what this was building toward.

"The rest is this," Roha went on, indicating the object with an outswept hand. "Calestri did burn down the Church and everyone left in it, but before that, he managed to capture Lehren Gelerte. Gelerte had fought valiantly in defense of his church and his people. He wasn't afraid to die in service to his beliefs, not if it meant rejoining the anima he so loved."

Cia nodded her understanding.

"But they took away even that. King Calestri ordered his men and mageri to hold Gelerte, and then Calestri himself bled him. He pulled out Gelerte's spirit, but he didn't take it for himself. Instead, he drew from the flagstones beneath his feet, cracking the very foundations of All Souls Church. He fashioned Gelerte's essence into a gem and then had that gem set into a prison. Both are indestructible. Gelerte will never be free. He'll never add his essence to the All. King Calestri took the stone with him and carried it atop his scepter and staff until the day of his final defeat."

Cia eyed her skeptically, "Why wouldn't I know of this? Why wouldn't *everyone* know this? It seems as though King Calestri would have made Lehren Gelerte's fate into a cautionary tale, like putting people's heads on pikes."

"Because the king's men were sworn to secrecy on pain of death. Calestri claimed to have made Gelerte's prison indestructible, but I don't think he wanted it tested. If it were known, his staff would have been a target for every true believer out there. It would have been a lodestone for the resistance."

"And now you have it?" Cia had watched the gem as Roha told the tale. It had glowed gold, pulsing in time with the story as through in emphasis. As though it was alive.

"Now the *Church* has it. Part of the carta that reestablished the Church involved the return of this artifact. The Church's great and secret icon. Another part established certain limitations on the Church to be sure that they'd never again directly oppose the Crown, never foment rebellion. That was, by the way, the reason Calestri gave for imprisoning Gelerte the way he did—that Gelerte hadn't achieved enlightenment, but preached division that was too *unhealthy* to add to the collective spirit of the land."

"Why are you telling me this?"

"Because the gem still holds Gelerte's essential essence, his belief in truth and his ideals. It pulses gold in the face of truth, red in the face of lies, and goes black in the face of betrayal."

Roha studied her carefully before continuing. "We need to know whether we can trust you. If you're truthful and well-intentioned, if you renounce any power and dedicate yourself to our cause, you live. If not, you will get the end Lehren Gelerte never achieved."

Cia's breath caught in her throat every bit as though Garif was present and squeezing. She'd been through so much, she hardly knew her own heart, and here they were going to test it. And passing or failing meant life or death.

She looked to the old woman for help, but she was watching the stone. She didn't meet Cia's gaze at all, yet she had the strong sense that if she bolted, the woman wouldn't hesitate to stop her.

She swallowed down her panic, forced in a deep breath, held it. Breathed in and out a few more times. Then she nodded agreement to Roha. She didn't have any choice, but they were giving her the illusion of it at least.

"Ask your questions," she said.

Roha didn't waste time. "Why are you here?"

It was an open-ended question, but she didn't see a point in playing around. Even aside from the stone, Roha seemed competent enough to judge deception.

"Will standing or sitting affect the response?" she asked back.

Roha huffed at the delay, but answered, "No. There is no cheating the stone."

"Good." Cia collapsed down on the hard stone floor of the altar. She was so tired that she almost didn't care if she lived or died, as long as sweet release came at the end. "I'm here because I killed my husband. He was abusive, a monster of a man, and it was kill or be killed. Like Gelerte, I'm not so afraid of death, but I wouldn't let my husband benefit from mine."

The gem pulsed gold. Cia spoke only the truth.

"Then I ran. I didn't come looking for the Restoration. I hadn't planned on killing Garif or on fleeing the castle. I didn't have a plan, except to escape, disappear, survive."

More gold.

"But you found us. How?"

"I stumbled upon Hostill in my escape. He hasn't done anything wrong. Just helped me, hoping I might have some word of his sister."

Roha's gaze shifted away. Just for a moment, down and to the right, as though looking for something...or avoiding whatever might show. It was the first time Roha had given anything at all away, and Cia had no idea what it might mean.

"And the other woman who came with you?"

"Ulan? I don't know her at all. She was on the run. The Crown must be after her as well." Ulan's secrets weren't hers to divulge.

"Now that you've found the Restoration, do you want to join? If you've merely come seeking asylum, we have none to give. As you've seen, there is no safety with us, and your presence increases our danger."

"Yes," she said, and the stone pulsed red, then gold before its light mutated to a swirling amber, as jumbled as Cia's thoughts.

"Explain," Roha commanded.

Cia blew out a breath. How did she explain? She'd had no time to absorb, to analyze. And to do so with an audience...what if she came to the wrong conclusion?

"I need to strike a blow." They were the first words out of her mouth, and they brought others tumbling, things she didn't even know she had bottled, that she'd pushed down so far they were now exploding out. "I kept quiet when they took my princess, my queen, when they called her a murderess. For survival. I let King Jannik marry me off to his mageri Garif and was *grateful* for the rescue." Her disgust tasted like acid on her tongue. She swallowed it down. "I stayed silent at the abuse because no one would listen. I was disgraced; Garif was the great man. I took the abuse until it nearly killed me. Until it killed him. There is something rotten at the core of the crown, and now they've got Hostill and Ulan, all of your people. Because of me. I can't stay silent any longer. If I don't act, I might as well die, because there will be no point to my existence."

The stone flared a bright gold and held it, and Cia felt warmed by the glow. Everything she'd said was so true it hurt, but in the way of a controlled fire, burning away what needed to be burned, making way for new growth.

"You will dedicate yourself to us, to our fight? You will not betray us?"

"Yes, I will dedicate myself and no, I will not betray your cause. I never lied about my princess to save myself, even when I faced her fate. And I never condemned her after my marriage to gain acceptance." But she did spend years with her lip bloody from biting it to keep her mouth shut when she should have defended her queen. Perhaps that in itself was a betrayal.

But maybe the stone couldn't read what she didn't speak. Maybe it was kinder to her than she was to herself. Not just a stone, but the essence of the scholar, the martyr who had been killed to create it. It flared gold. As dry as she was, her eyes stung with tears.

Roha looked to the woman behind Cia. "Do you have any questions to ask?"

The woman shrugged, looked at the tears in Cia's eyes and softened just a touch. "The stone is satisfied, and she seems sincere. My only question is whether she'll be an asset rather than a liability."

Roha looked to Cia. "What about it?"

Cia had been thinking about this. "I have no special skills. I know the castle, but not the dungeons, not the parts you'll likely need knowledge of to save your people. And I don't doubt that you have other inroads into the palace. However, I can be a distraction. Bloody Bess is after me. *Has* to capture me after the public spectacle of my escape and the hunt for me. I can pull guards away from their posts. I can be bait."

"And if you're caught?" the old woman asked.

"Then at least my actions will *mean* something. People will be saved, will be free because of me. One life for many. Balance. Atonement. Isn't that what this is all about?" She waved at their surroundings.

Roha pressed two-tone lips together into a hard line, thinking. "I have one more question. *How* did you escape?"

Cia went cold, hugged herself for warmth, protecting her core as though it wasn't already too late. How would they react when they knew? Did Garif still live within her, that frozen ember waiting to ice her over again, or had she burned him out? She could promise that *she* wouldn't betray them, but… was she bringing a spy into their midst?

The stone turned black, the sudden absence of light seeming to suck it out of the rest of the room. Apparently, it could read beyond what was spoken. Instantly there was a knife at her throat and Roha's eyes staring right into hers.

"Tell me *now*. My knife hand is very twitchy and my blade razor sharp."

Cia didn't dare swallow the lump in her throat. She fully believed Roha would make good on the threat. She didn't know where to start, but she was clear that hesitation would cost her. So, she told Roha the whole story. Quickly, in such a rush that she was not cautious about the blade. She felt it nick her, and Roha eased off fractionally, but never let up with that stare that felt as though it could see into her soul. Cia started with the haunting, the fear for her life, the…enveloping. She had no idea how to describe it or what it meant for her short term, because there would be no long term if Roha didn't like her answers.

The blade was still at her throat when she finished, and Roha was still staring into her soul. Neither looked to the stone. What could the stone do with all of that? It was the truth, but the meaning… It couldn't see into the future.

"Leave us," Roha said without looking at the woman who'd brought her.

"But—"

"I'm safe enough, and whatever comes next you don't need to see."

Cia's heart stuttered as the old woman turned to go.

Then the glass shattered above their heads, and the blade sliced into her neck and she screamed, too shocked to process whether her throat had been cut or just nicked in Roha's reaction to the exploding stained glass window.

CHAPTER NINETEEN

Ceramor

Ceramor lost himself in the pleasure of chasing rats. They were gamy and not more than a mouthful, but he reveled in the challenge of it. They were fast and small, and could outmaneuver because of their size, but he had cunning on his side. He could predict which direction their little tiny rat brains would send them, head them off or leap ahead of them or right on top. It was such fun. Ridiculous fun, especially after the oubliette and the starvation, the dehydration, the filth. Rats were filthy, but it was the crunch, his mouth flooding with juices, the meat… Oh, the meat. It had been so long. And these were fat rats. They'd fed well on…the meat turned rancid on his tongue. On bodies. Plague bodies. *People*.

The thought snapped him back to himself. Mostly himself. As himself as he could be these days. Some part of him was still howling, upset at being denied the hunt. Fresh meat. But another part of him remembered what he was about, and that was what had snapped him out.

People. Inside the church. Yes, he heard them now. Not well enough to know what they were saying. They weren't loud. But the night was quiet. People no doubt hiding in their homes from the patrols, uncertain what was happening. The streets weren't safe at night anyway. Not with so many abandoned buildings into which a person might be dragged. Not with so much desperation. And with a predator in their midst, the rats and other animals had gone silent.

Why would there be people at the church this late? Too late for services. He had to get closer. One could be his quarry.

There was a groundskeeper's shed not far away, and up against it, stacked pallets. Above that a round window of colorful picture glass, about where the sun would be at mid-morning, but that was still a long time away. He could feel the position of the moon without even looking up to confirm it. If he could get up the pallets without making a clatter and onto the top of that shack, he could hear, maybe even see inside.

He went to the pallets, adjusted one that might topple the stack, and clambered onto them as carefully and quietly as he could. He was not weightless, though, and they creaked, but the voices inside didn't stop. The pallets stopped shy of the roof, but he jumped, the top pallet flying from the stack as he kicked off. It hit the ground with a thud, then another as the other corner struck down, but all his focus was on pulling himself up with the tenuous handhold he'd gotten on the roof. There was no cornice. No gutter. Nothing really to grab onto, but his hands had become claws, his nails razor sharp, and he dug them into the tar on top of the groundskeeper's shack and swung a leg up onto the roof before he could fall. He edged toward the church, toward that window, and looked through a clearish glass pane now at face height down into the altar area.

There was the murderess! Right there. A knife held to her throat by someone who looked very determined to use it.

His instincts kicked in. All he could think was, *no, they couldn't kill her until he got what he wanted*! There was no time to find a better way in. He gathered his legs beneath him, ducked his head, threw his arms up to shield his face, and dove head-first through that beautiful glass window, shattering it on impact.

Cia

Cia's scream snapped Roha's gaze to the blood welling on her neck, and instantly the blade was gone, replaced by Roha's body, crushing her to the floor and then rolling them both against the altar to shield them from falling glass. Whatever had come bursting through the window landed with a crash and a snarl. Roha whirled to face it, the blade that had been at Cia's throat now aimed at the new threat.

Roha's transformation from peril to protector made Cia's head spin. One part of her brain screamed at her to run while Roha was distracted. If it hadn't been for the blood streaming down the acolyte's robe, the shard of glass that she could see embedded between shoulders that had been used to shield her, she might have done just that. But whatever Roha had intended to do to Cia, the acolyte had now placed herself—himself?—between her and danger, and Cia couldn't leave Roha to fight alone and injured…because the old woman who'd led her to the church had run for the secret passage, and the beast hadn't given chase. He'd chosen to face off with the bigger threat, the one holding the blade.

Cia jumped to her feet, her system flooding with terrified energy as she tried to make sense of the creature she could see beyond Roha——a hunched figure, the size and shape of a man, and then some. His upper back was bowed, his face long and filled with knife-like teeth, dripping froth flecked with blood. No doubt he'd been hurt bursting through the window, but it was madness rather than pain that showed in eyes the color of red clay. He flexed scythe-like claws at the ends of over-long fingers to draw their attention. He wanted their fear, savored and salivated over it.

But only for an instant before springing at Roha.

Roha slashed with the knife and he with his claws. Cia couldn't watch the outcome. She looked frantically for a weapon of her own and lit on the gem of Gelerte. The point of the twisted tines was the only thing within reach that she could see. She grabbed it from its pedestal and it resisted, heavier than expected. The metal grew hot in her palm as though to insist she unhand it, but she held on. She stabbed the barbed end into the monster's side as he slashed at Roha, who dodged out of the way, though not before the beast's nails raked bloody furrows into Roha's shoulder.

The beast howled and backhanded Cia without a thought. She went flying into the altar, her back cracking against it. Pain burst through her body, her backside hitting the floor so hard one leg went numb. In the instant she sat dazed, the beast sprang, and suddenly she was face to face with those clay-red eyes, the dripping teeth so close she could smell blood on his breath. And flesh going gamy. She bit back a gag, afraid the slightest movement would cause those teeth to snap down on her neck.

Cia saw motion behind him and instinctively looked up. It was enough to warn the beast, who whirled in time to catch Roha's knife in his arm rather than his back. He howled again, bloody spittle flying, and ripped his arm away, taking Roha's knife with it. The gem was still in Cia's hand, though. She realized it when it blazed with heat once again, and she swung back toward the beast's damaged side as he grabbed for Roha with those bladed claws.

His back arched in pain as the Cia pierced him again with the metal tines caging the gem, but he didn't let go of Roha, instead grabbing the acolyte by both arms and swinging the rest into Cia so that Roha hit hard, knocking the stone of Gelerte away and sending them both skidding across the floor.

Cia rolled to face the beast in time to see him pounce...and suddenly there was such a blast of air that it blew him into the back wall of the church, as though something had exploded, but if so, it had only blown in his direction.

"Quickly," Roha said. "It won't take him long to recover."

Cia was too stunned to answer. There was more going on here than she knew. Too much more. She didn't want to be a pawn again, battered around by fate.

Roha reached for her to help her to her feet, and Cia skittered back like a spider, going on arms and legs that wanted to fail her. Roha tsked and grabbed for her anyway, but instead of closing on her with an iron grip, the acolyte seemed to be hanging on for dear life, as though Cia's shoulder was all that was keeping Roha remotely upright. "You have to help me. I can't make it on my own. Neither can you."

Cia didn't know if that was true, but the vulnerability worked far better than any manhandling. Had Roha been hurt worse than it appeared? Or hit with that blast? What the holy spirits had happened?

Cia got to her feet and put a shoulder under Roha's arm, wrapping her own arm around the acolyte's waist. Roha had cut her but had also saved her. And in the end, it was an instinctive thing. Against all reason, she trusted Roha more than she trusted the urge to run. More than she'd trusted anyone since her princess. Maybe because she had no one else. Nowhere else to go. No other choice.

Her leg was still numb, but they leaned on each other and stumbled together toward the outer door of the church. They heard a rumble, and the ground beneath them shook. They clutched each other harder, pushed faster, but Cia's leg started to give out, and Roha had to release her or fall as well, not steady enough herself to hold Cia upright. Cia fell sideways into a wall that jumped under her hand, her heart lurching with it. Plaster began to rain from above, and she lost sight of Roha while shielding herself with her free arm.

When she peeked under it, she saw Roha unlocking the doors of the church and pulling at the massive oak panels. They didn't budge. Cia pushed herself off the wall and practically fell toward the doors, momentum all that kept her going in the right direction as great cracks split the ceiling and the ground continued to shake. It wouldn't be long before small bits of plaster became entire sections of the ceiling overhead.

She hit the doors hard, slamming one back into place just as Roha started to make progress, but then she grabbed the handle, hands over Roha's, and together they heaved. The massive door gave inward suddenly, and Cia went staggering back. A beam broke loose from the ceiling and swung down at her, striking her shoulder and knocking her to the ground. Roha reached a hand down to help her and ended up bracing instead on Cia's bad shoulder as the shocks continued. The pain stole a cry, but it was lost in the sound of cracking foundations and more splitting beams.

Cia reached for the hand gripping her shoulder and grasped it. She could feel Roha's muscles shaking with exhaustion and the strain of Cia's added weight, but Roha pulled, and Cia rose. Together they threw themselves through the open door and staggered into the night.

Roha went right, and Cia followed. She could turn aside, go her own way. The stone of Gelerte had gone black for betrayal when Roha asked how she'd escaped the Crownsmen. She might trust Roha, but there was no way Roha could trust her. Or that the Restoration would put its faith in Cia after she'd left their people behind when she'd fled, even if there hadn't been anything else she could do then, even if she hadn't planned to *leave* them imprisoned. No doubt Cia was the one the beast had come for at the church. But Roha hadn't abandoned her, and Cia would rather face whatever came next than run off and lose any chance to redeem herself. *And find out about that blast*, a small voice spoke up. But the voice was so small. Hardly able to break through the shock and make itself heard. It had been so long since she was allowed to question.

That almost stopped her.

What if the voice wasn't hers at all?

What if Garif wasn't truly gone? What if this was *his* voice, trying to make trouble?

But there *had* been an explosion that knocked the beast off his feet and allowed them to escape. And it hadn't come from her.

Maybe she wasn't the only one with secrets.

And yet...

The Restoration was against the use of mageri powers. Violently, zealously against it. Even more so than the Church.

And yet...

There was one person who might possibly have the answers.

Roha veered left at a cross-street, not wasting breath for directions. Cia, unprepared, overbalanced, knocking Roha into a building. The acolyte bounced off and kept going, limping and unsteady, one bad foot placement away from going down.

"Is it far?" Cia panted out.

Roha swayed with the head shake and put a stop to it quickly, nearly falling into a doorway halfway down the alleyway. Or Cia thought it was a fall until she saw Roha fumble for a key, only to drop it to the ground.

Cia bent to pick it up, and her head swam at the sudden rush of blood. She rested it against the wall for the moment, waited for her vision to clear, then picked up the key and fit it into the lock Roha had been trying. She and Roha fell through the door as it opened, and Roha slammed it shut again, locked it. Then the acolyte collapsed to the ground, eyes closed, breathing labored, smoothing out as sleep had its way.

Cia fell as well, but only to her knees. She wanted to lie down, but she had no idea where she was or whether she could relax, and she couldn't let Roha go without answers.

She slapped at Roha's cheek, and then a second time harder. Roha's eyes flickered open.

"Where are we?" Cia demanded, tone harder than the slap to keep Roha from falling away before responding. "What happened?"

"Home," was all Roha managed before going out again, this time for good.

If Roha could pass out with no true reason to trust Cia, then Cia could do the same. She didn't have a choice. Her body decided for her, run down to the last dregs of energy. She managed to control her fall to avoid landing on Roha, but that was all. She curled onto her side and spared a moment to hope that blood flow would return to her numbed leg, then she was out.

If the beast came for them in their sleep, at least it would be over quickly.

CHAPTER TWENTY

Cia

Light spiked into Cia's eyes, and she rolled to avoid it, only to be jolted awake by the pain in her head and shoulder. Her stomach flipped like it wanted to come up through her throat, but it was so dry it seemed it would crack rather than expand to accommodate the extra load. She worked her mouth, trying to find some moisture to swallow her stomach back down, lest it become stuck.

And suddenly she remembered…everything.

Her eyes shot open again, blinking uncontrollably against the light, grit scraping her eyes raw with every motion. She raised an arm, the one that was working, to brush the debris away, but it only seemed to rub things in until finally she irritated her eyes so much that tears eked out and flushed some of the detritus.

That was when she saw Roha, still in the same position as the night before, face to the sky, arms to the sides, breathing so subtly Cia had to hold her own breath to hear it. Part of her wanted to wake Roha to make sure she could, but self-preservation won out, at least for the moment. She wasn't certain what would happen when Roha woke. Before the monster had broken in, Gelerte's stone had indicated betrayal, and Roha'd held a knife to her throat. The knife and stone had both been lost in the battle, but that didn't mean the danger had passed. Cia'd had enough of being anyone's target. Escaping together didn't necessarily put her and Roha on the same side any more than Cia marrying Garif had aligned her interests with his.

She forced herself to her feet. Both legs were working again, but even the weight of her arm was too much for her injured shoulder, which shrieked in pain if she left the arm unsupported or moved it in the wrong way...or apparently any way at all. She cradled that arm by the elbow and looked for something she could use as a sling.

She was in spare quarters. Literally just a room to rent, or maybe one given to Roha by the Church. They'd passed out short of the sleeping pallet, but it did exist, up against the far wall, away from the window with the ill-fitting wooden shutters that had let in the light that woke her. It was as neat as she kept her own, the single blanket pulled taut except for a spot where the pallet's stuffing seemed to sink inward, as though worn down from someone sitting there regularly, perhaps while they dressed. There was a small fireplace as well. Enough to heat the room, and maybe cook an egg or so, but not for much else.

There were a few wood planks affixed to the wall near the fire that held supplies, but no clothing. Nothing that could be used for a sling. For that, Cia turned to the only piece of furniture in the room beside the pallet, a plain wooden chest. She bent to open it, her shoulder and entire body protesting the movement. She had a moment of anticipation, wondering what it would reveal about Roha, recognizing that it was an invasion, but...

She did it anyway, swinging back the lid of the trunk. She didn't know what she'd expected, especially when it wasn't even locked, but she was immediately disappointed. More white robes. She knew one thing at least: Roha really was an acolyte.

Or they were in someone else's quarters.

"So, you know my secret," Roha said, apparently awake, but not strong, if the near-whisper was any indication.

Cia didn't jump—she'd gotten good at covering her reactions with Garif—but the guilt made her flush.

"You really are with the Church. I thought only men—"

And she bit her lip. She couldn't think quickly enough for an end to that sentence that would save it. She'd known Nim went to the Church. It was said that they had an especially close relationship to the anima because they were so attuned, representing a balance of nature—the masculine and feminine in harmony. But she'd never thought about what role they played there. She'd never really thought of them at all. And come to that, she still didn't know... Not for sure.

Roha sighed, a mighty gust. "I knew it would come. It always does."

"What does?"

"Some don't ask. Or don't ask *me*. They'll stare in a way they wouldn't with others, as though I'm not worthy of that kind of consideration until they can label me, decide what respect to afford me. Others ask—each other, other priests, acolytes. Some quietly, some loudly enough for me to hear, giving me the chance to explain myself, as though I owe it to them."

"You don't owe me an explanation," Cia said. She didn't understand, not really, but she identified. She *knew* the feeling of people talking behind or around her, making assumptions because she'd come from Frizenze, because she'd served the Poison Princess. Or because she'd married Garif. Deciding who she was, how her life must be.

Roha took another deep breath, as though holding back, and Cia didn't understand. Hadn't she done the right thing? Hadn't she just said she wasn't like the others? That Roha didn't have to explain?

"Let me ask *you* a question," Roha said in a voice that was dangerously uninflected, the way that Garif's was when he laid a trap. Cia was instantly afraid. "Have you ever had to explain *yourself*? Or consider it a kindness that someone doesn't expect an explanation?"

Cia drew back as though struck.

What are you doing skulking in that doorway? What kind of hext did you use on Mager Garif to get him to marry you? To save yourself from the headsman's ax?

But that wasn't what Roha was talking about.

"No," she said quietly. Cia had never been asked to explain her very self.

Roha nodded. "Exactly. I am *Nim*. And yes, I embody both masculine and feminine. The Church will tell you that we combine both aspects of the divine, and so we can touch the anima within ourselves, feel the power that flows through all. Sacred. That's why we're given to the Church so early."

Cia had no idea how to respond. There was something in Roha's response, the pain weightier than the words. It struck a chord within her.

"How early?" Cia asked.

"As soon as they realize."

Roha started to roll to away, and Cia asked gently, "As soon as who realizes?"

"They," Roha said again, the word a seething mass of suffering. *"Whoever*—parents, playmates, people. *They."*

Roha's tone didn't invite further inquiry along those lines. But something else was off with what Roha had said, buried agony that couldn't be ignored. It had been so long since Cia'd had a real conversation. The courtly manners she'd been taught from the time she could toddle told her to let it go. Be polite. Be politic. Pretend that everything is fine, because it is. Of course, it is. What else could it be? But Roha's pain beat harder, resonating, pulsing in time with own heart, and she felt compelled to push on. "You said 'the Church will tell you,' as though there's more to that story."

Roha didn't look back. "The Church's words and their actions don't always match, any more than a man's. Their true meaning of 'sacred' is something that must be kept apart from the profane, the everyday."

"Then why were you serving at All Souls?" Cia asked gently.

"Oh, the Animist there is not so bad." Had Roha sidestepped the question? "I'm kept mainly in the background, but I'm not asked to call myself that which I'm not, though it's clear others would wish it so. I make them uncomfortable. Everyone wants a connection to the All, but no one wishes it for others. Where they can't admit to their jealousy, it oft turns to suspicion."

Cia nodded, though she wasn't certain about Roha's perception. There was a part of Cia fearful of those with a connection to the anima. Or not so much the connection, but what they might do with it. Not everyone was like her husband. She knew that. She thought she did. But she had a difficult time with the concept nonetheless. All she'd known were Crown mageri, who ripped the anima from the All to power their constructs to destroy their enemies.

"May I ask, what do I call you?"

"You call me Roha. '*Ni*' in place of she or he. '*Nim*' and '*nes*' where you would say him and her or his and hers. Easy to remember, or so you'd think." Roha muttered the last bitterly.

"If you don't want to talk more about the Church, I won't ask, but how about what happened back there? The blast of magic that knocked out that creature—"

Now Roha did turn toward the fire rather than to face her, so all Cia could see was the rise and fall of nes shoulders as ni tried to coax dead embers back to life.

"The wards flaring? Unless I'm mistaken, that was a feral mageri Bloody Bess sent on the hunt for you, an ankari named Ceramor."

"*Mager* Ceramor?" *The Hound?* They'd given him the name when he'd gone mad. After they'd discovered Jannik's hunting dogs dead or dying, and they'd traced the deaths back to him. The whole palace had been in a panic until he was cornered and captured – an especially frightful task since all the other mageri were off fighting the war. Ceramor had been King Jannik's Court Mageri, the only one held back from the battlefront to protect his royal person and the city itself. But who to protect them from him once he'd turned? It had been a terrifying time, and the only thing that had leveled the playing field was the Frizenzian potion used on the darts that brought him down. They'd been glad enough of Frizenze's specialty then. Bess had since refused to name a new Court Mageri. She pulled Erdain back from the battlefronts to coordinate his fellow mageri, but never brought him in as her close and trusted advisor.

Cia shuddered and wrapped her arms around herself. It was horrible enough to be haunted by one mageri, but to be hunted by another, and feral at that...

Something still didn't make sense. "The church protecting its own?"

"One truth at a time," Roha answered.

Cia almost spat.

She was starting to think that truth was the real myth and wondered whether anyone was well enough acquainted with it even to describe its attributes.

Ulan

It took two men to drag Vizi back to his cell, one holding him up on either side. Ulan caught sight of him only by pressing her cheek hard against the bars of her cell when she heard the door at the far end of the hall bang open. She gasped when she saw him. Vizi hung limp, naked to the waist. His entire torso was purple with bruising and gleamed red with blood, but it was hard to tell from whence it came. Perhaps his face, which she couldn't see, as his chin banged against his chest, his hair, ropey with blood, lashed it each time. A woman wailed, others cried out as he passed.

Ulan thought they paraded him past intentionally to show what was in store. To instill fear and soften them all up. It worked. Thoughts ambushed her like street thugs lying in wait, beating into her images of all that might have been done to Vizi, that might be done to her.

She realized she'd gripped the bars in her horror, as though she could pull them apart and get to Vizi. They bit into her bloodless hands, imprinting there as the image of Vizi imprinted itself upon her soul. She had to pry her hands from the bars so that she could shrink back. She hit Hostill as her arms fell away. He was pressed up against the bars as well, so small she'd not noticed him there. He backed into her now, as though needing her reassurance, and she risked putting a hand on his shoulder and squeezing. He looked up at her, his eyes huge and fearful, but his lips pressed together as though trapping everything in. Her heart bled for him.

With the hand on his shoulder, she steered him back from the bars, glad they were at the end of the row and no one was paying them any attention. No one had eyes for anything but Vizi and those guards.

If she helped Ruggerio, if he pulled her out to speak with him and she had something to give him, would the torture stop? It was a horrible thought. Vizi had just endured everything to keep his cabal's secrets. She didn't know why she was so certain he hadn't talked. Maybe it was the hardness in the guards' eyes. There was no sense of triumph. No taunting of the others that they'd broken him. Yet clearly they had, physically if not spiritually.

Even if she had the opportunity, she didn't have anything to give. The Crown had the only part of the Restoration she knew in custody. How many in the cells were thinking the same thing?

Vizi's cell door opened, and she heard him hit the floor without even a grunt. When his door slammed shut again, Ulan motioned for Hostill to stay back, put her hands behind her as though she was still bound, and pressed her face against the bars again to see what was going on. A pair of hard eyes met hers.

She stepped back as the guard stepped forward, hoping that putting herself out of sight would also put her out of mind, but the steps came toward her. Both sets of steps. Was now her moment? Had Ruggerio called for her? What could she tell him that would stop all this?

The guards halted before her cell, eyes scanning the shadowed corners. They stopped on Hostill, and one guard reached for the keys at his belt.

157

Ulan let out a cry and forgot that she was supposed to be bound. Forgot everything except how to put herself between a child and danger.

"No," she said, standing tall, hands out to either side, as though she could make herself too large an obstacle to circumvent.

The one guard snarled and grabbed her so quickly she couldn't even react, wrenching one arm behind her back and throwing her face first into the back wall of the cell. While she was dazed, he grabbed the other arm and brought it down to meet the first so roughly she thought her shoulder would pop out. His hands were big enough that he could hold both her wrists in one like a manacle. But it was Hostill she was worried about. Her face was turned to him when she slammed into the wall, so she could see him compressing himself into the corner of the cell as though he could vanish into the shadows.

Her guard used his free hand to grab her hair, to scrape his nails against her head in a parody of a caress. "Don't worry. He's a boy. It'll go quick. He'll break easy. And then we can come for you."

She tried to rip herself away from him, to fling herself like a shield over Hostill, but the guard held her too tightly. All she could do was watch as the other guard grabbed the boy, and lifted him by both shoulders, kicking and screaming. His gaze met hers, pleading for help, and she redoubled her efforts. The pressure on her eased, and she thought she was getting somewhere until the guard slammed her back into the wall and she realized he'd just been gaining momentum.

Her already abused head exploded inside, her vision went with it, and she lost what was left of her stomach lining on the cell wall.

Disgusted, the guard dropped her. She crashed to her knees and caught herself on one hand before her face could hit the floor. She tried to reach out with the other to grab a leg, do *something*. But she missed, and the cell shut behind the guards. Hostill was gone. She'd failed to save another child.

She let her legs and arm go out from under her and sank to the moldering reeds.

She was still lying there when the guards came for her. She'd long ago stopped twitching at every sensation of something climbing over her. She didn't bother slapping at bites or itching at the aftermath. She didn't even raise her head when the cell door opened.

Not until she heard Ruggerio's voice. "Get her up."

Then she did raise herself on both arms so that she could look up, try to read something in his face, but it was completely closed. Might as well try to read a pattern by moonlight.

The guards he'd brought with him grabbed her under each shoulder and hauled her to her feet, which she just managed to get under her before they dragged her off. They must have noticed that her arms were free, but they didn't say a word, as though where she was going, it wouldn't matter.

Bess

Hostill!

Bess flinched from the voice inside her head, ruthlessly slammed the door on it, but another blew open. Pain struck as the door banged straight into the walls of her skull.

Nooo, another voice wailed. Or maybe it was the same one. In extremis, they all sounded alike.

The slam of yet another door sent her off balance, and she swayed into Strego, who caught her as though she was a frail little girl. She shook him off, irritated at the look he gave her, like she was *sick* and he was concerned. Maybe he still saw her as the little girl he'd slipped candies to rather than the woman she'd become. Or he was catching on to the cracks in her composure. Maybe she'd been wrong to keep him around as long as she had, an unfamiliar sentimentality plaguing her.

She shook her head in denial of whatever he was thinking, but her head swam, and it took too long for her vision to come back. In the meantime, she swayed away, and Strego caught her arm to steady her and keep her on track.

The guard behind her asked if everything was okay, and it was all she could do not to whirl and strike him for the affront. She wasn't sure she could lash out and remain standing. And on some level, she knew it was uncalled for. It was his job to protect her. But from threats external. She couldn't afford them to notice any other vulnerability. There were people who would swipe her off the throne in an instant. Install a pretender or some distant relative rather than a girl…especially one with any inkling of instability. She had to control herself lest they control her.

"A headache. Nothing more," she bit out.

She turned off at the corridor leading to her quarters, quelling Strego with a look when he suggested she might want further escort. He jerked almost imperceptibly at whatever he saw in her gaze, and she exerted a little of the power she hoarded to quell him. She needed him compliant, but not afraid enough to move against her. It was a matter of balance.

But the expulsion of power blasted all her locked-down doors open, and the blowback hit her like a winter storm.

She hurried to her quarters as quickly as her doubling vision allowed and was relieved when she locked the guards outside. But her maid awaited her inside, and while she never said a word, her very presence was an irritant. Bess barely tolerated the removal of her gown, the rustle and scrape of the fabric abrading her senses, before she sent her maid away and fought with her bed curtains to collapse atop her blankets.

Immediately, she was ambushed. Accusations. Memories. Wordless cries of loss and pain. All in her head, all in her head. She tried to tell herself, but…

The face of the last maid whose name she'd never even learned rose up in her mind, her face paler even than it had been even in life. Lips as blue as her eyes. *Trecia.* The name hissed through her, and the woman struck like a viper. Bess stumbled back into a grassy field, pulling someone along with her, but those weren't her hands, and those she was holding… *She looked up at the man through the eyes of a woman in love. To her, his prematurely gray hair glowed in the moonlight, begging for her fingers to rake through, bring his head down to hers for a kiss. His dark eyes, usually so serious, softened just for her. She could see the passion and humor and everything he kept inside when he was standing at attention. Just following orders.*

Bess realized with a shock that she knew him—one of her guards—*just before he swung her around by their linked hands and pulled her into him, wrapping one arm around her waist in a way that made her heart pound against her chest. When his mouth came down on hers and his breath escaped into her, she gasped it down in place of the breath that caught in her throat. She let go his hand to clutch at his shoulders.* Only it wasn't her doing. Wasn't her thought. It was Trecia, and she was deeply, hopelessly in love.

Engaged.

They were engaged. And Bess had stolen all of this away from her, and she wanted Bess to know. She wanted Bess to feel her pain.

Bess was ripped away from the kiss, *and was holding another pair of hands, running and giggling down a passage deserted but for the two of them. The other giggle was as feminine as her own and the hand in hers so tight, as though she'd never let go. But did it mean what Inka wanted it to mean or...*

A baby's cry. Not the pitched, painful wail of deep unhappiness, but the fuss of need. She cradled him closer, kissed his perfect head, inhaled his scent like nothing else in the world. She sang a quiet lullaby. The babe quieted, cuddling in, nuzzling against her breast for a feeding.

Pain exploded in Bess at the thought that she'd taken a mother away from her child, before she heard, *No little one, you'll find no food here. Let me hand you back to maman.*

But just because she hadn't taken *this* woman from *this* child didn't mean...

She heard another cry and realized it was her own. She was back in her own body. Her own head. But the women were all around her. There were no doors anymore. No barriers. Her head hurt too hard for any constructs. There was just blinding light and flashes of her victims— angry or pained, ranting or wailing.

All except one, who sat with her legs drawn up under her and her head down, hugging herself so tightly her muscles strained. This one she had a name for. *Galina.* She recognized her by all that thick beautiful hair plaited down her back. It had caught Jannik's eye as well. It was part of the reason Bess had chosen her. She knew what catching the attention of either of her brothers could mean. She'd known since she was much younger and they'd first turned their eyes on her, thinking her to be a soft target, and she'd drawn her first blood in the panic of trying to save herself. She didn't know why the girl couldn't see that Bess had *rescued* her. Between her brothers and herself, she was the lesser of the evils. The girl might even thank her if she understood what she'd been saved from.

But there was another girl, on the ground, in essentially the same position as Galina. Maybe it meant something. Maybe not. She didn't know if she'd still be off-balance here in her own head, but she didn't try to stand. Instead, she rolled onto all fours and crawled toward the girl, ignoring the buffeting from all sides, resisting the pull into other memories by focusing on this girl, Annalisa, who ignored her, lost in her own misery. *In her memory of a young child toddling toward her.* Bess could see him now, Annalisa's arms her arms as she held them out to the child, chubby and perfect, his face a study in contrast. *Lips crooked as one side was caught in concentration between the two teeth already growing in. His eyes were on her, lit with triumph because he was doing it. He was walking on his own, and he was showing her. He broke eye contact as he wobbled. His lips puffed out, and his arms windmilled, and when he caught his balance, he looked up at her with such transcendent joy, her heart stopped.*

But no, it wasn't the joy. It wasn't the look on his face. It was the face itself. She knew that face. That smile. Those dimples. He took one more step and fell forward into her arms, and Annalisa jerked away, becoming distinct from her again.

Bess's arms were empty.

And Annalisa was staring at her in horror as if *she* was the one seeing a ghost.

But the boy... "Who is he to you?" Bess demanded.

Annalisa startled, and disappeared as Bess reached for her, ready to hold her or shake her or whatever it took to get answers. Instead, Bess slammed her fist into whatever passed for a floor, flinching as the pain reverberated through her. Annalisa was in *her* head. Shouldn't that mean that *Bess* was the one in control?

She snapped awake and sat up, the compress falling from her head. She bellowed for her maid, splitting her own head in two. She'd bind it up if she had to. Maybe counter-pressure would even be a good idea.

But she had to find out more about that boy.

Ulan

Ulan listened with all her might for the sound of Hostill's screams as the guards dragged her through the corridors. She didn't hear them and told herself that was a good thing. And it was. Of course it was, but... It was the *but* that twisted her stomach into knots. But what if whatever they were putting him through was so bad he'd already passed out from the pain. What if...

The guards force-marched her up a set of stairs, down a corridor and through a doorway into a low-lit room. Not Ruggerio's. That would be higher up and deeper into the castle. From the little she could see, this was a small chamber set up with two cots, a three-legged table with a washbasin between them, and a small fireplace from which came the faint illumination. Maybe a flop room for guards between shifts.

"Leave us," Ruggerio snapped.

The guards looked to each other, as if casting lots to see which would speak. The taller seemed to have lost somehow.

"She's loose of her bonds. Shall we—"

"I said *go!*" Ruggerio roared.

The guard who hadn't spoken cocked his head meaningfully at the beds and raised a brow, his partner shrugged, and they left her. Just like that. She spat at their retreating backs. She knew Ruggerio wasn't about to do what they imagined. But he could have been. And they'd have let him. And thought no more about it.

Maybe *that* was what the room was for. The thought disgusted her, and her body shuddered all over, as though it could shake off the horror.

Her vision doubled and tripled before coming back to almost normal. She waited until there was one Ruggerio again, though with a blur around him like an echo or an aura, and fixed him with a look of all the loathing she felt.

"So much for protecting me."

"Our deal was *if* you brought me the woman."

"There wasn't time before your guards came crashing in on me."

"Out of my control."

"Like what's happening to the boy?" she spat. This was the real issue. But she was afraid that if she started with Hostill, Ruggerio would use him against her.

"Nothing's happening to the boy," he said, disgusted with her. As if she didn't have good reason to think otherwise. As if she hadn't seen what had happened to Vizi.

"Are you sure or is that out of your control too? Your guards said he'd break easy. They said—"

Her voice broke. So much for Ruggerio not knowing how to get to her.

"You won't believe I am protecting him, so let me say that I have plans for him, and so he is safe. For now. But I need you to help me keep him that way. In order to do that, I need more than I've gotten from you."

"What does that mean?"

"It means that I can continue the torture. I don't think the boy will talk, but I might be wrong. Same for the others. Rebellions are so often structured as cells, so everyone only knows so much, the next links in the chain so that no one can give too much away."

Her head was still pounding. Maybe she was too dense to understand. "Then how do you imagine I can help? I'm not even one of them. I was their *captive*."

"A name. Just a name. Something you overheard, maybe. It's no more or less than I'll get from any of them, and it's something I can act on. But there's one thing you can do for me that no one else can."

She stared him down, waited. So far Ruggerio's help had been no help at all, and she didn't trust him any farther than she could throw him. Right now, she wasn't even sure she could lift.

"What is that?" she asked begrudgingly.

"I want Dazia to spy for me," he said.

She tried and failed to process that. "You want my daughter—my *dead* daughter, my *ghost* daughter—to spy for you? And you want me to promise you her services like I would lend you a blanket? I...I don't..."

Out of the corner of her eye, she saw something flicker, and waved her hand to warn Dazia away as though Ruggerio might see her, might somehow capture her. She had no idea what he might be capable of.

Ruggerio noticed the gesture and squinted where she'd waved.

"Roha," she said, hating herself the second it was out of her mouth. Some part of her had thrown the name out as a distraction, without thought to the consequences. Maybe she was saving Dazia *and* Hostill. Maybe if they no longer needed to rack him for information...

She forced her knees to steady when they wanted to give out on her. She couldn't let Ruggerio think that he'd gotten everything she had to give, that she was of no more use.

Instead, she met his gaze as though she was teasing out information. The name was already out there. She might as well make it count. "Roha is a name I've heard. The one who gave warning that your soldiers were on the hunt."

Ruggerio made a rude noise. "Roha is already known to us. You'll have to do better."

Before Ulan could answer, the door slammed against the wall, and two guards flooded in, followed by the Princess. It seemed like a flood anyway, because suddenly, all the air in the small room was swept away and she could barely breathe. In the glow of the fire, Bloody Bess lived up to her name, the flames catching the rosey tones of her hair and turning it the red of freshly spilled blood. It also made her loom larger, her shadow dancing behind her in a way not emulated by anyone else's in the room.

She heard a gasp from the shadows where she'd seen Dazia flicker earlier, but didn't dare look that way. Instead, she focused on the impossibility before her. Princess Bessory's shadow didn't move like one, but many, all trying to pull away from each other, but anchored inexorably by the Blood Princess. She suddenly had a very, very bad feeling about what had happened to the missing girls, but she didn't dare speak. She was so transfixed by the shadows, it took her another moment to notice the additional guards behind the Blood Princess, blocking her escape.

Bloody Bess and Ruggerio faced off, both with eyes like daggers, neither shielded nor restrained. Nothing blunt about either. "Why have *I* not heard about this Roha, and if you know of him, why was he not rounded up with the others?" the Princess demanded.

"Because Roha is an acolyte at All Souls, and the Crown can't afford an open confrontation with the Church right now, not with rebellion brewing. So we have kept watch. But now that Ceramor has forced your hand—"

"*What?*" she roared.

Her shadows trembled. Even the fire seemed to shrink back in the hearth. Ruggerio held his ground, but if his eyes were still daggers, they were no longer so sure of their aim. She had never seen Ruggerio at a loss before, and this more than anything terrified her. She wanted to fade into the deeper shadows with Dazia but had the sense that the Princess could penetrate them with ease.

"Strego was briefed," Ruggerio answered, "but he said that you were resting and didn't want to be disturbed. I assumed you had been told upon waking and that's why you were here."

"Assume I was not," she said, words dripping like venom from her tongue.

"You know already that Ceramor was able to track Cia to the Restoration, which had taken her. Unfortunately, they caught wind of our first approach and collapsed the building behind themselves, catching Ceramor and the guards with him. Strego's order was to focus on the living and go back for the dead, so we put our resources behind chasing down the rebels who escaped, and we caught them."

"And thus you make failure sound like success. We sent Ceramor for the woman, Cia. We've lost both. Get to the business I don't know," she said dangerously.

Ulan held as still as a rabbit in a field with a snake coiled close by. For the first time ever, she pitied Ruggerio, understood what it was that made him scheme as he did.

"Ceramor survived. And, apparently, he continued on his mission. He went after Cia on his own, tracked her to All Souls, and half destroyed it in his attempt to take her down. My men are even now picking through the rubble."

"So, you stand here interrogating this woman not knowing if our quarry is alive or dead, our asset is alive or dead, whether your mission is complete or incomplete."

"I am your Spymaster, not your foot soldier. I am gathering information. I assumed the rebel network took precedence over a murderess, especially when it appears they're together and two birds can be killed with one stone."

"Your job is what I say it is, and right now, it's to take personal charge of this hunt or become the subject of it. I *assume* that is clear enough," she snapped back.

Ulan wanted to look at Ruggerio to assure herself that he kept his usual perfect mask in place, afraid that any sign of resentment or rebellion would mean his death, wondering how she could distrust and fear him one moment and fear *for* him the next, but she couldn't look away from Bloody Bess. It was like taking your gaze off a spider, not knowing from which direction to expect it next. It hadn't always been like that. She and Ruggerio had grown up together, but he'd left early without looking back, and Ulan didn't know him anymore.

"Yes, Highness," Ruggerio said. "By your leave—"

She inclined her head and moved fractionally so that Ruggerio had to be very, very careful not to brush up against her on his way out. He did, however, brush into her shadow, and while he didn't give himself away with a shudder, Ulan saw him stiffen, as if he felt the wrongness, even if he didn't know just what it was he felt.

She wanted to cry out to him not to leave her alone but feared drawing Bloody Bess's attention. She could hope that she was beneath the Princess's notice entirely. She wished she could fade away, like Dazia. She wished she still believed in prayer, but the All hadn't answered when Dazia had the plague that had stolen her away, and if the spirits hadn't answered when her precious little girl's light was about to be extinguished – when so many other little lights…

"Send me Strego on your way out," Bloody Bess called after Ruggerio, not bothering to turn her head.

"He's already here," came a deep voice from the doorway.

Ulan finally tore her gaze from Bess and her contorting shadow to see a tall man replacing her cousin in the entry. His hair and beard were storm cloud gray, his eyes rain-slicked rock. She recognized him as the Regent, Strego.

Bloody Bess whirled, fury in her eyes. "You're keeping secrets," she accused him.

I shouldn't be here, Ulan thought. *I shouldn't be witnessing this. Why hasn't she sent me away? Unless...*

Unless it doesn't matter what I see, what I hear, because I won't be around to tell anyone.

Because I'll be one of the shadow girls.

Someone to fuel her power and her madness.

Ulan risked shrinking back into the shadows, and Dazia appeared at her side. They hugged each other for dear life, as though it might be the last time. If Ulan went, at least she would be with Dazia again, one way or another.

"Leave us," Bess ordered the guards, a perfect echo of Ruggerio earlier. Neither with any regard for Ulan, who wished she did have the mageri powers she was accused of. Then she could fade through the wall and make her escape while the power players were distracted with each other.

The guards bowed low and left, closing the door behind them, the thud as final as forgetting.

"I don't know what you mean," Strego said, his brows furrowed, the fire casting dark shadows there that mercifully behaved.

"You didn't tell me about Ceramor or the church."

"You were resting." He said it as neutrally as possible, and Ulan recognized the ploy from her own household where they'd all had to walk eggshells around her father. No inflection meant there was no need to correct their tone. "As soon as I learned that you were awake, I came to your side."

"And how did you learn that I was awake? Are you having me watched?"

He must have realized that he couldn't win, but he had no choice but to respond. "In this case, I asked to be informed when you woke so that I could brief you on the situation with the Church, knowing it to be dire. I didn't think that with the state of your head, you'd want to be awakened to deal with it. My apologies if I was wrong."

"And what *is* the state of my head?" The Princess's back was still to Ulan, but her shadow flapped and fought against the back wall, as though in warning. Ulan could only imagine her eyes, turned away now from the fire, were as dark as the abyss.

"Well, I hope, Princess."

And then she struck, her hand whipping out and catching him by the throat. He gagged, as though she weren't a head shorter than him and at least ten stone lighter.

Maman! Dazia cried, burying her head in Ulan's shoulder. Ulan was glad she couldn't feel it, glad for once that Dazia wasn't physically there and couldn't be hurt. It was odd to think her safe in death, but the horror that was happening with those poor girls trapped in Bloody Bess's shadow could never touch her. Ulan, on the other hand…

But right now, it was Strego trapped in her grip, Bess's nails digging into his flesh. Either they'd been filed to points or they were pressing his neck hard enough to sever the skin even blunt, because rivulets ran. White shone all around Strego's eyes, and they rolled in terror, finally meeting Ulan's. She raised a hand to her mouth and bit her knuckles to keep from crying out, hating herself for not answering the appeal in his eyes as they found hers in the darkness. She was certain he was calling to her, not to stay silent and safe, but to save him. Him with all the power and her with none, yet he wanted her to risk herself for him. Expected it, because that's what those with power expected from those meant to serve. The worst was that she would have if she had any ideas, any hope of stopping Bloody Bess. He wouldn't have done the same if their situations were reversed.

Maman! Dazia cried again, and Ulan snapped out of her rationalization. Fair or not, she could not just stand by and allow a man to be murdered. Not when she could do something, and not in front of her daughter. No matter who she had to fight.

She looked around and found only the tools meant to stoke the fire. She threw herself toward them and came up with a poker, but she no sooner had it in hand than Bloody Bess's head twisted as unnaturally as her shadow. Her lips pulled back from her teeth, and the blood that seeped from Strego's neck seemed to glisten between them like saliva, only that was impossible…wasn't it? Everything about her was impossible. Unnatural.

Ulan froze with the poker poised to strike. Tried to continue her arc and couldn't. It was as though she was made of the same unbending metal as the poker itself. As though she was locked in a vise. Terror infused her, running through her veins in lieu of her lifeblood.

Bess had the hand not buried in Strego's neck splayed toward Ulan, locking her in place. She ratcheted her neck back around to Strego.

Ulan didn't want to think about what she was seeing. *Mageri* tapped into the land for their powers, into people only on rare occasions of great need, but never like this. It was never supposed to be unwilling. And it was never supposed to be anyone in line for the throne.

Ulan would never live out the night.

The thought shouldn't terrify her. She'd join Dazia and together they could go to their rest. Return to the land. No more plagues or blackmail or rebellions.

But that left Hostill in danger. It left Vizi and the others to torture and execution. Bloody Bess to kill and capture more girls, imprisoned shadows of their former selves. She tried to think of that for Dazia and her heart cried out. It left the kingdom to be ruled by a madwoman.

Strego's head had fallen forward, and Ulan could no longer see his eyes. He murmured something that sounded like, "Would have told you; needed your rest."

Bess hummed deep in her chest, like a cat purring, before she retracted her claws and Strego fell to the floor, like a set of robes with the man no longer inside.

And Bess whirled on her, head first with her body following.

Ulan stayed frozen. Her muscles were starting to shake holding their position, mid-strike.

"Now, tell me about your powers and about this boy captured with you." Bess didn't just command it; she reached out with the power she'd stolen from Strego to compel her obedience. Ulan felt it as though someone had drilled a spike straight into her skull, a conduit straight into her psyche, but with no finesse, the difference between an apprentice and a master craftsman. One who would discard his piece once it had been practiced upon.

"What powers?" Ulan cried out. "I see the dead. That is all. And only the few restless spirits who don't go on to their rest. Only those who come to me. I have no power to compel them."

Bess's gaze bored into her, the fire reflected in her eyes so that they seemed to burn. Red like her hair, like her spittle. She was so close now that Ulan couldn't see her shadow and was glad of it. She knew the motion would distract her, and she'd give away that she could see the shadow girls as well. But now that they were close, she could hear them. Crying, wailing, begging. She couldn't make out the words, but the tones

169

were pleading, inconsolable. The healer in her, the mother, wanted to reach out. Wanted to help them all.

"We shall see," Bloody Bess said. "And the boy?"

Hostill? Why was everyone so interested in him? First Ruggerio and now Bloody Bess.

"You've stolen his sister," she said, the drill in her head keeping her from thinking better of it.

The Princess's face froze, even to the flames dancing in her eyes. "His *sister?*"

Something was not right here. Ulan hurt too much, was too terrified to figure it out.

"She worked for you. Or anyway, at the castle. She disappeared. The rumors say you're responsible." And she saw them to be true. She managed to hold on to that much, but only because she clamped down on the thickness burning its way up her throat. She didn't have anything left in her stomach. She was sure of it. Her body was eating itself, and she had to swallow it back down.

The Princess's power was eating her up as well. She swayed and fell to her knees. In another moment she would be lying on the floor. Like Strego.

"What rumors?" she snapped, staring down at Ulan, unmoved by her distress.

Her throat felt like she'd swallowed acid. "That you've killed all those missing girls. That you're as ruthless as your brothers." No one had even guessed at the truth. How could they? Ulan had seen it with her own eyes and even she could barely comprehend.

Bess smiled in satisfaction. As though Ulan hadn't just accused her of being a murderer.

"What do you want from me?" Ulan asked, more afraid of the unknown than the answer.

"From you, nothing. You say you are no mageri, and I accept that. You have no more than a spark. But your friend Cia…I saw what she did in the courtyard. I saw her escape, and I know that there is some of Mager Garif left behind. Enough to suit my purposes. I need the woman brought to me. My guards have failed. Ceramor has failed. This needs a gentler touch."

"I don't understand."

"Your daughter has spied for Ruggerio. I've heard as much. Now, she will do the same for me. She can sense out other spirits, yes? Communicate with them?"

Dazia? Her heart lurched. Did Bloody Bess know or was she guessing? Had Ruggerio told her, or had she overheard? These were much deeper waters than Ulan knew how to swim, and she was surrounded by sharks and sea monsters.

Ulan nodded, certain there would be no convincing Bloody Bess of any denials.

"She will communicate with Mager Garif. She will convince him to come in or give up his location to me. And only to me."

"But Mager Garif is dead."

"Not entirely."

She gasped, thinking of the shadow girls trapped inside Bloody Bess's sphere. Was it possible that the same had happened with Mager Garif? How horrible for Cia to be trapped in her own head with her abusive husband. Cia would never have swallowed him up intentionally, but in her panic, she might not have known what she did. Or Garif might have intended her to choke on him. Ulan didn't know how these things worked. Only that there had to be a way for whatever was done to be undone. For Cia and for Bloody Bess's victims. There had to be. She just had to live long enough to find it.

As though she had the power. The sheer arrogance of it hit her. But even stronger was the feeling that it *was* her problem to solve. Because she saw it. Because the universe had put it in her path.

"Why would I bring Cia to you? Why would she come?" The questions slipped out. She had just seen the Princess attack Regent Strego. He was still on the floor. Ulan didn't even know whether he was alive or dead. And the Princess thought she would lure someone else to her? But what if she didn't? Would Bess—?

The Princess lashed out, gripping Ulan by the windpipe and squeezing. But this time her nails didn't come out, didn't sink into the skin. Panicked, Ulan fought for air, scratching and pulling at hands that should have been soft, childlike, but it did no good. Bess cut off her air, and already it was only terror getting through. Weakness flooded her system, and she thrashed, using up her resources even faster, but what else to do but fight?

"It is not your place to question me!" Bess hissed in Ulan's face.

All Bloody Bess's cold beauty had been transformed into a horror mask. Her eyes were flat now without the fire to light them. A void, an abyss that might suck you in and never let go. Ulan shuddered in her grip, eyes fluttering, losing the fight to stay focused on the nightmare before her.

Bess gave one last squeeze before dropping her to the floor. She gasped in a breath that was fire. Wheezed as though something had been crushed and might never expand again. She struggled and found the strength to scuttle away from the Princess, putting both beds between them as quickly as she could. Bess eyed her with a gaze that made it clear Ulan's escape was only by her leave.

"I have a message for your daughter to convey when she finds the woman," Bess said. "She is here?"

Dazia flickered, her face fierce, her hands clenched in futile rage. She looked ready to fly at the Princess, but Ulan shook her head. She didn't want Dazia to spend strength she didn't have, and she was terrified that Bloody Bess's dark energy would suck her in somehow and not let her go.

The Blood Princess followed Ulan's head shake and addressed Dazia. "Tell the woman that I can give her back her life. I can clear her name, create a story and make the people accept it. She can become my hand-maiden, my closest confidante. No one will dare question or disrespect her. She can come to me and have everything...or stay away and be hunted down like a dog."

Ulan wanted to ask why Bess would make Cia such an offer, but her throat still felt half-crushed, and anyway, the Princess wasn't likely to share her plans. Dazia was looking at her with wide eyes, frantically shaking her head to say she shouldn't trust Bloody Bess.

She held a hand to her throat as though it would lessen the pain as she tried to speak. "Dazia...spirit. Limited energy...may not be...successful."

"I will make sure she is highly motivated," the Princess said with a smile that nearly split her face in two before she screeched, "Guards! Guards!"

They burst into the room, swords drawn. Stopping short as one nearly stumbled over Strego's prone body.

The Princess flung her arms toward Ulan, "She's done something to the Regent. She's a mageri witch. Throw her in with the others!"

The terror running through Ulan's veins nearly stopped her heart.

The guards looked from the Princess, who was much closer to Strego than she was, to Ulan, cowering by the beds, but didn't question their orders or how it came to be that she'd taken down the larger Regent but left the Princess still standing. The first two advanced on her, while the two still in the hallway called for a healer.

There was nowhere left to run, and no way out.

As the guards carried her past the Princess, Bess leaned in and said barely loudly enough for Ulan herself to hear, "Your daughter will come through or an accident will be arranged for you. You've declared yourself no asset, and so I have nothing to lose."

And then she was dragged straight over Strego's body and away into the unknown.

CHAPTER TWENTY-ONE

Ceramor

C eramor twitched as he raced all-out to catch up to the hounds he could hear in the distance, but he still fell behind with each step as his dream body reacted to the heaviness of his real one, which felt clumsy, sluggish. He fought against waking, sure he'd find he was still in his oubliette, dying of hunger and thirst, his body scabbed-over and lice-ridden. He could feel it shutting down, flattening, becoming one with the earth, sinking into it. He'd feared it for so long. There would be no Reina waiting for him at the end of it. If these were his last moments, he would make them count. He bayed, imploring the pack to wait for him, insisting that he was coming to join them.

"There, you hear it?" someone yelled nearby, and he thought *no. Oh, no, I can't be found.*

But he thought it faintly, without the energy to make it manifest. There was something about that thought. Something he needed to grab onto.

He stopped the baying. Stopped the twitching. Stopped the *breathing.* This was no dream. This was a nightmare.

He could not be caught. He had failed and he had betrayed them, and they would not give him a second chance. They wouldn't capture a wounded, feral animal.

They would *put it down.*

Maybe they'd bring his head back to the Princess. Put it on a pike to show what became of those who challenged her.

Weight shifted on top of him, and blood flow came rushing back in some areas, bringing with it biting, gnashing pain. When the torchlight hit his face, he snarled and snapped at it, and it retreated, but not far.

"He's all yours," a voice said.

There was no answer but a sudden pull. He gasped, a most human sound. He shouldn't have been surprised to hear it come out of his throat. He *was* human, after all. He just sometimes forgot it.

But right now, as the voice had said, he was not his own. Not wholly himself. Another mageri had tapped him like he had the guards back at the collapsed house, like he had his master's hounds. He was being bled away. If he'd felt flattened and hollowed before, it was nothing compared to this.

"You've been very naughty, Ceramor," said a new voice.

He knew that voice, the hauteur of it. Erdain? In his state, he was nothing against the Crown's head mageri. Instinctive terror had him reaching for the anima in the earth, but he couldn't pull it through the floors or the walls. The land was protected by wards. Sacred, so at odds with Ceramor.

Then what of the blast? From whence had that power been drawn? The questions bled away as quickly as his strength.

He tried to turn things around on Erdain, find a way in to drain *his* power. But Erdain was a strategist for his battlefield brethren, kept far back from the frontlines. He was fresh, unblooded. If he had a cut, a hangnail, a canker, even... But Ceramor had no way in.

He changed tactics, reached for the tether to the other mageri, pulsing with his life force as it ebbed away from him, but very quickly became lightheaded. If he ranged any further from his body he might never return, be locked inside the other mageri forever, like he'd locked the hounds inside himself. Panic flooded his system with frenetic energy that got him back to the shores of self but left him with nothing. He lay there spent, shaky. Breathing was little more than an illusion he couldn't relinquish. It seemed as though his lungs were a bellows with a hole in them, pumping fast, shallow, and ineffectively.

"What goes on here?" A new voice. Commanding. Carrying. Clearly unhappy. "What have you done to our church?"

Ceramor had never heard such utter silence as followed. Even the hounds seemed to understand that now was a time not to be noticed.

Then, "We are apprehending a fugitive and offering our services with the clean-up. You have been betrayed. Surely, you've received the Crown's messenger?"

Yes, definitely Erdain's voice.

"We've received no message."

Ceramor's eyes had been clenched tightly with agony, but it wasn't as though the pain took any notice of the fact. Or that he could meditate it away. He forced his eyes open. Focus was harder, but he needed to see what was happening. The distraction of the new arrival had slowed the stealing of his energy to a trickle, as though Erdain thought the priest could sense the use of his mageri powers on Church land.

The Church that despised Ceramor might yet be his salvation. He'd howl at the irony if it wasn't likely to puncture a lung.

"I'm sorry for that," Erdain said. Ceramor could only see the back of his head and not the look on Erdain's face, but he certainly didn't *sound* sorry. Actual contrition involved taking responsibility for wrongdoing. And Erdain was *never* wrong. "Perhaps we should step aside to discuss."

The priest must have acolytes or some of his congregation with him. The only surprise was that the guards and mageri had beaten them to the church. But maybe they hadn't? Maybe the believers had been watching and waiting for others to clear the debris and see what the Crown would do? To catch them at whatever acts they would commit?

"We keep no secrets at All Souls. Whatever you have to say to me, you can say before witnesses," the priest said, and again it was as though he was at a pulpit, his voice meant to carry.

Erdain's voice was not pitched the same way as he said, "Very well, then I challenge your assertion that there are no secrets here. There was certainly a traitor in your midst, which is why your church lies in ruins. A murderess escaped our custody today. She killed her mageri husband. Your Church is opposed to the mageri. You preach against us and our powers every day, every week with your sermons. Now your poison has borne fruit. At least one of your acolytes sympathized and sheltered this murderess, brought destruction to your door. We must even investigate ties to the Restoration, since the killer, Ciara né Respari, was with them when she was initially taken."

Before he was finished, the believers were shouting down his accusations, but the priest waited until Erdain was finished before saying with an almost inhuman calm, "This was not done by soldiers. And it wasn't done by the Restoration or any acolyte. The destruction here involved *power*. So I will ask again, and I won't be distracted or deflected. *What did you do to my church?*"

"*I* did nothing."

"The Crown, then." The priest's tone matched Erdain's chill for chill.

"I cannot speak for the Crown."

"Then get me someone who can."

"Who are you to demand it?" Erdain asked.

"Who are you to deny it?" the priest countered.

Oh, very good, thought Ceramor.

"You cannot order me."

"Once you are off Church land, I cannot make you do anything, though I presume you have orders to report what you've seen and heard, which will include my words. However, as you *are* on Church land, I can demand that you leave it. You have admitted that your people have damaged Church property and you have leveled accusations. If you return here, I will consider it trespass and a violation of the sanctity of the Church and the treaty between Church and Crown. We will conduct our own investigation. The Regent is invited to send a representative to discuss reparations and the sharing of information, but it will not be you."

"The Regent does not need to be invited."

"I will not argue sovereignty and extend your time here, which has come to an end. I have demanded that you leave, and I will consider any further delay a declaration of hostilities."

"And do what?"

Ceramor held his breath, but not for long, afraid that any cessation would become habit. Even with Erdain slowing the flow to a trickle, his life force was down to nearly nothing. If hostilities were declared, he would be the first casualty.

Something hit the ground hard, three times. It sounded like a mageri staff, but blunter. It didn't pierce, but beat, and then he could sense the life forces of many more around them, as though the entire congregation had gathered in support. Maybe they'd been told to stay back as the priest judged the church's structural integrity, but the tapping had been some kind of signal bringing them out in force. But why? What drove people? Drew people? He'd never understood.

But then, he couldn't. He'd always thought the Church was for those who couldn't sense the power of the anima. Who hoped one day to be part of it in death but found it easy to say that it was unholy to exploit it in life, because they themselves couldn't. It wasn't for them, and so it shouldn't be for anyone. Easy to say that it was wrong.

That *he* was wrong…

"Don't think this is over," Erdain snapped.

Ceramor had started to drift away, energy almost gone, but forced himself to focus.

"I could say the same to you."

He heard stomping then, and the whimpering of dogs leaving without their prey, a yelp as one was handled too roughly. His eyes were about to drift shut when the siphoning of his own energies stopped so abruptly the backlash sent enough of a jolt back to pop them open again. And then a new man paced into view. Not just a priest, as he'd kept calling the man in his mind, but *the* high priest of the region, the Animist. No wonder his voice had held such authority. No wonder Erdain had left with his tail between his legs.

"See that they're truly gone," the Animist said to his acolytes.

Then he turned, and looked straight down at Ceramor, as though he'd known him to be there all along. "Dump this one in an alley well away from here and then bar the churchyard. Set sentries. I won't give him over to Erdain, but neither will I have him here."

A man in a white robe stepped up beside the Animist and looked into the depths of the ruins atop Ceramor. He had to squat to see what the Animist saw. When he did, his eyes widened and he craned his head up to the Animist. "Who is he?"

"I can't be sure, but I heard that the Blood Princess released the Hound to hunt for the mageri's killer, and they couldn't manage him. Mageri can't be trusted or controlled, and certainly not after they've gotten a taste for blood."

"This is the *ankari*? And you want to set him free?"

Ceramor watched the Animist suck in his lips and puff them out again. "Want is perhaps too strong a word. But I couldn't give him over to Erdain. Or to the Crown to be used again. And we can't kill him. He looks to be on the edge of death. Let's let him die in peace."

"Surely we can send him somewhere more dignified than an alley?"

"We can't harbor him, even if it were safe. I won't risk our people, and I won't have him befouling our sacred ground."

"So we'll risk other lives?" his acolyte argued in a harsh whisper. Ceramor was surprised he dared that much.

"What would you suggest? We can't end his life before his time. It's against nature. We can't prolong his life and make the church responsible for whatever misdeeds he commits for the balance of it. We have to leave it to fate. From the looks of him, it won't be kind, but it will be over before long."

Another man came running up. No, a boy. Or somewhere in between the two. He looked terrified to interrupt, but also determined. "Animist! My apologies, but you'd asked for all support, and...Roha didn't show."

"Roha? You've sent someone to the lodgings?"

"Yes, my Lord. There was no answer. In all the flurry, we assumed that meant Roha was already here or on the way, but, well, ni isn't, and so..."

"Thank you. You may go. I'll deal with this."

The boy bobbed and backed away, running and tripping and then walking more slowly, speeding up again as soon as it seemed safe to do so.

"Do you think Roha is the traitor Erdain was talking about then, the one harboring the murderess?" the acolyte asked.

The Animist ran a hand down his face so hard he flattened his features as he went along. "For all we know, this murderess forced Roha's aid, but we can't know until we find nim, and we have to do it before the Crown does. We cannot allow Erdain or Strego or Bloody Bess to find nim and spin their stories, creating broader conspiracies that suit whatever actions they want to take against us. Dump the Hound. Find Roha. I will get at the truth."

"Are you sure that's safe? Won't we be bound to turn Roha over to them?"

The Animist drew himself up. "We are a sovereign power. We not *bound* to do anything. *At least for now,*" he muttered under his breath.

"What was that?" asked his acolyte, worried, Ceramor thought, that he'd missed a command. Ceramor would have missed it himself if the comment hadn't been aimed toward the floor.

"I don't think there's such a thing as safe any longer. The only thing left is what is right."

CHAPTER TWENTY-TWO

Bess

Bess was livid. She watched as Ulan was dragged away, as help was summoned for Strego. She drummed her fingers along her cheek as she considered her next move.

Her first thought was to order the removal of the boy. He looked enough like her brothers, Jannik in particular, that anyone acting against her could use him to their advantage if the rumor reached their ears. Ulan had said that Annalisa was his sister. No doubt she passed herself off that way. While it was *possible* her mother had been the one to catch one of her brothers' eyes – they were indiscriminate in their tastes – Bess knew the truth. Or suspected.

She could order a sketch of the boy, but that would only lead to questions. Others might notice the similarity. She'd seen it already, though, hadn't she? In the little cherub who had run to one of the shadow girls in her mind. Pudgy and perfect. Maybe, having seen this one, a sneaky sliver of sentiment that had kept her from ordering his death, especially based on a mere suspicion.

But now he'd grown into a problem, and not her only one. She knew what she had to do, but not to who she could trust to get it done.

Normally it would be Ruggerio, but finding him alone with Ulan, discovering he'd known for some time about the Restoration agent within the church made her question his loyalty. Maybe she shouldn't have sent him away. Maybe she should have kept him close, bled him the way she had Strego, turned his will to hers. She was growing more and more impatient with the fear that his will might be stronger than hers. Some day she would test it.

In the meantime, she had sent him off on the hunt. Either he would return successful and prove himself or his loyalty would no longer matter because he'd already have failed the question of competency. Despite herself, she hoped it was the former.

Ruggerio

Ruggerio walked briskly. He didn't run. He *never* ran except when absolutely and utterly necessary. Running said that a situation was out of control. And he was *always* in control.

Bess had ordered him to the hunt. She suspected something, but she didn't know what.

Because there was nothing to suspect. Thus far, he'd been the perfect spymaster—searching out information, collecting it, analyzing, piecing the jagged edges together. For the good of crown and country. Because usually a strong country meant a strong steerage. But...

There were times when he'd wondered. Doubted. Times when the pieces didn't quite fit.

Those pieces he'd socked away. Not anywhere they would be discovered, but in mental storage. He'd sometimes take those out and play with them, try to form them into a picture, a plan, but they never quite came together.

But now...

There was no doubt that the Regent wasn't the one in charge of the kingdom. Princess Bessory had some strange hold over Strego when she hardly had a hold over herself. Girls had gone missing in her presence. He knew that for fact, not mere rumor, but he had yet to discover what she was doing with them. No accusations had been made. *Who would dare?* No witnesses had come forth. No bodies had been found. Even if they had been, the Princess was the last in the V'Alban line. It would take more than a few deaths to unseat her.

Like a contender for the throne.

King Calestri had been dethroned, removed entirely from the line of succession, along with any descendants who might be tainted with his 'madness'. King Grammond's line had not been fruitful. He himself was an only child, and he'd been devout in his thanks to the All when his queen had given birth to three fine children. He'd have been horrified that he was down to the last, and, in his mind, least.

There'd been rumors of V'Alban bastards, but none had presented themselves to challenge Bloody Bess. Ruggerio had been sent by the Princess to deal with the rumored few. He'd deemed it expedient. Necessary. Best for the stability of the kingdom. The midst of a war was not the time for a battle for supremacy. If he hadn't taken out the challengers, she'd only have sent someone else, perhaps less skilled, who would have done the job with more collateral damage. Or the contenders would have taken each other out in their bid for the throne, along with the backers needed to fight Frizenze, leaving Jucar defenseless. Assassination was the tidiest option.

Tidy. Orderly. Efficient.

All lovely words. Thoughts. Ideals. Ridiculous in the face of reality. He sneered at himself.

Nothing about spywork was ever tidy, but he kept trying to make it that way, tying up loose ends, assigning himself the most complex missions to assure that they were done right, cutting problems off at the roots before they could grow.

That was what Bloody Bess was going to do with that boy. What Ruggerio would normally do. But not this time. The Princess was unraveling. It was in everything she said and did. It had been her idea to employ a feral mageri on the hunt, yet when Ceramor escaped and went rogue, suddenly it was Ruggerio to blame and take the fall?

He knew better than most what that meant. That he would not be around much longer to spearhead anything. And if Ruggerio succeeded, Princess Bessory would find fault with some other endeavor. She had begun to doubt. She would remember that her brother had installed him, and she would want her own man to take his place. Which meant his days were numbered.

Maybe Jucar's as well. Bess was overextending herself, her men hunting not just the murderess, but all women with power, and the Restoration rebels as well. He'd applaud it as powerfully ambitious if he thought they could take in all the rebels at once, but without being prepared to close the net, they gave those left behind the opportunity to slip through the cracks—to dig in deep, to hide, to plot, to mount an offensive all their own.

He would hold onto the boy. At least until he could be sure the contender really was the problem and not, perhaps, the solution. Maybe it was time for a change.

He hit his quarters and let himself in, grabbing the sack he kept always prepared, in case there was no coming back. He was in and out in less time than it would have taken him to use the garderobe. He only wished he could think of a way to save Ulan. Their families—brothers, wives and cousins—had moved up together from Cartesia in the farthest reaches of Jucar when he was a child and she still a babe in arms. They'd lived together, ten people in two rooms on the second floor of a tenement which stank all the year through from the dross everyone tossed out their windows which slopped up streets and gullies. Then one by one, their number dropped. First it was Ulan's father, a cartographer, commissioned by King Grammond to draw a more accurate map of their southern borders. He'd been a dark cloud on them all until he'd found the work and none had been too sorry to see him off. Then it had been his brother, Callo, joined up with the military and sent to a border outpost.

Ruggerio got out of the overcrowded quarters as quickly as he could. Already, he spoke Markens and Cartesian—their region only having been 'annexed' in Mad King Calestri's time. He'd picked up other languages within their tenement easily enough as well. It was how he'd first earned attention at court. He'd snuck in on a lark. He was good at sneaking, a prodigy at relieving people of their purses and sundries with no one the wiser. And if they did look, it was to see someone completely innocent or uninterested, engaged in some other activity entirely. It was the way he brought in money to the household after his father's hand was smashed and his uncle's advance had run out, and money and messages stopped coming. He knew he took a big risk sneaking into the palace while the King was holding open court, though it would also bring bigger rewards. But he'd been too fascinated by the spectacle and too amused that there were greater scoundrels at court than on the streets for much thieving.

"You know he's not translating accurately, don't you?" he said to the man next to him, unable to help himself as he watched the King hear cases. He'd vaguely noted that the man himself was extravagantly dressed but also that he was too smart to have his valuables hanging in a pouch where anyone could clip them.

"Oh, no?" the man asked, amused. "How would you translate His Lordship?"

Ruggerio told him, in all the colorful language included, and when the man stopped laughing, he said, "Come with me."

Intrigued and knowing he could take care of himself, Ruggerio did just that, and it was the beginning of his life at the palace. The end of his family's life in that tenement. He'd seen to it. Eventually, Ulan's mother, sister and brothers had moved back to Cartesia to be reunited with her father, who had become very ill with a sleeping sickness and been left behind by the expedition, word of which had only belatedly reached them. It left only Ulan, who'd by then become a camp laundress and stitcher for the army. His only family, the last of his ties. He'd made her promises.

Then left her behind with Bloody Bess. Allowed himself to be dismissed. As though he had any choice.

His intervention now would do nothing but make things worse. He had to consider the good of the kingdom. Right now, the kingdom's welfare might align with the wellbeing of the boy. He was sure Ulan would want him to proceed accordingly. That his brother Callo, who had given his life in service to Jucar, would expect no less of them.

Ruggerio jerked a nod of acknowledgment to the guards he passed in the hallway as he marched toward the dungeon and used his master key to burst into the cell he'd ordered the boy delivered to, the one with gaps only at the very top and bottom of the door, the bottom for food, the top for added air flow.

He was momentarily staggered at what he saw inside, then quickly entered and closed the door behind him. He had expected that Gernot wouldn't hurt the boy. Unlike so many of the other guards, Gernot never seemed to revel in the violence, but did what was expected of him as if he had no opinion on it at all and no ambition to do anything more or less. However, he never expected to reach the cell and find Hostill's hands no longer bound with rope, but with colorful strands of wool.

Both boy and guard jumped, and Gernot grabbed the wool out of Hostill's hands as though he could hide it away *now.*

"What the unholy ghosts am I seeing?" Ruggerio raged. "Did I miss the tea and cakes? Why isn't this boy bound?"

Gernot jumped to attention, stowing the wool behind his back with one hand while pounding his chest with the other fist and dropping his head to his chest in a show of devotion. "My apologies. You had said the boy wasn't to be harmed, and I didn't take him to be any threat. M'mam's sight isn't what it was, and she's made a mess of her woolens, so I'd brought them in my sack to work out on my own time. I thought I'd put the prisoner to use. He said he'd done such for his mam."

Ruggerio didn't even know where to start with that. Apparently, they'd had enough of a tete-a-tete that they'd worked out that little similarity. What else might they have gotten to? Clearly, Gernot wasn't quite the consummate soldier Ruggerio had given him credit for.

"Well, bind him again, and *not* with wool. The boy is coming with me."

"Sir?"

Gernot had picked a fine time to start questioning orders.

"Yes?" he said, in a way that did nothing to invite Gernot to continue.

He swallowed and did it anyway. "Will you need an escort?"

Ruggerio looked down his nose at the guard. "No, but I thank you for the offer."

Gernot stuffed the now hopelessly retangled wool into his sack and went to retie Hostill, who even turned his back to make it easier on Gernot, all the while glaring over his shoulder at Ruggerio. If he actually had feelings, they might have been hurt.

As soon as the boy was secured, Ruggerio dismissed Gernot with the warning, "Do *not* release any more prisoners or you might find yourself among them."

It did not escape him that his words echoed those of the Blood Princess. He'd become a product of his environs. It was perhaps past time that he was getting out of this viper's nest.

Gernot nodded his understanding, swept his rucksack up on his way out and didn't linger.

Ruggerio was left alone with the boy. Given everything he'd seen—his friends swept up in a raid, the aftermath of Vizi's torture, Ulan being ripped away from him—he was remarkably en garde. He watched Ruggerio not with terror or resignation, but with a fighter's readiness, as though he might have to strike or dodge or parry and didn't want to miss his moment. He didn't have a noble's expectation that opportunities would be granted, but an urchin's understanding that they must be seized.

"Where are you taking me?" the boy demanded, dodging as Ruggerio reached for him.

He sighed heavily. He didn't like explaining himself. No one could tell what they didn't know, but it would go easier if the boy went willingly. He could clout him on the head and carry him out, but knockout blows were never as precise as one would want, and deadweight never as light at the end of a journey as at the start.

"Away from here. Princess Bessory has become far too interested in you, and I think we can both agree that is not conducive to your long and continued life."

"In me?" His voice broke, and Ruggerio was glad to hear it. The boy was beginning to be a bit too impressive. "But why?"

"We'll talk when we're safely away—"

"But the others. I can't leave without them."

"You can't do anything for them from here. We need to get away. We need to connect with people who can help."

He landed a hand on the boy's shoulder and started to steer him toward the door, but the boy dug in like a mule and refused to be moved. "How do I know this isn't a trick to get me to lead you to the others?"

Ruggerio sighed. It wasn't too late to rethink clouting the boy and throwing him over his shoulder.

"Can you save your friends from here?" he asked the boy.

He received a blank stare in response.

"How about alone?"

Another blank stare.

"Shall we try it together then? You can always watch for your moment to double-cross me. You're currently bound, but I have to sleep sometime, yes? I imagine your odds are better out there than they are in here."

The boy mumbled something indeterminate.

And there it was, Ruggerio had just experienced all the joys of fatherhood in the space of a few moments in time. No need for the real thing.

When he pushed again at the boy's shoulder, he moved, all without conceding any of Ruggerio's points, which was fine. Ruggerio was perfectly capable of giving himself credit where it was due, especially if it distracted him from the life he was about to burn down behind him.

He had a choice. But not much of one.

He *could* return Hostill to a cell. Take up the hunt for Cia. Bring her in as the Princess commanded, and Roha with her. He could pretend that he hadn't been ignoring the signs of the Princess's growing instability and that he hadn't sold bits of his soul here and there in service to the kings and then to her. Everyone did, even if they didn't admit to it. Ruggerio was just more honest with himself than most. Or had less of a conscience that needed to be appeased.

But before his way had always been for the good of the kingdom. That had always been his salve. That and the recognition that his position within the kingdom was precarious. He'd seen that with his uncle. Stay useful and they would sweep you along – provide you the means to care for yourself and your family. Falter and they'd step over the body, leave you where you lay. He'd only been elevated to spymaster when Jannik had executed his predecessor for failing to prevent the Queen and her hand-maiden from plying their poison and killing King Cyril right under his nose. Oh, the zeal with which Jannik pursued the case was quite some-thing to see, spittle flying from his lips at his suggestion that Fenric's failure to stop the King's assassination was perhaps even an indication he was in league with the Queen. The bloodlust had been real enough. But Ruggerio had always wondered whether the rest had been a bit overplayed.

Cyril's murder made Jannik king, and, after all, he had never been overly fond of his brother. Or anyone for that matter. He loved a hunt. He loved his horses and hounds. He enjoyed those who joined in with his bloody pursuits, laughed at his poor jests, and matched him drink for drink and he had no use for those who did not.

When Jannik offered Ruggerio the newly vacated position, "We seem to be *a head* short! *Ha ha!*" There was nothing to say but yes. And nothing to do but please the King. He had to thrive so that he would be able to shelter others, like Ulan, within his shade. *Until they died from lack of sunlight,* a voice inside him said, but it was such a small voice and so quiet that he had no trouble silencing it.

Ulan was not dead.

He and the boy made it through the palace without incident. No one but the Princess or the Regent would stop the spymaster going about his business, and they were otherwise occupied. He might meet a little more resistance if he planned to take the boy out via any of the traditional routes, but that wasn't going to be a problem. There was a secret escape route near the royal quarters, but he wasn't going to risk getting anywhere near that one. There was another nearly forgotten hidden passageway in the north tower.

The north tower was bitingly cold in the winter, and so not used except when their numbers swelled in times of treaty or diplomatic visits, which hadn't happened since before the Blood War. Since they'd used it to cage a queen. After Inaya's execution, it had been given over to storage... until recently. When the Princess ordered the rounding up of mageri women, she'd also ordered the north tower to be prepared as part prison, part living quarters. But she knew about the secret escape. She wouldn't have quartered anyone in the Poppy Room.

He hurried there now, pushing Hostill before him. He turned again to ask where they were going, but Ruggerio hissed him silent, and the boy huffed, but complied. There were other voices now for the boy to listen to, in any case. Unless he had better hearing than Ruggerio, he couldn't make out what they were saying, but he listened. Ruggerio was fairly sure that it was those voices rather than Ruggerio's hiss that actually caused him to quiet. When they reached the room he wanted, Ruggerio applied his master key, and locked the door behind him. Everything that had been stored in the north tower had been moved to this one room to make space for the mageri women, and so it was packed to the rafters with out-of-favor furniture, discarded cradles, spindles and clothing, and entire lives that had been abandoned. He doubted all as willingly as he was about to do with his.

He let the boy go and pushed things around, making a path to the back wall, where he knew a heavy wardrobe blocked the way to their exit. He was filthy by the time he cleared enough of the room that he could get to the wardrobe, but that was fine. By the time he exited, he would not be Ruggerio the spymaster, and Hostill couldn't be seen as his prisoner. He grabbed his pack, and changed into a laborer's tunic, cape and woolens. He didn't have a boy-sized cape, but scrounging in the detritus of others' lives turned up something that would do. He shook the dust and drop-pings out of a slightly holey cloak before wrapping Hostill in it and covering his bound hands. Everyone should be heads-down against the winter chill. No one should pay them any extra attention, as long as the boy didn't call it to them.

On second thought, the kid was going to have difficulty navigating the tunnel with bound hands. Was it too soon to win himself some goodwill? He should offer a carrot and a stick.

"Are you hungry?" he asked the boy. They didn't have much time, but he'd come across some of the hard cheese he'd packed away while searching out his change of clothes, and the moments they'd gain with the boy's added agility would make up for any time lost.

He eyed Ruggerio suspiciously. "What do you think?"

"If I free your hands, can you be trusted?"

He was surprised to see Hostill consider and not instantly swear to whatever Ruggerio wanted to hear. "I promise that I can be trusted for as long as you can. Sound fair?"

Ruggerio cocked his head. "Eminently," he answered. He had faith in his own ability to appear trustworthy even when it wasn't so.

He freed the boy's hands and put the cheese into them. The boy eyed him as he bit in, as though he could read in Ruggerio's eyes whether he'd have to spit his bite out due to poison, but Ruggerio didn't have time for such games. He turned away to find and spring the hidden catch so that the stonework behind the wardrobe would slide aside, giving them a low, narrow ingress into a slightly broader passageway.

It was a given that castles had secret, secure ways in and out in the event of betrayal and siege, and discreet doors to allow for illicit liaisons. But some liaisons were more illicit than others. One might wonder why the desolate north tower would rate its own unsupervised entry and exit —if one weren't the spymaster and thus privy to the knowledge that an obscure path existed between the Poppy Room and a royal antechamber, where it was said a queen had once been impregnated by a king's cousin when the king could not do the job himself and yet required heirs. Many things were said. Or went very carefully unsaid. There was only ever one key, held by whoever wore the crown or circlet.

Ruggerio himself didn't have access. There might come a day when he would be motivated to try his skills against the lock, but that day hadn't come.

There was a shuttered lantern hanging from a hook just inside the passage, and he took and lit it before closing the doorway behind them. He hated surrendering the control but wanted his hands free and the boy at his front rather than his back, so he handed the lantern over and indicated that Hostill should precede him. There was only one path, so no concern about having to lead the way.

The boy seemed happy enough to have his hands free and something that could be used as a weapon in them. He'd need Ruggerio to work the catch at the other end of the passageway, but after that, he could, in theory, make a run for it. If Ruggerio wasn't prepared. If he didn't have reach and experience and ruthlessness on his side.

At the other end of the passage, the boy took in the situation, and decided against taking things any further. Ruggerio approved.

Ruggerio opened the far end of the passage, and the only fight he had was with the landscaping on the other side, where the hedge planted to hide the exit had grown out of hand. He called to the boy when he saw that the way was clear and motioned him out ahead. Ruggerio stopped only to scoop up a handful of dirt, rub it between his palms and apply it throughout his hair to rough it up and dim down the iridescent black of it that gave him away otherwise. He then clapped one hand against the other as though beating a rug, dusting his face with a fine mist that would suggest he'd picked up the grit from a day's labor. The boy's grime was rather more ground in, freeze-dried into creases.

They would do, as long as they were well enough away by the time any alarm was raised from the castle. *If* any alarm was raised. Bloody Bess couldn't afford to lose another prisoner. Certainly couldn't afford the suggestion that her own spymaster had defected. He was counting on it. It would take her time to rally, to come up with a plan. Normally, she'd have put Ruggerio himself on it, but…

He hurried them away.

It was dangerous to take them past All Souls, especially with the investigation going on, but he needed to see the sign board outside. He hoped that even with the partial collapse and the investigation that his contact would have left him a coded note on the board, which always had an inspirational message to be contemplated along with service times. Luckily for Ruggerio, the collapse had mostly affected the far side where services would be conducted, rather than the entryway, which still stood, the stone arch intricately carved with fruits, flowers, animals and people, all stemming from the same vine. The carving could be clearly seen, but the wooden doors themselves were blocked by a Crown guard and an acolyte, certainly not fruit of the same tree, watching the passers-by. Even the acolyte looked unwelcoming, and Ruggerio didn't linger. He didn't need to. He saw what he'd come to see, the message on the board.

Foundations must be seen to be strengthened.

Book of Light, passage twenty. The casual reader would see it as a reference to the building collapse and be comforted that all was as it was meant to be. That the church would rise up stronger.

But Ruggerio knew it for a message. The Book of Light meant the Split-Tree Inn. Passage twenty meant eight bells that evening.

Ceramor

Pain shrieked through Ceramor like the demon winds of the north, stealing his sanity and consciousness. When the latter came, the former was questionable. He seemed to be in some kind of cart, jouncing over the ground, some bones that used to be fused together fractured, jagged and poking through muscles and maybe out the other ends.

There were parts of him, stolen from King Jannik's hunting hounds, that crept out of the dark corners of his mind, sniffing hungrily as though to see if he'd make a good meal, determining that he was more meat than man. But not good sport. Fun to nose and watch flail, avoid a spasming arm, or a kicking leg, but not for long. So little fight remaining. Best left for scavengers.

But then, something else on the air. Something infinitely more interesting. Not him.

He was nothing. A rotting meat sack. Or soon to be. The Animist had said it himself. Not worth saving.

But the boy...

He didn't know how the dark corners of his mind even picked out the boy over the scents of blood and fear sweat and, yes, even urine that he'd released while trapped under the church. And the blanket under which they'd covered him in the cart—wheelbarrow?—wasn't too fresh either. Every jounce brought dirt and "fertilizer" sifting down to poison his wounds.

But the boy...

He smelled like the master.

He smelled like home.

Like something familiar. Another time. Before the plague. Before Jannik died from the battle wound, and Reina got sick and Ceramor tried to save her and ended up condemning himself.

If he could move, he would follow that scent rather than lose it. He tried, straining against weakness that reached somehow beyond the realm of passive exhaustion and into the active aggression of a vortex that grabbed him and pulled him repeatedly down and down until he was certain there would be a point at which he wouldn't be able to fight his way back to the surface. He didn't know whether his body had been pushed beyond its limits or whether the church had been right all along and whatever tethered him to the energies of creation had declared him close enough to dead to call him back to the collective.

Ceramor needed a hook to keep him from going, some way to claw his way back. He chose the boy. He swallowed down his scent. He remembered. He marked. If he surfaced again, he had a path if not a plan.

CHAPTER TWENTY-THREE

Ruggerio

R uggerio set them up at an inn on a street parallel to the Split-Tree Inn, where he'd stabled his horse upon past visits to the area. Infrequent though they were, he assumed from the wink and nod he received from the stable boy that the story he'd concocted for himself had made an impression—about an assignation close by and stabling his horse elsewhere for the sake of discretion.

Ruggerio was not stupid enough to get a room at the same inn where he was meeting his contact, but Grayven's Rest wasn't far down the way.

He'd have chosen somewhere he was entirely unknown if it wouldn't have meant scouting new escape routes and trusting that staff he'd had no time to investigate wouldn't slip in on them in their sleep for a bit of thievery or murder.

The master of the house, perhaps having heard the gossip that went around about him in the stable, was startled to see him enter not with a paramour, but a boy, filthy and swaying on his feet. Ruggerio, known here as Waru, was rougher around the edges than usual, and hardly seemed himself.

Indeed, he wasn't. As they'd approached the inn, Ruggerio told Hostill what he needed to know about their circumstances. Enough that he wouldn't seem surprised by anything Ruggerio might say and give them away. Anyway, not enough that Ruggerio couldn't improvise. The closer they got, the more Ruggerio adopted Waru's characteristics. First his steps, his pace, the way he carried his shoulders, the cant of his head. So different from Ruggerio's. He'd changed things up enough not to be recognizable as they moved through the streets; he shed himself like a snake's skin and put on Waru's mantle instead.

But it wasn't just about mannerisms. It was about bearing as well, and for that, he needed to weave in the elements of his story. The weight of the responsibility for his orphaned nephew, the added injury of being set upon by highwaymen on his way back from fetching the poor boy, who'd already been through so much. The loss of his horse. All the boy's belongings. The only thing the brigands hadn't stolen was the hidden purse that was paying for their night's lodgings.

Their home was in the countryside, but the boy was dead on his feet. He needed to sleep and to heal. Waru needed somewhere he trusted to leave his nephew while he went out into the city to replace the things the boy would need, that had been stolen from them.

Hostill watched him, expression flickering between horror and fascination. "How do you do that?" he asked.

"Do what?" Ruggerio said, distracted.

"*That.*"

"It's nothing. How did you learn to speak? You listened to others. You learned. You tried it for yourself."

"You're putting me off."

"I can't teach you all I know in answer to a single question."

"But you will you teach me?"

"Perhaps."

"Perhaps?"

"That's the best you'll get from Waru."

"Is that who you are now?"

"Yes, and you're my orphan nephew, Gint."

"Gint?"

"Do you do anything but ask questions?"

"I eat."

"Once we get there, I'll be sure that you do. As long as you play your part."

"Mourning I know well. I *am* an orphan. And I'm still grieving what you did to Vizi." His shoulders hung, his back bowed, and every line of his body showed the exhaustion Ruggerio feigned for Waru, yet his eyes blazed.

"Not what *I* did."

"No, you ordered it done. Worse, because you sullied someone else's hands and conscience."

"*Sullied*. Where did a gutter rat like you learn to speak so high and mighty?"

"Perhaps my sister brought her pretty speech back from the palace or my mam before her, and I picked it up like I do the dirt of the streets."

Ruggerio rubbed his jaw. He had a million more questions that would have to wait. They'd arrived.

As startled as the master of the inn was to see him arrive with Gint and his tale of woe, the mistress ate it up. She got the boy seated in the taproom and fussed over him with a damp rag, cleaning off his face and hands before she let him at a heaping bowl of stew and a heel of dark bread. She brought him a mug of watered ale herself and watched while he downed half of it as though to be sure he wouldn't die of thirst on her watch.

Then someone called to her, and she waved the rag now bearing the imprint of Hostill's face impatiently in their general direction. She stroked the boy's hair gently on her way to see to her other patrons' demands.

Ruggerio sat across from him, stewless, aleless, and amused nonetheless. Hostill didn't look up or pause in the spooning of food to mouth.

"Good?" he asked.

Hostill grunted.

Ruggerio signaled for a meal of his own and caught the eye of a boy nearly twice Hostill's size with the look of the innkeeper. Undoubtedly his son. His own stew arrived with so few chunks of actual meat or vegetables that he had to dig to the bottom for them. It at least seemed thickened with the flour left over from the bread and flavored with whatever ale hadn't found its way into Hostill's stein. The boy seemed happy enough with it for certain, because it was gone before Ruggerio was half through with his own, and Hostill was near to falling asleep in his bowl.

The mistress swung back around before he could actually collapse into it, and Ruggerio slipped her a small token to see that "Gint" was washed and tucked into bed so that he could be off on his errands and back before he was missed. She shot a quick glance at the tall but still gawky boy serving tables with only the newest sense of where his arms and elbows fit into the world, and he could see her remembering him at Hostill's age and knew she would care for his *nephew* as if he were her own.

He slipped out to his meeting. It was well past dark, and with a murderess on the loose and the Crown guards on the hunt, no one else was about. Unfortunately, that was true of the public room at the Split-Tree Inn as well. There were few travelers in the winter. Even merchants stopped making their rounds before the snows, mostly sold out of increasingly scarce wares. And while pubs seemed to do business even in the worst of times, the biting winds of winter frequently encouraged all but the diehards to do their drinking at home or close to it.

There were only two tables occupied, one by an entire family of weary travelers who mostly ignored him or glanced incuriously as he passed, all but an imp of a child, who looked like he still had energy and was in want of a playmate to expend it. He turned quickly away from the imp's surveillance, knowing any expression at all might be taken for encouragement. At another table in the back, a man in a dark woolen cloak and cowl waited, turning his mug in his hands three times at the sight of Ruggerio. It would have been a foreboding look if it weren't so cold outside that a man could be forgiven for continuing to feel the chill.

Plus, he knew those hands and that signal. He folded one of his hands over the other as he approached and tapped a knuckle three times in response. This was the all clear. Acceptable. What wasn't was that his contact was sitting at the bench against the far wall with his back to it, leaving Ruggerio the bench with his back exposed to the room.

"Move in," he demanded.

"But that would leave me trapped."

"You chose your seat," Ruggerio said. "You knew I wouldn't take the other."

"Did you expect that *I* would take the assassination seat?"

"Move in," he said again, looming now to make clear it was not a request.

The man glanced around to see what attention they might be drawing. The candlelight of the pub limned the outline of the church robes and hood beneath his cowl.

"Fine," he said with ill grace, perhaps assuming he could slip under the table and out the other side if anything happened amiss. It wouldn't be in time to save him if Ruggerio decided otherwise, but he let his contact come to his own conclusions. He slid over, and that was what was important.

"I can give you Roha," the churchman said without preamble, probably hoping to get this over with and regain his freedom as quickly as possible. "And the woman too. I know where they are. At least for now. The question is what will you do with them?"

Ruggerio freed a pre-filled purse from his belt and made sure that it clinked nicely as he did so. "I don't think that's any of your concern."

The man drew in a breath. "You won't kill them?" the man asked.

"I won't." He didn't even have to lie. It was not—for now—part of the plan.

The man grabbed for the money, leaving a piece of parchment behind in its place, and then tried to shove Ruggerio out of his way, but he wouldn't budge. He could be made of stone if he wanted to be. Immoveable. He made sure his contact knew this, but when he pushed again, Ruggerio felt inclined to give, making it clear that it was a choice. The churchman nodded his thanks.

Ruggerio refrained from smiling. He had intimidated the man enough already, and didn't want to scare him off entirely. He might need him again.

He had no idea what use the churchman had for money, or even whether he was truly in it for the reward. He seemed to take a special pleasure in informing on Roha to the spymaster. But so far his intel had been good. Ruggerio would find out soon enough whether that would continue. As soon as he collected the boy.

But when he got to Hostill, the boy wasn't alone.

CHAPTER TWENTY-FOUR

Cia

Cia jumped at the sudden pounding on Roha's door, followed by the near-panicked voice, "Hsst, let me in."

Roha gasped and fell against the wall, overbalancing in the attempt not to use nes bad shoulder in the effort to rise. Ni used the wall as a springboard to get to the door while Cia stood frozen with indecision. Her instinct to trust Roha didn't extend to whoever was pounding at the door, but in the end, there was no place to hide. She was caught in the center of the room when a young man with a sparse topknot and robes that had once been white but were now smeared with blood and other things she didn't want to examine burst into the room, leaving Roha to close the door behind him. The man was breathing so hard, she feared he might exhale his very soul before he could breathe it back.

"Ceramor. The Hound, the Bloody Beast," he puffed. "The church has just. Left him. To die. Blind alley at Tallow, backing on Wicking Way. Go now. Run. They're onto you." The last was almost a whisper, as if he'd run out of all his air. He doubled over, hands on his knees to hold himself largely upright.

"They're onto me? Then–"

"Probably not far behind me. Left me puking in the alley with the body. Told them I'd catch up and took a cut-through."

Which might explain some of the muck on his robes.

"Go!" he yelled, waving his arms as though Cia and Roha were a flock of birds he meant to scare into flight.

It worked with Cia, who was ready to fly straight for the door, heart pounding once more, but Roha dove for the fireplace, and reached for the hearthstone. With nes one good hand, ni yanked the long, smooth stone out of place to reveal a depression underneath, and a sack that ni grabbed before shoving the hearthstone back down. The acolyte must have planned for the possibility of having to leave in a hurry.

Roha slung the sack over nes head, the strap landing on nes good shoulder and the weight slapping against nes side, because there *was* weight. There was something squared off that Cia could see, something that might bruise if allowed to bang about. Then Roha grabbed the undyed woolen blanket off the pallet and wrapped it around nimself like a cloak, shutting down the white beacon of the acolyte's robes and protecting nimself from the elements all in one.

"Thank you, my friend. I won't forget you," Roha said to the other acolyte, sending him on his way. He was already half out the door, ready to vanish and come up behind the others he was meant to catch up with.

And then Roha was out too, and Cia realized that she hadn't been invited to join. But neither had she been discouraged or abused or anything else that she'd come to expect. Possibly Roha didn't want to be responsible for Cia and whatever might come next. But Cia, all evidence thus far to the contrary, could be responsible for herself. And intended to be from here on out.

Two steps out into the dark, misty morning and Cia could barely see the acolyte before her. Four steps and Roha turned on nes heel with a breathless "Run!" as Cia's only warning.

Two white-robed acolytes had stepped out of the alley and were bearing down on them like a steaming Torvus, a massive battlefield beast built of anima with clawed feet and rapier sharp horns. It was no wonder the two had been chosen to move bodies. They might have raised the beams for the church itself. She didn't know if the church had enforcers—she'd never heard of the need—but if so, surely these were them. It wouldn't have taken three to dump Ceramor's body, certainly not if these were two of them. She didn't know what that meant, unless the church had meant them to watchdog each other. If so, that effort had failed.

Roha didn't knock her down, but dodged as Cia stared a second too long at the bulk barreling down on them. Then she whirled and raced after Roha, just in time to catch sight of Roha's unbleached cloak as ni dodged down a side street, and then another. Cia raced to catch up. Her legs were shorter, but she'd lived a life punctuated with terror, and her survival instincts were finely honed. She ran, keeping Roha in sight, but she could hear the men just behind them, calling to each other to go left or right. They weren't losing the men, and it was only a matter of time before they came to a blind alley or crashed into some unforeseen obstacle.

The cold air sawed into her lungs like blades, and a stitch started in her side, growing until it would not be ignored. She tried to beat at it, knead it as she ran, but it did nothing but pull her off true, bounce her off buildings, slow her until she feared she would be caught.

Then suddenly Roha was too close. The acolyte had slowed for some reason Cia couldn't see, and she plowed into Roha's back and now clung to avoid falling. Roha's muscles were like ropes, so odd for a servant of the church, who she'd expect to be soft. She would have to revise her conceptions, but not now. Now they were just a distraction.

A door was open to their right, and there was a hand beckoning them. There must have been a call or maybe a face peering out that Roha had responded to, but neither was evident now, and it seemed far too convenient. Maybe this was one of Roha's Restoration contacts. Maybe it was the acolyte who had gone ahead.

Cia didn't trust it.

But she trusted the men chasing them even less. And they were gaining.

Roha reached back for Cia's hand and ran for the door. Cia had no choice but to follow or be pulled off her feet. Which was a lie. She had a choice. She could yank her hand back. Go her own way. Or, more likely, get captured. But she didn't. Not taking her hand back *was* a choice. She wasn't going to do herself the injustice of pretending otherwise.

The door closed behind them quickly, but without slamming. The figure shutting and locking it was cloaked and hooded in a covering so voluminous all Cia could tell was that the person was tall and of unremarkable girth. He—Cia felt that somehow, though she couldn't say why—then turned to the side and motioned as though they were to follow this mystery person even unto death, but she wasn't having it. She didn't like this. Not at all. And she would have no more discounting of herself.

She stepped up to the figure to pull at the hood, and he chopped her hand away with such ease that sweat broke out on her brow. She tried with the other hand, and he chopped there too, but while he was busy with her, Roha stepped up behind and yanked his cowl down.

Cia gasped and stepped back from the man they called the Blade.

He grabbed her and whirled her around, her back to his front, knife tip pressed between her ribs, angled to go straight up under them and into her heart so quickly she choked on the rest of her exhale.

CHAPTER TWENTY-FIVE

Dazia

D azia finally sensed the ghost man. She'd grown more and more frantic as she couldn't find him anywhere, torn between going back for Maman and continuing on to find him so she would not disappoint her, when suddenly he flickered into faint life. Dazia tore through the mists, the haze of nothing and everything that called to her, but never so strongly as her watch upon Maman.

But then suddenly, there he was. She flew out of the ani-mists, trying to carry some with her, to hide herself with. She landed spitting distance from the terrified woman her uncle threatened with a knife. The woman's eyes were wide, but almost more resigned than terrified.

"No," Dazia yelled, waving her arms to get her uncle's attention, releasing the mist. "No, no, no. Stop! Uncle, Maman sent me! She says—"

But her uncle spoke right over her. No one saw or heard her. Except that when she looked again at the woman to see if there was some way she could divert the knife, she noticed someone *paying attention*. Not at all in a nice way —but in a murderous, dark, dangerous way.

Somehow, the ghost man was staring out of the woman's eyes.

And when he lunged for Dazia, the knife aimed at his wife's chest slid inside.

Her uncle's knives were ever sharp.

No one heard Dazia scream.

Cia

The pain was lightning through her body, and Garif let it strike, let her feel the impact, the branching agony, as it started in her chest and took over her entirety. But Garif kept control. She tried to jerk away. Fall away. Anything. But her body would not obey. He had shoved her back, locked her away, but kept her aware. Made sure the power was his but the pain was hers. As always.

Ruggerio dropped the knife before Garif could impale her entirely. It was all that left her alive.

"What the bloody bells did you do?" Roha shouted, ready to launch nimself at Ruggerio.

But Garif wasn't finished. Not nearly. Terror wrestled the pain as he had her diving for the knife. She knew what he would do with it if he grasped it.

He had done what he'd always threatened. He had taken her over, only from within. It was her nightmares come to pass. Maybe Cia should let him pick up that knife. As though she could stop him. She shouted and banged, only to have an after-strike of the pain spike through her, blacking her vision. When it cleared, Garif was a hairsbreadth from the knife. Ruggerio reached for it as well, and Garif grabbed him by the hair, yanking, snarling, pulling him away from the thing _he_ desired to end her with.

Garif hurled the other man to the side as best he could and reached again for the blade, but from the corner of his/her eye caught Ruggerio going for the dagger in his boot. There was an instant of hesitation, she thought, as though the spymaster didn't want to use it, but he overcame it, whirling with it in time for Garif to come up with the one on the floor, only he didn't turn it on Ruggerio. He turned it on her.

There was a great flapping from above them, as of a blanket being beaten and aired, and suddenly, she could barely breathe. _He_ could barely breathe, smothered and swaddled head to toe in the cloak Roha had been wearing. Bound without breath, tightly enough that he couldn't fight, couldn't draw air, possibly while bleeding out from the knife wound to the chest, Garif surrendered her to her fate.

The release had Cia sagging in her bindings, and she panicked, trying to fight her way out, weak with blood loss and the strength Garif had sucked out of her. But she gave all she had, panicked. She did not want to die. Not like this. Not with Garif polluting her. Would they go to the anima together, bound for all eternity? Would she be aware? It was an unimaginable horror.

A sharp blow to the back of her head sent it slamming forward, rolled her eyeballs like knucklebones and sent her vision to black. Her thoughts scattered. Limbs went limp.

Someone did something, and air struck her face.

"You didn't hit her too hard?" came a voice, fearful. *Roha?* The name floated around, bumped her brain.

"Just hard enough, I promise you. I don't know what came over her. She went mad," a man said. "*I* didn't cut her———"

"I see that now," Roha snapped. "But why?"

"Remorse? She did kill her husband."

"She said it was kill or be killed."

"Still," the man said.

There was silence like a weight. The binding around Cia was tight. So tight. Maybe keeping in some of the blood spilled. She couldn't remember why she was bleeding. Was too tired to get worked up over it.

"I don't think so." *Roha?*

The man sighed. "I miscalculated with the blade. I knew Cia wouldn't trust me. I thought it expedient to get her under control so that I would have the opportunity to explain myself. I had no idea it would come to… that. Let me begin again—I have a friend of yours by the name of Hostill. I would like to take you to him, if you will allow it."

"And *I'm* to trust you, after *that?*"

"There are better places to talk, and I would rather not leave Hostill unguarded for long."

"You truly have Hostill? He's escaped?"

"I helped him escape, burning down my former life. Will you come?"

"Go," Cia managed.

It came out only as "Oh," but she got her point across. For a moment, at least, she could stop fighting.

Ruggerio

Ruggerio led the way as the rebel, Roha, carried the murderess like a child. Less conspicuous that way than over the shoulder like a sack of potatoes...or a dead body. Their relative sizes were such that it was possible, if burdensome. It was certainly easier on the wounded woman, but Ruggerio still wasn't certain that was a good thing. A person seeking death might not notice who else they took down in pursuit of it, and they were in enough danger already.

He didn't like bringing them back to the inn, but he disliked the idea of moving Hostill and Ceramor right now even more. He'd trussed up the ankari when he'd discovered him, and dosed him with something that ought to keep him docile for long enough, but one never knew with ankari. Not really. He'd have quite happily slipped a dagger between his ribs and dispensed with him entirely if the boy hadn't waked and if he wouldn't then have had to deal with body disposal and explanations.

He went in first to make sure that the host and hostess were busy elsewhere while Roha snuck up the staircase with the key to his room, trusting that the lure of the boy would keep the rebel from running off with the wounded woman. It might be tricky for nim to juggle the body while unlocking the door, but he couldn't be sure that Hostill would unlock it to Roha. He might fear a trick. Or Ceramor might try something if given the distraction of a knock at the door.

The inn's mistress was nowhere in sight, and the master had joined the single occupied table that was well into their cups, and simply gave a nod that was more of a wobble. Ruggerio—Waru—nodded back, letting the exhaustion of the hour show on his face, and vanished to his room, hoping the door would open to him. The exhaustion wasn't entirely feigned. Staging a one-man rebellion came at a cost he supposed he was still too numb to feel.

The door did open, but there was a reluctance rather than an alacrity to it. As though it would rather not. But, like any tool, what mattered was not the thing itself, but the will behind it. Like weapons. Like words.

The door closed behind him, and he moved to put his back to it, but the position of power was already taken. It had been Roha who'd opened it and Roha who closed it, standing there now, blocking his escape, hands loose and ready almost as though ni'd been trained as he had, which was impossible. The Church didn't shape their people that way. Not that he'd ever heard. But he had no reason to test his knowledge. He'd be a poor spymaster if he'd chosen an inn where the door or window, both blocked at the moment, were his only means of egress.

He walked to the one spot where he could see the entire room and be out of easy lunging distance from any of the other inhabitants—the far wall from the head of the bed, not that anything was terribly far. There were no fireplaces in the room. The central hearth of the inn and a bedwarmer filled with hot coals were supposed to do for them, so he leaned against the peeling plaster walls and took in the room.

Ceramor was still bound, still tucked under the window, trussed like a turkey, wings and things pulled in tight. But the analogy ended there, because he was awake, despite the hefty dose of henbane Ruggerio had given him. And staring. His gaze was that of a predator. But not a raptor. No, the flared nostrils, the slight twitch of the forehead as though ears would be swiveling were he wearing a different shape, and the lips pulled back from the teeth gave him a more lupine look. And it wasn't Ruggerio on whom he was focused, but a spot between him and the door. Ceramor had become ankari by draining the lives from King Jannik's hunting hounds. Cats and dogs often focused on the unseen—some said they were sensitive to the anima, could see bright spirits or flares, and maybe that was what it was. Or maybe Ceramor was still out of it. Either way, he wasn't free and fighting, and for now that was all Ruggerio needed to know.

He focused on the bed, where Cia lay unconscious with Hostill beside her, staring with eyes too big and bright with unshed tears.

"Can you help her?" Hostill asked. "You must know some medicine. Something. Being a spymaster. I mean, you'd know poisons, so it stands to reason…"

And then it all went to hell. From the corner of his eye, Ruggerio saw Roha pull something from nes topknot and lunge for him. He pivoted, grabbed nes wrist and twisted, causing a gasp, bringing nim to the ground. Ceramor grunted through his gag and threw himself against the bed, knocking it hard and sending Hostill, who was off balance, ready to fly off the bed to Roha's aid, into a hard crash. Ruggerio released Roha to catch the boy and cushion his fall, to keep the sound from alerting anyone to check on them. It brought the boy up against his chest, no worse for wear, and brought all the action to a stop.

Roha couldn't move against him with the 'shield' of the boy. Ceramor's kick had done nothing more than topple him to the floor and knock the bed out of his own reach. Hostill was no worse for wear, already fighting to free himself from Ruggerio's grip as though he hadn't just been rescued from a good knock on the floor if not deathly harm.

"Now, can we get on with things?" Ruggerio asked Roha, pushing Hostill the rest of the way to his feet as though it was all his idea. "If I'd wanted to hurt you, I'd have finished Cia off in the street and done for you as well."

Then he approached the bed on the far side from Ceramor to check on the wounded woman.

"Why is *he* here?" Roha asked. "You didn't mention the ankari when you told us to come."

Was *that* what had set off the acolyte?

He didn't bother to answer. If Ceramor's actions and bindings didn't tell Roha they weren't on the same side, he didn't know what would, and he didn't like to waste breath. He kept on as he intended, going for the cloak wrapped tightly around Cia, and pulling it back carefully from her wounds. The blood was still seeping, which made the fabric sticky but supple. The first layer pulled away easily, but the last had become one with her flesh, sinking into the wound, but too porous to seal it.

When he pulled, a hiss escaped the near-dead woman's lips. He looked to assure himself that she hadn't just breathed her last, and found her eyes open and staring. Shining. Incandescent, even. But not with pain or fear or even focus on prayer for a smooth passing. No, they were bright with...calculation. It set him back, and for a moment he could have been staring into a mirror. Then the gaze shifted, and he followed it. To nothing. To that same nothingness that held Ceramor's attention.

"You have a spy," Cia said, and the voice was...wrong. Twisted, but not from pain.

"We know already that he's a spy," Roha said impatiently. "But we had no choice."

Cia laughed, but it was brief and ugly and ended on a ragged cough. Ruggerio watched for blood. If the knife had pierced a lung...but no blood came, and he was relieved to see it.

"Not him." Cia's hand twitched where it lay beside her on the bed, and while it didn't rise far, it hovered high enough for one finger to point where she was looking. Just where Ceramor's gaze was fixated. "There. The Ghost Girl. She has a message for you." There was another cough, and while the blood hadn't reached her lips, Ruggerio thought he could hear a wetness in it. And then the words hit him. *The Ghost Girl.*

"Dazia?" he asked, turning away from the woman on the bed, who he was no longer so sure was herself.

"You can't see her then? Or hear her? I..." There was a choked off pause, as though the pain of the body must finally have gotten through to whatever, whoever was riding the mind. Ruggerio thought he knew, though the how... it was horrifying to think. If this woman, this normal noblewoman, had been locked in a fight for her life with Mager Garif, it wasn't just conceivable that he'd found a way to continue the war after losing the battle, it was almost inevitable. "I'll make you a deal. I pass along her message, and afterwards, you finish the job. Kill off my bitch wife. She's nearly dead anyway. At this point, it would be a mercy. We all win."

"*Mager Garif?*" Roha gasped.

That incandescent gaze burned a hole right through Ruggerio, as though he could see Roha beyond, and Cia's lips spat such invective that it was amazing blood and bile didn't pour out with it. There was too much hate and too little sense for him to determine whether Garif's consciousness was reacting to Roha as a member of the Church or as one of the Nim or both, but neither was he concerned. He used the moment of everyone's distraction to reach for one of his hidden blades, in case... He wasn't yet certain what he would do. If Dazia had a message from Ulan, who was back at the palace with Bloody Bess, he needed to hear it, but killing Cia would lose him Hostill and Roha, he was certain of it, and he needed to begin building allies.

"Don't do it," Roha said.

Ruggerio stilled. "It's not for Cia," he lied. Or maybe he didn't. But first he had to explore all options. He moved around the bed, blade no longer hidden, but where Ceramor could see it. "Don't try anything," he told the ankari. "Don't drain Cia. Don't lash out. Don't do anything stupid or this is for you."

Ceramor's eyes shifted to the blade, and he snarled around his gag. Ruggerio bent, knees cracking loudly in the suddenly silent room, and pulled the cloth out of Ceramor's mouth. The beast-man snapped for his hand, but he pulled it back before he could catch it and waved the blade as a reminder.

"You see a ghost girl?" he asked the ankari.

"Smell her," Ceramor grunted, nose twitching. "Sense her. Know she's there."

"She?"

"Lavender. Topped with mustard and mint."

Ruggerio stuck the gag back in then, and Ceramor caught his fingers, hard enough for him to bite back a yelp, but not to break skin. Ceramor was useless, then, but for one thing. He'd confirmed that the ghost girl was Dazia. Ulan had kept dried lavender everywhere, used it to soothe, ground it into lotions, infused it into the compresses she'd applied to calm Dazia's fever. The mustard and mint had been part of the poultices spread across her frail chest to draw out the sickness raging through her. He'd been chased away by those very scents himself. Strange that they'd followed Dazia into death. And beyond.

Ruggerio turned back for the bed to check Cia's condition, but Roha was there ahead of him, bending over her. *Looming* was the word that came to mind.

He couldn't hear what Roha was saying over the woman, prayer or good-bye, because the mager was muttering as well, spending the body's strength on invective if not volume.

"You can't ease her way just yet," Ruggerio said, rising. "Her death must count for something."

Roha glared such that if ni was going to speed anyone to the anima, it was clear it would be him. "She will not die."

Ni kissed the woman suddenly on the forehead, nearly as fast as a viper's strike, and the invective cut off as though an arrow had shot it through. Cia's head lolled to the side, and the woman was unconscious. The lines of pain and fury raked into her face dashed away in an instant.

"What have you done?" Ruggerio asked, rushing the bed, but Roha vaulted the body to intercept him.

If Ceramor hadn't kicked the bed, there'd have been no room for the two of them between it and the wall. Even as it was now, there was just space to lock them together, his blade at nes throat, nes hand gripping his balls so tightly there were tears in his eyes.

"There's another way," Roha said, staring into his eyes.

He could see it for truth. Roha's truth, anyway. And what choice did he have? Lunge for the bed and pray that his manhood wasn't ripped off in the attempt? Slap Cia, pray she survived the rude awakening and that it was the murderous husband and not the murderous wife who came back to consciousness? And that the mager could be trusted to convey Dazia's message accurately?

"What other way?" he asked.

"I'll show you."

He stashed his blade. He could draw it again in an instant if necessary.

Hostill watched them both. He'd scuttled into the farthest corner and curled almost to a ball, knees to his chest and hugging them with his arms. Binding himself as tightly as Ruggerio had bound Ceramor. He looked young and vulnerable.

Roha walked back toward the door to retrieve the satchel ni'd brought, and Hostill's eyes followed without moving his head. He wasn't going to miss anything.

Neither was Ruggerio. The last thing he wanted was the boy bolting for that door.

Roha brought the bag back toward the spot on the far wall where Ceramor and Cia had been staring and peeled the flap covering it to reveal the corner of a book, bound, it appeared, in tooled leather. Ruggerio would know more of that book, but that could wait. For now, he watched as Roha squatted near the wall at what ni must have guessed to be child height.

"I'm Roha," ni said. "I know that you want to talk to us—some of us, anyway—and I have a way you might do that. If you'll reach out and put your hand on this book, you may find a little boost of power that will allow us to see and hear you. We won't hurt you, I promise. I don't even think we could if we wanted to."

"Well, *that's* reassuring," Hostill mumbled.

Ruggerio focused on that spot between the wall and the book, not moving lest he frighten her—the ghost girl—his niece. He realized he was holding his breath when he found he had to let it out to take in air again. He believed in the abstract. He had to. She'd successfully spied for him, listened in on other bosewights for information. He'd heard the results. But to actually see the dead returned...

To see little Dazia... Ulan had always thought him cold, and she wasn't wrong. He'd never known what to do with a child. Never dandled Dazia on his knee. But he had brought her sweets, had played ogre for her a time or two. Lighting up her face somehow lightened his heart. And she'd been the image of her mother at that age, not so long after they'd first come to the heart of Jucar.

There was a glow. Just a glow at first, so faint he wondered whether he constructed it from the light shining through the high shuttered window, and then there was no mistaking the shape of a girl. The features formed, faint and faded, as though moonlight clung to her, cold and silver rather than warm and gold. But they were hers—Dazia's. Eyes large for her face, chin pointed, curls irrepressible. The only color was her eyes, which seemed to gain a little more of the light, turning them the indescribable purple of twilight.

Dazia turned them on Ruggerio now, and while he hadn't had much use for hugs or displays of affection while she'd been alive, he suddenly wanted to open his arms to her, wrap them around her, hold her to him and breathe in that lavender scent, even if it meant the mustard poultice came with it.

"Uncle," she said, her voice like winter wind gusting through a drafty window, "you have to help Maman!" She looked to the woman on the bed and back to him. "The horrible princess sent me to deliver a message to the lady—join her, and she'll give her life back. She's building an army of lady mageri and wants this woman to be her right hand. If not, she'll kill Maman."

She pulled her hand from the book to reach for Ruggerio and instantly started to fade, so dropped it back again.

Ruggerio took two steps toward Dazia to make it easier, and reached out so that she could put her free hand on his. It was so cold, like the water of a mountain stream that immediately stole all feeling upon stepping in. Even so, his blood boiled. How could Bloody Bess have been planning this without his knowledge? And to come for Cia so soon – how could she know that Garif had taken up residence in her body, when they'd only just learned of it? Unless she thought that Cia herself must be a mageri-in-hiding to have defeated one so powerful?

"But Uncle, I don't believe her," Dazia went on, "I think she'll kill Maman anyway. Or hold her hostage for me to spy for her, and make Maman her slave. She has...she's *eaten* others like me. I don't know how to say it, but *their shadows are part of her.* Like with this lady." She gestured toward the bed and looked up at Ruggerio with pleading eyes. Then her gaze slipped past him, and her already impossibly large eyes widened. She took a step back, and almost lost contact with the book again. Roha shifted forward to keep it in reach. "And this man..."

Luminescent tears glistened in the corners of her eyes. If he had a heart, it might be breaking. "Uncle, there are shadows everywhere." The first tear fell. "They're horrible. So much suffering. You have to stop it. Stop her."

"The Blood Princess?" he asked, to be certain, because she'd just said that the princess would kill her mother if the woman on the bed didn't do what she wanted.

She nodded. "You have to. She won't stop, and... She's going to use Maman, use me, to do horrible things. You can't let her. But you have to make her believe you will."

From the mouths of babes.

"I'm very, very good at that," Ruggerio said.

The second tear fell.

"What should I tell her?" Dazia asked, making a move as though she would wring her hands, but stopping herself in time.

"Stay while we plan. For now, it's best to say you haven't found Cia. If you report back that she's been badly hurt and can't come to her yet, Bloody Bess will send healers. We'll—"

Suddenly, Roha swayed, barely catching nimself.

"Are you okay?" Ruggerio asked.

Roha looked at him, irritated. "Fine," ni snapped. "I should have put myself in a better position if this was going to go on, is all. We should probably wrap this up."

Ni looked about five years older than when the conversation had started, and as though it wasn't the muscles in nes legs, but nes entire strength that was about to give out.

Roha was part of the Rebellion, part of the Church. It *couldn't* have been a spell rather than a prayer that ni'd whispered over Cia. It couldn't be anything but the book—a relic stolen from the Church?—that was strengthening Dazia now. But maybe the book drew the power it was feeding Dazia from the closest living being, the person holding the relic. Maybe that was why Roha hadn't just laid it down, but stayed in that awkward position.

Dazia glanced up into Roha's face, saw what Ruggerio saw from his side view and gasped. She dropped her hand away, and Roha, suddenly released, fell backwards. It was a controlled fall, but ni didn't get up again. Roha came to rest against the foot of the bed, eyes closed, head sagging chin to chest, travel sack clutched like a security blanket. Ruggerio had a feeling that if he tried to pry it away, Roha would come up fighting, even as exhausted as ni was. And so he left it. For now.

He had a lot already on his plate. Because if Bloody Bess wanted Cia alive, then so did he.

Lifesaving was becoming a bit of his thing. It sat oddly upon him.

CHAPTER TWENTY-SIX

Cia

Garif surrounded Cia like a huge Malacostra, a segmented battlefield construct like a cross between a spindle crab and a scorpion, the stuff of nightmares. Its legs caged her in, and she cowered, hoping that if she made herself tiny enough, central enough, neither the front pincers nor the back stinger could tear her apart or shoot her through with venom. She curled tighter and tighter until she compressed like sheets of dough that could no longer be separated from each other.*

Then came the piercing, stabbing pain, not from behind, as expected, but from before and below, from just under her heart, up and in, pinning her like a pike. Now she would never get free. The Malacostra had won. At least she wouldn't be conscious for the feasting.

She was aware at first only of the pain, a sharp savaging of the chest that threatened to rip her apart. It radiated outward from there until her entire upper body was aflame, and she was lost in the haze. Eventually, voices penetrated. She let them swirl, meaningless until they weren't.

But she worried they were a trick to draw her fully back to consciousness, so that Garif could revel in her pain, his victory.

"I've done what I can," a man said.

"And what is that, exactly?" *Roha.* That voice was almost worth surfacing for, but Garif would know that if he was in her head. Would punish her for it. Roha hadn't left her when they were running from the Crownsmen. Had taken her hand and pulled her along. Was she that starved for any act of kindness that she would apply so much significance to it? "I don't trust you as far as I can throw you."

"I've cleaned her wound, and I've packed it. All wounds can be dangerous, if infected, but as far as I can tell, this one is not profound enough to put her near death or to sink her so deeply into herself. *That* is something else entirely. Possibly shock. Possibly fighting on two fronts, the pain and the man she murdered." It was that man again, his voice familiar. She could almost bring to mind his face, but only almost.

"Is there something you can give her for the pain?" Roha's face she imagined vividly. As it was in the church right before the acolyte sent that blast at the ankari who'd burst in on them through the stained glass window.

And *that* brought her several levels closer to consciousness. The blast had come from *Roha*. She was sure of it now. If only she didn't leave the knowledge behind when she crossed the veil back to where she could communicate it.

"I can't give her anything until I know what you did to make her sleep. I don't know if it's safe."

"I did nothing. I said a *spiritu,* a special prayer for the spirit, an appeal to the anima to restore balance. That is all."

"I have heard that the *Nim* have a special relationship to the anima."

"I claim nothing special for myself but what the Church has taught me and nature has granted me," Roha said.

Cia snorted, but it was all in her head, apparently, because the conversation went on uninterrupted.

"False modesty," the man said for her, and she could visualize him now, hair as dark as a shadow, features sharp as knives. The Spymaster. The Crown's Blade. Was it he who had bitten her with his dagger? If so, she was lucky to be alive. But why?

"Let's talk about you and the Church, since it looms so large. If you truly claim nothing but what the Church has given you, then why are you tied to the Restoration? You claim not to trust me as far as you can throw me, but how far is that? Already, you have stood between me and what you perceive as my only exit. You've fought me hand to hand, and yet here you avert your gaze and claim to be only an acolyte. You are not. You can dispense with that fiction. It won't play. I knew you for more even before today. I'd have been a piss poor spy otherwise."

There was a growl, and Cia realized that Roha and Ruggerio weren't alone in the room, but who...

"And you, boy, what do you bring to the table? If we're going up against Bloody Bess, I need to know what my assets are."

Boy? Could it be...Hostill? But she'd thought him imprisoned.

Cia swam closer to the surface. She was just about there, but all around her was darkness and pain, and the closer she got, the more crippling...

"I have a name," he said.

"And where will that get us? Should I list that among our advantages? One boy with a name, a treacherous ankari, an acolyte who swears to be nothing special, a murderess with a death wish, a magical book, and a spymaster about to leave you all to it because no one will answer his perfectly reasonable questions?"

She was getting dangerously close to the surface now. Their argument had distracted from the agony continuously shooting through her as though her mind wanted to make up for the memory she'd missed of the knife going in, and so kept replaying it. But the more alert she became, the greater the pain and the harder to ignore.

She tried to focus back on the argument around her.

"What about you?" Roha spat at Ruggerio. "Why should we trust you with our secrets. Why should we list *you* among *our* assets? You left your power at the palace gates. Since we're listing things out, it seems all you have is this beautiful bolt hole, a traitorous ankari, and a price on your head. Given your lack of personal charm, I doubt that you've developed a vast and loyal network outside of those you paid to work for you, so I'm guessing that you're well and truly on your own. What do *you* bring to the table?"

Cia hadn't registered the talk of an ankari the first time it came up, but now she gasped, and all talk in the room stopped.

Then three faces peered at her from varying heights, one hungry, two hopeful.

"You're alive," Hostill said with wonder. She drank him in. If she'd been able to move without torment and thought he'd allow it, she'd have grabbed him to her to prove to herself he was real.

"*You're* alive, more to the point," she said, but talking hurt, and she vowed not to do more than she had to. "How?"

Hostill shrugged at the other man in combined explanation and bafflement. Her lips quirked in amusement. She'd found the one motion that didn't cause her pain.

"Heard something about a tonic for this pain," Cia said, meeting Ruggerio's avid gaze.

"I don't think you want the kind of relief I can administer," he said, and she shivered.

Hostill knocked into him the way kids will with each other, as though he wasn't large and terrifying. "Here, that's enough. You're a spymaster, right? Which means you're capable of putting on an act. You can at least pretend to be human."

Ruggerio bristled. "I thought you preferred that I drop my act."

"With me. Not with the ladies."

The surprise chivalry startled a laugh out of Cia that choked off on a sharp spasm like a blade through her belly and ended with her gasping for breath. As soon as she caught it, she rolled her gaze to Roha to see how ni'd taken Hostill's words. It was sweet, though misplaced, that after all she'd been through in her life Hostill felt that he had to protect her, but to misidentify Roha... She wondered if Roha got that all nes life. Ni's not like *me*, so ni must be *the other*. But Hostill knew Roha. Did he struggle under such a deeply ingrained idea of either/or that it came out when he wasn't thinking. Did it mean that much to all of them, deciding whether someone was *like me* or not? Needing to label someone to decide where they fit?

But she already knew the answer. As a woman, society didn't allow her the same space as a man. In turn, a scullery maid wasn't the same as a handmaiden, who wasn't the same as a dutchess. A princess was not a queen. Neither would ever be a king.

Roha's face gave away nothing. Was ni ever-ready with shielding in place?

Cia wasn't going to ask. Not in front of the others. Maybe not at all. If Roha had secrets, who had earned the right to them? Certainly not Cia, who literally didn't know her own mind, not with Garif living in it. What she knew he knew, which was a horrifying thought.

"Wait!" she said frantically, and all three looming over her looked concerned. "You said..." Pain ripped through her again and momentarily stopped her breath. She had to swallow it down, along with some blood that had gotten caught where she needed to breathe. "I heard...you need me to go to Bloody Bess."

Ruggerio nodded. Hostill shook his head. Roha remained neutral. "I'll go, but you have to make the plans without me. None of us can trust what's in my head."

Roha turned on Ruggerio. "But why does Bloody Bess want Cia? Does she know about Garif possessing her? Can he—" the horror in Roha's voice gave Cia some idea of what ni was going to say before ni said it "— still wield power from in there?"

"Maybe she believes Cia has hidden powers to have defeated him in the first place," Hostill said.

But it was Ruggerio's face Roha was watching, not as though she trusted whatever might pass his lips, but as though she might see something there that would lead her to the truth.

"I don't know what she believes," he answered. "Only what she wants, and that is to be Queen. Princess isn't enough for her. She doesn't want a Regent. Or a council that can bicker and decide. She doesn't want votes or justifications. She doesn't want challenges. She wants absolute power. I'm now convinced that she will do anything it takes to get it and will kill anyone in her way. And that this is bad for Jucar."

Cia wanted to ask how this was different from her brothers, but they were dead, and it no longer mattered. Ruggerio seemed to be using *bad* as in *the wrong way to go about things* rather *than the enemy of all that is good*. She didn't think anyone who had so faithfully served the Jucari crown was suddenly going to undergo a crisis of conscience.

"Well, whether she wants Cia or Garif, we can't know who will come out on top," Roha said.

It hurt because it was true.

They all looked at Cia, and the pain that ripped through her this time was nearly her undoing. Her chest pierced with pain, as though she was being stabbed over and over again. A cough started in her lower chest, and bursting forth, ripped something loose with it. She could feel it, a chunk of something coming up, clogging and choking and propelling her upright in bed. Hands reached out to support her, pound her back, but her vision went red-black with blood. She retched up a chunk of something ripped from inside her, wheezed in air that cut like knives. Weak and deflated, she fell back against hands that lowered her to the bed, consciousness going the way of her vision.

Roha

Roha gasped at the raw, bloody chunk of flesh that landed on nes once-white blanket, red racing along the fibers as though they were veins. Cia collapsed into deadweight, and Roha tore nes gaze from the blood to make sure Cia's chest still rose and fell.

"Everybody out," ni ordered.

Three sets of eyes stared as though Roha'd suggested they call down the moon.

"Out!" ni said. "I need the book, and it's sacred to the Church. You've already seen more than you should."

"Then perhaps you should never have removed it from the sanctum," Ruggerio said.

"And yet, I did, and I think we're all glad of it."

"Where would you suggest we go? And how do we take Ceramor without raising a ruckus?"

"Fine, turn him toward the wall and take the boy. Do what you have to do. But do it fast."

Ruggerio's eyes blazed. He was clearly used to issuing orders, not taking them. Yet he understood expediency, and Roha'd left no room in nes tone for argument. No doubt he'd try to listen or look in, but the door was solid wood with only a peephole ni could easily block.

Roha caught Hostill's look of betrayal that ni would send him away, but ni didn't respond to it. Ruggerio took two great strides toward Ceramor and swung him ungently around like a naughty child put into the corner to consider his actions, strode back toward the door and grabbed Hostill under his arm on the way, somewhere between an avuncular hug and a horse-collaring. He closed the door behind them, but as expected, Roha didn't hear their footsteps recede.

Roha made a show of pulling the book from nes satchel, and then positioned nimself between the peephole and the bed, leaning with it over Cia.

Ni was still exhausted from nes earlier working. This would all be easier if Roha had been trained in the use of nes power, but ni hadn't. Not by nes parents, who'd never even told Roha what it meant to be Nim. Certainly not by the Church, where the only training ni'd received was in how to use nimself up protecting the Church and its lands from future King Calestris, creating and setting wards, after which ni needed to fit nimself into the regular workings of the Church. Become only what it was convenient that ni should be.

Ni didn't remember much about nes parents—the cardamom scent of nes mother when she'd cradle Roha close, the basso rumble of nes father's voice that ni could feel vibrating against nes breastbone when he spoke. That ni heard crashing against nes head that fateful night that shook apart nes foundations.

"They know, Lyra. We can't keep the babe any longer."

Ni was always 'the babe,' even though ni hadn't been so for some time.

"Then we'll go to Markens, to my people. Roha will be accepted there. Trained. Even revered. We've talked about this. We knew we couldn't keep the secret forever—"

"You've talked about it." This time when the timbre of her father's voice set up a vibration, it was at a different frequency. "My business is here. The one that supports us. Our lives are here."

"Our lives? Is Roha not our life? If our child is not here, then my life is nothing."

"So I am nothing?"

"You're saying that what I want is baktru," *she spat. "My people, my country, our child is nothing. Only your livelihood, your place in the world."*

They had put Roha out—told nim to go and play, but ni had only swung around the back of their house so that no one could see, and mashed nes ear up against the garden door. Ma and Da were at the back of the house as well so that no one would hear their raised voices. But Roha heard them just fine. Tears didn't hurt Roha's hearing. They only blurred nes vision.

They wanted to send nim away? What had ni done?

Well, Da wanted to send nim away. And they lived in his house, in his land, where people spoke his language and looked at nes mother as though they were good to treat her with the respect they did. It was a small thing, but something Roha noticed—that people acted differently toward nes father than nes mother. Da they treated like everyone else—hailing, laughing, chatting. Ma they watched, and when they dealt with her, they waited, as though looking for thanks at their graciousness.

"Roha will be revered here," he said. As if that was the last word. "The Church honors the Nim. They will make a place. What kind of life will the child have with us? Never a family, never finding acceptance. In the village, there will be prejudice, bullying. Already people shy away. Roha needs a place to belong, to be useful."

"Yes, that's what every child needs—not to be loved, but to be useful."

"It's the best thing for the child."

Roha didn't hear what nes mother said, possibly because she'd turned away. Ni heard footsteps moving away, and then heard nes mother bang out of the front door. She called nes name, but Roha didn't want to be found. Ni went to an overgrown part of the garden, curled into a ball and tried to find that deep, quiet place within nimself.

And so, ni went to the Church. Ni never hugged her father again. Ni held on to nes mother, who held nim back, their tears mingling until they were both sodden and salted, but in the end, Roha's mother gave nim up as well. She elicited a promise from the churchmen who came to take good care of Roha. That they wouldn't try to make Roha other than ni was. That Ma would be able to visit.

The churchman agreed that she could, but only after a year, and that they had to understand that Roha was no longer theirs. Ni belonged to the Church now.

Belonged. Like a possession. Something that could be given or received. Bartered or bought.

Nes mother was dead inside of a year, so said the one letter ni ever received from nes father. In lieu of a visit that never came.

Ni really did belong to the Church then, until ni came to realize that there was no true belonging.

Not until ni found Lehren Gelerte's treatises hidden away. Here at last was someone who understood. And where there was one, there must be others.

Roha held the Gospel of Gelerte as a talisman as ni worked over Cia, drawing from nes own well of anima. As tired as ni was, Roha's head swam and nes muscles shook as though ni swam through a strong current physically rather than spiritually, magically. Roha pushed some of nes energy across and into Cia.

Roha couldn't do as much as ni'd like. Ni wasn't trained in healing. All ni could really do was shore up Cia's strength, give her the ability to hang on a bit longer while the body did what it needed to do naturally. Instinctively, ni reached out to trigger a few reactions, starting the body knitting itself, but nes power was limited, especially with what ni'd done already. Roha pulled back before collapsing entirely.

As ni fell away, Roha felt Ceramor's stare like a physical thing and raised nes head one last time before allowing it to drop to the bed. Ceramor had wriggled and twisted until he had turned sufficiently to watch, and while he couldn't speak around his gag, his eyes said it all. *He knew.* He'd seen what ni was about.

Like it or not, they now shared a secret, and Roha was going to have to find out what he wanted for it.

Then Roha did collapse onto the bed, half on top of Cia, hoping that nes efforts had been enough, because ni had given everything ni had.

CHAPTER TWENTY-SEVEN

Bess

Princess Bessory V'Alban thought that she would very soon go mad. They had tried to close her out of the Council yet again, something she normally allowed, with no patience at all for their bickering, knowing that she could influence the decisions and discussions through Strego and hear all about it afterward, but today was crucial. Her plans were finally moving forward, and there could be no errors. No cracks in Strego's foundation.

Yet he was looking decidedly gray and still not fully himself as he stood before the lords designated by their dukes to represent them.

"So, we're to understand that on *your* watch, one of our principal mageri has been murdered, and his killer still not captured, even though we had her on palace grounds. We've lost the ankari sent to collect her, who partially collapsed All Souls on the hunt, putting us further at odds with the Church, and we now have the Hound loose in our city. And our spymaster has defected with all of our secrets. Is that right?" asked Lord Ruland, his overgrown eyebrows raised entirely into his out-of-control hairline so that they met in a bramble. No matter the overblown tailoring of his clothes, he always reminded her of an owl or some other bird who wore his nest upon his head and went around mantling and calling out

"Who?" as in "Who is responsible?" or "Who will take care of this problem?" Always questions and never answers.

"My watch?" Strego asked. "Am I to understand that you are abdicating all responsibility? If there is no help to be found here, then pray, let me be about my business. I do not have time to waste on those who lay no claim to it."

Lord Ruland sputtered, and another man wearing a skullcap over a perfectly clean shaven head—Lord Cristanus, talked right over it. "Now, now, don't be ridiculous. Lord Ruland is just expressing the frustration we're all feeling. These are strange, unsettled times, and we can't afford further unsettling. We have to get things under control, and the more productive discussion is *how we get there* not *who do we blame."*

Well said, Bess thought. She'd have to keep an eye on him. This sort of political savvy could be very helpful, provided it wasn't combined with too much ambition. She'd never seen Cristanus in anything but robes of the utmost black, relieved only with a sash, insignia or trim in the purple that represented his duchy. With his skullcaps always coming to a point between his brows, reminiscent of a beak, and his tendency to perch rather than settle into his chair, she thought of Cristanus as the raven.

"But sometimes," Lord Ruland reinserted himself, "we *need* to know where to root out the rot."

Princess Bessory stood, using some of the power she had stored to turn all heads her way. Let them begin to feel her presence, her power. Let them begin to tremble before her, even if they didn't yet understand why. "Are you suggesting that *The Crown* is at fault here?" she asked, quietly.

They had to lean in to hear her, but they could not mistake the danger in her voice. Their lords would not have sent fools.

She felt the shadows within her shift and bristle in discomfort. She watched the same ripple all around the table as her councilors shifted, and she took note. Some eased away from Ruland, as though distancing themselves from whatever was about to fall on his head. Others leaned forward in their seats, eager to see. Cristanus just sat all the straighter, gaze darting between her and Strego, as though starting to grasp where the real power shift was taking place. He definitely bore watching.

Lord Ruland opened his mouth again, and she nearly roared when the knock at the door interrupted what he'd been about to say, because she really, dearly would have loved to hear it.

"Come," she and Strego barked at the same time, and she had to tamp down on the glare that she wanted to shoot him, but Cristanus noticed;

she caught the sly brightness in his eyes. She let him have her glare instead, so it didn't go to waste.

The guards at the door opened it to one of their sergeants she knew not by name but by insignia, and he strode directly to Strego. He whispered in his ear as Bess stood and seethed, but he hadn't said much before Strego pulled back and directed him, "For the gathering, if you please."

If the sergeant was startled, he didn't let it show, but rose to his full height, straightened his tunic, which had gotten out of sorts from bending, and cleared his throat before giving his report like it was a proclamation, "We have found the murderess, and, as you've commanded, we've brought those who have turned her in to you for questioning."

Strego himself rose, pushing his chair back with a sound that gave the shadows in her head hard edges that dug in like daggers. She closed her eyes and breathed through the pain and sudden urge to kill the cause. Strego's time had not yet come.

Her eyes snapped open again as Strego addressed the lords, "You'll have to excuse me, my Lords. Since some among you feel that there are wrongs I must right, I will be about it, swiftly and decisively, as I'm sure you'd prefer. I will leave you to argue the rest amongst yourselves, and we can pick this up again when I have the information gleaned from our interrogation."

"I would prefer to be present for whatever is revealed," Lord Ruland said.

Princess Bessory stood corrected—some Dukes were perfectly willing to send fools. Perhaps they hoped that they would advocate for their duchy so annoyingly that others would give in simply to shut them up. Or even that they would be such a thorn in the royal backside that the Crown would rid them of their unwanted lords.

"As would I," said another. Lord Sorvain. He came from Morvais, one of the oldest and most respected duchies, closest to their northern border with Frizenze. Now *he* made her think of a peregrine falcon, fast and deadly. You'd never see him coming, but all of a sudden, he'd swoop in and latch onto his prey.

"Yes, I'm sure you would," Strego responded, moving with the guard toward the door. She knew that even without her prodding him with her power, Strego was a strong advocate for the Crown, else he'd never have been chosen Regent by the Council. But it was rare that she saw him in action or as anything but her pawn. She had a momentary twinge about what she'd done to him and what she planned to do, but it was *her* power after all. Her power that he held in trust with no intention of returning it, just of passing it on to the next man in line. And the next. And the next.

Unless she grasped it for herself. Thus, she ignored the protests that rose loudly and stridently behind her that interrogations were no place for a woman, that if she was to be allowed, they should be too.

"Where are they?" Strego asked the sergeant.

"I've brought them to your quarters, Regent," he responded. "They flagged down one of my men and turned the murderess in willingly. I hope I did the right thing."

"The woman, where have you put her?" Princess Bessory cut in.

"The...woman?" the sergeant asked. "You mean the murderess? She's in the dungeon, though I don't know that she'll make it to the gallows. Someone patched her up, but then left her for dead, by all accounts."

"That won't do," Princess Bessory said, rubbing at the hollow above her eyes and between her brows. "She needs to be in the North Tower with the other mageri women. But isolated, a room of her own. Send Erdain to her, and my own personal physic. With an entire guard contingent. She's not to be trusted. But she is to be healed."

"Princess?" he asked, but he looked to Strego for the actual approval of the orders.

"You will look to me," she snapped.

The sergeant only gave her a sidelong glance before returning his attention to Strego. She whirled, her shadows fluttering, and grabbed the sergeant, her sharpened nail sliding straight into his wrist with no resistance. His eyes widened and he tried to pull back, his strength nearly breaking him free before she clamped down with her will. Then he froze, quivering, as did Strego beside her when she flexed her will. "Is that understood?" she asked.

She was so angry that it was an effort to hold her will to an infection rather than an infestation, to an inchworm incision rather than a slither of serpents. She wanted him to know her power. She wanted them *all* to know her power. To be her creatures. But it was not yet the time, and he was not the place to start.

"Yes, my Queen."

She released him with a smile that left him dazed. Or maybe it was the power she'd tapped into through his blood, empowering her will and depleting his. Though potentially more had transferred than she'd intended, like her vision of herself as Queen. She wasn't too concerned. They would all see it soon enough, and the sound of her true title on his tongue heated her blood, warmed her all through the chill halls as the sergeant led the way to Strego's antechamber.

There, two guards awaited in house red and gold watching over two peasants who could best be described as...peasants. Their faces were deathly pale, possibly in fear at being called before their Queen...or, for as far as they knew, their *Princess* and her Regent. Their hands, oddly, were slightly darker, as were their clothes. Their hair was pale and strawlike. The woman's overdress had dust or perhaps flour in a plume across the front. The man's had a wet spot from anxiety or ale—she had no intention of discovering. Nor did she have the chance before both man and woman dropped to their knees at the sight of their sovereign.

As it should be.

"You discovered the murderess?" Strego asked as the door closed behind them.

The man looked up, but only as far as Strego's knees, and the woman seemed very intent on the inlaid floors. The guards hadn't brought them in even as far as the rug that eased the winter chill, and so their position couldn't be one of any comfort.

"We did, Regent, though not through any efforts of our own. One of our patrons had only paid for a night, and when another came and went, and he'd neither paid for another nor appeared to vacate his room, we went to collect our fee. You can imagine our surprise when instead of the man and his nephew, we found an unconscious woman! And then my lady wife realized that she bore a resemblance to the woman on the proclamations about town, and we hailed your guards."

"Looking for a reward?" Strego asked neutrally.

"Looking to get a murderess out of our establishment and our room back to let!" His voice trembled with indignation, but his gaze went right back to the ground. "By your leave," he added, much more humbly.

"How did this man and his—nephew, you say—" something tingled at the back of Bess's brain. Not a man and his nephew, but a man and a boy, traveling together... "come upon this woman?"

"We didn't even know that they had. It was quite a shock to us!" the man said.

"Can you describe them?" Bess cut in, before Strego could ask any other questions. "The man and his nephew. What did they look like? Did you know them?"

The woman glanced up, just for an instant, and caught Bess looking at her. She snapped her gaze back to the floor, but that was enough. When her husband started to answer, Bess stopped him. "Not you. I want to hear it from her."

The woman raised her gaze again, but only to Bess's slippers.

"You have my permission to look at me," she said. "I want to see the truth in your eyes. And you can stand, both of you. You came of your own will. It's all very gratifying to have you grovel, but it's not very conducive to questioning. Get up before my neck bends like a swan's."

The woman flashed her a look of thanks before the pain of movement caused her to grimace instead. The man immediately put a hand to his wife's elbow to help her up, and her gratitude changed focus. Then they were standing before Strego and Bess, the guards behind, between them and the door, the sergeant on the other side of Bess like the protection she didn't need.

Neither husband nor wife would quite look at their Princess, but as she'd ordered it, neither would quite look away. The woman settled her gaze on Bess's cheek and would look no higher.

"Now, tell me your names, the name of your inn, and everything you know about these men."

She did, and the descriptions fit Ruggerio and the boy from the dungeon, the boy she suspected now to be her nephew, her rival. Or at least, the boy she'd have to dispense with to eliminate any doubt. How had they met up with Cia, and why had they left her behind? Had Ruggerio been the one to stab her? It didn't make sense. Ruggerio wasn't in the habit of leaving his victims alive. Or patching them up after running them through.

If he'd allowed Cia to fall into Bess's hands, he had to be playing a deeper game. Bess would have to play it better.

Ruggerio

"We can't bring you, and you can't bring *him*," Roha said in no uncertain terms.

"Yeah," Hostill said, his nose wrinkling, "he smells like the shitter."

Ruggerio, carrying the bound man over his shoulders like a sack of potatoes through the back streets of the city, couldn't disagree. He was going to have to burn Ceramor's clothes. Burn both of their clothes. Breathe fire to burn out his sense of smell. It still might not be enough. He wasn't just filthy. The clothes and soot, blood and…other items staining his clothes said that Ceramor had been through more than they could imagine.

"I could dump him somewhere. The Church was ready enough to do it." He might not even wake. Ruggerio had given him another knockout dose so that he could carry the man without him snapping and snarling and trying to escape, but that didn't make his burden much more pleasant.

"He's too dangerous. *You're* too dangerous. The Restoration would never trust you," Roha said to Ruggerio

"They'll have to trust me sometime, if they want the information I have."

"Maybe. Once we prepare the way," Roha said. "Get Ceramor cleaned up and let us know where we can find you. We'll send word."

Ruggerio glanced sidelong at Hostill to see what he thought of Roha's promise. He believed nes word. Or seemed to. That didn't mean Ruggerio could trust it.

They were at a literal crossroads, a broad thoroughfare that most months out of the year would be a marketplace, but with the blustery winds of winter, everything was shuttered and deserted. No one set out blankets or stalls. There were no beggars or buskers. There were store-fronts, but with no new shipments, their stock was denuded, and it would take desperation to venture out. Visits were probably by appointment only. He had no cause to know.

His closest bolt hole was not far. He might make for it, if he weren't carrying a smelly, heavy, feral ankari he'd just as soon knife and leave for dead, but he had a sense for assets, and for some reason that defied logic, he felt that Ceramor would yet prove to be one. Something about finding him asleep at Hostill's feet… The Hound had been Jannik's man. Maybe he sensed that the boy was Jannik's son. Maybe he had some remaining loyalty that could be exploited.

And maybe it didn't matter right now, because if Ceramor suddenly disappeared or turned up dead, neither the boy nor the acolyte would ever trust Ruggerio, and his rift with the Crown would all be for naught.

So he told them about the bathhouse and breathed through his mouth as he carried Ceramor off. He was both sweating and shivering by the time he arrived, his teeth chattering so hard he thought they would shat-ter. The bathhouse would have turned him away at the door if he hadn't had the right amount of money and the right passcode for the secret rooms he knew existed for the things that were not supposed to go on. He was shown to a room, told the attendant what he wanted, slipping him an extra coin not to be curious, and then dropped his burden to the floor and dropped with him, suddenly shaking beyond control, so cold he thought he might never be warm, despite the roaring fire.

He forced himself to rise when the attendant knocked. He'd requested only a hip bath, not wanting to soak Ceramor in his own filth, but also accepted linens, oils, and a strigil before the attendant bowed his way out.

Then Ruggerio was left with the dangerous and demeaning task of untying Ceramor enough to bathe away blood and released bowels. If he believed in purifying himself for his eventual reunion with the anima, surely this would count toward his redemption. He could hardly think of anything more humbling.

He kicked the ankari to be sure he was still out. The body rocked away and back, settling like a stone. Like deadweight.

If his eyes were open, Ruggerio would know whether or not that was wishful thinking. If he'd died en route, it was none of Ruggerio's doing. He could not be held accountable, but... He dropped down beside the body, despite the stench, and watched closely for the rise and fall of Ceramor's chest. Listened for the breath. It took longer than it should have to come, and then was so faint. So shallow. He was surprised by his own relief. Had he given the ankari too much? Perhaps it *would* have been his fault if he'd died, and maybe that was the reason behind his relief, but whatever it was, there was life there still, and so no cause for alarm, as long as he kept the man on this side of the veil.

His lip barely curled as he shucked the man's clothes. They came only reluctantly. Some of his wounds had continued to ooze. Some of his... effusions...seemed to be more recent. His shirt and pants were half-clotted to him. If Ruggerio had not before seen men wearing their insides externally or trying to hold them in as they fought him to the death, he might have had difficulty finishing his task. But he separated himself from the work, treating the body like a carcass, trying to figure out where to make the first cut...or swipe.

The strigil is not a blade. The strigil is not a blade, he repeated over and over to himself. Although, he *had* used it as such. Once. Not the easiest thing to slip between a man's ribs, but not impossible.

It was a curved piece of metal, meant for scraping off accumulated dirt and sweat and excess oils from the skin. It would work just as well for blood and feces.

And so he began. It was surprisingly soothing work. He destroyed the first of the linens using the water from the hip bath to remove the worst of the gore from the body, but after the initial rough swipes, he had to go more carefully, clean and clear for a better view of the body and the abuse it had suffered. It was more difficult than it should have been. Ceramor's skin in places was nearly the color of old blood—purple-black—and in others the almost indescribable yellow-green of healing bruises and pus, cut through with trauma. From blades? From glass shards from the church? He couldn't yet see. There was a horrible protrusion from his chest, as though one of his ribs was trying to escape past his heart, and one of his legs was half-crushed, as though someone had put it into a press.

How had he ever made it to the boy? It was clear he hadn't intended him any harm. Had he lain down to die, and then Ruggerio had bound him up? No wonder he'd snapped. Ruggerio felt something resembling regret at the thought. The least he could have done was let the man die in peace.

The real mystery was that he hadn't healed himself somewhere along the way to Hostill or once they brought in Cia with all of her lovely wounds. Wounded and embattled, Ceramor could have stolen her life force. Cia could have died before their very eyes and they would have attributed it to the damage Ruggerio had inflicted. The others would have turned on *him*. Or possibly blamed the husband who rode her even after death. They'd never even have suspected the ankari.

So why hadn't he tapped into Cia to heal himself?

The question repeated itself as Ruggerio studied the protruding rib. He'd have to put it back into place, and carefully. Gently was out of the question. Pressure had to be applied, but judiciously or the rib would slip and puncture a lung. If it hadn't already. Ruggerio would never get his answers if he allowed the man to die.

If Ceramor was so loyal to his former king's son, how loyal might he be to the man who saved him? A mageri, even an insane one, would be an extremely useful ally to have in the fight ahead. He needed to start gathering allies. As Roha had been so quick to point out, he wasn't a man who made friends, only maintained networks. It would be much more lucrative and conducive to long lives for the people in those networks to work against him now. He did not have the wealth to outbid the Crown. And no one was going to work for him on the basis of his non-existent charm or because their mythical hearts were in the right places.

He was half atop Ceramor, two hands on his displaced rib, half his body weight risen up, ready to crash down *just so* when the man's eyes popped open, staring straight into his. Their only color a glowing gold rim around the edges. Otherwise, the blackness at their center had taken over completely.

"They're here," he said, voice nothing but a wheeze.

Ruggerio's nature was to finish something once he started, and he didn't know what to do but to rise and fall, as he'd intended. He did so, and heard the rib snap into place.

Ceramor's outgoing breath turned into a howl of pain, and Ruggerio was off him in an instant, lest those jaws, which suddenly seemed less human, come snapping at him again. This time there were no bindings to hold him. He reached for a towel he'd saved to clean himself but was stopped in his tracks by those eyes—the wildness in them, the terror.

"They're *here*. You must go. *Now.*"

"Who's here?" Ruggerio asked. These could be the ravings of a lunatic. Impossible to believe that Ceramor, who'd just been unconscious, could know anything at all, but he was an ankari and close to death, who knew what connection he might have to the anima that wound through all?

Only Roha and Hostill knew where to find them. They had no love for the Crown, but they *could* have contacted the Crown guards, even wanted as they were, for the bounty likely on his head and Ceramor's. They might have gone through an intermediary, hoping to rid themselves of danger and fill the coffers of their cause all at once. But he and Ceramor could also have been recognized at the bathhouse, where discretion was certainly for sale. They'd taken the money to provide him a private room and keep his secrets, yes, but if they felt he endangered others they could easily justify calling in the Crown. As if the reward wasn't justification enough.

Anyway, the *who* was not so important right now as *how* they would escape. There were many ways out of the bathhouse, but only one out of this room.

"Can you walk?" he asked Ceramor. It didn't matter that he was naked. As he was, the condition of his body—skin and bone, bruises and blood—would scandalize before anything else. His flesh hung on him like fabric, so that his nudity might not even be immediately noticed. The *guards chasing them* would draw enough attention.

Ceramor closed his eyes, and Ruggerio thought he might not open them again. He squatted down and slapped the ankari. Ceramor snarled, showing there was life left. "Leave me. I won't take life again. I am done. I am dead. Go!"

Ruggerio rocked back on his heels. "What about energy? This is a bathhouse. Heat is energy, yes? What about the furnaces below, heating the water for the hot baths? Can't you steal the heat, transform it? There must be something you can do—for the boy. I've seen how dedicated you are. You almost killed yourself getting to him. Do you want to leave him with the likes of me?"

His eyes sharpened at that. "Or the *Nim?* Roha has secrets, you know. Not all contained in the book."

"Tell me," Ruggerio said.

"No time."

The ankari closed his eyes again, and Ruggerio cursed. He took two steps toward the door when he felt it, the drop in temperature. By the third step he'd reached the door. He exhaled before opening so that he could hold his breath when he cracked the door open to see into the hallway, and his breath came out as mist in the now icy air. Ceramor was doing it. He'd gotten through to the crazed ankari.

He cracked the door as intended and saw three of the bathhouse's largest attendants stationed outside, but instead of keeping watch on the door, as they were no doubt intended to do, they were clustered, watching each other's breath. One argued for going to see whether something was off. Another ordered him to stand his position. The third hugged himself for warmth, alternately rubbing his upper arms or placing his hands over his cheeks and nose in the attempt to heat them.

Ceramor's healing was its own distraction—the sound of popping ribs and grunts of pain. If only he'd hurry. But once he did, what then? Probably his body would go into a healing sleep, and Ruggerio would be left with Ceramor in much the state he'd started—unconscious and needing to be carried. It wouldn't do.

Ruggerio left the door as it was. They hadn't noticed so far. He reached for one of the moderately unfilthed towels, dipped it into the hip bath, and wrung it out, but only so far, then spun it until nicely twisted. It would make a fine wet-whip. Then he grabbed the strigil. They hadn't taken his blades when he entered. Those would be backup. For the Crown guards. He needed at least one attendant with robes unblooded.

"Excuse me," he said, back at the door, opening it wider, giving himself the full range of motion, letting them see that he was no threat with nothing but the tools of their trade. "Could we get fresh linens? We've soaked these through."

And then he snapped the whip in the face of the attendant to his left, slashed the strigil toward the throat of the man to his right and sent a kick between the legs of the man in the middle. The first fell back, clutching at his eye. The second gurgled and choked and went to the ground. His aim was just off center on the third, who clutched himself, but didn't go down, so he aimed for the knee, and heard a crunch that meant the man likely wasn't getting up again.

But the attendant on the left lunged back in, grabbing at the whip. Ruggerio snapped it at the grasping hand. The man fell back when it connected, and went haring off down that hallway, hollering for help. Ruggerio cursed, and when the attendant with the bad knee came at him despite it, nearly falling forward, he made sure the attendant met his swinging fist. The man's nose caved, blood gushed, and he dropped like a stone.

The man with the half-crushed windpipe grabbed for Ruggerio's leg, but he kicked him off and pivoted back for the room, prepared to find Ceramor unconscious again while his body recovered from the healing.

What he discovered was hardly human. Thick fur now covered Ceramor's naked body, which was...not right. Ribs still protruded, now over a sunken stomach and legs that bent at awkward angles. Eyes and ears swiveled toward him as he entered, and he froze. Human ears should not be able to swivel, and indeed these were no longer human, but elongated and pointed, the skin stretched until it could be seen through, something like a rat's. His teeth were pointed as well, in some twisted sense of symmetry, but there were a lot more of them, and they crowded an elongated mouth that could best be described as a muzzle, as though he hadn't used the energy in the air to heal, but to draw out the beast within. Or beasts?

Ruggerio couldn't stay frozen until he knew whether Ceramor was enough in his right mind to identify him as a friend, if he ever had been. He took the risk of gesturing to the ankari to come. "Quickly–"

The beast sprang, and none of Ruggerio's training or instincts were enough to pivot him out of the way in time.

CHAPTER TWENTY-EIGHT

Ruggerio

Ceramor threw him aside, and it was only as those distended hands slashed at him that Ruggerio saw they were transformed as well. Fingers and nails together curved into something resembling meat hooks. If the beast had wanted him dead, he suspected he'd be well and truly shredded, but he was just in the way.

Even so, he felt an instinctual fear that buzzed through his system, insisting on action. Ruggerio dove as much as he was thrown, and rolled to his feet again to see the monster-that-was-Ceramor come face to face with the Crown guards. They could only come at him two abreast in the narrow hall, and the first two barely had time to register their terror before he ripped into them. The first he grabbed by the throat and hurled over his head. The guard landed at Ruggerio's feet and lay stunned or with back broken. The second Ceramor slashed with his claws, sending up a spray that lashed all the others.

But the absence of the first man allowed one of the other guards to step up. The Crown had the numbers, and Ceramor would tire.

Ruggerio had a decision to make: Escape in the other direction while the guards were distracted with Ceramor or stand and fight. Ceramor was terrifying. Deadly, dangerous, unstable. He could have become a killing machine at any time. *And the boy had slept in his presence.* He'd be a powerful ally if harnessed, but Ruggerio didn't think such a thing was possible. Yet, he couldn't bring himself to leave. He had some instinct that the man, or whatever he'd become, would be of use. He'd need him to find the others now that their meeting site was discovered. Ruggerio did know of a few other Restoration sites, but he could guarantee they'd been abandoned the second the Crown raided the first stronghold.

He reached for the sheath at his waist and pulled the blade he'd been saving, then raced for the guard pulling his blade from Ceramor's shoulder. Before he reached him, Ceramor's jaws opened as though they unhinged, and he clamped those piercing teeth down on the man's head. He lifted the guard and shook him like a ragdoll, throwing him to the side when he was finished so that Ruggerio had to step over him.

Another guard was shoved into his place, and Ruggerio took him down before he could so much as get his feet under him and his sword into position. The next was better prepared but went down just as easily. It was over so quickly, and then he and Ceramor were vaulting bodies and slipping in a sea of blood and slicker things that rolled beneath their feet as they fled before reinforcements could arrive. The man who'd taken their money at the door was nowhere to be seen, and there were no mageri with them. Clearly, no one had recognized the unconscious man with the spymaster as the Hound, or the Crown would never have been so careless. Ruggerio cursed, realizing that they'd left the unconscious guard alive to tell Ceramor's tale. They wouldn't make that mistake again.

There were screams as Ceramor burst out onto the street, naked but for the hair that had sprouted over his body and blood from the soldiers he'd slaughtered. He also seemed to have grown so that he now towered over most men. There was no missing him or mistaking him for human. A woman covered her child's eyes and whipped him off the street. And then Ceramor's meat-hook claws came for him, and Ruggerio had to pin down his instinct to defend against them. He still had his blade in hand, but Ceramor might be signaling a direction change or reaching to pull him along. If he attacked and Ceramor was well-intentioned, he'd lose an ally and probably even his life.

The claws locked on his blade arm, grabbing and swinging him like he was nothing. The blade fell from his numb hand. He cursed sharply as his arm dislocated from his shoulder joint – not for the first time or the pain would have been blinding – and he was suddenly thrown over the beast's shoulder like a sack of potatoes. He called himself every kind of idiot for trusting the ankari, twisting and pounding at him uselessly as Ceramor took a bounding step and then another, getting up to speed and then bolted through the streets, Ruggerio's face bouncing off his bony spine with every footfall. His nose bloodied before long, vision blurring.

If he was a praying man, he would have done so now. He did not want to end up like King Jannik's hounds.

"Ceramor!"

"Stop!"

"Where?" he tried each as he swung away from the beast's back, but either he-who'd-been-Ceramor didn't hear or wasn't inclined to answer.

A few more bone-jarring bounds, and the beast set him down on the ground. The world continued to jump around Ruggerio, his head throbbing in time with the pounding of his pulse. His vision hadn't resolved yet except into concepts of light and dark. For a moment, *dark* loomed over him, bringing a hot breeze he was sure would carry the scent of copper if his nose was working; then it was gone, and he breathed a sigh of relief. Maybe in Ceramor's feral mind he'd been *rescuing* Ruggerio, and now that they were safely away his job was done.

He lay still for another moment, waiting for the world to stop spinning, for his vision to clear, for his stomach to stop trying to claw its way up his throat. He hadn't quite accomplished it all when he rolled onto his side, determined to get up and get his bearings. Suddenly those claws closed again, this time on his ankle, and hauled him straight through shrubberies he had to break through with his body. One particularly sharp twig pierced his thigh, sending fresh agony spiking through his body.

He was thrown to the ground again with finality, feet first, and the world stopped moving. He risked opening his eyes. Ceramor stared down at him, eyes bleeding back to human, fangs and hair receding. Ruggerio didn't take his eyes off him as he regained his form, and not only because the transformation was so incredible. Ankari or other, Ceramor was dangerous and unpredictable.

And still covered in the blood of their enemies.

Still naked and now shivering.

Roha

"They're gone now, and good riddance," Hedric growled, facing off with Roha over a covered table in a manor some family had left for the season and the Restoration had claimed for their own. Perhaps someone within the rebellion was the one caring for it in their absence. "You heard what that *cadic* did to the king's hounds. What he'd have gone on to do to men if given the chance." *Cadic* in the language of the Seleni region meant, literally, shit-eater.

Roha knew Ludvin would call men from the other Restoration cells to the meeting; ni only wished Hedric hadn't been one of them. Ni'd never warmed to him, and the feeling was entirely mutual. But ni had to put up with him as another member of Ludvin's inner circle. Vizi had been the public face, but Ludvin was the Restoration's head and heart. Ni wondered what would happen now. Whether they'd ever get Vizi back, and in what condition.

"Let nim speak," Ludvin said mildly, putting a hand to his friend's forearm to settle him.

Hedric expelled a great puff of air through his lips and threw his arms up, dislodging Ludvin's hand roughly before walking to the far reaches of the room, as though to say they could do what they liked, but he'd take no part in it. Ludvin watched him go, his eyes, already deep-set, seemed sunken by recent events, the flesh about them bruise purple. His gray-blond hair was pulled roughly back in a leather thong, but several strands had escaped and lay sweat-slicked to his neck despite the cold. They had lit no fire, and hoped to be gone and the place closed up again before the chill could set them to the shakes.

"Listen, we have been building and recruiting, stockpiling and saving, but since our victory against the Magery nearly a year ago –" Roha repeated, trying again to make nes point.

Hedric whirled, ready to thunder back, his face so red Roha thought his heart might explode, as though he anticipated whatever ni might say next as a personal affront. Ludvin's other lieutenants leapt in to hold him back.

Roha went on as though Hedric wasn't being restrained within rushing distance, "Since that victory, we have taken nothing from the Crown, and yet Bloody Bessory has taken so many from us. We can't think to liberate them on our own. We can't be sure that none of them will break, which means cutting ties to all of the locations they have known, and we don't have so many. Unlike the Magery, we cannot just pick up and move."

It had been their greatest victory. The mageries were by their natures itinerant, moving as they exhausted the anima of the nearby lands with their training. Roha thought of them like traveling circuses, only rather than come through towns, they stayed as far away as possible, in case the students went too far. It had happened once, an entire town, dead. Possibly more than once, but one name was infamous. Redarsa.

The Restoration's attack had ensured that it was far too costly to maintain and protect two Mageries. What remained was folded into the Magery of the north.

"Your solution?" Ludvin asked

"I'm not saying that we trust those from the palace. Or that we link our fates. Only that for now, we use Bloody Bess's strength and her people against her."

But Hedric had had enough. He tore loose of the men holding him, tearing up to Roha and looming – or trying to, but they were nearly of a height. "We *become* her, you mean!"

He spat it in Roha's face, and ni bristled, debating how much to take, when suddenly the whole villa shuddered. Then again. And there came a terrible rending.

An answering tremor shot through their gathering as they drew their weapons and turned on the back of the villa and the courtyard there from which the concussion had come. Everything else was momentarily forgotten as they turned on a common enemy.

Ludvin had brought Roha's daggers. Not as good as longer weapons, but nes weapon of choice. What ni'd been trained with by the Church, which had never anticipated…*this*.

Roha couldn't make sense of what bounded toward them – a large figure, covered in blood and bruises, and not a stitch of clothing that ni could see. Ni raised nes daggers, ready to launch the first blade and strike with the second if the man went for Hostill, when suddenly the boy shouted, "By the All, Ceramor!"

The bloody beast himself dropped to the floor, going to one knee and letting his head fall to his chest, covering most of his naked body. Bowing to him like royalty.

Ceramor said, "You can kill me. The Crown has already tried. I'm an aberration, but I offer myself into your service. Between the two of us," he looked back at Ruggerio slyly, and then at the bladed men, "we know secrets, including that one of your own should sit the V'Alban throne."

Ruggerio stopped cold at that point, the eerie stillness of a predator before he springs. Roha had the sense he'd gladly kill the ankari himself right then and save them the trouble.

"Is this true?" Ludvin asked, looking to the non-naked man for an answer.

Ruggerio's face was as frozen as the fountain behind the villa. Roha had no doubt he'd wanted to hold this information back for bargaining. And here Ceramor had just blurted it out. Now, he was rearranging everything in his head, plans and placements.

"It is," he said, and his gaze dropped to Hostill.

Roha gasped. The men caught on an instant later, and all now stared at Hostill until he said, "What?"

"It can't be," Hedric said, stepping back. "His mother wasn't even working at the castle by then. His father—"

"Wasn't his father, and his mother wasn't his mother," Ceramor snapped.

"That doesn't make any sense at all," Hostill sniped back.

"Doesn't it, though?" Ceramor asked. "Your mother was a bit beyond her childbearing years when you were born, wasn't she? But your sister worked up to the palace. Were you ever allowed to visit her there?"

Hostill looked like he was going to be ill. Some boys might fantasize about themselves as princes, but in Jucar, heirs or rumored heirs had funny ways of dying or disappearing. Roha would guess that most children preferred to imagine themselves as alive rather than dead.

"No," Hostill said softly, a denial of everything. All of it.

"You are King Jannik's son," Ceramor said. "I am mageri. I *know*."

"You are *ankari*," Hedric said. "Even if you were still mageri, your motives would be suspect. As ankari, it's your motives and your mind."

Ceramor's eyes gleamed. "And him?" He cocked his head backward toward Ruggerio. "He betrayed his Princess for this boy."

Ludvin had been watching it all, assessing. Now he turned to Ruggerio. "So far he has spoken for you. What have you to say for yourself? You have betrayed your Princess. You have imprisoned and tortured our people. What possible reason would we have to trust you now?"

Ruggerio looked Ludvin in the eyes, relaxing his body language, no longer looking as though he would commit bloody murder. "You can trust me as far as our interests align. I want what is best for Jucar, and that is not Bloody Bess and this ongoing war with it's attendant plague and deprivation. But neither do I think it is ridding our kingdom of all mageri so that others will see us as weak and open for conquest."

Roha thought it was a nice trick, him adding that bit of truth at the end to lend credence to his sincerity. Ludvin looked to Roha for nes thought, so ni asked the question ni knew would be next on everyone's minds. "So you would set the boy on the throne as your puppet and make yourself his Regent so that you can rule the kingdom in his stead, thinking that you can do better?"

"*The boy* has a name," Ruggerio said, in lieu of *yes*.

Hedric growled. "And you can just keep it off your lying tongue."

Roha struck a hand through the air as though ni could cut through the tension. "We need to discuss this, but *not here*. Ceramor could hardly have been inconspicuous running naked through the streets. More Crown guards will be showing up, and this time they're likely to bring an army. With mageri. They will surround us. We need to leave."

Ludvin nodded. "We can agree on that much, at least. Luckily, there are tunnels."

Roha breathed a sigh of relief. Hedric indicated that Ludvin should lead the way. He would not put his back to Ceramor or Ruggerio, so Roha took the lead by Ludvin's side and Hedric and the others took up the rear. If those from the palace made a move, Hedric and his men would cut them down. Roha only hoped they wouldn't do anything pre-emptively. For now, they were united against a common enemy. Ni had to keep it that way. Ni had a strong sense of things aligning. If they could build on that, keep anyone from doing anything stupid... That seemed like a terribly tall order.

CHAPTER TWENTY-NINE

Cia

Cia choked on blood. Her eyes shot open, and she was staring into the bloodshot eyes of…no, it couldn't be. She was back in the palace from which she'd escaped, Bloody Bess shockingly close, her own arm sliced open, forced between Cia's lips, the Princess's blood sliding, slug-thick down Cia's throat. She tried to clamp down with her teeth, but Garif rose up within her, starving and loathsome. She could feel his thrill, brought to the fore by her distress, her terror, his thirst for the power coursing through Bloody Bess's blood.

Cia thrashed, desperate to escape what would come, but was barely able to move. In her head, Garif laughed. It boomed, echoed. Bloody Bess's eyes lit up.

"Yes, come to me!" she cried, the 'yes' booming, the rest fading as though Garif raced away. But Cia knew she was the one receding, shoved down as Garif used her as a springboard in his rush toward the princess.

Cia had told the others to send her back, but now she was a bird flying into the bars of its cage, prepared to escape or die trying. Her heart pounded hard enough to explode, and she knew she needed to be calm. There'd been a plan; she remembered that now. She'd returned to save Ulan. Perhaps there was more she might do, if she could just wrest control.

"My Princess," she said, in a mocking tone.

Her lips. Not her words. Garif had control over her voice, her head. But not her heart. He left that to ache.

Bloody Bess pulled her arm away from Cia's lips, ran a finger up the cut she had made and uttered some words. The wound closed as though it had never been.

"Why am I here?" Garif asked.

Cia feared she had made a terrible mistake.

Bess

Bess smiled as she felt Garif rise to her blood, then pulled aside the bedding and ripped down the bandages she'd allowed her healers to apply. She'd only ordered the minimum work on Cia thus far, enough to stabilize her. No need to do more until Bess knew whether she'd be an asset or a liability. Now, she pried apart the edges of Cia's knife wound to the chest and slid her fingers inside, using the connection to drive her consciousness like a long briar right into Cia's body and snake it toward her mind. The landscape was a roiling gray with sweating walls and flashes of fears, storms of angry purple and brilliant blue, lit with lightning that seemed as though it would take out the world in a single, ever-branching strike, leaving behind an after-image of eerie twilight before descending into unremitting darkness. Garif or a manifestation of the battle between him and his wife? Even in purely power form, she balked at continuing on. Better she call the mageri forth.

"Mager Garif," she *called* into the void. It wasn't that she had a voice here exactly, but that her thought had form, volume. It illumined the landscape for an instant, lit it as though she'd exploded something that reached into the sky. "I've a proposition to make. Your life was pledged to the Crown. When your wife stole it, her life was forfeit to me, your Princess. That means her life is now mine to take or do with what I will. I offer it to you. Take this body in lieu of your own, repledge your service to *me*, and only to me. I will feed your power. I will make a place for you."

She thought she heard a gasp from somewhere, and maybe she did. No doubt the lady would continue to fight for herself. Normally Bess would applaud her determination, but Cia had nothing to offer her. No power of her own. *Garif* had power and nowhere to go with it. He was perfect for her purposes. No one would accept him as anything but unnatural. No one but her.

She had long ago learned that the only thing that could be trusted was power, and only in her own control. Power in anyone else's hands would be used against her.

Her words gathered into new clouds above her that shot sparks which other clouds answered. All around her was electricity. If she had a physical body in the space, she imagined her hair would be standing on end or dancing about with it, popping its pins. The lightning started to shoot down, and she flinched instinctively. Could her power be singed, burnt to cinders? She didn't know. It was terrifying and thrilling all at once. She waited as the lighting shot and fractured and flashed to the ground, but didn't go out, instead taking the form of a giant stick insect or spider that crouched to look at her, as small in his presence as a speck of dust swept up in the storm.

"I can destroy you," the insect said, eyes like tornados spun of fire, legs of shimmering lighting. It was fearsome. If he could be translated to the battlefield, their enemies would run screaming.

"Maybe, and what then?" Bess asked, standing her ground. "If you destroy me and wreck your wife and blow yourself out, then you go with her. No legacy and nothing to show for yourself. But if you serve me, I rise from Princess to Queen. From Jucar to an empire. With you by my side, training a new army of mageri."

"In this body," Garif thundered, and the landscape shook.

"For now. Who's to say what we will learn in our conquest of other lands?"

"How are you even doing this?" he snarled. "You can't be mageri. Not and accede to the throne."

"That is an old rule, soon to be outdated, like the one that doesn't allow women to rule."

He continued to tower and flare, and she sensed that he was trying to stretch his power, because if he could take over his wife's body, why not hers? But she had already considered that. She'd fed him once to draw him forth, knowing he couldn't resist, but never again. Henceforth, it would be others sacrificed for his strength. She'd closed her wound and left him no other opening. And she'd ordered Cia bound to the bed so that she wouldn't burst her bandages thrashing in her sleep. There was no way for Garif to reach Bess. None at all. Once he was freed…well, she would have to remain ever vigilant.

His eyes spun faster in frustration. "You had better not cross me," he warned at last.

"Who would dare?" she answered.

He laughed, a crack of thunder. It blew her back through Cia's veins, back into her own body. It took Bess a second to stop the world spinning. She felt as though she'd been ripped up in the whirling fire of the storm-spider's eyes. And then she opened her own and was staring into the gaze of the woman on the bed, her eyes now open. *His* eyes?

"Garif?" she asked.

"*Mager* Garif," he answered. "Some ale, if you please?"

"I'll call for it."

Outwardly, she was calm. Inwardly, she was not as certain. She had just bottled lightning. The trick would be keeping it contained.

There was a terrible ruckus out in the corridor, and Bess withdrew her bloody fingernail and threw the bedsheet back over Cia's bound body before drawing the nail into her mouth and sucking the rest of the blood clinging to it. She was just in time as the door burst open, and one of her guards preceded a tall, self-possessed Lord Sorvain, swooping in, as she'd always known he would at some point, with a surprise inspection as though he had every right.

"The Lords demanded to see the prisoner," the guard said, pleading with his eyes for her understanding while keeping his voice and bearing neutral.

Lord Ruland blew rudely past Sorvain and immediately locked eyes with Princess Bessory on the other side of Cia's sickbed. "What are you doing alone with the prisoner, and why isn't the murderess in the dungeon? I hear you called for a healer. Why, when she is only to be executed? Or do you feel that killing her mageri husband somehow warrants our compassion?"

Lord Cristanus's gaze was on the finger coming away from her mouth, but he said nothing, watching and waiting. Four others and a guard lurked in the entryway and in the hall, witnesses as well. Surely, someone had called for Strego. She didn't need him, but he'd make a convenient distraction.

She fixed Ruland with the look she used on him so often it was there without summoning, the one that said he made her weary and it strained belief that the next words out of her mouth even had to be spoken. "You know your history, I presume. Political prisoners have often been kept in the North Tower, particularly through the cold winters when it's good for

little else. The dungeon is full of rebels. I can send her there to conspire—
a woman strong enough to beat a court mageri—but it didn't seem the
wisest course. If you'd like to take personal responsibility for such an
action, I will gladly have her moved. As for the healing, I called for
enough to keep her alive, as it's hardly a spectacle if the prisoner dies on
the way to her own execution. We can do it now, when it's so cold the
people stay away or freeze to death themselves in the public square. That
would be a spectacle, though perhaps not the kind we're looking for.
However, if you in your infinite wisdom feel differently…"

There was a snort, but she didn't glance away to see from whom it had
come.

From the other side of the bed, someone suddenly threw the sheet
back, revealing the bedsheets wrapped around Cia, swaddling her to the
bed… and the nightshift open in the front with the bandage pried up
where Bess had tapped into her.

Bess gasped and whipped the sheet back up, as though to protect Cia's
modesty. "She fought against the healing, and so had to be tightly bound,"
she said, staring into the face of Lord Ruland, who held the other end of
the sheet.

Cristanus looked at the hand the princess had dropped to her side and
half hid behind her hip, the one with the sharpened nail that had
conveyed the half-dead woman's blood. He *knew*. He knew but didn't
speak. Why? Would he blackmail her later? Was he waiting for his
moment? Something was not right here. She didn't like it at all.

"I'm sure you understand that we had to see about the capture and the
arrangements for ourselves," Lord Ruland said. "So much has been kept
from us."

Maybe he hadn't seen the bandage? Or believed the explanation? Garif
had closed Cia's eyes the moment everyone had burst into the room and
kept them closed. Or maybe he had given the body back to let Cia suffer
through the lingering pain.

"Nothing has been kept from you," Princess Bessory snapped. "And I
don't know what you expected to see, but as you feel free to burst in upon
your Princess at will, I will take it as permission to intrude upon your
persons as my curiosity demands. *I'm sure you understand.* You are
dismissed."

She nodded to the guard, but hoped the Lords would accept their
dismissal and leave, because she didn't want to expend the power to force
them do so, and she wasn't sure that her guards would actually lay hands

on the Council Lords even at their Princess's command. Not without Strego's reinforcement. It made her want to break something herself.

As soon as they left, she did as well, ordering the guards not to let anyone in or out. They looked at her oddly, since she was telling them their jobs, but she had to be sure. She was exhausted. Spirits help the next person to cross her path. She hoped they wouldn't be missed.

Cia

"No!" Garif snapped, smacking the semi-rigid rod down right beside the woman's ear, uncaring whether he caught any flesh along the way. She flinched back sharply.

Inside the body he'd stolen, Cia flinched with her. She knew the pain of that rod. On her spine, her backside, her thighs…anywhere the welts wouldn't show. These women were coming to know it as well. "Again."

Bloody Bess had left Garif alone with the mageri women her witch hunt had gathered.

Inside, Cia burned like a flashfire.

But she couldn't speak, couldn't shout out what he'd done to her. What he might do to them. What he would do even to the *Princess* if he had the chance. He had tasted Bess's power, and wouldn't care if he took down the world to get at it. She could feel him there, plotting, planning, looking for an opening. Just one. She didn't know what he would do then. Maybe he didn't either. He was *dead*. What could he do? But death hadn't stopped him so far, and Bloody Bess had given herself entirely over to the forbidden side of the mageri arts. The part only proscribed, never taught by the Magery. Maybe he felt he had something to learn from her – something to learn and nothing left to lose.

But Cia was learning as well. She had always wondered why Garif had chosen her. She'd always assumed it was because she'd been Queen Inaya's handmaiden, implicated and set to die alongside her. That Cia's life was his and he could do anything he liked to her and no one would protest. But he was a man and a mageri at that. Short of killing her, who would have gainsaid him even had she been anyone else? Even killing, all he would need was justification. There would be no one left alive to contradict him.

But on the first day Bloody Bess set Garif to training her mageri women and Cia had seen Garif working magic through her body, the idea kindled like the fire he used to train/torture them.

Bloody Bess wove in and out of the women like a cat, caressing a head or stroking a shoulder with the back of a hand, in such a way as to claim them, leave her scent behind. None dared shudder or shrink from her touch.

It wasn't a large room. The North Tower hadn't ever been comfortable. Even at the height of its use, it had been for less favored guests. But the largest of the chambers had been made into a dormitory for the mageri women, and that's where they were now. Cia stood before them, but not as she'd ever stood before, never being so bold as to fill her allotted space lest Garif take her down a peg for temerity. No, with Garif guiding, her legs were spread until it seemed two people could have stood where she was standing, and her arms were crossed most belligerently until he pulled them apart so quickly she nearly flinched from herself. Garif loved that so much he threw his shoulders forward and thrust his arms such that some of the women shrank back, and he laughed, her own face muscles contracting, and she hated herself, hated him. Hated Bloody Bess.

And then the princess's speech began, and she had something to focus on, choked it down as a chaser.

"I am your Queen," Bloody Bess began. No word of princesses or regents or the coming coronation. "I am sorry for the means by which you were brought to the palace, but the fact is that you are here now. It cannot come as any surprise that the war against Frizenze is not going well. We have made progress, yes, but still we struggle, and if we do not do something big, bold, and decisive, our supplies will continue to shrink and supply lines to lengthen. I have decreed that we will begin recruiting female mageri. Men have been impressed into service before now. I cannot ask any less of Jucar's women. Not if we are to show that we are on a level with them.

"My Lords will say you cannot. I say you *can* and you *will*."

There was an immediate murmur, which Bloody Bess silenced with a look that could cut glass, and an order of *"Silence!"* that Cia felt in her breastbone. "There is no time to send you to the Magery and have them gentle you along, after battling to convince them to train you at all. We must show them why you are a force to be reckoned with. Why *we* are a force to be reckoned with, because you will be *my* force, answerable to me. Which also means that your triumph is my triumph. Your failure, my failure. So *do not fail.*"

Bess made eye contact with each and every woman. Following her gaze, Cia was shocked to see Ulan. She'd expected her to be down in the dungeon with the Restoration rebels. Ulan looked equally surprised, and mouthed *Cia?*

Cia did her best to shut her attention down, move along before Garif could notice, but already her heart was kicking at her chest in panic. It was too late. He'd seen, and he'd marked Ulan. Recognized her as the same woman who had helped Cia during her escape. Cia felt her lips stretch and knew that Garif would make Ulan pay.

Bess left the women to Garif. They couldn't draw anima from the land – for one, the palace was warded, and for another, there was a good reason mageri weren't trained at court. Or anywhere near the palace or central cities. Anywhere near *civilization.* Power had to come from somewhere. The Church and the Restoration weren't wrong—mageri could be dangerous. Ripping the anima from the land had repercussions beyond killing all life, making it infertile, inert, dead. It could fracture the land itself, dry up underground springs, opening sinkholes that would swallow things whole, crack foundations.

Garif went down the line of women. He wanted their fear. Their respect. But it was Cia they saw. The murderess. If they'd seen the wanted posters about town, they would know her that way. Or maybe as the handmaiden to the Poison Princess, as Queen Inaya had been named, stripped of her name and rank, left with nothing but her falsely accused crime.

"I will mold you. I will shape you," Garif said with her voice. "I do not have time to coddle, and do not think to hide your powers. You will not like where it will get you. I promise that *home* is not the answer. You're each here because you've been marked. Because you can reach the anima. Let's see it."

He took a piece of kindling from beside the fire and lit one end, holding it up before the eyes of his first victim, making sure all saw the glow.

"We will start small. Take only the force of the flame. Snuff it out."

And he tossed it at the woman. She cried out and batted at it before it could catch at her dress, but Garif swatted her hands hard with the rod, and she yelped.

He grinned – grinned with Cia's lips, showing her teeth. Cia died inside, and he felt it. She wanted to sink to the ground, curl around herself as though it wasn't too late to protect her soft center, but she could only witness. Watch. Learn. And wait for him to weaken. The second she could take back control of her body, it would be hers. The instant she could make him pay...

She'd killed him once. She would find a way to do it again. For herself. For these women.

The woman's gown started to catch. Her eyes were huge, tearful. She was collapsing down on herself as Cia had wanted to do.

Then suddenly the flame was out. *Thank the All.*

But Garif whirled on the others. Cia felt his rage like a storm. Lightning cracking like whips in her head, rumbles of thunder. Her whole body prickling, lit up, flooded with ferocity. "Who did that?"

Cia was so stunned she went still inside.

All was stillness in the room as well. None of the women so much as breathed.

"I sensed nothing from this one. Who helped her?"

There was no answer.

He cracked the rod against his hand in anticipation, threatened them with it, hoping they would not respond. Thrilled when he got his wish. Cia never felt such horror.

He beat every one of them with a blow across the lower back with the rod – one of the places Cia knew from experience hurt the most. For helping the woman. To drive home the lesson that it wasn't to happen again. Each of them was on her own. They would learn or they would pay the price. This was war, and as of now, he was the enemy.

Cia was the enemy. They all looked at her that way. Side-eyes full of hatred, looks that said they'd kill her in an instant if given the chance. She'd been there. She'd struck that blow against Garif. She couldn't let it weigh on any of their hearts.

The second day was much the same, except with less resistance. Already, Gareth had begun to beat it out of the women Bloody Bess had gathered. Or the rumors of the people who'd disappeared in her presence had frightened them into submission.

On the third day, Cia woke in control of her body with no Bloody Bess to call her out, but as shaky as a newborn colt. She blinked against the faint light coming through her bed curtains. It seemed so long since she'd seen it. Her mind, for once, was not a storm, not a nightmare of crackling energy and a multi-limbed monster made of lightning ready to strike her dead. It was an illusion, the way Garif's hate and hurt and vengeance manifested, but it was as though her mind was a gameboard someone had upended, so that her own pieces went flying. She had to gather them back again, set things to rights.

Quickly, she threw off the bedcovers, but it took two tries. Her hands had to remember how to respond to her again. Tears threatened, but she would not cry them. Or so she told herself. They spilled over anyway, like a cup overfilled. Nothing she could do about that, but she would not give in to them. Would not fall into the heap her legs wanted to. Unsteady, shaky. Wet noodles that should be solid. But the world jogged under her. She lurched, held to the bed until it stopped or at least settled.

She closed her eyes. Breathed in, held, breathed out. Tried to clear her mind, as she did when she had to go out after…something had happened with Garif and she knew she had to present herself as though everything was fine. She could do this. Walking. Leaving. Finding a way out for the others. This was nothing.

Another breath, and she heaved herself away from the bed. Steadier now. Walked to the armoire, and opened it, thankful that she'd been locked away in a private room with no maid. There was a burgundy velvet dressing gown in the closet, and she got into it hastily, along with the slippers that were there as well.

Garif had had a big day yesterday with the women, teaching them how to transfer energy—nothing could be stolen from the anima of the palace or it's grounds, which left only elemental energy that could be transferred from one place to another, but not used up in any transformation. The problem was, Bloody Bess had given them Ulan as a plaything to drain for *her* unwarded anima. Magic so dark it was proscribed by the Magery. But it wasn't their choice. Do it or take her place. That was the only choice they'd been given.

Cia had to save Ulan.

Her scattered thoughts were coming back to her. She'd been learning the lessons, and if Garif could steal Cia's power, perhaps she could steal his. Or reclaim her *own* power. Because in the palace court-yard, when he'd first taken her over and she'd lashed out, she had felt powerful, and that power had run hot, where Garif had always been so cold. He'd threatened to warm the bath with her blood. Maybe it hadn't all been metaphor. His lessons with the flames had called to her. Maybe...

It was time to do away with maybes.

She stalked to her door, listening at it, knowing there were two guards on the other side. Her hearth was blazing. Back in her old quarters, she'd never had enough fuel, had always been kept just this side of freezing to her death. Maybe that had been by design. But now...Cia reached out. She felt the fire. It answered something within her that burned. She called it, raged with it, though fire didn't truly rage. Fire didn't care. It was energy that ate away, released what it burned. It transformed, and she liked that. Wanted that. She called, and it answered. Came to her in a way she could only feel, not express – as though in an instant, all of her was alight, alive, tingling, burning, breathing, racing, rushing. Everything in opposition to feeling dead, neutral, nothingness.

The old her wanted to burn away to ash, leaving a new Cia in its place, forged in fire. She understood in that moment how Bloody Bess might want to hold onto this feeling, but to steal it from someone else, the way Garif had wanted to do to her... It was the worst kind of evil.

That fueled her to the chamber door. It was locked, but that didn't matter. She pounded on the door, shouting that she was in need, and it was opened, the guards expecting no trouble from the Princess's little puppet. She aimed her fire, her rage, at the first Crownsman to step into her path, and he leapt back, swatting at the flames. The other flashed his sword at her, trying to strike with the flat, knowing Bloody Bess wanted her alive, and that gave her the advantage. She lashed again with the fire she had left, but it wasn't enough – only a spark remaining. She hadn't managed it well. It smoldered but didn't stop him, and the pommel of his sword hit her on the temple. She reeled and felt Garif waking to her pain.

She stumbled to the opposite wall, catching herself with the palms of her hands to keep herself upright. She pushed off again, desperate to make her escape. That blow had done something to her vision, made her already shaky legs want to buckle, but she wouldn't let it happen. She propelled herself down the hallway, one hand to the wall to keep herself steady, the Crownsman close behind her.

Three long strides and she was at a stairwell, but someone was coming up, and she was suddenly looking down on the furious gaze of Bloody Bess on her way to call Garif forth. Her time had run out so soon. Bess reached the top and mantled like a bird of prey, gaze piercing Cia and continuing straight through. With a motion, she put out the still smoldering guards and motioned them off before focusing back on Cia. Pinning her sharply in place.

"I don't know whether to be disappointed or impressed with you. First you kill my mageri and then you become one." Bess struck quickly, grabbing Cia's chin in her hand and squeezing hard. "Remember, Cia, your life was forfeit when you aided your Poison Princess. It was forfeit again when you killed the Mager. I could strike you where you stand. You live at my sufferance. And so, you will conform, or you will die. It is all very simple. Come, you will have a royal escort back to your room."

Bloody Bess released her chin, but Cia stayed still, poleaxed in place. Bess had just done what Garif had been training the mageri women for, and with nothing but a wave of her hand. More stunning than Cia's own revelation of magic, which had been dawning on her, ever brightening and becoming, this was blinding, devastating understanding – the Princess was a mageri herself. Well, of course she was. If only Cia's thoughts hadn't been so muddled and Garif foremost among them, she'd have realized that much sooner.

Bess saw the moment the realization broke over Cia. Her eyes narrowed, and she clenched the nails of one hand into a fist, and with the other, she struck like a viper, latching onto Bess's wrist right under her dressing gown. There was a sharp slice and then Bess was pushing into Cia's mind as she pulled her along bodily back to her prison room.

She cried out at the pain, not hopeful that the guards would help her. Not against their crown princess. Had they even seen what she had, realized the implications? Would it matter? The Princess had disappeared others –

Bess whipped her back into the room, shut the doors on the guards and slammed her against the wall. But it was her *will* that was rushing Cia like gale force winds, shoving her back, thoughts like laundry left on a line, ripped away, sent flying in all directions. She tried to grasp one, only to fly off herself, thrown against an illusory wall and smashed there, compressed. Then boxed away, walled off.

Garif, Bess called in the meantime. All pull and intent rather than sound, but Cia felt him there, the segmented monster of thunder and lightning. Hate and horror rising with the storm.

She kicked and screamed and clawed, but it was Garif who walked out of there with the Princess after dressing for the day.

She collapsed when Bloody Bess withdrew, and she was faced with only one monster, but not because she had given up. Garif would be sharpest now, alert for her attacks, and Bess's cage seemed impregnable – for now. Cia needed time to recover her strength. Time for Garif to tire, to grow distracted, time to weaken the walls of her prison. She *would* make another move, but she would have to be ready.

No one had seen the woman who'd failed with the fire since the first day. Bess had hauled her away. Not the guards, but Bloody Bess herself, and that was a thousand times more terrifying. One woman had had the temerity to ask where she'd gone, and Garif had answered, "The same place you'll be going if you fail."

Most had heard the whispers about town of the missing girls, those who'd gone to the palace and never returned. No one knew what Bloody Bess did with them, but Cia now suspected.

No, she *knew* with a winter-cold dread, the kind that crept through the veins to stop a heart. Bloody Bess drank the women down, every bit of their anima. She drew their life force into her own, used it to power her abilities. Whether it was madness or malice that had started her on the path, there was only one end to it. And she would take all of them with her.

So, the women worked harder, and each learned the lessons. No matter how long it took. How scorched or bruised or battered they became along the way.

But Ulan was not going to survive the day. Not without Cia's help.

Bloody Bess hadn't taken her when she failed, when it became evident that, as Ulan had always said, her only power was in speaking with the spirits. She'd left Ulan to Garif's tender mercies. To the women. They could not take the anima from the land and had come to the limits of what they could do without fuel quickly enough. They would take from Ulan. Garif would teach them the dark side of the mageri arts.

When a woman fell to her knees in prayer, pressing her forehead to the floor, calling out to the All, vowing she would never do such a thing, Bloody Bess had nicked her with that long nail she'd used on Cia and whispered into her veins that she would and that if she didn't, she would be next. The woman rose, her breathing jagged, her mouth working but no sound coming out, eyes darting from one person to the next as though searching out safety. But she stepped back into line, and she didn't protest again.

Bloody Bess had at least ordered Garif to stop short of Ulan's death. "We need her left alive."

But Cia's relief at that was short-lived. She felt his calculation instantly. Mistakes could be made.

"Again!" he told the woman trying to lift a table.

He cut into Ulan again, as though a fresh welling of blood might help the woman draw more out of her. At her cry, Cia threw herself once more against her prison wall, and thought she felt some give this time.

Garif was distracted, watching the blood. He licked his – Cia's – lips. They were not *his*. They would never be his. She shut down her thoughts. Locked them down. He would not be privy to them. She would take her mind back over, lock *him* down. Then and only then would she be free to think again. To feel.

She kicked, launched, fought, screamed.

Ulan's legs gave out – too much blood loss or too much of her anima being drawn out by the woman grunting as though physical exertion was required to lift the table – and she sank against the wall. She looked gray, her flesh practically melting away as the day went on.

Cia couldn't help it, she did think then, did yell. *Stop it, stop it! Bloody Bess told you to stop! Can't you see you're killing her?* Though she knew it wouldn't work. Knew he wouldn't care.

Knew it was exactly his intent.

He laughed at her pain.

The table rattled as if it fought the rising – a thing of the earth wanting to stay rooted to it. Cia fought just as hard against her husband. Three legs of the table rose and then the fourth began to lift shakily. Cia tried to rise with it.

"About time!" Garif said. "Next."

The mageri woman, sweat broken out all over her face as though she'd done the hard work, stepped back, and another took her place, shooting a glance at Ulan.

"Mager, I think the lady may need a break," she said timidly.

Garif took in a breath to blast her, and Cia seized it. Held it. Garif had always liked to steal her breath. So, that was how she found him, traced him to his source. Felt *his* fear. He was still the monster, still the storm, but he'd been raging for too long and he'd nearly blown himself out for now. Even squalls came in waves.

"Mager?" the woman asked when he didn't answer. And maybe she'd seen something in his – her – face. Maybe it was frozen. And, of course, his breath had caught.

Cia felt Garif reach for their power, reach for the fire in the room's hearth and felt it flash for them. Garif didn't care what he did to their body if she was going to be the one left to face the pain. She let it come. Reached for it, cupped it. Now that she knew the power was hers, she stole the energy from the flame as it raged, drinking it in. She felt strong, buzzy. Alive. Before Garif could steal it away, use it himself, she took the lessons he'd taught her, all unwittingly, and fireblasted him.

He roared. His multi-legged Malacostra construct in her mind struck for her with those spindle-crab like pincers, but it couldn't get close, not with the hungry fire raging at him. Even with his limbs of lightning, he couldn't breach the fire, as though it was an impossible barrier, a firewall burned to stop the lightning. Garif was driven back, lightning no longer strobing, growing smaller and smaller, and curling protectively in on himself as she raged and did not let up. She took back her control, fired off her anger. For Ulan, for all the women watching.

The fire in the hearth flickered and died, and Cia's own fire gave out, leaving the Malacostra a small curled husk and Garif with it, his storm a small flare on her horizon. But it hadn't blown out. She stood tall, the first smile of her own curling her lips. Her chest expanding to fill its own space. She could stand against him. The storm said he would blow back, but it would take time for him to recover. For now, Ulan was alive, and that was what mattered.

"Mager?" the woman said again.

"Not for now," Cia answered before she could stop herself. There would be guards on the other side of the door – enraged and ready for revenge. She covered as quickly as possible, "But we will pick back up again as soon as possible. Be ready."

They would have seen the fire shoot for her. But they'd also have seen it go out. Would they know what it meant? Would they talk amongst themselves? Even if they did, they were unlikely to talk with the Princess, and that was all that mattered. But *Garif* would talk. Which meant her time was limited.

She strode to the door and pounded on it as Garif would have done, calling to the guards that the woman Ulan was done for and that they should cart her away. As soon as they entered – new guards who kept as much fearful distance from her as possible – Cia made certain they knew that the Princess wanted Ulan kept alive. Then she tried to emulate Garif's strides as she escaped into the corridor and back to her room. She would have liked to leave the palace entirely, but even if she could get much further on her own, she couldn't leave Ulan, and there was no way to simply carry her off.

Garif had punished Ulan because of Cia.

And she knew who Bloody Bess was now. *What* Bloody Bess was.

She had never forgiven herself for the choice she'd made when she'd married Garif rather than die with her queen, even though it had seemed right at the time. Nothing had been right until she'd struck her blow against Garif's abuse, even if it had led her here. She needed to strike another blow now.

Bess

Bess watched Mager Garif work.

If she'd known about the mager's wife – about why he'd married his wife, what he'd been doing to her, *what she was capable of* – things would never have come to this. Bess would have saved her. Made her the cornerstone of her new mageri army.

And if she'd said 'no'? Well, Bess would have made certain she didn't.

But now, here they were, and she was shackled with this brute who reminded her so much of her brothers. And not even as a whole person, but as a bosewight possessing his wife even beyond death. And Bess was aiding him. She'd drawn him forth again, even after Cia had beaten him back.

Some day, her ends would justify her means. Someday, after she ruled Jucar, had conquered Frizenze and Galitrüd, she would make life better for all women. Give them more to which they could aspire. Change the laws, hold men accountable... Oh, there would be a new day.

For now, she could not stand another moment in the room with Mager Garif and his *techniques*. He was moving quickly with the mageri women, but it was not fast enough. Presumably, like her, they'd had their powers all of their lives. Yes, some would have discovered them later than others, and there were degrees of power. But wouldn't they have experimented? Learned? Grown? Yes, yes, in secret. The Church had a lot to answer for, preaching that the anima should go untapped. So, for that matter, did the Crown and the Magery, insisting that women couldn't be trained. *Couldn't*, in fact, *be mageri*, all evidence to the contrary. Perhaps mere hextes, witches – small, untrustworthy talents that should be quashed rather than encouraged.

Bah. If they were any of those things, it was *because* they were untrained. Of all the stupid, self-fulfilling prophecies.

Garif threatened the woman before him with an open hand as she failed the test he's set for her, and Bess caught his arm before he could unleash his fury.

"You will *not* abuse my women," she said, glaring into eyes that, if she was not mistaken, had been gray rather than murky green when it had been Cia controlling her own body.

He glared back and ripped his arm out of her grip, but lowered it into a fist he banged into his side instead.

Yet, she understood his frustration. The trainees needed to tap into more power. When Ulan's anima ran out, there was a dungeon full of rebels, though Bess would have to be careful—one or two might die of injuries. More than that would be remarked on. Anyway, she had plans for the rest that would assure the Restoration lived up to their name.

She was already heading for the door when a knock sounded, and if she hadn't long learned restraint, she would have been tempted to use Cia's trick of stealing the flame from the fire and lighting up whoever was on the other side. She was in a foul mood. But the mageri women didn't yet know that she was one of them, so she reigned in her power. Only Cia, and Bess had thrown her back into a cage inside herself, stronger than the last from which she had escaped.

No one would dare interrupt their Princess if it wasn't truly urgent. Bess knew this, and yet. And yet… The headaches, the voices, the sounds and smells and pressure that pushed and screamed at her all the time, the constant need to hold herself back were becoming too much. She wanted to lash out at everything. She was sure that if only she could release it all —BECOME who she was becoming, then silence and sanity would return. Peace would settle over her like a cooling cloth for her head, one that actually worked.

She ripped the door open, but only far enough for them to see her raging visage and know that they risked her wrath if their purpose was imperfect.

She had to look down almost to the ground to see who had interrupted her, and then spotted only the top of a man's head and the red and black of his tunic in the Crown colors. "My Princess," he began, raising his head only high enough that he spoke to her knees rather than the floor, "the Regent asks whether you will attend the Council today."

Her gaze sharpened on him. It was an important message indeed. The Council generally preferred that she *didn't* join so that they could talk about her in her absence, or at least without her interference, and Strego was more than able to represent their interests so that she could go about her pursuits. If he was signaling for her presence, there was something afoot. With Ruggerio on the loose, it was bound to come sooner or later. She'd have preferred later, but if she wasn't quite ready with all of the resources at her disposal, then neither was he. If they went up against each other, he would lose.

She would make certain of it.

Princess Bessory V'Alban drew herself up to her full height, and said over her shoulder, "Come when I call for you."

Garif nodded and continued on with the training.

She stepped into the hallway and closed the door behind her. The guard on his knees had to back away and rise to his feet quickly or be trampled, which he did with enough grace to credit his training. Then he led the way with the other two falling in behind her. To protect her, she knew, but what should seem like safety felt like knives at her back ever since Ruggerio's desertion. If this was an assassination attempt, and she was an ordinary princess, she'd have no defense against two soldiers at her back. And she couldn't always trust to her own powers. She'd be helpless if hit by one of her blinding headaches.

Plots and prevention took her all the way to the Council doors, and while she would have liked to throw them open and make an entrance, they would be locked from within.

The guard leading the way gave the proper knock and was answered in kind. Codes exchanged, the doors were opened.

Princess Bessory swept in to an ominous silence.

All eyes were on her or on the council table at which only two men sat. All the rest stood, and there were papers littering the table. Not a stack before each man for their consideration. Not one or two maps over which they were all bent, but a litany of pages spread across the table as though they'd been thrown down in challenge.

She didn't allow herself to pause, though she was as thrown as the parchment pages.

She thanked the guards for their escort and approached the table closest to Strego, glancing everywhere for cues to what was going on. He moved aside fractionally to let her see things from his vantage point without ceding his position.

On the page closest to her was a face, and it froze her in place and stopped her breath. It was an artist's rendering, done possibly with a spymaster's eye for detail. But worse, it was a face she saw every time she closed her eyes – Galina, her childhood friend and first victim.

Missing or Murdered? the page asked above the likeness, and below, *Last Seen in Service to the Princess.* There were holes at the top and bottom where it had been nailed or knifed to a post. She threw it down and picked up another page. This one was of another girl whose name she couldn't recall. One of her shadow girls. Not all of Jucar's people could read, but there were enough, and those who could would certainly spread the word to others.

Ruggerio had to be behind this. Her fists clenched hard enough that she drew her own blood. She would kill him herself. Her men would find him, and she would kill him. She would drain him and restore him and do it all again. However many times it took until she was satisfied. She didn't even know if this was possible, but she would find out.

"How many?" she asked through gritted teeth.

He was just one man. Only days had passed. He couldn't have put up many of these. It would take time to draw them, post them. He was a wanted man. The risk was too great.

"The watch has found them all across the city," Strego said.

"And that's not the worst," Lord Cristanus said, watching her closely. "There are rumors of an heir right here in town, King Jannik's son by one of the maids."

There was a roaring in her ears. She could not have heard him right. How many maids had she eaten up over the years? How many rumors had she chased? How could she have missed one?

But that boy... She'd known. Or she'd strongly suspected. And Ruggerio had him. The only way they could have gotten the word out and posters spread so far so quickly was if they had help, organization, and that meant what was left of the Restoration.

At least Ruggerio didn't know her deepest, darkest secret. Even she didn't know, not really. She only feared – that maybe she wasn't truly King Grammond's daughter. Maybe that courtier she'd never seen again...maybe that was how the wild magic had gotten back into the royal line. Maybe that was why her father had never loved her.

She'd been afraid all her life that someone would find out about her magic. That King Grammond would discover her or learn of her mother's infidelity and disavow them both. Or worse. Well, the King and her lady mother were dead. Her brothers were dead, and if there was already unrest, already talk of displacing her, what did she have to lose?

She was tired of hiding. Tired of appearing less than she was. She was never to be *given* power. She had to take it.

The men were still talking, blissfully unaware. "Plagues and hunger had the city on edge already, and the attack on All Souls seemed a sign to many more," Lord Grose said from the other end of the table. "And now we have Crown guards running through the city, rounding people up. A tactical error. As we feared, the Restoration have used this as a rallying cry for recruitment. As fast as we arrest them, others sign on. I'm afraid we'll soon be at war with ourselves. We need to rebuild. Start with something the people have wanted for some time."

He looked to Lord Trük to finish what he had started. One never began a thought or an argument that the other didn't take up, as though they only found the strength in solidarity. "Your marriage, Princess," he continued the old refrain. "With such unrest, the people need a strong leader. We need a king on the throne. We need an assured succession. Once you have provided male heirs, there will be no need for this talk of others."

It was all she could do not to strike them where they sat. Now was time to spring her trap. Seize the crown that should be hers. Even if her mother had played her father foul, she was related to the V'Alban line, a second or third cousin. King Grammond had pruned the branchings of the line to prevent any challenges to his own power. And anyway, the throne should go to one who could hold it.

The hammer she'd feared all her life would finally fall, but she would not be the one beneath it.

Come to me, she called through her bond to Garif.

In the council room, she kicked over the chair Strego wasn't sitting in to be certain she had everyone's complete attention.

Everyone froze. Everyone stared. She used the sudden stillness and her slightness of build to insert herself between her Regent and the table, usurping his place at the head of it in no uncertain terms. She banged both palms down on the table. It hurt, but the papers jumped, and all the men twitched to varying degrees. Whether they were horrified, stunned, amused or intrigued, she didn't care. They were *paying attention*.

"You will *not* brood me out to pacify the people," she said, meeting each gaze in turn. "We will *not* offer the pageantry of a wedding and coronation in lieu of practical solutions. The people are hungry. They are afraid. Of me, of the depletion of our land from the Blood War, that what the rebels say is right—that our way is bad, that the mageri harm instead of help. I will show them another way. A better way. And they will love me for it."

One of the council lords who'd been standing fell into his chair. "I don't understand."

"Lord Ruland, you wanted an execution, did you not, to entertain and distract the people?"

She watched him run it through his mind, looking for the trap. "I did. You can't let the murder of your mageri pass without punishment. Especially with the Restoration emboldened, we have to show the consequences of such actions."

"Then I think you'll agree we should hold a memorable demonstration that my mageri are not so easily defeated. We should show that the consequences of attempting to kill my men will be highly personal and unpleasant. We will provide the sort of deterrent that no one can ignore."

She used her link with Garif and knew that he was right outside with her mageri girls and the guards coerced to accompany them. It took hardly any of the stolen power she'd stockpiled to unlock the doors of the council room so that her newly minted mageri could expend a little of their own power to blast the doors open, announcing themselves with a bang.

At first there was abject confusion in the council room, as the Lords saw Cia standing there, the murderess free and in their midst. They ran over each other rushing to put the council table between her and them, unable to tear their gazes from those eyes that seemed to spin and flare or that smile that invited madness.

None of them stared too long.

"Hello, my Lords," Garif said, managing to shape the words around a vaguely sinister smile. It was his inflection in his wife's voice.

One Lord took his seat rather roughly. Then another.

"And who–?" asked Lord Sorvain.

"Mager Garif, dead but not gone to his rest. With him are my women," Bess said, gesturing them into the room. There was no reason for them to remain out in the hallway and for the whole palace to know their business. She was fairly certain that the one spy she cared about, her little ghost girl, would already be present. "The townswomen rumored to have mageri powers. Some of those we *rounded up*," she said, referring back to Lord Grose's objections. "I pray you all be seated, my Lords, because I have an explanation for all, and I would hate for your legs to give out before my voice."

She looked to the guard who had led her here. "Please see to it that more chairs are brought for my people." She nodded to Garif, "Thank you, you may go. I know you still need your rest."

To be honest, he shook like a *vranish* addict on the edge of control. Any second, he would fall upon one of the Lords, doing him violence and stealing his life force to fuel his continued control over his wife's body, and Bess was half-inclined to allow it as a show of her power. But she wasn't so certain of the other Lords. If they piled on as one, she might lose one of the truest arrows in her quiver, and she wasn't ready for that. Not yet. Her women warriors, her mageri-in-training, were far from ready to take his place. He had to go quickly before he lost the battle against Cia. She breathed a sigh of quiet relief when he followed her order.

Strego recovered himself enough to bark at the guards, "Please accompany...er, her."

He waved over one of the guards who'd hesitated, and issued private, whispered instructions. The guard's eyes widened as he glanced from Cia back to his Regent, clearly not confident in his ability to stop a mageri who'd somehow overtaken the body of his murderess from doing whatever he decided to do. But he had no choice, so he bowed and went on to whisper the instructions to the others, who had similar but quickly quelled looks of terror.

Bess was left with a council full of Lords and a line of mageri women between them and the door. They were bound to her more by fear than loyalty, but were hers nonetheless. Just as the council would be hers once she explained.

Once they were seated, she drew herself up to her fullest height and gave them each a direct blast of her gaze, making certain that none could escape that it was she and she alone to whom they were now listening. Not Strego or Bowstan. But their Princess, soon to be Queen.

"We have an entire dungeon of rebels doing us no good at all. They are giving up nothing about the Restoration. They might be used to provide power for my new mageri trainees. But I have something bigger in mind, which will benefit all of Jucar. Something that will draw out the Restoration and rid us of them once and for all while restoring some of the deadlands whose anima had been drained by the Blood War. There is no point simply killing the traitors on the gallows or otherwise when their deaths could mean so much more."

There were mutterings around the table, but only Lord Sorvain risked raising his voice so that she might hear. "Human sacrifice, Princess Bessory? But – "

"Merely changing the site of their executions to where they will do the most good."

If Dazia did as she expected and passed along her plan, then when the rest of the Restoration came to save their people, she would be waiting for them. One very large, living sacrifice delivering itself to the slaughter.

She would restore the lands, as her people had wanted.

They would love her for it.

And if they did not, who would remain to resist? Who would dare, seeing what became of the last to do so?

CHAPTER THIRTY

Dazia

It was amazing that Bloody Bess's head didn't explode with the Shadows crowding her eyes like everyone rushing the windows to see out. Only the Princess herself was in the way. Any second now, Dazia thought they might push her straight on through, and take over themselves, the way Garif had with Cia. She hoped it would happen. She prayed for it, even as she knew it was wrong.

Or thought so.

She didn't know what she knew anymore.

The longer she was away from her body, weaving in and out of the anima, the more she lost herself. If Maman didn't call so strongly, didn't need her so much, she would join. It was everything. Life and energy and peace. Belonging. Self didn't matter, but it didn't have *to matter. She wouldn't really be* part *of the whole like a wheel on a wagon, taking on weight, cracking under stress, but like a droplet of water in a huge ocean. Eventually, part of the whole would break off into something new that would join back up later. The way things were meant to be.*

This life wasn't forever. But what she did with it mattered. Maman had taught her that. Because what she returned to the anima affected it.

So, she watched Bloody Bess in the council meeting, and watched the others too. Maman and her uncle and everyone else was counting on her. And the others were NOT happy with the Princess.

"You can't be serious," General Bowstan said. "Marching prisoners off in mid-winter, knowing that you'll be set upon by the opposition. And not even sending a show of strength. Suggesting that we appear vulnerable. What if the Restoration aren't the only group to attack us? We're practically asking for an ambush."

"I didn't invite you to the meeting so that you could question my authority. If you plan to go the way of my spymaster, remember that you can be replaced just as easily, and you won't have his head start." Her tone was as sharp as daggers. It was a wonder Bowstan didn't flinch at her words. "You are a general. I expect you to plan for every eventuality. That is your job. Can you do it or will I need to replace you with someone more competent and less fearful?"

The General looked as though he could break the council table into kindling and still not grow calm, but he didn't move a muscle until he bowed so low that Dazia thought he might break in half.

"Yes, your Highness, I will see it done."

"Dismissed," Bloody Bess told him, followed by, "my Lords." She inclined her head to them, but only incrementally, and Dazia might be the only one to know why. Any more and she might spill shadows from her eyes.

Bloody Bess hurried away, accompanied only by her own guard, and Dazia could see the pain on her face now that she wasn't trying to hide it. She saw the shadows split her head, too many, too restless to be contained. She wondered if the Princess knew what she'd done to herself.

Dazia both felt for and feared those shadow girls. Living like that, they couldn't be right in their heads. Could she reach out and pull them with her into the anima or would they yank her in if she tried to save them? She was too afraid to find out.

So she stayed behind, and listened to the men.

"I have already written to my Lord. Come the spring –"

"Come the spring, I fear it will be too late."

"She cannot refuse to meet suitors. She certainly won't refuse this one."

"If only her brothers hadn't been too busy to arrange a marriage for her."

"Too busy or too calculating."

"They could have sent her away. It would have been better for all."

"And then who would we have on the throne?" It was the strongest voice she'd heard, and it cut across all the others. He was the Regent, but she didn't really know what that meant. They treated him almost like a king, but he wasn't, because they didn't have a king right now.

Everyone else hushed, and looked to the man who'd spoken, who looked like

his head was trying to retreat down into his robes. "My Lord is a distant relative,"
he said very quietly.

"I wouldn't push the strength of his claim, if you value his life," said another
man in dark robes, also in a hush.

"As you say," the first man said, giving up making his head disappear. "I only
mean that the sooner wed, the sooner she's in hand. Whether she marries into
another kingdom or takes a consort and provides heirs to ours, a family would see
her settled."

The man in the dark robes shook his head pityingly. "My Lord, if you were
married yourself, you might not be so sure."

Others cleared their throats or shifted away, and Dazia felt as though there
was suddenly another ghost in the room, only the man didn't know it yet.

Roha

Roha was bent over the map Ruggerio had drawn when Ceramor started
to sing from his place in the corner of the warehouse where they were
now gathered. Ni'd been impressed when Ruggerio had drawn the
women's faces from memory—if not all the girls who had gone missing, a
good number of them. He was the one who had come up with the idea of
the whisper campaign. An heir, he said, couldn't come from nowhere.
There had to be rumors, ideas planted, imaginations sparked. Hostill had
to grow until he became legend. And for Hostill to properly be the hero,
there must be a villain.

That, of course, was no problem at all. There was Bloody Bess, and all
of those missing girls. The only problem was that few dared speak of the
Princess for fear of summoning her like some sort of bosewight whose
name couldn't be said thrice. And the girls—the first and second girls
were said to have run off. By the third, inquiries were taken as treason,
questioning the Crown, implicating its adherents in wrongdoing. Anyone
who so much as asked could be beaten or locked up or disappeared themselves, which kept anyone from asking, except possibly in hushed breaths
to those they trusted very, very well.

But now, Ceramor sang:
"Come little ghost girl
Hither, hither
Speak little ghost girl

Wither, wither—"

"What are you babbling on about?" Ruggerio asked, whirling on the ankari.

Ceramor didn't shrink from him. Or even seem to notice. He was focused on a spot to his right, and not far from it. "The little girlie is back. Lavender and mustard seed, the smell so strong. Urgent, I would say. You need to hear her."

Ruggerio looked to Roha, who glanced around the table. Their numbers had grown, even with the Crown's raids, even without Vizi and his wonderful speeches in the squares. People were finding them. Whispers could be as powerful as shouts if they were the right words in the right ears. Their posters and the rumors of an heir were bearing fruit.

"Everybody out," Roha said.

Ludvin nodded when they looked to him for confirmation.

Ruggerio, of course, held his ground. The ghost girl was, after all, his niece. Roha could hardly breathe for an instant, nes heart feeling as though it was being squeezed in a press. If they were making a mistake trusting Ruggerio, if he hadn't truly switched sides, now would be the perfect time to close his trap, when the Restoration was mostly gathered in one place. If Roha really believed that, Ruggerio would be dead already, but there were moments like this, where ni expected to hear screams from the next room as the Crown burst in. Or smell the smoke of all the walls being lit and the doors barred. It wasn't the first such moment.

"Since when does Roha give the orders?" Hedric asked, hanging back.

Ludvin stared him down. He didn't look like he'd been sleeping any better than Roha, but his gaze was sharp enough to cut. "*I'm* giving the order, and I say go. Guard this room. Make sure the warehouse is secure. I will fill you in. Have I ever left you in the dark?"

Hedric glared at Roha, at Ruggerio and Ceramor and back at Ludvin, his lip pulled up toward his nose, which wrinkled toward his brow in a way that suggested someone had defecated nearby. Then he drew a blade and went for the door. "There will be a reckoning," he said to Roha, turning toward the door.

"I'll await the day," Roha said, bowing to him.

He snorted and slammed the door with finality.

Well, it had taken Roha's mind off of Ruggerio's potential betrayal, at least. Ludvin shot nim a glance, "It's such a shame. He was such a big fan of yours *before* you brought us a spymaster and ankari."

"Just imagine if he'd stayed," ni shot back.

Ludvin was the only one in the Restoration who knew Roha's secret. When ni'd come to the Restoration – like most, after hearing one of Vizi's speeches – and met Ludvin, Roha had known ni could bring to the rebellion something no one else could: *nulls*. Ni couldn't steal them from the Church. They were precious enough that they couldn't just be found lying around or unaccounted for. However, they were created by the Nim. It was why Nim were so precious to the Church, which believed the very reason for their existence, their connection to the anima was so that they might create wards and nulls to protect it.

As a child raised in the Church, it hadn't made sense to Roha that 'the only proper use' for nes power was to cut off access to the All, but when Roha saw how people used and abused the anima, ni'd come around. And when ni felt the Church wasn't doing enough, Roha had offered nes skills to the Restoration. Still, it wasn't something ni thought the others needed to know or would understand. Ludvin agreed. But Roha would have to tap into nes connection to the anima to talk with the ghost child. If Hedric was angry already, this would send him over the edge.

What would he do then? What would Ludvin do? Roha believed in the cause, but was terrified the cause wouldn't believe in nim, not if ni actually used nes powers in the battle against Bloody Bess. They were different from those of the mageri, but ni might not be given the chance to explain before being cut down. Different had never been welcome in Roha's experience.

Roha grabbed the satchel that still held the book. At least Ruggerio didn't need to know nes secrets. The book was important. Just not in the way Roha needed Ruggerio to believe. Ceramor, ni was pretty certain, knew or sensed the truth already, but he was staring fixedly at the same point.

Roha held the book out in that direction and closed nes eyes for a moment, sensing inwardly for that quiet place ni had always known. It wasn't truly a place, not an *anywhere*, but when Roha's parents fought or ni was at the end of nes reserves, ni would search it out instinctively. It was almost like an entrance to a well, in the way it promised refreshment, and in the sense that drawing from it diminished it, at least until it replenished itself. The Gospel of Gelerte—hidden, proscribed, locked away in the Church archives, liberated by his most recent and fervent devotee—had been a revelation in so many ways. About why Roha could do what ni did. Why the Church both revered and feared the Nim. But it didn't tell Roha how to find others like nimself or how to make people accept. It didn't say what would happen if ni went too far.

Roha fed some of the power ni drew from that inner well into the connection with the ghost girl, then opened nes eyes to see the girl, Dazia, glowing as she had before, with silver limning her like the halo of the moon.

"They're killing her!" Dazia said immediately, doe eyes wide. "Worse, they're going to kill them all. All of your people."

Ruggerio dropped to one knee, and Roha watched his face transform, go almost gentle. "You mean your mother? Is she–"

"She's alive for now. She says they want her that way, but the Princess plans to take her and all the prisoners to the fields that have been killed by the fighting, and sac'fice them to restore the land with their anima."

"Will that work?" Ludvin asked Roha. "If deaths were all that were needed, wouldn't those on the battlefield have restored the stolen anima?"

Roha gasped. "It's madness! The Church would never stand for it."

"The Church has stood for quite a lot," Ludvin reminded nim.

But ni was lost in the horror. "It's...unthinkable. Isn't it? I thought that the lands killed in the Blood War couldn't be brought back. Maybe it's just that with the anima ripped out and nothing left alive there's no way to restart the cycle of life? Perhaps in a generation or two, vegetation would have returned and brought animal life with it. The absolute evil of it aside, mass sacrifice *might* be a way to start the restoration of the land, but the Blood War has already ripped away at Jucar's anima. Now Bloody Bess wants to cut other lives short, so that they can't return the fullness of their energies to the All. This is a perversion of everything. She may restore the fields in some small way, but... How long before we don't have enough anima left for new life? Seedlings, kits, pups...babes?"

There was dead silence in the room.

"The Council Man said something like that," Dazia said, pulling on her uncle's sleeve. Even though it didn't have any physical effect, he leaned closer. "He called it human sac'fice. The Princess looked like she could have killed him for that. Then she said that the prisoners are scheduled for execution already. She's only moving it where it will do the most good."

Ludvin squatted as well so that he was on the same level as everyone else. His knees cracked loudly on the way down.

"But this is good, right?" He looked from Ruggerio to Roha. "*Not* that she plans to sacrifice our people, but that she'll march them out of the palace. Easier for us to ambush the guards and prevail. Inside the palace, there would be multiple choke points and minimal escape routes. Not to mention, we'd have to storm both the dungeon and the North Tower. Out in the open…"

"She'll know that," Ruggerio said. "I'm not saying that restoring the land isn't a reasonable plan. She needs to do something to help the crops and sway the people against revolt." He ignored Roha's hiss and Hostill's curse. "But now? In winter? I would guess that we've forced her hand, which means that she's moved up her timetable. She's not as ready as she'd like to be, which gives us an opportunity. But she's a V'Alban. Even if she wasn't raised to rule, she learned those lessons. She doesn't play any game she can't win. Her dungeon can't hold enough to replenish an entire battlefield, which means that she anticipates that you'll come after your people with everything you have, and plans to add you to her tally. This has to be a trap. If I was there, I could guarantee it to close seamlessly, but I'm not. She can't possibly count on us joining forces. She'll never suspect that you would trust her former spymaster – and even if she could imagine it, she could never truly anticipate *me*."

"You don't think too highly of yourself," Roha mumbled.

"False modesty is a waste of breath," Ruggerio responded.

"So you'll save them?" Dazia asked, her eyes shining.

"Find out where and when," Ruggerio said. "And tell Ulan to hang on. We will come." He looked to Ludvin belatedly, but he was already nodding his agreement.

"Any other questions before I let her go?" Roha asked.

"See if you can find out how many she'll have with her," Ludvin said. "Men as well as mageri."

Dazia nodded. "She's ordered the mageri who don't winter at the castle be called to her."

"So we'll have them all in one place," Ludvin said with a gleam in his eye.

Ruggerio's eyes narrowed and Ceramor growled. Neither of the rebels missed the signs. This was where their ideologies diverged. Where their alliance might fly apart. And it had to hold. Ruggerio knew the powers and the players and the inside workings in a way the Restoration would never be able to grasp on its own. But Ludvin had the people and their passion. He had the pipeline and the basic bones of plans that had been waiting for specifics to flesh them out for some time.

"Thank you, Dazia," Ludvin and Ruggerio said at the same time, two commanders acknowledging her contribution and releasing their asset.

The ghost girl looked from one to the other, and bobbed her head, gaze lingering last on her uncle, who ended up with a smug smile as though it proved who was in charge.

As though any of that mattered in the face of Dazia's revelations.

Roha tucked the Gospel of Gelerte away before seating nimself on the floor. *Not* sinking this time. Better rested and not following an enervating blast of power, the half-collapse of the church and a narrow escape. But ni did feel the support of a wall would be appreciated, and the nearest patch was close to where Ceramor rested. Ni trusted him well enough, loosely trussed as he was, to rest nes head back against the wall. He scooched a bit closer and leaned in like a big dog might, his warmth oddly welcome.

Ruggerio

In the aftermath of Dazia's announcement, the Restoration was a whirl of activity. Ludvin's attention was demanded for every little thing, so the actual tasks were thrust on his lieutenants. The bloodthirsty Hedric was set upon drills; Roha pulled together allies, risking nimself to recruit those in the Church who'd been most outspoken about Bloody Bess's attacks upon the anima; Hostill worked with some of the others gathering supplies and going over the logistics of escaping the city with them. Ruggerio's own work was with secrets and skullduggery, and he set about that.

He used all the paper and charcoal they could spare to make more fliers, easily evading Crown soldiers and the watch who were spread thin looking for him and the boy and Restoration rabble-rousers. They couldn't be everywhere, and the winter wind now howled and tore through the streets as though as hungry and heat-starved as the citizens. The watch would rather be keeping 'order' in a tavern or guard tower than patrolling the city. The better provisioned soldiers from the palace were not nearly as visible in the streets, preparing as they were to move out.

Ruggerio blended into the crowds at various taverns – always the louder, rowdier sort–before the curfew kicked in, listening to the gossip and spreading some of his own, always tales he'd "heard," about a *boy-*

prince, born on the wrong side of the sheets. Or maybe it had been a secret marriage for King Jannik. Hadn't they heard the same? Many of them had. The rumor had taken on a life of its own.

As for the missing girls, no one would have listened had it been just one. But ten? More? The tale grew as it was told until the missing and presumed murdered girls had become about the hunt for the boy's birth mother and the silencing of anyone who'd witnessed the birth or had a hand in helping her escape or in hiding the babe. Ruggerio almost smiled.

There was no stopping it now. The story was now as powerful as that of the Poison Princess.

Ruggerio did one more thing while he was out and about sowing discord, spreading information and disinformation—he sent a message. It was a risk. Bloody Bess was offering a reward for his capture, and Lord Sorvain could very well set a trap rather than send a message in return. However, Ruggerio had come to know the Lords well through his spying, and this one had been heeded less and less as the Regency wore on. Old King Grammond V'Alban, father of Kings Cyril and Jannik, had not engendered love so much as a brutal respect and the kind of loyalty where it would never occur to a person that they had any other option in life – the alternative being disloyalty and death. The sons hadn't ruled long enough to inspire much loyalty, and Princess Bessory none at all. She'd always been intended to be temporary, a figurehead for only as long as it took to marry her off so that she could produce an heir who could be groomed for the throne.

Maybe that had been a mistake. Maybe if they'd seen her promise and given her a path to real power she wouldn't have had to grab it so ruthlessly for herself. All those missing girls… Maybe there was just something rotten in the core of the V'Alban line. Or with the entire monarchy. Because Bloody Bess and her brothers hadn't been the first. There'd been King Calestri. And his father before him.

If Lord Sorvain saw that too, he might be willing to talk to Ruggerio. It was a risk. If he thought it was best for Jucar, he might turn in the former spymaster. Betray him, and let Bloody Bess carry through with her plans to restore the land, end the Restoration and the resistance. But fertilizing the fields with the people's blood and feeding the anima with their spirits wouldn't smooth over Jucar's rising anger. Relieving shortages wouldn't bring people back or make those remaining forget the lives exchanged. However, it might make them afraid to do anything about their resentments. For a while. People wouldn't stay down forever. Eventually, they would rise up.

Lord Sorvain would surely be smart enough to see that. If nothing else, Sorvain had always struck him as a man smart enough to keep a foot in both camps—to be able to say to whichever side might win that he'd been with them all along. If there was a way that he could stay on one side without losing the other... Ruggerio could live with that. He'd worked double agents before. And so, he risked checking the drop site he'd set for Lord Sorvain. His heart beat a little faster when he saw the tiny slip of parchment waiting for him there.

An encoded message said *'Ambush set for Grunder Pass'.*

That was all he needed.

It was after dark and past curfew when he slipped back into the Restoration safehouse. He gave the signal and was allowed entrance, grudgingly, by the woman keeping watch, but that didn't bother him. What did was the question of whether the information he'd gained could be trusted. Responding didn't mean that Lord Sorvain wasn't playing Bloody Bess's game, under duress or of his own volition. Before Ruggerio could act on the information, he had to verify things for himself as best he could. Bess knew about Dazia, which meant he couldn't entirely trust anything she brought them. Bess was clever enough to be sure Dazia overheard whatever she wanted her to and to find a way to keep from her anything she didn't. Lives depended on accurate information.

Speaking of which...

Those in their central cell of the Restoration basically slept in one room in shifts, Roha and Ludvin were never both down at once, and there were always at least two people on watch. As Ruggerio entered, as silent as death, he saw Roha closest to the door so that ni wouldn't disrupt anyone else if ni had to be awoken to whatever new emergency called. He also saw that for once, the satchel and the book were vulnerable. Roha had used them as a pillow, but had rolled away, head resting on nes hands, and so the book lay abandoned in his path, almost as a test.

He didn't spend even a moment debating what to do—the "noble" thing by walking away, thus justifying any mythical trust Roha might have in him, or the intelligent thing by garnering information by stealing the blasted book and doing his own legwork. Wars were won or lost on information and intelligence, and damned if they were losing this one because he was too principled for their own good. Roha was never going to trust him anyway, which was smart, though inconvenient to be sure. If ni caught him…well, he'd be certain not to be caught.

He swiped the satchel, eased the book out, slipped the bag back into place, and made away with his prize to the other end of the room where the hearth spat and struggled to keep up with the chill. Hostill lay closest to it, crying out in his sleep and twitching so hard that if the hearthstones were flush with the floor, he might have thrust a hand or foot into the fire. Ceramor, of course, slept at his feet. He was trussed up with a null strapped to his chest to keep him from trying anything they'd all regret. He was whimpering softly, as though in sympathy for the pain Hostill was feeling through the odd bond he'd forged with the boy.

Ruggerio avoided both and sat by the other side of the hearth, making space on the floor between the legs and arms of two other sleepers and their nests of blankets and belongings. He opened the book and tilted the pages to catch the firelight as best he could, a challenge when the shadow of his own big head kept getting in the way, but what he saw…

He risked getting up, brushing aside arms and legs, trusting to the exhaustion of the sleepers. Closer to the fire. So close he felt the heat on his hands. The pages would dry but surely weren't close enough to catch.

Men and women each hold part of creation, one side or another, and so it is only externally that they can access the anima. The only explanation I see that we, the Nim, can access the anima in and of ourselves in that we are both sides of creation, male and female, come together.

It hit him like a thunderbolt, and he had to reread. To make sure he'd grasped it correctly. But he found the book rising, being ripped right from his grasp. He grabbed on tighter, but he'd been caught unawares and tightened on it too late. Robbed of his prize, he burst upward, ready to fight for it back. He was shocked to come face to face with an enraged Roha. He'd never suspected ni could sneak up on him like that through a maze of entangled sleepers. He must have been lulled more than he'd thought by trust or familiarity—or maybe Roha had used some of nes powers.

"Thief," ni hissed, trying not to wake the others, but Ruggerio could feel at least a few sets of eyes on them already.

"I had to know," he said in his defense.

"You could have asked."

"Would you have told me?"

"You will not wake the boy," Ceramor snarled from right beside them, and then snatched the book from Roha's hand and went running for the door, leaping hands and legs and other body parts as though they were nothing, as though he never even touched the ground.

Roha took off after him less successfully, and Ruggerio less so still as people woke to Roha's landings or were awakened by their neighbor's cries or thrashing about.

They burst out into the hallway. Ludvin and those with him would be in the room they'd designated the council chamber to the right. Ceramor headed for the storeroom to the left. Roha waved off the guard between the two who startled at their sudden appearance and reached for Ceramor. Ruggerio barely spared him a glance.

The door to the storeroom closed on his back as he ran smack into Roha, who'd stopped just inside the entrance. There wasn't much farther ni could go with supplies taking up the meager space and Ceramor taking up the rest, holding up the book tauntingly, which they could see only because it produced a very faint light, as there was none in the storeroom itself.

"How are you even free?" Roha asked Ceramor.

His whole face twitched as though to scoff at the question. "I'm a mageri. Did you think your bonds would hold me?"

"But the null—"

Ceramor looked smug. "Search me."

"I won't."

Obviously, if he was free, he'd gotten rid of the null they'd placed on him, but had he gotten free of his bonds and stashed the null or worked the null loose and then gotten free of his bonds? It was in the ankari's best interests not to tell, but... Ruggerio had seen him nibbling and biting at his own neck like a dog with an itch. He'd attributed it to his feral, canine instincts, but now it became clear. And Roha, all this time leading them astray, having power of nes own, even as one of the Restoration? More than that, the revelations about the Nim...

"I told you ni had secrets," Ceramor said, glancing past Roha to Ruggerio as he stepped out from behind.

"Roha, I'll tell you how Ceramor got free if you'll tell me what's in that book, and what you can do," Ruggerio said. "I need to know what assets we have against Bloody Bess."

"How can you trust the spymaster with your secrets when he'll give up mine?" Ceramor wailed to Roha, sounding like a baying hound.

"A valid point," Ruggerio said. "What I propose is this, then. Ceramor, you give up your own secrets. I think you'd rather we consider you an asset than a liability. Give Roha back the book as a show of good faith. Tell nim about the null—or I will, to prove that I've figured it out and am not bluffing. Roha will tell us nes secrets. And I will tell you both where Bloody Bess's ambush is supposedly set, though I will want to confirm for myself before we pass the information along to the others. Agreed?"

The door opened, and Ruggerio whirled. Hostill's small, pinched face peeked in. "Did you really think I could just fall back to sleep and let you plot without me?"

Roha sighed. "Come in then. We started this together. I suppose we should continue as we mean to go on."

Hostill entered and everyone shuffled until there were four of them in the small space, illuminated by one glowing book.

"But first, we talk about me, yes?" said Ceramor. "I nibbled the chord tying the null to my neck and swallowed it days ago. Pooped it out yesterday. No more null. Nothing can hold me," he said triumphantly. "Ha ha!"

Roha looked horrified. Hostill stifled a smile, and Ruggerio made a mental note about null placements for future reference. But for now, Ceramor was on their side. He was an asset. As long as they had the boy, he could be trusted. More or less.

"Here's your book," Ceramor added, handing it over to Roha.

"Book?" Hostill asked.

"Shh," Ceramor said. "It's not magic. Ni is. Listen and learn."

He plopped himself down on the floor and looked up at Roha like he was a student and ni a great orator and he was settling in for a speech. Hostill, still half-asleep, sank down next to him with that boneless grace of children, and leaned in. If times hadn't been so dire and Ceramor weren't half-feral, it would have been a sweet domestic scene.

Roha closed nes eyes, took two deep, slow breaths as though looking for inner strength, and then opened them again. "Fine. I suppose you've all seen *or read*," ni said, glancing pointedly at Ruggerio, "enough by now to suspect some things. There's no reason that the world shouldn't know except that where there are people, there is prejudice and it always seemed safer to keep the truth hidden away."

Ni paused, taking another deep breath before continuing. "The Nim can access the anima within ourselves. We don't have to steal from the land or the air or from others. It's like there's a well deep within we can draw from that refills slowly, naturally. If we take too much, there's nothing left for ourselves. It's not like the unlimited power of tapping into the collective anima, though our way harms none but ourselves.

"I liberated this book from deep within the Church archives. It was written by Lehren Gelerte himself. It's called a Gospel but is really more of a treatise. He was working on a theory about how and why the Nim are as we are. He posits that the Nim are given to another form of creation. Nim are male and female come together, and it's the balance that puts us so close to the spirit and the anima. But he wondered whether there was a way for men and women to tap into their powers as well, because they're also a combination of their mothers and their fathers. They are not simply one or the other. If King Calestri hadn't destroyed him, he might have changed the world."

"You say, he, but in the book, Gelerte says we, indicating that he was one of the Nim," Ruggerio said.

It was as though the lighting of the book flickered with Roha's mood. "In Gelerte's time, Nim were even less accepted than in ours. Nim children were often killed, because they were deemed useless. Unable to marry, produce heirs to carry on a line. Aberrations. Some, as you know, were given to the Church. In theory, ni were accepted. Sacred and celebrated. In practice, ni made people uncomfortable, even more so because of our abilities. It was impossible to prove that the power didn't come from elsewhere, which would have been anathema to the Church. And to prove that the power came from within nemselves...well, how do you prove the intangible? It seemed to others implausible. Unnatural. To avoid the lifelong isolation and stigma, Gelerte did as many Nim did who went to the church, chose to live as him."

But Gelerte wrote the truth. The Church knew the truth. And they hid it away.

"But you're with the rebels. They want to do away with all mageri. How does this fit in with their philosophy?" Ruggerio asked.

"I want to stop the killing of the anima, the creeping desolation of the land, the deadness of the crops and the plague and the suffering of those left behind, who've lost everything that matters, including their own will to live. I don't want to kill mageri if there's another way. But if that's the only way to save the land and the people, then I am prepared."

There was a knock at the door, followed immediately by Ludvin opening it and appearing in the entrance. "Anything I should know?"

They all stared at him, and Ruggerio wondered how much he knew already. "Tell him about the ambush," Roha said.

CHAPTER THIRTY-ONE

Bess

Princess Bessory reached her chambers, guards opening the doors before her, and marching behind her. Her maid was already inside, awaiting orders, but as she opened her mouth to give them, her head split open, and she howled in such a way that her maid fell back in horror. The shadows in her head launched themselves for the rift, clawing to be the first to escape, shredding everything in their way.

But one shadow moreso than all the others. It was all articulated points, reminding her of the spider that was Garif. Each joint of the legs and body was made of blades, like armor fashioned to pierce rather than protect.

The room spun with the melee in her head, and she must have spun with it. She panicked, tears in her eyes, everything too much – too much pressure, light, pain. The cries from her maid like spikes through her head.

The room canted, and she was going down. Hands that were so hot— boiling, corrosive acid that might burn right through her clothing—lifted her and dropped her again onto a bed that felt like needles. They sank into her skin until they became part of her. The shadows in her head were a deeper darkness, the red of spilled blood against the blackout haze of pain.

Someone said her name and it was torture. Another someone laid a cloth against her head that was made of bees and ice. She hissed and flung it aside. There was whispering that came as loud as a shout. If she wouldn't explode with the sound, she'd order everyone out, but either she did or they sensed it, because finally they retreated.

She was left alone, but for the shadow girls clawing and flinging themselves against the sides of her skull. Howling or shouting, wailing, screaming or praying. It went on like a storm, buffeting winds, rain that blew sideways, knocking against shutters and penetrating every crevice into the palace as though it might tear right through. That shadow that was all articulated points, still girl-like but with arms grown and narrowed like a stick-insect's, probed at the rift she could feel in her head. It was horrible. Invasive.

In agony, she cried, "Stop!"

It was so sharp, so loud that it was like a concussive force inside her head, turning her mind to jelly. The pain so intense it blinded her.

But the fighting stopped. Either she had finally split her head, releasing the pressure within or she'd knocked out her shadow girls. For now. The echo died away, and the waves of pain receded enough that her vision was becoming her own again, her eyes adjusting to the scene inside her head. She checked to see that all of her women, all of their power was still with her. None had escaped through the rift she would have to repair, but all had collapsed into a heap. There was one figure still conscious atop the bloody pile, narrowed arms becoming all human again.

She was young.

Twelve. Galina was twelve. The age she'd been when...

Her hair covering was sewn with fake pearls that would someday be real. It was askew, cocked in the opposite direction of her hip. A minor lord's daughter, deemed suitable enough company.

Until the day...until the day...

She'd gone missing.

Bess's father, the King, discovered who his daughter was that day. *What* she was. She was mostly locked away after that, where her brothers couldn't touch her. The few times she saw them, their gazes were full of knowledge and fear. Mostly fear. It suited her well. A marriage was arranged for her far and away, where no rumors could reach.

Not that there were any. Not then.

Her father had paid Galina's family well to keep things quiet. The story they'd bring back was that their daughter was so well-loved that the princess had asked her to stay and be Bess's constant companion. It would have been true. She was so starved for attention, and Galina was so full of life.

Or had been.

Galina jumped down from the pile, as glowing bright in shadow as she'd once been in light, as though the sun had clung to her. Her eyes in particular were like someone had carved out twin suns to set just so. They were too painful to look at directly, but Bess refused to look away until it felt as though her own eyes burned.

"What do you think they talk about when you're gone?" Galina asked, her head cocked as it always had been.

Galina was never straight on to anything. A circuitous route, a rule reexamined for ways around, a hiding hole no one had ever found before. She was certain that her brothers had been looking for Galina that day.

It was a horrible thought, and it didn't justify anything at all.

"I'm sorry," she whispered, falling to her knees before Galina. She'd wanted to say it so many times. So, so many. But Galina would never show her face. All the other girls wouldn't stop, wouldn't quiet. And Galina would never appear at all. As though she was gone. Truly gone. Beyond anger or forgiveness. And now she wanted to play a game?

"I said, what do you think they talk about?"

Was she purposely mistaking the apology for a lack of hearing? It would be just like Galina to come up with her own interpretation.

"I mean—"

"Just like you, Bess, to think only of what *you* mean. To think only of yourself and your plans and your power. But they have plans as well—the Lords, your councilors. Don't you think? Power all their own, in their way. Your mageri too. You can't eat them all."

"I don't *eat*—"

"Don't you?"

The pile of bloody bodies, her shadow girls, leveled again in their uprising against her, started heaving, moaning. Those from the top rolled to the bottom and from there to their feet, rising as though forming from the bottom up, like a Torvus swirling up from the battlefield.

Only instead of a Torvus, they were their own righteous army, a first line of fighters advancing on her with murder in their eyes. One skipped like a child, as though killing Bess would be fun. Two dripped the salty water of the North Sea. Had they been alive when Bess had sunk them below the waves, watched over only by the inconstant moon and distant stars? Even the wind had whipped against her as though trying to turn her back from her terrible course. Perhaps it had known? Maybe it cried to her in a language she couldn't understand. She could think of no worse fate than sinking beneath those waves, sucking water instead of air, feeling her lungs fill and being able to do nothing about it.

Helpless.

Suddenly her air was sucked away and she was gasping, that terror washing over her in a great lung-collapsing, brain-blowing, limb-quivering quake. She faced the army robbed of breath, trying to hold her ground, testing her bladed nails, preparing to slice her way through the advancing girls if she had to. Only they were already dead. She'd already done all the harm she could do and now she had nothing. She cut only herself, her skin suddenly so thin it was translucent. She bled in rivulets that flowed to each of the shadow girls, feeding them until they grew to the size of monsters. She ebbed with the flow until she was a flicker of her previous blaze, set to go out.

As one, they sprang and she screamed with the last of her breath.

Bess startled awake, her heart erratic as a moth beating itself against a lantern. The pain pulsed, but she didn't have the energy even to curse it. She lay with the salt of earlier tears stiffening the skin at the corners of her eyes and new tears threatening. *Galina.*

She'd killed Galina. She'd lashed out as a child in pain, in need, in fear and even—she'd always shied away from admitting the ugliness even to herself—in completely misplaced, horrible, sickening anger that she'd been the one her brothers had found. She tried to excuse herself that she'd been in extremis. Untrained, lost in the moment. All she knew was that she hurt…so much…that she was broken. And here was someone whole with *so much life,* and if she could just tap into it. Take a little bit. It was instinctive. Galina was right, she hadn't thought about anyone but herself. She hadn't thought about what it would do to Galina. She hadn't intended to hurt her or kill her, hadn't considered that being untrained or too damaged to know what she did or when to stop she might go too far…

It had been an accident.

But had it? Had it really?

Was that her voice or Galina's? Was Galina poisoning her against herself or making her see truth?

She couldn't afford to think now, suddenly, that the same sadistic streak that ran through her family ran through her own veins, whether she'd inherited it or learned at their hands. She couldn't acknowledge that she had used and discarded Galina, only in a different manner than her brothers would have done, that her father had paid off the family the way he had others. That maybe she was, truly, her father's daughter. No. She had done what she had to do.

She had survived them all because she was stronger, that was all. If she held power over everyone, no one would ever hold power over her again.

She rang the bell beside her bed for her maidservant and then ordered her to tell the guards outside her door to bring Ulan, who didn't look much more than a ghost herself when she arrived, half supported, half escorted by the guards.

"They're plotting against me," Princess Bessory said from her bed after waving the guards away, leaving Ulan swaying beside her bed. "Tell your daughter to come back to me with what they're saying and who is saying it."

"If you kill me, your spy will follow me into death." Ulan didn't say it like a threat, but as fact.

"Then she must give me reason to keep you alive."

"May I sit?" Ulan asked.

"Sit down or fall down, as you like," Bess responded, and Ulan took her at her word, falling like a rag doll who'd been dropped suddenly by a child, sliding gracefully to the floor until her back fetched up against the chest beside Bess's bed, legs sprawled before her.

"Go," Ulan said to the air before her. "I'll be fine. I'll just have a little nap and be waiting here for you."

Dazia

Dazia flitted around the palace, frantic to find something to take back to the mad princess and save Maman, but she didn't know what she was looking for. She wasn't trained for this. She was a girl. Just a girl. And there almost wasn't anyone anywhere who wasn't talking about what was going on.

Bloody Bess wasn't interested in what was said in the kitchens or the servants' quarters or whatever. She'd want to know what her people were doing or saying. So Dazia concentrated on the noble parts of the palace, where people were whispering so they wouldn't be overheard or pulling each other behind closed doors.

Bowstan, the general, who always sounded like he was bellowing even when he wasn't, was saying to someone that he wouldn't discuss it. That he'd already said his piece and been ignored and now his job was to plan for all eventualities.

But the tall, scary mageri guy—Erdain or something like that—didn't seem to have the same problem. At least not based on the Lord who knocked at his door, glanced all around to make sure no one was looking—as if that wouldn't give him away, and then was let in. She didn't need anyone to open the door for her. She could ghost right through. Thinking about her mother in trouble gave her all the strength she needed to stay present, and it didn't take much to observe. If she wanted to affect anything, that was huge, but just being was natural, even if the anima and peace called to her like sleep or thirst had while she was alive.

"We can't afford to be seen like this," Erdain said by way of greeting.

The Lord, puffy and red-faced, said, "No one saw me. I left even my own guards behind."

"Won't that seem suspicious?"

"To whom? Everyone discounts me. No one is paying attention."

"I wouldn't underestimate the Princess."

"I wouldn't overestimate her either. Everyone seems ready to let her have her way, as though there are no other options, but you can't possibly be fine with all of this."

On the contrary, Erdain looked about ready to eat up his own lips, he'd sucked them so far into his face. He let them out now to answer. "I wouldn't say that, but it's not a bad plan—restore the land and do away with your enemies in one grand move. What ails me is that she's started her very own army of these untried women with rudimentary training by a revenant and very possibly mad mageri. It's unheard of."

"You mean Garif. One of yours."

"One of mine. Murdered and only living on in the body of his killer. His own wife. Asked to train an army of women. What would that do to a man?"

"What would it do to you?"

"Exactly."

"That's not an answer."

"Do you really need one?"

The men studied each other. Dazia didn't understand what was going on, but it didn't sound like what the Princess was looking for. She already knew all this.

"Do you think it will work?" the lord asked.

Maybe a little longer.

"I don't see why not. As long as the women don't mess it up. But...we're already at war with Frizenze and Galitrüd. The people are rising up. The last thing we need is to go to war with the Church as well if they take issue with the path Princess Bessory has taken to restore the anima."

"Do you think they might?"

Erdain shrugged.

"What if there was another option," the lord asked.

"Do you mean the boy child that's rumored in the city?" Erdain asked, the twist of his lips showing what he thought of that.

"I'm not talking about treason or usurping the Princess's place. Her father never had time to arrange another marriage after her first betrothed died, and so it falls to our Regent and her Council. My own Duke is a cousin to the crown–"

"Your own Duke is married –"

"But, sadly, I've just had a letter from him, and it seems that my Duchess is not well. It's not expected that she will last the winter." The Councilman sounded sad, and yet, there was something else to it...

Erdain must have caught it too, because he said, "Not expected by whom?"

"It may be that he will arrive in the spring to petition for a new arrangement."

"And you're telling me this why?"

"So far, the Princess has been unwilling to discuss a match, though we all know it must happen. Jucar needs a king, and heirs. The ascension must be assured. My Duke has spoken of bringing back the position of court mageri, and all of the benefits associated."

Erdain studied him, trying not to allow the smile that wanted to form on his lips. "I would learn more of your Duke and whether he would be a good choice for Jucar. I will certainly consider what you say."

"I look forward to talking further."

Dazia raced off ahead of the Lord leaving. She wasn't exactly sure what she'd heard, but she thought the Princess would want to get a look at that letter from the Duke, and if she could prove herself that way, then maybe her mother would be safe.

CHAPTER THIRTY-TWO

Ruggerio

That was the last time Ceramor allowed himself to be bound. For the rest of the preparations, he either stayed by Hostill's side or, if locked out, as close to him as doors, walls or windows allowed, snapping and snarling at anyone who interfered.

When that did no good, he bothered Ruggerio, dogging his heels.

Unlike the Princess's party, which could march out of the city with a show of force, the Restoration had to be canny about their departures, hide their numbers in dribs and drabs. So much easier to do in softer seasons, but now traffic into and out of the city had slowed to a trickle. They were oddly aided by the Princess's own plans. Rather than shut down the city and trap them in, she'd set an ambush far outside it. Why go to the trouble and expense of marching her enemies to their doom when they'd gladly feed and escort themselves?

It was diabolical. Something Ruggerio might have come up with himself. He shuddered to think he was feeling pride, but perhaps something akin to it. Or maybe it was the satisfaction of going up against a worthy adversary more directly than in a game of kingdom against kingdom. Still, appearances must be maintained, and there was no guarantee the guards were instructed to let *everyone* leave quite so easily.

Hostill, small for his age would hide in a smuggler's cache beneath the footrest on a wagon headed out with some of the supplies he'd wrangled. He'd taken to the idea like a cat to water, fighting and hissing. He wanted to sit the wagon, ready to take on the Princess's men and cost them dearly if they came for the rebels, but he was overruled. One day he might be king, but that day hadn't yet come, and wouldn't if they didn't survive to put him on the throne. But the wagon would be well guarded by a girl who was twice as good with knives as Hostill on his best day, perhaps even as good as Ruggerio; one of Ludvin's hulking lieutenants; and a woman neither large nor small. Impossible to see her form beneath her gown, but the muscles straining at the neck as she held her own loading the wagon suggested that she threw down with the men, and her sharp eyes as they darted about dared all comers to give her an excuse to take them on. Ruggerio knew better.

Roha rode out with Ludvin and would meet up with Hostill's party and the others of the Restoration along the way.

Ruggerio and Ceramor rode silently behind two Restoration soldiers who were dressed in the whites of the Church. Not in vestments, since they were bundled for traveling rather than officiating, but still in the bleached white representing the purity of spirit expected of them. One wore a cap that curved low over his forehead to protect it from the cold and then molded over his cheeks to do the same, edged in gold embroidery, clearly marking him the higher status of the two. The other held his horse a pace back to further that impression. Ruggerio and Ceramor rode behind, looking like any other guides or guards for hire, expected to take the lead only once they'd passed the gates.

'Acolyte' Ekland reached the gate first. He halted his horse, the others following suit behind him, Ceramor's making a lot of noise in the doing. It had not accustomed itself to the ankari yet. Ruggerio hadn't wanted to take him at all, but Ludvin had insisted that Ceramor's place was with him, and Ceramor had insisted the same. Ceramor could see through any illusions and dissect any spells. The Restoration soldiers Ludvin trusted were to both protect and keep watch on them and ride like the wind to report back on what they found. So Ruggerio was saddled with three unknowns.

"State your business?" called the guard at the gate.

Eckland peered down at the guard and at his partner coming up on the other side to hold his horse by the reins until satisfied with his answer. He glared when the man's other hand came up to stroke his mare's neck, as though to reassure her, even while silently provoking her rider.

"You must know that our church has been half-destroyed by an agent of the Crown. We've been sent to negotiate for Markensian marble for the rebuilding."

"Now? You'll catch your deaths."

He huffed, and the air plumed out of his lips and up into the air in a visual show of disgust. "We're not going all the way to *Markens.*"

The guard waited for more, and he huffed again before continuing.

"The war's destruction of Ingver extended to the church there. It was almost fully demolished. They've brought in a master stonemason already who has an importer for the marble. If we can reach him there then we won't have to wait until the spring for the merchants, then summer for our order, and probably autumn by the time we have bids and plans and masons free from other sites."

For all Ruggerio knew, that was even true. Roha would know better than he would. Ni had come up with this plan and supplied the robes. He had to hope that if the Church really was planning to order new marble from the stonemason at Ingver, they'd send out messengers when different guards were on duty.

"Enough," said the guard holding Eckland's horse, bored already. "A noble cause, but in winter winds, and taking so few? Surely you know of the rebels about?"

Eckland drew himself up. "We're hardly foolish enough to have the money for all that marble on our persons, and from what I understand, the rebels are more likely to take exception to the Crown than to the Church. Isn't that right?"

He danced his horse to the side so that the guard either had to release him, mince forward or fall off balance. The guard let the horse go, but his cohort caught the horse on the other side, unamused.

"Search them," he ordered, and he himself started with Eckland. When he found the man's money pouch, he helped himself to a coin. "To make you a touch less tempting...just in case."

Ceramor's horse tried to take a bite out of the guard that came for him, and Ruggerio had to stifle a laugh. Maybe it wasn't the ankari who bothered the horse. Maybe the beast was foul-tempered by nature.

Eventually, though, the guards let them go. Ruggerio's roll of potions and poisons was well hidden in his bedroll and packed so that nothing clinked to give it away. Truly, he didn't know what they expected to find. He and the others weren't so foolish as to have insignias or notes labeled "plots to foil the Princess". Ruggerio was a master of masking his appearance. The ash raked carefully through his dark hair and the beard he'd been growing added decades to his appearance, as did turtling of his neck to give himself a scholarly hunch. Ceramor – no one recognized a mageri without his long hair and beard, and hardly anyone had seen him since he'd been released. Clean-shaven and with his hair in an acolyte's topknot, the concern was more that he not begin itching at fleas than that he be recognized.

They were as anonymous as they could be.

Out past the gates, they turned in the expected direction. Ingver *had* been ravaged by the war and was in the direction they needed to go. Roha had chosen well. There was no reason for them to meet up with others from the Restoration, and every reason to avoid it in case they were followed, though there was no reason for anyone to bother. Princess Bessory counted on the Restoration coming for their people. The only question was where she'd set her traps along the way.

That was what they were to determine. Was the ambush set where they'd been told or was that a ruse? There were only limited routes to the Dobrens Valley, where Princess Bessory was going to perform her first resurrection of the land. The Restoration had to know which path would safely get them there, preferably ahead of Bessory's forces so they could lay their own traps.

Once the city was far enough behind, they raced against invisible enemies. Even Ceramor's horse forgot to snap at him once it had the wind to nip and kick at instead. They pushed their mounts until they reached the foothills of the Dobrens Peaks and had to slow to watch their footing and pick their trails. It was early yet, and dry, so the snow hadn't fallen as low as they were on the mountains or had already been blown away by the wind that howled and stole their breath as it left their lips. They wrapped scarves around themselves to keep as much of their heat in as they could, so that only their eyes showed, but the wind stung tears from them, and the biting wind threatened to whip the moisture straight away until their eyes felt as though they would crack like ice.

Eckland offered them each a strip of fabric they could wrap around their eyes, so thin they could see through it. On the treacherous ground, the thin textile shield might be enough to make things even more hazardous, but it was better than trying to see through the tears.

They passed the first day quietly. Not speaking—they'd never have heard each other over the wind and with mouths and ears muffled by fabric. Their vision adjusted quickly to the veil around their eyes, not that there was much to see. The others. Rocks. The occasional leaf-bare tree growing straight out of a fissure in the rock as though to show that life would find a way and cling to it against all odds, branches rattling in the wind like skeletons warning them of what would happen if they too should stop along the way.

They did, though. As darkness fell and shadows lengthened, Ruggerio, who had taken the lead, explored a shadow that seemed longer than the others and turned out to be a cave. Not deep and clearly not undiscovered, but unused at the moment. They took shelter. Eckland built a small fire in one end of the cave, and they all brought their horses to the other end and watered and cared for them as best they could. The poor things were exhausted, and Ruggerio, who would have given himself credit for being hardier, wasn't much better off. The constant cold had been harder on him than he'd realized, and now that he was down, he realized that he wanted to keep going, straight to the ground and just sleep. Which wasn't an option. Not yet. He'd do what he had to do. He always did. Even if his legs, which seemed to be made of overcooked noodles, didn't agree with him.

Eckland's companion, whose name he finally remembered was Morley, gave them each a small, slightly gray and very gnarled carrot like a hexte's little finger from a pouch at his side. "For your horses. Not for every day, but I have a few. Go ahead. Make sure to hold your hands out flat, so they don't mistake it for a finger."

As if they didn't know how to deal with horses.

Ceramor looked at the carrot like he'd like to eat it himself, but his horse didn't wait to be invited. The big roan swung his head around and nipped for Ceramor's hand before he could get his fingers flat—nearly, as Morley had warned, taking more than a carrot for his treat.

"Whoa, boy," Ceramor said, snapping his teeth at the horse, as though in warning.

The horse had swung its head away to chew, but now brought it back, snapping his teeth so close to Ceramor's nose he could probably feel the displaced air.

He stumbled back, and both Morley and Ruggerio laughed.

Ceramor smiled. "Your teeth may be bigger. For now. But mine are sharper." And before their eyes, Ceramor's cheeks began to lengthen into a snout, his teeth began to grow, as did he.

Morley cried out, his hand going to his waist, only this time he wasn't reaching for a carrot.

"Ceramor!" Ruggerio warned. And he did the only thing he could think of at that moment—he twisted Ceramor's ear like a naughty school-boy, bringing him down to one knee.

"Ouch!" Ceramor growled. "What was that for?"

Morley stared down at him, his blade only half drawn, but not going back into its sheath. He was breathing hard, clearly undecided whether or not to use his weapon.

"He's sorry," Ruggerio said.

"I'm—what?" Ceramor looked up to see Morley thundering down at him, the horror and complete incomprehension on his face. "I'm...I was just trying to show him who's boss. I wasn't going to *eat* him."

That wasn't making it better.

"I was making a joke."

"You were making a joke to a horse?" Morley asked, his voice as tight as a bowstring about to break.

"It made sense at the time."

Morley's gaze slipped to Ruggerio's, but only for an instant, like he was afraid to take his attention off the ankari. Ruggerio couldn't say that he blamed him. Ceramor really wasn't safe or sane. Certainly not predictable. But at this point, they were stuck playing with the cards they were dealt.

He shrugged. "I'll vouch for him."

Morley made some kind of criss-cross gesture that he thought might have come from the Church, and Ruggerio wondered if the acolyte's robes were his own. Maybe the reason Eckland and Morley played their roles so well was that they weren't roles at all. Maybe they'd defected from the Church with Roha. Or maybe the Church had some place in all this he had yet to learn. He was already reexamining everything he thought he knew. Or, at least, everything that he stood for.

They took turns at watch, except for Ceramor, who no one trusted not to take off or kill them while they slept, and emotions were running high when they set out in the morning, but no one had the energy for them as the day went on, and by the third day they were close enough to Grunder Pass not to be thinking of killing anyone but the enemy. Not that it was their job. That was just to observe and report. They'd taken the higher, narrow road to get a bird's eye view of Grunder Pass and avoid the Princess's larger force. Another group like theirs had gone out to scout the longer way around the mountains and into the valley. That had its own challenges and choke point later on. They had to know which was the set-up, where the Princess's forces were and where they could plan their own surprise.

They had seen and heard *nothing* on their way thus far, and Ruggerio was starting to get a very bad feeling in the pit of his stomach. What some called instinct, he knew to be the mind subconsciously analyzing a million signals even before the consciousness knew what it was reacting to. Something was wrong here.

His spyglass was frosting over, so he pulled the cold metal from his eye, warmed it with his breath, wiped the condensation off with the interior of his sleeve, did the same with the protected glass inside the end of the tube and tried again. Ceramor plunked down beside him and tried the trick with his hands, holding them like a spyglass to his eye and gazing down on the pass as well. Ruggerio wondered how he fared with it.

"We need to get closer." Because from here, even with the spyglass, he couldn't see a thing. Nothing moving. And yet—

"Too risky," Eckland said.

"Then don't risk it. I'll go," Ruggerio said. "If there's nothing there, there's no risk. If there is, better I spring the trap, don't you think, and leave you alive to report back? They'll expect scouts, so I won't be giving anything away, and you'll be well rid of me."

Eckland didn't look so certain of that, and Ruggerio was almost touched.

"At least allow me to pray over you," Eckland said.

Almost touched. "Knock yourself out, but only if I don't have to stand still for it."

He'd have to leave his horse behind. Inexplicably, the wind had died down, leaving near silence on the mountainside. The hoofbeats would be heard for miles and give him away in an instant. He'd have to travel by foot. And speaking of which... He whirled at the sound of someone behind him and found Ceramor right on his heels.

"What are you doing?" he hissed, even though he was not near enough to Grunder Pass to be overheard.

"Following you. If there's illusion or deception, I can sniff it out, and if there's magic, you'll need me to fight it or get a message back. Besides, for some reason, the boy likes you. He probably wants you back in one piece. Maybe two."

It would take longer to argue than to accept his help. "Just be quiet and take my lead. I mean that. No going off on your own. Going out of control can get us killed."

"I swear," Ceramor said, holding up a hand as though to take an oath.

Ruggerio didn't believe him for an instant, but Ceramor *could* come in handy, as sniffer or distraction. Or he could be a liability. At least Ruggerio wasn't going in with a precision plan.

Together they wound down the mountain, going single file, sometimes doubling back when the way Ruggerio had chosen became a sheer drop off or a pit of brambles. At one point, they turned around and down a ravine that was no more than chest width and no promise of an outlet on the other end, but Ruggerio trusted his instinct that there was an outlet. Ceramor, on the other hand, entered with a low rumble of distrust that rose in volume as they went on until Ruggerio was afraid he might manifest his claws and teeth and try to climb the sheer rockfaces to either side of them as he'd tried his oubliette. They were lucky enough to squeeze out the other end before the ankari tried to tear apart either Ruggerio or the rock.

Then finally, they were just above the pass, behind a rough outcropping of stone that hadn't been worn away by whatever had created the pass—a long-gone river or glacier or, some said, mountain wyrm that had hunted the mountain until devoid of life and then moved on. And still they saw nothing. Not that they would. Ambushes weren't meant to be seen, but...

"Anything?" Ruggerio asked, mouthing it more than making an actual sound.

Ceramor didn't answer at once. His head was cocked. His nostrils flared as he took in great gasps of the cold air and let it out again to coil up into the sky. His eyes were fixed on Grunder Pass, but not as if he was seeing it, at least not with his normal sight.

It was disconcerting, that Ruggerio had come to this–his life, the potential future of the kingdom here on this mountainside, and somehow he was entrusting it to this madman. Not entirely, of course. Ruggerio trusted nothing and no one entirely. But even so far–

They both heard it, a rumble like thunder. A flash like lightning, and suddenly, a whip-crack of pain sliced into Ruggerio from behind. He was catapulted straight over the rocks that hid him and thrown into Grunder

Pass. He landed hard, the agony crashing through him in waves, but he forced himself to roll to his feet to face the danger, gripping his sword in his dominant hand, his dagger in the other.

Something leapt over him, its shadow nearly freezing him in place. It whipped around as it landed, putting itself between him and Ceramor, cutting off his aid. His mind skittered, trying to make sense of what he faced. The backend of a beast or the front end of several, it was hard to say. There were several stalks snapping at him, and at first he thought that they were hissing, fanged serpents, but then realized that they were vines ending in needle-like thorns, glistening with menace. The hissing was the sound they made whirling in the air.

That left Ceramor facing off with the other end of the monster, he presumed something catlike by the thunder he guessed to be a roar. If Ruggerio had the tails, Ceramor faced the teeth.

A *Caturnine*, then. A mythical creature said to come from the deserts of Arthran. Not native to the mountains, which meant magic.

Cursed magic. The Restoration had the right of it.

The whip tails came for him before he could test the extent of his shoulder wound, but now that he knew it for a Caturnine, he also knew he'd have to end the fight quickly, before the toxin in those barbs could take effect. If he went down, he would die. The vines moved as though they had minds of their own, more like the snakes he first thought them to be. Some went left, some right, some striking straight for his face or his chest, where the toxin might blind him or stop his heart. So close in, there was no way to counter every strike.

He did his best, pushing away the terror as non-conducive.

He couldn't die here. Not now.

He had a job to do.

He fought on.

Ceramor

Ceramor had known something was off. Smelled it, felt it, but couldn't identify it until it was too late. Until he heard the roar and the lash of the Caturnine's tails and dove under them, coming up on what he expected to be the back end, but it had whirled, whipping Ruggerio and sending him spinning out of sight. The beast dripped mist in lieu of saliva, its teeth like daggers, canines oversized like the two that split his own lip as he transformed. A two-legged dog-man now facing the four-legged cat-creature.

He tasted blood, licked his lips and grinned at the beast. It was mageri magic that had created a desert cat in the mountains. He knew that, and so this Caturnine wasn't his true enemy, though his instincts said otherwise. There was someone behind it, but he was willing to go through the man-sized kit to get there.

He discounted the poor blade they'd given him, primarily for show—a mercenary soldier wouldn't be terribly convincing without a blade, but they hadn't trusted him with anything serviceable. This one was dull and pitted and all but useless. Not that anyone would have been able to tell with the weapon in its scabbard. He wanted to *feel* the not-skin of the cat rend and peel back and the anima spill over him. His claws would do very well for that.

He and the cat screamed challenge at the same time, ringing out over the mountainside, carried in the clear cold air, and it sprang, teeth out, claws out, ready to pierce him one way or another. He bent back, claws above him to rake the cat's soft underbelly. The tips of his nails caught, ripped furrows, mist shed over him like a fog. He never saw the back claws coming for him.

Suddenly, his own chest was on fire, the pain so unbearable there was no thought, no comparison, just the collapse to his knees, and the cutting of sharp stone into them, and then the falling onto his face and the bleeding onto the mountainside, an offering of his lifeforce back to the stone so recently robbed of it.

He hoped there'd be something left for himself.

Ruggerio

Ruggerio slashed at the vine-whip tails with his sword, yelling for all he was worth as he watched the creature bunch up its hind legs for a leap, knowing it was going for Ceramor. If he could make it turn on him and keep its attention, he could give Ceramor time to work, find their real enemy, the mageri behind its manifestation.

But he was too late. He swung, and the beast leapt, screaming its anger, but not stopping as two of the poisoned barbs fell from its tail, dropping and rolling on the ground, where they instantly took root, shooting up stalks as though nourished by their own venom. And at the end grew tiny barbs that sought out prey, homing in on him. He cursed, dodged them, hoping they wouldn't grow like kudzu, taking over the whole mountainside. Or that they'd die when he killed their host. Which he *would*.

He saw Ceramor go down and raced for him, yelling like a fool to get the Caturnine's attention. It was probably already too late for Ceramor, and he'd now given the beast notice of his attack, but idiotic instinct said to draw it away from the injured man. Sentiment was a killer. Possibly literally in this case. Not something he could afford. But what was done was done, and the creature was already glaring murderously at him.

The thing about beasts was that they didn't waste time on banter. It sprang instantly, and there was no way Ruggerio was going to outrun it, so he did the unexpected, he ran *in*. And *stumbled*. Oh great fumbling fires, he'd forgotten about the barbs. About the poison. It was slowing him down. Making his feet drag and get in the way of each other. He was going to have to finish this quickly. And carefully. But those two things didn't often go together, especially not in the heat of battle.

The beast's teeth and claws missed him by a hair's breadth, and instead of driving his sword through the Caturnine's soft palate and up into its skull as he'd intended, he was suddenly crashing into its shoulder. New plan. He sank his dagger in as high and as deeply as he could, and swung himself upward, using the dagger as he would a hand grip on a mountain climb to pull himself upward onto the beast. The Caturnine snarled and whirled suddenly, snapping to rid itself of the pain and the cause of it. Ruggerio used the momentum of its sudden turn to propel himself the rest of the way onto its back. Once there, he yanked the dagger out and plunged it in again at a better angle to steady himself in his seat. Mist poured out of its wounds in lieu of blood, streaming somewhere toward the earth. Maybe back to the land or to the mageri who'd created it to allow for the formation of some other menace. He couldn't look right now. He had to kill the creature before it could unseat him and stomp him to rubble.

He raised his sword, prepared to drive it straight through the Caturnine's spine or whatever substituted for it in a magical construct, but two barbs of the beast's tail struck him from behind, dead center, upper and lower back, and then others joined them until he was a pincushion, a nest of needles.

The pain was searing, excruciating, like being ripped open, exposed to fire ants the size of plague rats whose feet were covered in acid. Next, he was sliding from the beast's back, falling to the ground, head torqued to the side, facing the creature, which was rearing, claws lashing the air like a Caturnine rampant, like it was posing for some sort of flag or pennant. Its tails were streaming, whipping in triumph.

Then he saw the impossible, an equally rampant dog-beast rising. He knew it was Ceramor. Had to be Ceramor. But he was no longer even half human. He stood shoulder to shoulder with the Caturnine now, three heads— three!—to her one, but one tail to her nine, because her lost barbs had grown back.

They came together in a clash of claws and teeth, blood and mist.

Ruggerio forced hands made of mountain rock—heavy, immovable, unmalleable—toward the roll at his waist. He had to have something to counteract this poison. Something. He couldn't die here.

Ceramor

The heads were hungry. Bloodthirsty. The anima bleeding off the Caturnine had fed his transformation, but not decided the shape he'd taken. The dogs that bayed within Ceramor had risen to the fore, coming to the call of the hunt. Bones popped and cracked with incredible agony, muscles tearing, stretching, reforming. Then heads to either side snapping and snarling, knocking left, then right, fracturing skulls and battling for dominance, fighting the wrong enemy.

He fought back, fought with himself. Knocking heads, biting, bleeding. It took a monstrous effort to raise his forebody from the ground, but he took control. The Caturnine facing them was rampant; he couldn't allow it the upper hand. Monumental to rise, but nothing at all to fall, the greater mass of three heads and the muscle it took to support them crashing down in a clash of snarls, teeth and claws. Flesh filled his mouth, and he bit hard, ripping and shaking his head as though he might snap his prey's neck. Instantly, mist blew up around him so that he couldn't see what damage he was doing. He only knew it by the grip of his teeth and the flood of anima that he gulped down in the absence of blood. It tingled and popped, made parts of him come alive, but dissipated, wasn't something he could swallow down with satisfaction. He missed the blood. And the Caturnine wasn't some smaller prey who could be killed off so easily.

He was left with nothing but pain to his chest from the claws that ripped and tore, frantic to force him to disengage.

He came away with the Caturnine's borrowed essence, her anima, and she with nothing but blood, which, freely flowing, was maybe his essence too, pouring out upon the earth.

He and the Caturnine came down hard, and suddenly, the head to his left was taking over the attack, but his neck wasn't long enough to skirt her jaws to get at her jugular—not with his other two heads attached, and so they were just biting at each other. If he and the Caturnine continued to meet head on, it would be a bloodbath. They would fight until one of them lost too much blood or anima. Until one was too damaged to go on. It wouldn't be a clean fight to the death. He had to get to her back or sides. Or he needed to track whoever had control of her.

But she wasn't going to let that happen.

Ruggerio

Ruggerio managed to move incrementally and then stopped dead. He hoped it was only a figure of speech, but he was very much afraid that it wasn't. The only things still working seemed to be his heart and lungs, and they were uncertain. He was lying face down, and either the poison or his own weight were putting a lot of pressure on them to stop entirely. So much easier, and really. If only he hadn't bought into his own sense of importance – that *he* could save the kingdom. That he had to be there to guide the others, the boy...

So his heart, his lungs and maybe his eyes were still with him, though he wasn't so certain they weren't playing tricks on him when he saw the human figure running across the battlefield where the two beasts were locked in combat. It seemed too risky for reality.

Then he feared that it only made sense for one side to race out onto the battlefield—the one that could control the Caturnine. Why wait to see who won the battle when they could try to tap into Ceramor through his wounds? It was a dark magic, but Bloody Bess had shown no qualms at all about using forbidden rites.

This was no kind of ambush—or if it was, it was set only for them. There was no army here or it would have been sprung. The message left for Ruggerio must have been meant to draw him out to investigate. He'd miscalculated, and here he was near-dead on the ground. He'd been out-maneuvered, and by a mere girl. Had Bloody Bess known or guessed that the Restoration would also send their other misfit, the Crown's other defector with him, leaving themselves magically defenseless? Was she *that* good?

Had Eckland and Morley gotten away? If they'd seen the Caturnine, they might have ridden off believing in the ambush at Grunder Pass and that the other route was safe. He had to survive. He couldn't let them convey that message and risk all the others. He couldn't let Bloody Bess win.

He made another desperate attempt to move, and while his upper body refused to respond, his feet scrabbled at the rocky ground, at first catching nothing but scree which slid out from under him. One foot finally locked on a jut of stone that stuck out enough to allow him to roll over onto his back—where he caught sight of Morley coming up on him and a man right behind him with a dagger raised, ready to bury in his back.

His eyes widened, and he tried to grunt a warning.

Apparently, it was all Morley needed. He whirled in time to block the fall of the dagger and swing a blow to the man's jaw. As he reeled with it, Morley sent a kick to the side of the man's knee that crunched bone and crumpled him halfway to the ground. Morley launched himself at the man then, sending them both rolling across the stony ground toward the dagger. Both reached for it, but Morley rolled the man on top, pulled a dagger from a sheath at his own side and buried it in the man's throat before he could find another. It had all happened so quickly that Ruggerio tracked it at only half the speed and caught up only after the man was dead.

He carried the weight of the mountain on his eyelids, and now that he was safe, they wanted to slide shut.

A sharpness stung his cheek, rocked it to the side. Another rocked it back. His cheeks stung like hornets had been at them, but only for a moment. His eyes opened on a blur. A face.

He tried to close them again, but someone pried open one eyelid and held it that way. So rude.

"Antidote?"

He shrugged. Thought he shrugged?

"Green vial," he tried to say. But it came out more like "een isle," if it came out at all, and he wasn't even sure what it meant. It had come without thought. He had a distant idea that he'd been poisoned, and that's why he wanted to drift off to sleep, but he didn't know with what or why, so he certainly had no conscious idea of what would help. Sleep was also a good way of conserving strength.

The hand on his eye went away, and it snapped shut again. His body rocked. Maybe. Or maybe it was the clash of the great beasts snapping and snarling at each other shaking the earth, and then someone was prying at his lips. He didn't have the energy to resist, but he didn't help either, and then something poured into him and someone rubbed his throat to make him swallow. He wanted those same beasts to come trample that someone to dust, but it didn't happen.

What did happen was that the same something or someone grabbed him under the arms and pulled him away from any hope of a trampling or quiet death and over sharp rocks he could barely feel, because while his body was waking up again, it seemed a case of the cure being worse than the disease. His skin, his veins, his very *self* was on fire, as though someone had injected a serum of stinging nettles and snake venom into his system. His stomach was made of churning magma, wanting to burn its way out and liquify everything on the way. And it was making great, ghastly noises. The someone—Morley, his brain supplied—pulled him around a bend and dropped him like he too felt the fire. Immediately Ruggerio rolled onto his side and began puking up gobs of black gunk.

His eyes squeezed shut and teared up with the violence of the expulsion, and the biting cold wanted to freeze them that way. If it weren't for his feverish body fighting the chill, it would have succeeded. It took all he had to pry his eyes back open, to push himself up on his arms, shaking like a newborn calf, and look for the figure that had run across the battlefield, but the two beasts had fallen to the ground now, and were locked in battle, mist streaming off the Caturnine, and blood running in rivulets from Ceramor, who seemed almost to lose mass as he watched. Ruggerio's mind was still sluggish, shaky like the rest of him, but the conclusion was obvious enough—what he'd seen was a mageri running across to collect Ceramor's spilled blood, using proscribed magic to tap into him. Ceramor didn't have long.

Ruggerio's arms weren't going to hold him for much longer. They'd gone from shaking to shuddering. He pushed back onto his knees, and from there sat back on his heels, swaying, but grabbing onto Morley, who knelt beside him on one knee.

But Ceramor's triple heads suddenly rallied, throwing the Caturnine this way, and Morley launched himself upright with his sword to put himself between Ruggerio and danger, leading with his sword. It pierced the Caturnine's side, but that only enraged it. The beast snapped at Morley, catching his sword hand between its jaws, causing an awful crunch and scream, but leaving its neck wide open for Ceramor's jaws.

Ruggerio saw it all, heard it all, and seized the moment. He was shaky, weak, but he saw the direction Ceramor's spilled blood wanted to flow, and he thought he knew where their mageri was hiding. He could either end the Caturnine by ending the mageri or draw its attacks to give Morley and Ceramor a chance. If he couldn't be dexterous, at least possibly he could be crunchy.

He'd underestimated the difficulty he'd have just getting to his feet, just closing his hands around the grip of his sword, walking two steps without vomiting. He did vomit again as he staggered toward the mageri's hiding place, feeling weaker but less hot and horrible afterward. He couldn't have been inconspicuous, but he must have been non-threatening, because neither the magic man nor his creation took any notice of him, caught up in the raging battle.

Ruggerio kept going only by using his sword as a walking stick. He had a certainty that if he stopped, the battle would be over with none of his side left alive to help him up again.

He skirted the only outcropping he saw that could be hiding the mageri and then had to lift his sword as it had been intended, knowing that any drag would be heard. He'd had to pick up his feet for the same reason. It cost him. But now that he was here, now that he'd come up behind his prey and could see the back of the hooded figure crouched behind a rock, looking down over the "battlefield," such as it was, his heart was beating a little faster again, and his blood was pumping. The fever and chills seemed to have reached an understanding.

He swung his sword, and in the stark light it cast a shadow that he couldn't help, giving warning. The figure gasped and rolled to the left, hood falling back to reveal that it was a woman under there, cowled under the hood, but it didn't matter. His dagger was instantly at her throat, his sword now pinning her in place so that she couldn't slide out along that one side—not that he couldn't slit her throat faster than she could escape him in any case.

"Cease your workings," he commanded.

"She'll kill me," the woman said. There was terror in her eyes, but a determination as well. She believed what she said, and knowing Bloody Bess, Ruggerio did as well.

"I'll kill you sooner."

"I'd rather it come from you," she said, forcing her neck up into his blade.

He was so shocked he twitched his blade back, but not quickly or far enough. His weight was forward, against the sword arm that had her trapped against the rock. There wasn't time to shift it all back and himself away before she'd thrust herself onto the dagger, and when it met resistance, her hand came up and curled itself around his own, pulling the blade into her neck with a strength born of desperation and fear.

She'd rather die than live on as one of Bloody Bess's shadow girls. Rather impale *herself* than let the Princess drain her away, spirit and soul. He couldn't blame her. But to be the vehicle...

He ended it quickly. She'd made her choice, and she would only suffer if it was half done. There was no saving her now. He saw her exhale her last breath and watched as it plumed in the frigid mountain air. It had to be fancy that he saw her spirit escaping, but unlike his breath, it didn't quickly dissipate in the whipping winds, but flew out to meet the anima now streaming out of the Caturnine, flowing from its wounds. Buoyant, he would have said, as though partnering with the breezes, dancing with them. They whirled together for an instant, before floating down to the ground. They settled through Ceramor, wounded, heaving, half the size he'd been when the fight had started, and Morley, now on the ground as Ruggerio had been when the man had found him, and straight into the earth.

Ruggerio shook from the aftermath of it. From what he'd witnessed or the sudden burst of battle strength leaving him or whatever, it didn't matter. There was still work to do. He stumbled onto the battlefield, using his sword again as a support. Ceramor was transforming, losing his heads, limbs popping and cracking, hair retreating. It was the stuff of nightmares, though it had been years since they'd visited themselves upon Ruggerio.

Thus, he focused first on Morley. Morley's eyes didn't even flicker as Ruggerio tried as gently as possible to pull back the jagged remains of his once-white cape to see what was left of his arm. It was missing from the elbow down, broken bone jutting out, the meat raw and purple-red around it. So much blood. Ruggerio couldn't even conceive of the pain. A break was one thing, but this...

301

He had saved Ruggerio's life – killing one mageri and putting himself between Ruggerio and the Caturnine when it charged. Ruggerio had a responsibility to save Morley's life in return if it could be done.

Ruggerio went to Ceramor now, leaning over him and calling the man's name, patting his human face, now that he had it back. He was afraid to be harsh with him, lest he come up fighting tooth and nail. The man was fully naked, clothes probably shredded in his transformation, but he'd seen everything before. There were two bodies he could steal coverings from. They'd never miss them. But first things first.

"Ceramor, are you alive?" he said. Perhaps *that* was the first thing to be determined, but he was fairly certain that nothing short of a full-scale war would kill the ankari, and this had been but a skirmish.

"Mmmn," he said.

"Can you heal yourself? Or others?" Ruggerio asked. "Morley sacrificed himself for us. He may die if you can't help him."

There was another noise that turned into a deep snore. Ruggerio didn't waste breath even on a sigh.

He went and roughly stripped the cloak from the man Morley had killed, rolled Ceramor onto it, and dragged him to behind the outcropping where the dead mageri lay, where he'd at least be protected from the worst of the wind. Then he bundled Ceramor the best he could to keep him warm and returned for Morley.

He had an idea there at least. He wasn't sure Morley could survive the shock of cauterization, but he had to stop the bleeding and hold off infection. Oddly, the outcropping of barbed vines that had grown up from the Caturnine tails Ruggerio had cut had not vanished with the beast but flailed about looking for prey. If he could harvest them safely, the poison he suspected they held would work to keep off infection—safe enough when applied to the skin, poison when ingested. Given the dangers inherent in his craft, he had to know what healed every bit as well as what harmed.

The mageri who'd caused all the trouble wouldn't be needing her cloak either, and as he stripped it from her, he got a better look. He recognized her as someone his network had investigated due to reports that her entire household had gone untouched by the plague while all around them had withered and died. They'd not found evidence that anyone had powers – not her or any of the children; her husband, as in so many Jucari families, had never come back from the war. Not that power would have mattered to the Rot, which didn't care a fig for magic. If mageri magic could have healed it, they'd have ended the plague well before it took so many lives. But an *entire family* overlooked by the plague?

And now this woman's abilities were lost to the world.

Cloak in hand, Ruggerio went out to face the poisoned vines. The mageri he'd taken it from wasn't a large woman, and so the cloak wasn't voluminous. He wouldn't be able to double it to smother the vines but hoped a single layer would be thick enough to protect him.

CHAPTER THIRTY-THREE

Roha

The Restoration had left the royal city in dribs and drabs and their numbers were still growing, fed by members from other cities and villages, some of whom had joined them in the successful attack on the Magery before disappearing back into their old lives until called on again. The Restoration had a reliable messenger off High Street who had some means to get messages out with amazing speed. Everybody had a secret, it seemed.

Growing numbers were good. Not good was the fact that neither scouting party had returned, and time was running out. If they didn't make a decision soon, there would be no way for them to reach the Dobrens Valley before Bloody Bess's troops. It might be too late already.

Ludvin stood beside Roha, scanning the peaks and passes, each with their own spyglass. Others were set up elsewhere on the mountain. One twist and turn of the trail could conceal or reveal multitudes.

So it was that they weren't the first to catch the movement. A runner raced to tell them where to look, since they couldn't risk shouting it across the mountain. Roha and Ludvin angled their spyglasses to see a horse, stumbling, exhausted, but making its way down the mountain. Without its rider.

It was coming from the direction Ruggerio, Ceramor, Eckland and Morley had set out. Four men and none had come back.

"Grunder Pass," Ludvin said, lowering his glass.

"All dead," Roha said, lowering nes.

"We don't know that."

"No," ni admitted. "But—"

"Yes."

They both hung their heads. One quiet moment of reflection.

Then Ludvin whipped his head up.

"Get that horse!" he ordered, voice raised, but not enough to carry too far across the mountaintop. "Start preparations. We travel via Vraily Way."

"But we don't know that's safe. Restin's crew hasn't returned either," Roha protested.

"We know Grunder isn't, and we're out of time. We'll face whatever comes."

Roha's thoughts and feelings were like a bladed pendulum, swinging from the knowledge that he was right to the certainty that he wasn't. That something here was very wrong. But the only thing ni had to go on was the missing scouting party, and that could be anything. A landslide, white-out snowfall, or other misfortune delaying them, having nothing to do with Bloody Bess. Each swing cut Roha until ni was raw and bleeding. Ni would never be equipped to do what Ludvin did, make decisions that meant life or death to the people who believed in him, in his cause.

But then ni saw the state of Eckland's horse – completely knackered, gear listing to the side as though his rider had fallen and nearly pulled his saddle with him. The horse was more staggering than running, sheer momentum all that kept him upright. As soon as the man leading him into camp stopped, his legs gave out, collapsing under him like sticks that broke in the center. From there, he rolled to the side, his eyes likewise rolling in their sockets, sides rising and falling like a bellows. There was blood smeared on his neck, but not his own.

Roha knelt to look for other signs, evidence, but there was nothing.

Three days to the Dobrens Valley.

Two days to the most likely ambush – where the way opened to a path large enough for soldiers to descend, but tight enough to be a choke point.

They would know soon enough whether they made the right decision. Bess wanted them in that valley for her sacrifice. But she'd want to be sure that she had the upper hand. That there were no surprises and that they wouldn't be able to escape once Bess had them where she wanted them. They had to be ready for anything.

Vraily Way was the more obvious of the two routes. Where Grunder Pass was only a section of Regenary Peak that had been worn flat while the surrounding rock had held its ground, leading to a gentler decline through the range and into the Dobrens Valley, Vraily Way was a wider expanse between two of the peaks. It was longer around, though. Less favored by travelers, though possibly more favored by an army. It was difficult to know what went on in Bloody Bess's mind.

Roha wished they'd had another visit from Dazia. Ni'd watched for it. But there'd been nothing, and ni feared for Ulan's life. If she died, her daughter would have no reason to stay. It was selfish to want her to do so. She should go on to the anima. And yet... Those who stayed behind had so much depending on her. Could it be, though, that Ulan had no energy to lend her? Or that Bloody Bess was using Dazia herself? Threatening Ulan to make that happen? Could she...could Dazia be spying on them?

Without Ceramor to give warning, there was no way to know. Roha never thought ni'd come to miss the ankari.

As the gathered Restoration army approached the Way, they could see signs of Bloody Bess's army having passed – hoof prints, horse droppings, broken branches. They would not beat her to the battlefield. Their caution had seen to that. *But Eckland's horse had come back bloodied and alone, so the caution hadn't been misplaced.* Pain pierced Roha's heart like the dagger ni wanted to thrust through Bloody Bess's. Roha didn't even like Ruggerio particularly, but somehow ni felt a pang at the thought of his death. Worse even was the thought of Eckland and Morley's loss. Roha had recruited them nimself. Ni was responsible for their deaths.

The Animist would have told Roha that was hubris. That every person made their own decisions and that as long as they chose the right rather than the easy path, they were doing what they needed to do. If their deaths saved hundreds of others, then they certainly would bring light and life to the anima. Wasn't that all anyone could ask?

Wasn't that what Roha believed?

Hedric and a woman, one of the Restoration's members from outside the city, came thundering up on their horses. They'd been sent ahead to see whether they could find any sign of the earlier scouts – or of the ambush they'd been looking for.

For once, Hedric wasn't sneering, but he looked spooked. "Nothing," he said, as soon as he was within hailing distance. "Nothing at all. Not a rockfall. Not a body. No sign of them."

Roha held up a hand to halt the procession so they could talk. To give time for Ludvin, who was guarding the rear, to ride up from his position. He'd want to hear this. To decide...there was nothing to decide. They'd move onward. But with caution. *More* caution.

"Maybe the Crown captured them," the woman said. "They may still be alive. For now."

"What's the story?" Ludvin asked, after some shifting of positions with the horses, to allow for his progress.

They told Ludvin what they'd told Roha.

His face – inset with lines of grief as though a master carver had incised them there when he'd been told about his sons, first one and then the other, would not return to him from the Blood War – didn't so much as twitch. He'd expected the news.

"We continue on. This changes nothing. I – we – must go on. But...our Vizi is gone, and I do not have the words to rally the troops. I never have."

The sadness in his face, in his eyes. No, he did not have the look, the words. He had the motivation. Roha now understood that his thirst went beyond ending the mageri and the desolation of the land. It might only be quenched by ending Bloody Bess and the V'Alban line responsible for ending his own. Ni wondered whether even he knew himself.

Ni and Hedric looked at each other, communicating silently for the first time, together rather than at odds. He nodded as though granting Roha the boon. He would gladly lead the people into battle, but he would leave the speeches to others. He had decided that ni was good for one thing, at least.

"Let me," Roha said, inhaling deeply, trying to breathe in the anima all around, feel the cold air fill nim, ripple across the well somewhere inside. Not that ni would draw from it, but it centered nim knowing it was there.

Ni turned on nes horse, faced the army, saw those closest looking at nim expectantly. And at Ludvin, Hedric and the woman, whose name ni just remembered was Dré. Those at the front had seen Hedric and Dré ride up without the former scouts.

"Good people." Roha almost winced. It sounded warm when Vizi said it. Round, encompassing, sincere. His voice was larger than he was, than the space he filled. It was electrifying. Roha had spent all of nes time in the background at the Church. Assisting. Seen but not heard.

Ni cleared nes throat. Forced nimself to stand straighter. Shoulders back, chin up. Take the space, fill it. Expand the chest, expend the air. "You are here for a purpose greater than yourselves. You are here not just to save your compatriots in the Restoration, but to save Jucar." Roha grew louder as ni grew more fervent, as ni said what was on nes heart. Maybe *that* was what Vizi did every day.

"Too big a task, you say. Impossible. There is too much set against us. To that I say, *remember the Magery*. Anyone would have told you that was impossible. If you told anyone in advance – anyone at all – spouses, sisters, brothers, I'm sure they did just that. But we took it down, didn't we? *The Restoration did that.*"

There was a shout from the army.

"What's that? I didn't hear you?" Roha called out.

Another shout, louder.

"That's right. Without magic. Without ravaging the land. Now, Bloody Bess is out there with her mageri and our people. If we let her, she will use both. She will –"

"Roha!" Hedric shouted.

Beside him, Dré screamed, and Roha looked beyond the vision in nes head, beyond the next words crowding themselves. All of them fled in an instant. Instead ni ordered, "Run!" wheeling nes horse and leading the way. Fear sweat instantly rose and chilled nim to the bone as the wind whipped up.

At the back of the army, Bloody Bess's mageri had summoned a mighty Torvus, a beast with a great sloped back something like an oxen but at least four times as large with huge clawed hooves it stomped and gouged across the rock. It snorted a massive gust of ani-mist from its nose, which flew up to razor-sharp horns that matched the lower set of tusks.

It was like a dread beast had come charging out of a nightmare. Ludvin and the others were already off, the rest of the army racing with them.

Bloody Bess's ambush had sprung, and the Torvus was herding them exactly where she wanted them to go, where the final battle awaited.

But it would be madness to stand and fight the Torvus. At least the Dobrens Valley was devoid of any anima. At least it would be a level playing field.

Roha had to believe that as they raced for their lives.

Cia

Cia fought like never before as she was held between two guards beside Bloody Bess, who stared off into the mountains, a spyglass raised to her eyes, not trusting anyone else's report. Cia had waited for too long to escape, never finding the right moment. Now she stood on the eve of battle, Garif like a flickering madness, infecting everything within her. He'd left her the body as she'd been trussed up and thrown into the supply wagon alongside Ulan. Crates and other supplies crashed into them as they traveled, despite the thin blankets that were supposed to protect them but instead bunched beneath them at the first jounce. The important thing was that they lived, not that they enjoyed the experience.

The large, decorated man beside the Princess whipped down his spyglass and drew in a breath, his barrel chest expanding to shout his orders, but she beat him to it. "They come! Troops to the ready. As soon as they hit the valley, we attack!"

He glared, but only for an instant before he was on the move, shouting his own more specific instructions.

Cia's own breath stopped and her heart along with it. Whatever they had seen, whatever sign Bloody Bess had been waiting for, it had come, which meant things had gone against Roha and Hostill, against the Restoration. She and Ulan were out of time.

No, not out of time. Not while they still lived and breathed.

The General's orders caused a great commotion. Men mounted or drew up into formation, spread out and advanced, their weapons drawn, at the ready, leaving the captives down the field from where the Restoration would come for them.

Cia gasped in as her air ran out and managed a single breath before Bloody Bess turned on her, her eyes daggers that pinned Cia in place.

"Now you," Bess said. As Cia struggled to understand, the Princess added. "Guards, bring him forth."

They dragged a man forward and threw him to the ground. He raised himself up onto his elbows but didn't try to get to his feet. Exhausted or beaten down, she couldn't tell. Neither did she recognize him. Was he one of the rebels? Someone they'd sent to scout Bloody Bess's camp who'd been caught?

"Bleed him," Bess ordered.

"Princess?" asked a guard, looking to his companion for aid.

If the glare she'd snapped at Cia was a dagger, the one aimed at the guard was a full and freshly sharpened sword. "Bleed him, and now. His blood or yours, I won't wait, and I am not particular."

The Crownsman dropped to his knees, and lifted the man's head by his hair, taking the dagger from his belt to nick the man at the neck. His victim offered no defense.

"Now feed," Bess commanded.

Cia tried to back away, but she was held fast. The Princess gave a nod, and the guards holding Cia kicked her knees out from under her. She crumpled, landing hard beside the man.

"Her hand," Bloody Bess ordered. "Lay it over the wound."

Cia wondered what the guards thought, but whatever they felt, it wasn't enough to stop them from grabbing her palm and manhandling her with all vehemence, mashing her hand straight onto the bloody gash. Garif oozed like blood to the surface of her mind, not through her pores, but from all of her hidden places, those she thought she'd locked off, hidden away from him. He was poisoning them, polluting them with his presence. He seeped from them now only to do more harm, tap into the man through his open wound and draw on his energy to allow him to possess Cia's body and hold it. To use it to sustain himself to do Bloody Bess's bidding.

Cia had to watch in horror as the living man was drained of his essence. He lifted his face to her once, a plea, and she could see the color leach out of his skin, his cheeks go hollow. Faint lines began to form, then become crevices, cracks. Everything grew dry, desiccated. The flicker of light in his eyes went out, filmed over, drawing the veil from life to death. She wanted to shut her eyes, turn away. But Garif wouldn't allow it.

All while the man withered, she felt Garif grow bloated on his essence like a tick.

*Not me...us...*he said in her head. She didn't just hear it, but *felt* it. Pulsing like a heart. They were one now. If he grew distended and sanguine, or gangrenous and unnatural, so did she. If she retreated before it, she yielded ground to him. Perhaps he counted on horrifying her into nonexistence.

She had to fight it. He thought he could repel her into virtual death; perhaps she could starve or exhaust herself into actual death. If she died, he went with her. A tick starved or suffocated would fall off the body, and absent another host, it would shrivel and die. But better yet if she could find another way. Live victorious with the power and the knowledge she had gained from watching him.

She felt her lips stretch into a grin. Bloody Bess's childlike fingers pulled Cia's chin around to meet her gaze. "Ah, Garif, how nice to see you again!"

Then Bess was blasting Cia into the mental cell she'd constructed for her, which she'd fortified since Cia's escape. She could see and hear everything and affect nothing. No matter how hard she kicked or clawed or screamed herself hoarse. No one could hear her, and not a single muscle would obey.

"Shall we join the battle?" Bess asked with a bloodthirsty grin.

Garif, of course, offered his arm.

Cia flung herself against her prison walls as guards wrestled a struggling Ulan up the steps of the watchtower they'd built for Bloody Bess's viewing. Garif ascended behind the Blood Princess. Ulan, her feeble struggle now spent, was tied to an upright beam meant for the purpose. She raised her head once, catching Cia's gaze, but Cia was not the one looking back, and the fear in Ulan's eyes said that she knew it. She let her head fall again to her chest.

Bloody Bess went to the rail of the watchtower and allowed Garif a moment for a bird's eye view of the killing field.

Then she said, with her gaze on Garif, but a casual flick of her hand to her guards, "I'm sorry, but I can't let you remain free, in case..."

And Garif was being manhandled toward the upright beams next to Ulan and lashed there, arms pulled behind his back, shoulders straining. Cia knew for a certainty he'd have drawn her forth from her box to take the humiliation and the pain, but she was locked away, and this was his lot now.

He was useful to Bloody Bess as a bed curtain was useful – lashed to a frame. Easily forgotten.

Roha

"What do you think of your damned spymaster now?" Hedric shot the words like darts, the only way they might hit home in the whipping wind as they fled the Torvus, racing to outpace the horses behind them. Especially dangerous on the uneven terrain.

Really? He wanted to do this now?

"No!" Ludvin snapped. "We will not set our swords against ourselves. Save all of your vitriol, all of your violence for *her* and her men. It is clear enough she set an ambush at both choke points, and it seems likely the spymaster gave his life investigating Grunder Pass. Respect that and move on."

Hedric growled, and spurred his horse even faster, anxious to get to the bloodshed. Behind them the Torvus bellowed and blew, and there were cries from men, women, and horses alike as the monster caught those unable to get out of its way.

"Is there anything you can do?" Ludvin asked Roha quietly enough so that only the wind could hear.

Nes instinctive reaction was to say *no, nothing,* but ni stopped. Was that true? The Torvus was made of ani-mist, and though ni would never steal anima from the land or the air or any living thing, stealing it from a construct was an entirely different matter. It might even be possible to feed it back to the earth.

"Maybe," ni said. "Go. I will do my best."

Roha pulled nes horse around, causing consternation all around as people nearly crashed and had to quickly wheel to each side. Ni took deep breaths, the first two as shaky as the mountain beneath the Torvus's rampage. Ni searched for nes center of power, letting people flow around nim, running from the danger behind them straight into another.

The construct loomed larger now, no further away than a furlong. It would be on Roha before ni could take another two breaths. The time to act was now. No more thinking, just feeling. Roha reached for the peace and power at nes core. Ni could see ani-mist escaping where someone had already pierced the Torvus. Ni pulled it to nim as though breathing it in, and it came.

Roha felt it there – tingling, alive, *the potential to become.* To be shaped. It was indescribable – like the sun on nes face after weeks without. No, more. Like the charged sky after lightning had rolled through. A tsunami following a quake. The first meal after a fast. All of it and more.

And this was how it felt partially depleted, already used for a construct, already running out.

Then the Torvus was on Roha. One leap, one bound, and ni would be –

Nes horse gave a cry, whipped its head back, the reins pulling from Roha's slackened hands, and it was wheeling away. It was no warhorse. It was not going to stand its ground to be trampled. Roha's concentration wavered, and the ani-mist leapt in nes hands like a live thing, which it was, especially with a mageri, maybe more than one, wrestling it back.

Roha dropped low over the horse, hugging for its neck rather than fumble for the reins, keeping nes focus on the inner well and reaching through it for the anima, using it to fight for the ani-mists bleeding off the Torvus. Ni felt the pull again of the other mageri, but they had nothing to offer the mists. They could insist, but not with the same allure as belonging to the All. Not like one of the Nim.

For an instant, Roha was tempted to take in that extra anima, to replace what ni was depleting, use it to keep fighting. Mostly it was frightening, even the moment's temptation deeply disturbing. It might fill nim up until ni was something else. Too much to contain. Like Ceramor. Like Bloody Bess. More, yes, but no longer nimself.

Roha had to return the stolen anima to the earth, but ni couldn't focus on that as ni rode, grounded to that earth only by the horse's hooves. Taking a deep breath and holding the ani-mists close, Roha threw nimself from the horse on the inward side of the mountain. Ni chanted a silent spiritu as ni fell, praying ni wouldn't roll straight off the cliff or beneath the Torvus's hooves before ni could take it down.

The impact crushed the air out of Roha as ni hit, rocks tore through nes side, but ni ignored it all. Ni forced nes hands down, fingers splayed as soon as ni could manage, driving the whirlwind straight into the land, feeling the phantom claws of the Torvus as it seemed to trample overtop of nim as it fed back into the earth.

When it was done, Roha collapsed, forehead to the ground, body boneless. Ni had to pry nes eyes open. Roha didn't know how far behind ni'd left the enemy mageri, how far ahead nes horse might have gotten, but ni couldn't stay. Ni needed to catch up to nes people, had to arrive before they were pinned down in battle.

Roha had stopped the Torvus, but it had done what Bloody Bess had needed it to – herded the Restoration army where the Princess wanted them and weakened them with no cost to her own people. They would arrive to an impossible situation. Bess had beaten them to the Dobrens Valley, where she had every advantage except one – no mageri constructs. But she had trained soldiers on her side. And she'd had time to choose her ground.

Roha pushed nimself to nes feet, brushed nimself off, and began to run after the retreating army; and then to walk and finally to stumble. When

Roha sensed no pursuit, ni could only think that the fight with the mageri had left them as exhausted as ni had been. Or that the Torvus had done all they'd needed it to do. Ni caught up with nes horse when it stopped running to chomp at a trampled patch of winter-brown grass. The animal gave nim the side-eye, side-step when ni tried to approach, clearly not trusting anyone who had ridden it so close to the Torvus or who wanted to take it away from food. Eventually, through sweet talk and the offering of great handfuls of the same grass the horse had found for itself, it allowed nim to mount and ride again. Maybe it felt there was safety in numbers, but that safety didn't last for long.

The cries and clangs and howls of battle reached them first, and Roha's horse shied again. Rather than deal with a balky horse in the midst of the fighting, ni slid to the ground and let it go. Hopefully, ni would be able to find it again to retreat – or someone would – but ni was not going to tie it to a tree and leave it to bash itself senseless in panic.

Ni drew nes blades and said another spiritu. That they would win this. That they could do it without mageri, without the ankari, All rest his soul. They would show that it could be done.

Roha would never have sought to kill for the sake of killing, despite nes belief that the mageri must be stopped from their desecration of the land. But ni'd willingly strike down anyone who'd ambush nes people. Ludvin, at least, had *seen* nim. Had accepted nim. Ni'd come the closest with the Restoration of finding acceptance, of finding a family. And ni would strike any blow in defense of the All. Those in Bloody Bess's service had chosen their paths.

Ni gave a great war cry as ni raced in with nes blades at the ready to find a bloodbath already in progress. The Restoration was beleaguered, outnumbered. Ni was at the back, but the Restoration had been chased onto the field where an army awaited. They'd never had a line to hold. Already some of Bloody Bess's men had pushed in among them. Before nim, Artis, a man Roha had brought into the fold, went down with a sword strike between shoulder and neck, nearly cleaved in half.

Roha hollered and would have leapt to take down his attacker, only ni was immediately fighting off an attacker of nes own. A Crownsman vaulted another bloody body, his blade aimed to cleave straight into nes neck. Ni blocked the blow, but it reverberated down nes arm, striking it momentarily nerveless. Ni struggled to keep hold of nes blade and kicked for his knee. He leapt back, but it gave nim room to swing again with nes sword, still determinedly clutched in nes hand.

Out of nes peripheral vision, Roha saw another man closing in, and ducked, whirled out of range. Ni now faced two attackers. There was nothing of ice about nes body now, nothing of crystal. Everything was heated, fluid, molten. Ni flowed, blocking one blow, another, dodging, twitching to the side so that one Crownsman's blade caught another, whirling, biting into one soldier with nes blade in the sweet spot where the protective padding connected between hip and thigh. Then a blow out of nowhere struck Roha's skull just behind nes ear with the flat of a blade, exploding nes head with the pain of metal colliding with too-fragile flesh and bone.

Nes vision went double, and ni stumbled into the horse of another soldier who had ridden in, careless of the downed – or to assure they stayed that way. Two swords were aimed Roha's way, both heading for nim at once, except that there were four or more in nes vision, and ni couldn't tell which to block. Something—a dart or, more likely, a dagger —came out of nowhere and buried itself in the second guard's eye…one of them. Ni couldn't tell, and then someone was yanking nim out of the path of the second—third?—sword.

Ni tried to whirl to see what new threat held nim, but the hold was too tight.

"Ludvin says you're needed against the mageri. Find him at the standard."

It was Hedric, and he was *not* happy about it. He growled the order and pushed Roha in the right direction, which was lucky, because the world was spinning now. And everything was doubling or tripling before coming together and dividing again, like a deck of cards that looked like one and then fanned out, only to come together again. Both were the reality, but… Right, Roha'd been hit on the head. Ni had to find Ludvin. At the standard. Even if there were three or more, they'd be in the same general area, and one would be right.

Ni headed for it. Green banner. Golden sun.

Roha dug for nes own little golden sun, deep down inside. More of a golden sun shining off a pool, a reflection of sunlight on water. Ni tapped a little bit. Nim, heal thyself. Could ni take some of nes power to power nimself? It seemed recursive.

Ni drank from the stream. Just a sip, nothing more, and instantly nes head cleared enough that there was only one standard, and ni could see it and head there without feeling as though ni might throw up or nes skull might explode along the way.

Then ni heard the singing, and started to run.

Ni'd heard of Sirens, but they were mythical. Mageri didn't construct them in battle because the other side had mageri as well, who used their powers to protect their soldiers against things like a Siren's magical song. But the Restoration had no mageri, and so no protection, only a few null disks – though not enough to go around. Likewise, the Dobrens Valley had no anima. What was Bloody Bess using for power? Was Bloody Bess... Could it be that now that their side was blooded, the Crown mageri were tapping into them directly? It was unheard of, but then, so was human sacrifice, and that wasn't stopping the Blood Princess.

No, Roha could not let it happen. Ni was their only defense, and nes power was finite.

Ni could not possibly be enough.

⸻

Cia

Princess Bessory was a terrifying figure. She seemed to revel in the bloodshed, a few times running her hands over herself unconsciously, as though it was a physical experience that she was rubbing in like a lotion. Perhaps Bloody Bess and Garif deserved each other. What a truly terrifying pair they would make. Bess had both a military advisor and a scribe beside her, along with a chute so she could send messages to a runner waiting below for orders. A pulley system assured the scribe could retrieve messages from below with alacrity.

She'd already sent a few orders or inquiries, more satisfied each time a response came back. When she turned to Garif and said, "It's time for the Siren," Cia's heart stopped.

She sensed Garif's pleasure like a spreading sickness. And because he was within her, she could *see* the power, watch him draw the red-tinted anima out of the living beings on the battlefield, at least those who had been blooded and not warded, which meant those on the Restoration side. From that red mist a woman formed at the front of their watch-tower. Or a half-woman, anyway. The upper half was a naked female, flesh dead white in the frigid winter air—frostbite white, almost blue, hair blowing in the breeze, tying itself into knots that would never come undone. The bottom half—at least the part that she could see, was a tumult of scales and matted feathers, hazy blue-green, freezing over with

316

ice. A Siren, like on the masthead of a ship, to sing them smooth sailing. She couldn't see the face, but she could hear the voice, and it was haunting—high pitched and naturally melodic, almost as though the wind and water themselves had a voice, capricious and wild, inviting you to play with them on the rocks. Insisting upon it. Mere mortals couldn't resist.

Cia didn't want to resist. She was *behind* the Siren, and not within the full force of the blast, only blooded in the sense that her wounds were not fully healed, but if she wasn't locked away, she would dance to the song straight off the edge of the watchtower. On one level she knew it, and on another, it was such freedom, it made more sense to do than deny. And then the song changed, calling for rest rather than abandon, for sinking into the sea. She looked to Ulan, who swayed in her bonds. Cia watched longing, and then the peace wash over her...followed by annoyance, as though something was interfering. Maybe her little daughter Dazia was trying to sing over the Siren, or holding ghostly hands over her mother's ears. Cia couldn't imagine that doing much, but maybe...

Down below, people were beginning to stop, to sway, and were being struck down where they stood.

Cia wanted to yell but couldn't.

Wanted to sleep but was denied.

Wanted to shout, but Garif allowed her control only of her thoughts and her rising fears.

Roha

"You have to wake her *now*," Ludvin shouted over the Siren's song.

He had a null, and the inner circle with him, but they were the only ones. The others were being struck down where they stood. Roha wanted to rush back into the fray. The Crown wanted the Restoration rebels alive for the sacrifice, not fighting to their deaths. It was only the thought that they were being stricken but not killed that allowed Roha to keep going.

"I'll be defenseless while I do it," ni said. "You need to keep me safe."

Roha looked Ludvin in the eye, driving the point home. He knew it, but not like this. Not when it was down to this little cadre of protectors with the rest of their army falling to enemy blades.

"Do what?" Hedric asked.

"No time!" Ludvin said. To Roha, "We'll do all we can. Hurry."

The others looked from one to the other in bafflement, but their plan was need to know. Roha's *power* was need to know, and they didn't. Ni'd saved them from the Torvus, but they'd been able to outrun the construct while ni worked. This time they were trapped in the valley. Ni could see Cia up there on that watchtower with the Siren, which meant Garif was guiding it. It was time for a showdown.

Ludvin nodded to the others, and while Hedric didn't like it, he joined those closing ranks around Roha. Ni nodded nes thanks to him, but he didn't acknowledge it. Wouldn't, ni was certain, until he knew what he'd gotten into and whether ni was truly welcome. Even in battle.

Ni dropped to the ground, knowing from the past it might be best to sit before collapsing. Ni put nes hands to the earth, grounding as best ni could, though there was no anima there to reach for. So ni searched within, finding the sunlit stream at nes center and tracing the almost imperceptible line ni'd rooted there that ended at the hook ni'd buried within Cia when ni'd healed her back at the inn. Not just so that Roha could find her again – so that Cia could find herself. Ni'd hooked it to that brightest part of Cia, the central spark. Ni hadn't gone inside others the way ni had Cia. Never. In the rare times ni'd followed anyone else's stream, they had protection, the equivalent of a cap or a grate to keep animals or detritus from getting in and fouling the water, but Cia's protections had already been blown through, leaving her bare. Spirits curse that husband of hers.

Roha had certainly never hooked anyone, never done anything like this before. Ni could only hope it was more help than harm. Ni couldn't see that ni could do worse than Mager-bloody-Garif already had. But now ni was putting that hope, that theory to the test.

If Roha thought about it any further, ni'd outthink nimself. Instead, ni let the stream carry nim. Ni fought the feeling of discordance as ni flowed farther away from nes own center and toward the growing wrongness of Cia's spark.

***

Cia

Garif had Cia's legs locked, her chest straining against the ropes binding them, eager to rush to the rail of the watchtower for a leap off or maybe a better view of his handiwork down on the battlefield. He could do it in an instant with the least little expenditure of stolen power. Cia didn't even realize what she'd done at first. Then her thoughts reverberated over and over in her head – 'the ropes binding *them*'. They didn't fade off like an echo but grew louder, blasting her with their power. She'd linked them together, as though she and Garif were truly one, as though she'd resigned herself to that fate.

Garif knew exactly what she'd done, and his triumphant laughter rattled her within and without, not disrupting the Siren's song, which was lilting, haunting. Cia's gasps within her prison went unheard as Roha's army began to waver. They still fought, but Bloody Bess's men pressed hard, unaffected by the Siren's song, each warded by her mageri placed about the battlefield. The Restoration couldn't possibly last.

Cia's heart pounded with fear. If, in fact, it was still her own.

Inside, she stared out through her prison at the monster Garif had become. The monster he'd always been. The Malacostra was not just a construct. He was not made of ani-mist, but of darkness struck through with lightning. When Garif had torn his way to the forefront of her mind, he'd created a terrible storm. Rolling thunder boomed through her head. When she tried to beat against her barriers, the storm broke against them, lashing them with concussive sound and tremors, throwing her off her feet and shaking her foundations out from under her. Lightning forked, red-purple afterimages searing her eyes. He sparked at erratic intervals, disrupting her thoughts.

As Cia battered and beat, she grew hot, she grew angry, and she *grew*... He thought he would diminish her. Bess thought she would wall Cia away. Both thought they would use her body and lock away her mind.

She. Would. Not. Have. It.

People would die, people like Hostill, like Roha.

There had to be something she could do.

Between the blinding flashes of lightning, there came another sudden flare of white light. As far away as a star, but when Cia looked again, it was a will-o'-wisp, an illusion, floating toward her, fighting through the storm Garif created. Was that – it seemed to be *Roha* pressing toward her, garbed in the Church's white robes, but glowing as though they were made of sheer starlight, particularly as ni was keeping to the darkest edges of the storm, hoping to avoid the monster's attention.

Roha looked like an Anima come straight down from a church mosaic, but no representation ever lofted a sword, and ni raised it high, long and glowing, bathed in the same pure white starlight.

Was this some new trick? Something to distract Cia from her struggles while Garif finished off the Restoration army? But just as she had the thought, she felt the storm pressure build, and knew her attention had drawn Garif's. She cried out as a spike of lighting shot straight for Roha.

Roha hurled the sword in Cia's direction and dove, rolling over and over like an acrobat as the lightning balled toward nim. Roha narrowly missing being struck, maybe only because Garif's attention was divided. As soon as the lightning flashed itself out, ni leapt to nes feet, scooped up the sword, and ran serpentine for Cia's walls.

"Cia, get back!" Roha hollered over the whipping winds of the storm.

Cia was large now with her anger, too large to hide in a corner, but she turned away, crossed her arms over the back of her head to protect it in case the walls shattered like glass. She didn't know the rules of the prison. Didn't know what Bess had done, what Roha could do. But she felt it when Roha slashed at the wall, and it cleaved in two, dissolving like a construct with its mist stripped away.

"What – ?"

She had so many questions – how was Roha here? What did they do now?

But Garif wouldn't give her time for answers. Thunder boomed, and her whole head shuddered. Her whole body, for all she knew. She and Roha fell together, and the Garif-Malacostra, the crab-spider beast made of lightning and fury, stared at them through compound eyes, hatred as toxic as his poison. He struck out with one of his segmented legs, and they dove apart rather than be skewered together.

He leapt like a spider to trap Cia, all eight of his legs surrounding her like a cage. "You've found someone to fight your battles?" he thundered down at her.

"Cia!" Roha called, and Cia tore her gaze from Garif's monstrous form to see Roha hurling the sword at her. It wasn't like a dagger or a throwing knife. It didn't sail smoothly and slice cleanly through the air. Garif saw it coming, and swiped for Cia as she leapt for it, but she flew straight into the path of the sword, snatching it out of the air. He struck her as she caught it, and she went skidding to the ground, landing hard on her face. It heated, and so did the sword.

No longer like starlight, she thought. *Firelight.*

It flared. With her anger. With her rage. With her power.

"This is yours now," Roha called. "It always was. Your mind, your weapon. Your battle. I've got my own to fight. Take him out, but quickly. Because the watchtower is going down."

Cia gave a grateful nod, and Roha's light winked out.

Cia focused on the monster overtop of her. Even in his inhuman eyes, she could see Garif's calculation, watch him spark with fury and pain at her resistance. Her ability to wound him. He readied two pinchers to come at her at once, one from each side. Cia whirled like a dervish to slice at one, quick as thought. She'd never handled a sword, but this was a construct. It was *her* mind and *his* monster, and she'd beaten him once.

He was on her field, and he'd only kept it because of Bloody Bess, who couldn't help him now. Cia sliced a leg and it was nothing but vapor. The only substance was hers, and she stole it back, raced for the next, taking out as many pillars as she could to bring him crashing down before he could in one of his strikes against her.

With all of her strikes, he should have dissipated by now. He should be dead. He should have joined the anima when Cia ran him through the first time. But he hadn't. Cia didn't understand how he or any spirit survived the pull of the collective energies, but somehow...

The Malacostra started to sway. It would come crashing down any moment now. Something dripped on Cia, burning, biting, and Cia locked up to see a cavity that opened and shut, lined with teeth, poison and dripping things. Maybe saliva. Maybe blood and bile. Maybe acid or ichor or all of the above. Nothing she wanted any part of, but with every exhale there was a flickering. Irregular, jolting, painful in appearance, as though every spark might be the last. Or as though it might jump out and strike her at any instant. The cause, no doubt, of the lightning effect. Deadly, dangerous and in this case unnatural, and precisely what she was looking for. Her heart quailed, but she'd come this far.

"I'm right here. So close!" she taunted. "You're not going to let me defeat you, are you?"

She had to do this quickly. She banked on him not giving her the body while they were on the battlefield. Bloody Bess had no use for those who failed her.

His remaining legs shook at the effort to hold him up. All he had to do was drop, straight over her to swallow her up – straight onto her flaming sword. Perhaps it was mutually assured destruction, but as long as she could take him out.

She felt a tremor.

And then a spike in Garif's spark. The tower!

She couldn't wait. She'd forgotten Ulan. She'd forgotten the battle. Everything in her need to rid herself of Garif.

Now there was no time. Not even for fear. Cia closed her eyes, tried not to think, only feel, only go on instinct, which said that Garif's power was hers, and that lightning was the closest to her power. The next time he sparked, she grabbed it, yanked on it, and ripped it from him, pulled it like a whip to propel herself into the air where she could slice him open with her flaming blade, tear through him with the lightning, cut his power into pieces that sank back into her. His screams faded into nothing as he fractured the way he'd wanted for her. Her whip died, her sword dimmed and disappeared, and she fell back into herself, the mindscape disappearing until she was looking out of her own eyes and quaking with her own body atop the watchtower as it shook itself apart.

Roha

When Roha got back to nimself, ni was disoriented, as though still in two places at once – back there with Cia and here on the battlefield. Ni could still hear the Siren, but the song was faltering. Cia had lit that sword on fire. Ni had seen it. Cia had beaten Garif once. She could do it again. Roha had to believe.

The fighting closed in. Roha was jostled, and nes protectors forced aside to fight oncoming attackers. Someone stepped on nes leg, grinding it into the ground.

"Hurry!" Ludvin gritted out.

Hurry. That would do wonders for nes concentration. Ni didn't even know if ni could do what ni hoped. There would be little enough life left in the beams of the tower. If ni could suck it dry, crack the timbers, ni could topple it. In theory. In practice, ni had never done anything like it. The Church had never taught offensive magic. Ni had never been to the Magery, and if the watchtower was warded…

Roha opened nes eyes just long enough to refocus on the tower, saw the Siren flicker, and nearly crowed. It bolstered nim enough to close nes eyes again, feel for the beams at the base of the tower. Ni tuned out nes fear for Cia. For Ulan. They would survive or they wouldn't. The tower was still coming down. If Cia couldn't take out Garif, take out the Siren, hopefully the toppling tower would, and the Princess with it. But there was no guarantee there either. It wasn't so high that they couldn't clamber down the ladder or even jump, though limbs would likely break. But ni had to try, and ni couldn't wait any longer. Ni had to bet on Cia. Had to believe.

The beams...it wasn't like feeling for nes well, where there was warmth and power. Or like the anima of the All, which was light and life. The beams were dead things, yet some were still moist, still somewhat green with the remembrance of life. There was a faint thrum, a peaceful chord in the midst of the violence that ni could aim for. Ni called what little life there was out of it. It came sluggishly, but it came to nim, pulled toward the stream of nes anima as though hungry for it. Ni was sad to deny it, to drive it instead down into the deadened earth below, so denuded by the violence of the battle fought before this that it didn't even have the means to welcome it. It was as though the anima dissipated on impact. The beams split as the life flowed out, and the tower began to tremble.

The fighting around Roha rose to a crescendo, but ni held on, focusing on the tower. Someone overran nim, and ni jerked back to nimself to see Ludvin standing over nim, deflecting a sword blow that would have cleaved nes head in two.

Then a swordsman hit Ludvin from behind, and he went facedown, leaving Roha in the midst of a circle of Crown soldiers. The Restoration forces had fallen. They had taken the tower, but they were too late.

CHAPTER THIRTY-FOUR

Bess

The Siren vanished with a great gush of vapor into the air, and Bess whirled, ready to lay into Garif, only to find him sagging in his restraints. Or *her*. Somehow she sensed that Garif was gone. Maybe she'd asked too much of him and he'd exhausted himself, giving the body back over to Cia. Whatever it was, it didn't matter. He'd done what she'd meant for him to do.

"Cut them down," she ordered, sweeping an arm to include Ulan as well. "Throw them in with the others."

And then she turned back to the edge of her makeshift parapet to watch just as it started to shake itself apart.

"Now!" she yelled to her people.

There was a commotion behind her, but she didn't wait on them. She tested the structure, but there was nothing she could do to steady it, nothing of her power that would be strong enough. Something had been done. The tower was coming down on them.

Erdain came running from where she'd ordered him out on the field, as though he could do anything without anima. She waved him away, used the handhold of the ladder only as a ruse, expending her power to ease her precipitously to the ground, feet sliding past the rungs. One of her men fell screaming past her, striking the ground with a horrible sound of meat and bones passing through each other in a way never meant to be. More haunting than the Siren's song, which had cut off abruptly.

Bess hit the ground and raced away, looking back to the tower to see which of her people might escape or be pulled from the wreckage. Beams were dropping away, the side sheering off, the front edge of the platform tipping down. Another of her men tried to make it down the ladder – without either of the captives – and got most of the way before the tower gave a great crack. It seemed to hover in the air for a breathless instant, and in that moment, Bess was certain she saw Cia's head whip up and the bonds fall away, saw her dive for Ulan before the whole tower collapsed.

She didn't even wait for the air to clear, for the beams to settle, before she was ordering men to look for survivors.

Bowstan's lieutenant came racing up, "Princess, are you all right? I saw the tower go down!"

"Quite all right," she said, brushing dust from her hair, splinters from her gown. "Report."

"We have won the field. Between your Siren and our men, we have them."

Bess nearly fell to her knees, and that was *not* an appropriate reaction. Not for a Princess. Not for a *Queen*. But her body was suddenly shaking with reaction – the controlled fall from the tower coming down around her, the defeat of her enemies, the fruition of her plans...

She stopped her spinning mind, steeled her legs, straightened her back and took in a full breath. She had done it. Drawn in the rebels, defeated her resistance. Soon enough, the Restoration would be all collected, disarmed, bound and separated so that they couldn't conspire and rise up again. Under heavy guard until it was time.

"Be certain General Bowstan has mageri stationed on each shift around the camp to watch for any magical disruption," she told the lieutenant. She didn't expect any disruption. The Restoration did not trifle with magic, and Ceramor *had* to be dead. The tower had to have been Cia. Somehow she'd escaped the prison Bloody Bess had fashioned, but it hadn't gotten her far. From one imprisonment to another. As for Ruggerio...well, it was too bad he hadn't survived to see her victory. Or been the match for her that she'd hoped he might be.

"One at each compass point, Princess," he promised. "General Bowstan says there aren't so many that he can put them any closer and allow for sleep and changes in shift."

She growled. She supposed it was true enough, if she considered that there had only been so many battle-proven mageri they'd been able to call back in from elsewhere in time for this march, and supplemented with her women...but it was incredibly inconvenient.

"We can sleep when our enemies are dead," she snapped. "I start the ritual at first light."

Though Bowstan knew this, of course.

The soldier gave her a look that said as much, but he just bowed so deeply it was a wonder he didn't fall over and slipped away as though he couldn't get back to his duties–or, perhaps, escape her presence–quickly enough.

<hr />

Ruggerio

Ruggerio had passed out beside Ceramor and Morley, who would live or die, he couldn't tell at this point, though he'd done all he could. When something startled him awake, he was more irritated than alarmed. At this point, he was fairly certain he hadn't regained the strength to grapple even with his conscience—should one inconveniently arise—so whatever was going to kill him could very well have done so in his sleep.

Apparently, his instincts felt otherwise. His now-blunted blade was already in his hand, and pointed in the direction of the menace, but fell at the sight of what he faced.

"Dazia?" he said in a hush. "But how–?" He'd never been able to see or hear her without help before.

The fire was down to embers, and the moon hiding behind one of the mountain peaks. Stars provided some illumination to the night, but the little ghost girl came with her own. She was luminous, like a constellation come to earth.

"I don't have much time," she said, voice choked with tears that he could now see pelting her face like shooting stars. "Roha gave me what power ni could, but it's a long way, and ni doesn't have much left. Maman said to tell you the battle is already lost. Everyone is dead tomorrow morning unless you can get there in time. Unless you can do something. *Please.*"

"Is there a plan?" he asked.

But Dazia was already turning toward Ceramor, whose snore was the only thing to show that he was more asleep than dead. "I need to talk to him," she said.

"I don't know that I can wake him."

"He knows I'm here."

She went to him, floating more than walking, and Ruggerio watched as she squatted beside him and whispered in his ear. He cocked his head as a dog might, listening, though never seeming to wake. Ruggerio strained to hear as well but couldn't make out a single word.

"Secrets?" he asked when she finished.

"Suggestions," she answered, and then she was gone.

Just gone, and he was aware just how cold the night had grown with the fire burned down. Then suddenly, there was warmth on his leg, and he was afraid some wound had broken open and was bleeding. He looked up to see Ceramor's horse returned and peeing on Ceramor with Ruggerio catching the side-stream. He cursed, rolling quickly away and to his feet, but the harm was already done. He was wet, now wide-awake, and smelling of horse piss. He'd already been planning to stalk downwind of the enemy camp. Now it would be an absolute necessity. Damned horse.

It nickered in laughter as Ceramor snarled and leapt into a crouch, flashing out half-heartedly with a clawed hand. The horse danced back toward two other horses that waited nearby as though to see how the joke had gone off. One of them Ruggerio recognized as Morley's big gray, unmistakable with the half black, half ashen mane and black stockings on two feet. It stepped forward then to nose at Morley's belt, looking for carrots. It pulled back at the scent of the cauterized wound where his right arm had once been, before moving to nuzzle Morley's cheek and blow into his face, as though giving him breath.

Morley's eyes fluttered, and his remaining hand came up to scratch at her chin. "Cinder, you came back for me."

She tossed her head as though to agree with him and then put it back in his hand.

Ruggerio's horse stayed back with Ceramor's roan. Cursed thing.

"Since we're all awake –"

He passed on to them what Dazia had said, even assuming Ceramor had already heard. "We have to leave. The moon will rise shortly. It should give us enough light to ride by."

"I may slow you down," Morley said, looking to his half-missing arm, and cringing in pain as he moved it instinctively.

"You may fall behind, but you won't slow us down, because we can't afford to be slowed. Keep up or catch up as you can, but we ride."

"Do you need us to lash you to your horse?" Ceramor asked.

Morley raised himself to seated using his one good hand, biting back the pain this time, though Ruggerio saw sweat break out on his brow despite the cold. He glared daggers through Ceramor. "I've learned to fight one-handed while keeping my seat. I'm fair sure I can ride."

Ceramor smiled, and it was feral. "Ah, there's the fire. Let's go then. Shall we dance?" he asked the roan, rubbing at the spot where the horse had peed. The horse peeled its lips back in what Ruggerio would again swear was a laugh.

"Do whatever it is you need to do to ready yourselves. We ride as soon as we won't lose ourselves in a crevice."

That, and he had it in his head to make poisoned darts with what remained of the barbs he'd stolen from the Caturnine vines. It shouldn't take long to cut and core the mageri's staff to make a passable blowpipe. Swords were fine, but he was one man – with maybe two, two and a half, depending on Morley's health and on Ceramor's dependability – against an army. He would need stealth and ranged weapons. Ceramor's powers wouldn't do him any good on earth devoid of anima. It would be the level field the Restoration had always wanted…if only they weren't already in chains.

Ceramor's mount snapped at him good-naturedly as he mounted, and he, oddly, caressed the roan as through rewarding it for a trick well played. Ruggerio's horse stomped as he approached, nearly on his foot, but did nothing else, and Morley's horse swung her head as far around as it could to rub up against him like a cat.

Then they were off, hoofbeats echoing off the desolate mountain peaks. The moon lit the path so that they had to be cautious but not overly so. The larger concern was the way sound carried. Mostly, it rose up, and he had to hope the sounds of an entire army below would cover the approach of three horsemen from the peaks above.

CHAPTER THIRTY-FIVE

Roha

The prisoners had been bound and roped off like cattle in smaller groupings, kept apart from each other during the night and well-guarded. At dawn they were dragged out, their knees kicked in as they were made to kneel, dropped to the ground of the battlefield, in the blood that had been spilt.

Roha bit nes lip to keep from crying out as ni caught sight of Hostill, still alive, but his own lip cracked and bloody, one shoulder hanging as though a Crownsman had bashed a pommel or the flat of a blade into it. Not that it would matter soon. Not if Bloody Bess had her way. Not if Dazia hadn't gotten through with her message. She'd never made it back, so Roha didn't know if the girl had found help. Or if she did, whether they would make it in time.

Here and there, a head raised in Roha's direction or Ludvin's, looking for a signal, for hope, only to have a soldier forcibly bow their head again. Bow to the Princess. Bow to their inevitable doom.

"Be ready," ni and Ludvin mouthed in the flash of time they had before they or others were taken down.

Ni reached for nes well, kept nes thread of power close. Tried to believe in the hope ni promised those who looked to nim.

Two guards had brought out a crate, like a makeshift stage for Bloody

Bess to stand on. She was going to make a *speech*. Here they were about to die, and she was going to gloat.

Could Roha use nes power to blow up Bloody Bess's heart right now? Would it make any difference or only begin the bloodshed? Would it be the worst kind of sacrilege to use the power of creation for destruction?

Everything within nim said that it would be. That ni couldn't do it. That the precipitant death would only lead to more death. Roha couldn't kill. Not like that. Not someone who wasn't trying to kill nim. But Bloody Bess *was* trying to kill nim. Kill all of them. Coldheartedly. From a distance, through the command of others. Rather than justify things for Roha, that just seemed to make it more wrong. It would make nim like Bloody Bess. There had to be another way.

The Princess mounted the crate, accepting the help of the two guards as though it enhanced her status and not as though it was required. She seemed to loom even larger than her diminutive height, not because of the extra elevation provided by the stage, but because of her presence. The sun was behind the Princess, but rather than provide a halo, it threw her shadow before her to fall over those gathered, much larger than it should have been, wider too, as though she contained multitudes. Roha thought of what Ulan and Dazia had told nim about the shadow girls and hoped that what ni was about to do was right. That it would work. Ni hoped Ceramor still lived and had gotten nes message.

"My people," Bloody Bess began, "as you know, our lands have been drained by our war with Frizenze, by the valiant and monumental efforts of our mageri to fight off those who seek to weaken us. And yet, there are those amongst our own people, within our own borders who have challenged and fought against us. They say that they want more food for the people, more crops, less hunger, the land restored. We will show them the cost, and they will pay it. Today we accept their sacrifice."

She raised an arm and opened her mouth to say more when there arose cries from the back of her army. Roha could see some disruption there. Hope beat at nes heart. It could only be Ceramor and Ruggerio. Eckland and Morley. Ni hoped it would be enough.

Ni turned back toward Bloody Bess in time to see her general step forward as though he'd pull her off her crate, but she sent him back with a glare and a slashing gesture that needed no words for understanding.

Bess straightened, looked out over her army, only a fraction of whom were now facing her way, the rest turned toward the commotion at the back. "Kill them," she said. No more preamble. "Kill them all!"

Roha yelled, "Now!" and reached into nes well to draw from nes power. At once, all of the ropes between prisoners were severed, and they were ripping their hands free of their bindings as Bloody Bess continued, oblivious, voice rising to be heard above the din.

Close in, her men began to slash at the rebels, and farther out, something was happening. Men were falling, others engaging with whatever disruption Ruggerio and the others had kicked off.

"Let their anima and energies feed the land. Let it be known that Bloody Bess *is* the Restoration and the Salvation of Jucar!" She raised both hands as she uttered the final words, inviting a rousing response from the troops, but mostly they were too busy to respond. There were a few cheers, but Roha nimself had little attention to spare for the Blood Princess's disappointment.

The rebels were free, but still weaponless. Bess's men turned on them with sharp steel flashing. But Cia had found her strength, and pulled the sparks from the camp fires still burning and blew them like embers into the eyes of the Crownsmen. The Restoration was fighting for their lives and their land. They crashed straight in under the swordsmans' guards, gouging for eyes, bladed hands aimed for groins or the soft sections of throats. Weight was thrown, insoles were stomped. Any and every street fighting trick was employed.

"Roha!" Ni heard the call but couldn't respond. There was a soldier coming straight for nim.

Ni dove in under the wide swing, driving hard into the soldier's breastbone, hoping to take him straight to the ground. He aimed the pommel of his sword at Roha's back, but ni twisted, bringing up nes hands and catching the hilt first, wrestling the Crownsman for control. Roha threw back nes head, straight into his nose, and heard the crunch. Ni didn't wait to revel, but stomped on his insole with all nes weight.

As he started to go down, Roha relieved him of his sword, swinging it to be sure he stayed down. Ni hated the feel of cutting into another person, the resistance of the meat and muscle. But there was no time to dwell. Roha would fight or others would die. Already, a Crownsman had a baker named Fermi down on the ground, ready to take her head. Fermi would never have raised a weapon but to fight for what she believed. Roha raced in, nes blade swinging. The soldier turned in time to catch nes blade, but the vehemence of Roha's swing drove him back a step, and Fermi scuttled away and to her feet.

Ludvin called Roha's name again, and ni cursed him. Now was not the time for distractions.

The soldier watched the two of them, as though unsure. Perhaps he was a newer recruit. He was certainly young enough, almost a child, really, and the years of the Blood War meant more seasoned men growing sadly scarcer. But he'd been willing enough to commit human sacrifice.

And he'd decided his current course. Roha saw it in his body language, the shift in his eyes, and knew where he would leave himself exposed. Ni was ready.

Ni wasn't ready for Fermi to come in with a great cry wrung from the depths of her soul, running and leaping for his head. He saw her, grabbed for a dagger at his belt, but didn't adjust his target, perhaps judging Roha the larger threat. But Roha was no longer where he expected nim to be, and it was too late when he saw nes sword slashing down at him, slicing him from throat to ribs. Fermi was on him by then, wrapping her arms around his head.

He staggered, overbalanced, spurting blood. He went down hard, first to his knees, then falling to the earth, sending Fermi rolling away. Hating nimself, Roha brought nes own blade to bear on his bent neck, severing his head from his body. He wouldn't take another life.

Ludvin called again, more adamantly, as Fermi grabbed up the soldier's sword, gave a nod and disappeared into the fighting. Roha ducked, spun, avoiding another blade coming nes way and striking down the man wielding it, pivoting to search out Ludvin.

Ni found him standing nearly over Hostill, and nes heart leapt as though the sun of their standard had risen again. "Go, I've got the boy!" Ludvin said.

As Roha watched, he destroyed another attacker, toed aside the body he'd just downed and insisted that Hostill hide under it. Ni saw the rebellion in the boy's eyes but couldn't stay to see how it turned out. Hostill needed to stay safe. They needed him on the throne, but the boy had spirit and clearly didn't want to hide while his friends fought and died around him.

But Roha had nes own part to play and felt the air displacing behind nim. Ni whirled, catching a blow meant to take off nes head in a way that reverberated through nes whole arm, maybe even cracking the bone. Something else came flashing for nes stomach, and ni caught that hand in nes, using a trickle of power to crack the bone in nes opponent's hand, the dagger falling to the ground and the soldier falling back in pain. Roha used the opening to flash nes own sword down, slashing it at the man's exposed neck, dropping him to the ground. Bloody Bess wanted to feed the land with anima; she could do so with her own men.

Ni stooped to pick up the fallen dagger and raced for the Princess, hacking and slashing nes way through until ni was covered in as much blood as cloth. Until ni felt nimself joined on the right by another figure hacking and slashing and moving toward the Princess. When Roha risked a glance, ni saw Ruggerio. Ni smiled, cracking the blood that had frozen on nes face. It had to be a fearsome sight.

Something big was bounding up from behind. Ni felt it in the change of the air, in the rising of the hairs on the nape of nes neck. Ni whirled, sword raised, to see a man-beast, standing a head above anyone else on the field, looking half wolf with a muzzle and a mouthful of blood-stained teeth.

"Don't!" Ruggerio shouted to be heard over the cries from the rest of the field. "It's Ceramor."

It shouldn't be. All the anima was gone from the area. Unless he could pull from an inner well like Roha. Or was using blood magic. But of course, he was *ankari*. Ni should have expected it. There was so much blood to go around here, and he had already crossed that line.

Ni shivered, knowing that ni'd crossed it by association, by using nes power to reach into a man and break his bones. If ni lived there'd be time for atonement. Now there was no time for anything but turning and running and hacking and slashing.

Ceramor and Bloody Bess and... were they all just sides of the same coin?

CHAPTER THIRTY-SIX

Cia

The Crown cavalryman slashed at something on his far side, and Cia picked up the dagger of a fallen soldier and cut through his girth. Overbalanced as he was, he and the saddle slid right off his horse, leaving the reins in place. She'd beaten Garif and drawn from her own power. She was more alive than she'd ever been, but still so weak. He had not been good to her body while he'd had it. She'd be cut down in seconds if she tried to stand and fight, but she could swing herself up onto the horse. It had worked for her once. She could do it again.

She cut through her garments to give her the necessary movement, then grabbed the reins and some mane with it to help anchor her. She gave it everything she had, jumping to splay herself over the back of the horse and pull herself up and over. It wasn't elegant. It would have been so much easier with the stirrups and the saddle still in place, but she managed it. She righted herself and took stock as quickly as she could, knowing that as soon as she was spotted, enemy horsemen would run her down, and she had only a dagger with which to defend herself. She spotted Ulan about to get struck down and gave the best war cry she could manage, hoping to turn the attacker her way, since she'd never make it on time. She kicked the horse hard, spurring him on, racing the fall of the sword.

Because it did fall, the attacker not knowing the cry was for him. Or not registering it in the midst of battle.

Ulan fell, and Cia ran the man down. Or rather, ran the horse right at him. Instinctively, it stopped just shy and reared, front hooves lashing out, catching the man in the face and chest and dropping him like a stone. Cia held on for all she was worth, thighs and calves trembling, chest pressed to withers, arms wrapped around the horse's neck, and her cheek mashed into the horse's mane. She jolted when it landed, and sat up, breathing hard, staring at the ground to see if Ulan lived, afraid to slide from the horse and see for herself, lest it rear again and use those hooves on her or bolt and take away her protection.

To her shock, Ulan rose like a ghost, swaying, shaking, holding a hand out as though she'd lean on the horse for support. Her other arm hung limp, bloody. Useless. One more blow and she'd have been gone. Might still bleed out.

Cia stroked the horse's neck, hurriedly trying to make friends, to reassure and gentle the beast before reaching out a hand to Ulan. "Here, hurry."

Ulan looked from her hand to the horse as though trying to figure out how the hand would help. Then she struck on something, and stepped aboard her downed attacker like a mounting block. She took Cia's hand with her good one. It was still a struggle, but the melee of battle held off long enough for her to pull herself up and mount behind Cia.

"Toward Bloody Bess," Ulan said. "She's the key."

Cia wheeled her horse in that direction.

That's how she thought of the big bay now. *Her horse.* It had saved her. It had stayed in place for Ulan. As if somehow it knew. *Animals. Anima.* Maybe there was some connection.

Bess

The general had run off yelling orders, commandeering a mount, leaving Bess in the company of standard-issue soldiers, who tried to hurry her off the field. To get her away and guard her. With their lives, if necessary.

Would they have done this with Cyril? With Jannik? For certain her brothers wouldn't have gone. Jannik had died from wounds received on the battlefield. She had to show that she was stronger. Better, and more fit to lead. She would not let her people see her fleeing the field. Coddled and cared for. Protected. She was the one to be feared rather than to show fear.

"No!" she yelled to be heard over the battle.

The word split her head. Or maybe it was the wrongness of the land. Her heels dug into the earth like a mageri pike, finding only nothingness. Emptiness where there should be life, energy, anima. It was what she was there to rectify. The Restoration was supposed to be all about that, restoring the balance, only they weren't willing to die for it. Hypocrisy. They would kill others, the mageri, but not let themselves be sacrificed.

And yet they *would* die. Maybe those deaths would come in battle, taking some of her people with them. Maybe that would further feed the land to her greater glory.

Either way, she would win.

The shadow girls inside her howled. Some cried out with names. Some in horror, some in wordless terror. As if her victory wouldn't be theirs. As if they weren't a part of her now. They wanted to split her down the middle, pour out into the battlefield. To help or haunt or be dispelled in the chill mountain breeze. Yet, she felt feverish. On fire, as though she might melt the icy caps of the mountains and bring an avalanche down on them all.

She had to vent some of her heat, unleash some of her fury.

"Back!" she cried to her shadow demons.

"Princess?" one of the guards asked, looking at her like she'd grown a second head.

She lashed out at him, backhanding him with a strength that sent him sprawling. He stumbled with blood on his lips where his teeth had cut into them at her blow. She smiled slowly, and it discomfited him. "Give me your sword," she said very distinctly. She had to be careful, because the shadow girls were howling like the winds, battering at her locked doors, and she was afraid they would blow them open and come howling through her lips. She had to keep them back, keep control.

The soldier looked to his compatriots but found no help there. He handed his sword over, and Bloody Bess turned it on him, burying the tip into his shoulder so quickly he had no time to defend, and sliding the blade out again and her hand into the wound, drawing on his blood and his energies.

She saw her enemies approaching—Garif's half-dead wife riding a bay horse, Ulan mounted behind her, a running figure in a topknot covered in blood, flanked on one side by the ankari Ceramor in a bestial form and on the other by Bess's former spymaster. If she could do away with them all at once, she could take the crown free and clear. No one could stand in her way.

"Get them!" she ordered the guards. There were five left, since she was draining the sixth of their number. They were slow to turn from the horror of her to greet her enemies.

She didn t expect them to stand. The ultimate destruction would be up to her.

Ceramor said something to his companions but didn't wait for an answer before leaping straight over her guards to face her. They didn't get the chance to engage him, too quickly caught up in fights all their own as the others took them on, though one tried and was instantly struck down.

She didn't see by whom, faced as she was by a slathering beast almost twice her size. As the ankari raised a clawed hand to strike her—*his Princess, his Queen*—she borrowed the guard's blood and power, drew on the energies the shadow girls had given her and gave up on trying to hold her head together.

Suddenly it exploded outward as it had always threatened. She gave vent to all the monstrous, needy, deathly shadows, and they burst forth, her head and neck transformed into a nightmare of seething tentacles, but instead of suction cups, there were pustules along their lengths bubbling and bursting into poisonous pools.

She lashed them at the ankari. He reared back at the sight of her, but it was as though she was somehow everywhere, as though she had *eyes* everywhere, all along her whirling tentacles. It was jarring, but powerful, as though she was omnipresent. She struck and he whirled and she struck again.

Then the blood, that lovely blood. She wrapped him with a tentacle, ready to tap into all that power.

Roha

Roha faltered at the impossibility before nim, taking a ringing blow to the head before the soldier fighting nim registered the horror on nes face

337

and turned to look. His distraction allowed Roha to cut him down, but another snuck in from the side and slid a blade right into nes ribs.

The shock of it came before the pain, and Roha knew ni was going to die before ni could respond with a blow of nes own.

There was a thwack of displaced air, and then a spurt of blood as a dagger lodged itself in the soldier's neck, and then he was falling. Roha looked up to see Cia nodding at nim.

Roha nodded back and looked around. Between Ruggerio, Cia, and Ulan they'd taken out the rest of the Princess's guards. But then, it looked like *she* was the truly dangerous one as the battle raged with Ceramor. The ankari was already wounded, exhausted from his earlier battle at Grunder Pass and from previous months of captivity. He staggered under Bloody Bess's assault…or the *thing* that had once been Bloody Bess.

Roha didn't have long. Ni dropped to nes knees and signaled the others. Cia and Ulan slid from their horse and kept sliding, straight to their knees, right there in the blood of their fallen enemies.

"Clear a space," Roha ordered.

They did, pulling back bodies, brushing away rocks and grit until there was a fairly battle-free, almost peaceful place in the midst of the battle. Ruggerio kept watch over them, ready to slay any who came near. It wasn't ideal. It didn't seem very holy, but it would have to do.

Spells are prayers with power attached. It was the line in the Gospel of Gelerte that had stuck with Roha more than anything, and ni'd memorized most of it. Now that seemed a very good thing.

Ni heard a cry, the kind that was all the louder for the attempt to stifle, to smother, and looked up to see the faintest flicker of the little ghost girl, outlined in the mist of frigid air and the kicked-up dust of battle, her arms thrown around her mother's neck. Ulan was hugging her back for all she was worth, sobbing quietly at first and then crying unreservedly, shoulders heaving.

Roha started the ritual. There was no time to waste. Ruggerio's defense could fail at any time, and they'd be lost.

Ni shut out the world, reached for that well of power, and then for the little ghost girl. Dazia had to unhand her mother to take both of Roha's hands in hers.

"I can dive into the well," Roha said to her. "I can ride the anima. Will you be my guide? Help me find the others like you?"

"If you can see me, I think you can see them. But can you find your way back after?"

Roha didn't have an answer, so ni gave none. "Are you ready?" ni asked instead.

A tear ran down Dazia's little pointed face, and she reached a final time for her mother, who joined their circle. Ulan had the ghost sight. She could help. Ulan beckoned Cia in as well and grasped her hand when she came near. Dazia joined Cia's hand to Roha's when she didn't immediately offer it, and Cia moved as though she could feel the ghost girl's guidance. As soon as their hands clasped, Dazia returned to stand within the circle of her mother's arms, resting her hands on top of her mother's, as though they stood as one. All in the circle closed their eyes, and Roha chanted the spell-prayer that was part Gelerte's and part nes own. The book had suggested a spell for helping unquiet spirits along to the anima, but that was one on one. And voluntary.

While Dazia had consented, Roha had no way of gaining the agreement of Bloody Bess's ghost girls or Ceramor's swallowed spirits...if there was enough of them left to consent. And Roha's way would be significantly less gentle than Gelerte's. He could never have conceived of the horror that was Bloody Bess.

Roha found the bright spot within nim. The river that right now seemed winter-barren, down to a trickle, as though most was bound up in ice and would be released again on the spring thaw. Ni had used up that much. Or nes All-given gift was drying up, not meant for the use to which ni had put it. Ni couldn't think like that. Not now when so much was at stake.

Ni wished ni had had time to track down more of the writings of Lehren Gelerte. If ni lived... But for now, ni had to trace nes own anima to the source, to the All. Roha waded in, not that it was truly a stream, but ni imagined it that way, a natural spring that bubbled up, an elemental power ni could feel, dive in and follow it to the source. With Dazia's help, Roha was doing just that, could sense nimself coming to it. Not a spring now, but a powerful torrent, like a vast waterfall – inexpressible, awe-inspiring, overwhelming. Roha might not survive the plunge. Deadly and dangerous and so compelling. If the fall didn't take nim, then ni might be forever carried along by the swiftly flowing currents out into the vast ocean of anima or caught up in whirlpools and eddies or...

But can you find your way back after? Dazia had asked.

Ceramor

Ceramor reared back at the sight of the Princess's head erupting into a violent explosion of tentacles, blood and flesh, ichor or acid that burned on contact being flung off as poisonous byproducts of the transformation.

He howled as they hit, lashed this way and that. He rallied, grabbed for the next tentacle that came at him, but it grabbed back, snaking around his hand and then his arm. It burned on contact, corrosive and sick, like the Princess herself. The closest head snapped at it, ripped it half off with its teeth, but yelped at the sting of acid, the sharp rotten-sweet taste of poison. His tongue went instantly numb, and he shook that head hard, expelling drool and tentacle, trying to cleanse himself, but it was already too late.

He frothed. If poison was going to get him, he was going to rip her to shreds first. Like the hounds with their prey. He unleashed his feral side. *Ankari*. It was his curse. He would make it his strength. He reached for the pack within him and howled. He felt them rise up.

His beast responded. His chest expanded, and the grip of the tentacle that wrapped him, trying to squeeze the breath from him like a serpent, struggled to hold. He ripped at it with his claws, slashing, even at the risk of catching his own chest. Two of his heads bayed. All three snapped even more furiously, biting, tearing. Trying to rip her apart before she could poison the life out of him.

But her tentacles slithered around his hands and legs, suckers latching onto him like leeches, and he could feel the sting of their corrosion, their burn just before the pull on his power. His tongues weren't the only things going numb. His jaws could hardly lock, and the pain was spreading. Everywhere was pain, shadows were spreading across his sight. But still, the instinct to live… Over the scent of corrosion, of putrefaction was blood. His own, others, but more immediate – Bess's. The blood that burned.

It was tainted. Rotted. But it was a way in. All his instincts called for it. Food, essence, life. He was hungry on all levels. Every one. Blindly, he struck again, but not merely in defense. Not to rid himself of the whipping tentacles coming for him, but to consume. Bess thought she could come for his blood. His anima. Well, that worked both ways. He could feel her worming in already, the poison creeping, killing.

They were so close now, locked in a final embrace as she drained him to death. She thought she had him. She had every right to think so.

Ceramor forced the jaw on his central head, *his* head, to unlock and bite for her again, shaking her like a predator shakes prey—to break a neck or a spine. She no longer had a neck, but that didn't mean she couldn't be broken. He reached for her through her blood until he had her. Her taste, her feel, underneath it all.

A lashing tentacle caught him across the eyes, across the nose, one wrapping around his neck, tightening, tightening. Even if the pain and poison allowed him sight, he'd be blinded now. Weeping blood from his eyes, his nose. Flailing and failing for air. He ripped at the tentacle with his claws, but already it was so embedded, it did as much damage to him as it did to her.

But that wasn't the real fight. He felt for her, where she was vulnerable because she was focused on him with her power and her poison. He could feel her now, not just pulling at his anima, but whispering her will, telling his body to slow. His heart to stop beating. His breath to cease.

Ceramor had to keep her busy, give the others time. It was his job. Save the boy-king. Redeem himself, and he could join his Reina with a pure heart. It was all he'd ever wanted.

Keep his heart beating. Just a little longer. For Reina.

Your heart will seize.

For Reina.

Now! Bess breathed into his blood

No! He thought as he started to seize, and he tore at her anima with all the wild fury born of desperation, and said, "Yours!"

Roha

Roha dove into the torrent, ready to sacrifice nimself if need be. Life had never been about nim. It was service and beliefs and ideals. Ni tumbled, end over end until there were no ends, no beginnings, no ups, no downs. Ni surged with the torrent, with the power until ni learned its flow. Here and there were things dipping in, catching, snarls and eddies of dark things, and ni knew they were the unnatural places the mageri had caused.

With no voice, but only will, Roha chanted nes spell, nes prayer. Immersed in the anima, ni called all souls back to where they belonged. And kept chanting, kept calling. Ni'd never done anything like this and had no idea how long it would take or how ni'd even know if it worked until ni backed out again to see whether Dazia was still there.

At first, there was nothing. Ni was alone trying not to be swept away.

Then ni was looking down onto the battlefield, at Ceramor and Bloody Bess locked in a battle to the death. Ceramor was somehow a three-headed dog, and Bloody Bess's upper body had become a mass of tentacles, wrapped around him, squeezing him until they were both on their knees in blood and agony. They were lit up, a burst almost of starlight crowning their heads. Nes view scoped out, as though a spyglass were adjusted, as ni was seeing more of the countryside, other bursts of starlight – other spirits, Roha realized, not gone to their rest. And ni felt a presence next to nim there in the anima.

Dazia.

"Ready?" ni asked.

The little ghost girl was only a light, a feeling, an impression, but she flared, and Roha had the feeling of peace. It was time. It had to be.

Ni focused, said nes prayer again, focused nes intention, and released nes power.

Ni watched as all those lights spread across the countryside became a shower of falling stars, focused on the Dobrens Valley. Ni marveled at the beauty, following them to the battlefield, heart falling as ni came to Ceramor and Bloody Bess, still locked together.

Then Ceramor shrank down into a man, just a man, and looked off at something only he could see. He said something that looked to Roha like, "I come, my love," before collapsing to the ground. His lights joining the others, sinking into the Dobrens Valley, joining the anima, reunited with the All at last.

Bess collapsed, her lights sinking as well, but Roha couldn't tell if hers was among them.

Roha's heart swelled until ni thought it would burst. Ni had done it. The field glowed with life now like morning mist, the light diffuse and magical. Now ni could rest. The last of nes energy exhausted, Roha floated, drifted. So at peace, ni never wanted to leave.

Never...

Something tugged on nim, and ni resisted.

Ni was happy here. If ni waited, ni too would dissolve and join with all of this peace.

But the pull came again, and ni knew that there was something more, and nes time was not now. But this would be waiting. Whatever came, it would be here. It would wait.

Reluctantly, ni let the pull carry nim back upstream, against the lovely current, back into nimself until ni was sprawled out on the ground, two worried faces above nim. Just two—Cia and Ulan. No little ghost girl. Then they were joined by a third. Ruggerio.

"Did we win?" ni asked.

Pain crossed Ruggerio's face. Ni wouldn't have thought him capable of it. "We lost Ceramor. It might have been the battle with the Princess. Or that without his other souls, there wasn't enough of him left. He was too far gone."

Roha wanted to close nes eyes. To sleep. So exhausted. And to come back from such beauty to such fresh pain... "And Bloody Bess?"

"She collapsed, and her general called a retreat. They've taken her from the field."

"So she lives."

"She lives," he confirmed.

"And Hostill?"

"I'm here too." And a fourth face popped into view.

Ni could rest on that.

CHAPTER THIRTY-SEVEN

Bess

I t was so quiet inside Bess's head. So, so quiet that she would have thought herself dead if it weren't for the buzzing outside, rising in volume until she thought her head would collapse inward from the sound with no more pounding pressure within to counterbalance it. When swatting at the source of the buzzing availed her nothing, she pried her eyes open and saw the faces. Bowstan, along with some other soldier with elevated insignia to show that he was in a position of power. She didn't know him. Didn't want him bending over her, either of them.

But the noises stopped. Until she spoke, and it was too loud. All of it too loud. She started again, more quietly. "General…*General, report.*"

He looked at her and then at her head, as if he understood, as though he knew something, and she was sure she knew something too, only not what. Her head felt empty, hollowed out, and not gently. More as though something had clawed it and scraped it from the inside, and while her mind had to remain, because she was thinking, hearing, *feeling*, it hadn't yet healed from the breach.

The final word bounced around in her head, and she held up a hand to stop the general before he started. Remembering. Reliving with a horror that had her gasping.

"Bring the Princess water!" Bowstan ordered.

"Queen," she said, hoarsely, forcing her mind to quiet again, forcing herself to sit, despite the pain shooting throughout her body, the surge in her stomach that suggested the contents were ready to erupt as her head had not long ago. Unless she'd been out for quite some time. The thought caused a sound reminiscent of thunder none of them could have missed, and the soldier wasted no time doing Bowstan's bidding.

"I'm sorry?" Bowstan said, as though her words had been a symptom of her wounds.

"Queen," she repeated, more strongly.

She remembered enough now. There'd be time later for the actual count of bodies, but she had to fill in any blanks before he did so for himself. Before any of them did. Before rumors became truth.

As soon as the soldier returned, hand determinedly steady as he offered the wooden cup of water, she swiped it from his hand and downed it. She wanted her voice as firm as possible when she issued her orders. She handed the cup back to the soldier without a glance in his direction, keeping her gaze on Bowstan.

Instinctively, she reached for her power, for her shadow girls, and fought to keep the shock off her face when she found nothing. Less than nothing. A void, a whirlpool, a vortex. An emptiness that sucked away at her. Had it been there before she'd stoppered it up with her first kill? Could she fill it again? She would find out soon enough. For now, it was just her—Princess Bessory V'Alban. Her father's daughter. The poisonous fruit didn't fall far from the tree.

"We will have the coronation directly upon my return with the court and council as witnesses. The dukes will swear their fealty and come for a coronation ball at the first thaw. I have no more need for a Regent or council of keepers. I am your Queen."

Bowstan's eyes nearly popped, and she saw the opening and closing of the decorated soldier's mouth in her peripheral vision. She let the moment stand, heavy with possibilities. She was unarmed and at the moment powerless, but they couldn't know that. They'd be remembering her on the battlefield, striking down her guard to steal his anima and gain his power, becoming the tentacled monster, taking on Ceramor in his bestial form. Ceramor, who had very nearly killed her. She remembered being locked together, her heart feeling like it might explode, and then...

Then nothing until she woke up here, her tentacles gone, her head lashed back together. Did the poison pustules all burst and empty or were they pulled back inside, poisoning her even now? Had they come from within or were they a side effect of the blood magic, taking in anima that didn't belong to her? Would they make her ankari like Ceramor over time? Would knowing the answers change anything? She couldn't imagine surrendering such power now that she'd tasted it. But nothing needed answering now. This moment.

For now, it was enough that they'd seen and they feared. That none dared stand against her.

"Yes, my...my Queen," Bowstan said, testing it and hastily hiding his dislike of the taste.

"Tell the people—the land is restored," Bess said. Because she could feel it. She didn't know how, but her enemies had done *something*—called out all the unrestful spirits, returned them to the anima, and put a protection over the land. The mageri wouldn't be able to mine the anima of this particular place again. It was untouchable. Like whatever protections the Church put over their lands. She hadn't done it, but she could take credit for it. Who could say otherwise? "The Restoration is dead or on the run. They won't be back to our city. I will see to it. And Bowstan?" He bowed to show his attention to the special acknowledgement. "We *will* crush our enemies within the next year and we *will* have peace. This I will promise."

When Bowstan rose from his bow she studied him for belief, for excitement, for admiration or even determination, but saw only an acceptance of orders. It was enough for now. He didn't know enough to believe in her yet.

But he feared her enough to follow. And, really, that was all she could ask. For now.

Blind devotion...that could come later.

RESOURCES

If you or someone you know needs help, consider reaching out to one of these organizations. Please don't ignore warning signs or try to go it alone when things get too tough. There are people out there who want to help.

National Domestic Violence Hotline
Thehotline.org
1-800-799-SAFE (7233)

RAINN (Rape, Abuse, and Incest National Network
Rainn.org
1-800-656-HOPE (4673)

Childhelp: National Child Abuse Hotline
childhelp.org/hotline
1-800-4-A-CHILD (4453)

The Compassionate Friends
For loss of a child.
https://www.Compassionatefriends.org

Grief Speaks
Helpful information and a list of other organizations based on specific types of loss
www.griefspeaks.com/id76.html

ACKNOWLEDGMENTS

Writing may be a solitary endeavor, but agonizing and revising certainly is not! Many thanks to my husband, Peter Wheeler, who reminds me that I've suffered before and I will again and that I do not, in fact, suck. (Your mileage may vary.)

Thank you to Debra Fleming and Kathy Hennessy, who help me solve plot problems simply by listening while we walk in the mornings, and sometimes by asking questions that lead me in the right direction.

Thank you to Jackie Williams and Deidre Knight, formerly and currently of The Knight Agency, who have helped me revise and shape THE SHADOW GIRLS, and who are marvelous cheerleaders.

Wholehearted appreciation to Tiffany Yates Martin and Laura Crenshaw for their incredible insights, which brought the novel leaps and bounds forward. To Amy Christine Parker and Amber Hart, Christina Farley and Vivi Barnes, who've bolstered me as well. Thanks also to Lynn Flewelling and October Santerelli, who have also given THE SHADOW GIRL reads, one so early in the process I shudder to consider how things read at that stage!

Also, thank you *immensely* to my publisher John Hartness, who believes in THE SHADOW GIRLS and in this series, who made comments on the manuscript that gave me life and helped quell the doubt-demons that plague me. You are amazing, and I hope that I live up to your faith in me!

ABOUT THE AUTHOR

Lucienne Diver is the author of the *Vamped* and *Latter-Day Olympians* series, which Long and Short Reviews calls "a clever mix of Janet Evanovich and Rick Riordan". She also writes young adult suspense – **FAULTLINES**, **THE COUNTDOWN CLUB**, and **DISAPPEARED**, where two teens investigate the disappearance of their mother and the story their father tells about the night she went missing.

On a personal note, Lucienne lives in Florida with her husband, the two cutest dogs in the world, and enough books to some day collapse the second floor of her home into the first. She likes living dangerously.

More information can be found on her website www.luciennediver.com.

FRIENDS OF FALSTAFF

Milton Keynes UK
Ingram Content Group UK Ltd.
UKHW042204280824
447585UK00012B/286/J

9 781645 543183